Dedication

For Lee, my son, who would read my stories and always suggest certain improvements, if needed. I lost him tragically a few years ago, but I know he is always reading over my shoulder as I work on my computer.

Also a mention of Anne, my partner, who keeps me positive and is always ready to offer advice if the storyline gets difficult.

Other Books by the Author

Ludden

Les Marles

MARTHA'S CHAIR

REVIEW COPY
Not For Resale

AUSTIN MACAULEY PUBLISHERS™
LONDON * CAMBRIDGE * NEW YORK * SHARJAH

Copyright © Les Marles (2018)

The right of Les Marles to be identified as author of this work has been asserted by him in accordance with section 77 and 78 of the Copyright, Designs and Patents Act 1988.

All rights reserved. No part of this publication may be reproduced, stored in a retrieval system, or transmitted in any form or by any means, electronic, mechanical, photocopying, recording, or otherwise, without the prior permission of the publishers.

Any person who commits any unauthorised act in relation to this publication may be liable to criminal prosecution and civil claims for damages.

A CIP catalogue record for this title is available from the British Library.

ISBN 9781786297686 (Paperback)
ISBN 9781786297693 (Hardback)
ISBN 9781786297709 (E-Book)

www.austinmacauley.com

First Published (2018)
Austin Macauley Publishers Ltd.
25 Canada Square
Canary Wharf
London
E14 5LQ

Chapter One
The Beginning

Mid England 1643

Martha Budd shook her auburn hair and several sprigs of hay dropped to the ground. Jack Spicer had only started pulling his pants up, as Martha, still dressed, started skipping away back towards the village a quarter mile distant. A warm mid-September sun fanned the greenery of the recently cropped hayfield, with several stacks of hay neatly positioned, awaiting the carts to haul it to the village feed stores.

Jack Spicer cursed as a button on his pants broke away, dropping to the hay covered grass. He was desperate to run after Martha and get his tuppence worth of fun with the best looking young woman in the village. He spotted the button and picked it up, but Martha was too far away to catch. He had earlier pulled his pants down, after a few minutes kissing and fondling with the teasing young woman, hoping she would respond in kind and remove her lower clothes. After all, he had handed over his money and a full-blown romp was what he had paid for.

Martha Budd was no fool and not an easy catch to hold on to. Going on eighteen years old, above medium height, with long auburn hair and full figured, but not overweight. Her laugh was infectious and her sense of humour, slightly wicked but not offensive. As far as looks were concerned, she had no rivals among the other young women in Towton Meadows. No best friend, but she was happy to share tales with another eighteen year old, Maisy Duckworth.

An orphan from the age of five, after her mother had died of smallpox; her father a rogue and a petty thief, who had perished at the end of a hangman's rope for stealing a pig, Martha had been taken in by the Reverend Jonas Brooks and his wife, Elizabeth. They were a childless couple who, from the start, tried to indoctrinate the feisty little Martha with regular sermons on the merits of the Holy Book. It was always bedtime reading of the Bible for Martha, but she resisted the single minded attempts of the couple to fill her head with religious facts and figures.

By the age of twelve, Martha was a full-blown rebel and though one of the brightest pupils at the village school, she was never happier than to be in the company of a travelling Irish tinker called Fimber O'Flynn. Elizabeth Brooks had all but given up on making Martha an ideal adopted daughter, the constant battle of wits between the two sending the vicar's wife to an early grave.

Jonas Brooks tried his best to educate Martha in the necessity of being a good Christian, but it was a losing battle.

Martha stopped going to church and when Fimber O'Flynn was in the village selling his wares, she would help him to make money. The old Irish tinker would pass over a few pennies for her efforts and this infuriated Reverend Brooks. It was the Devil's money, he would say, and tried to ban Martha from seeing the tinker. It was to no avail and just made young Martha more of a rebel. Girls in the village were ordered not to associate with her, but this actually pleased Martha and by the time she was fourteen, her only friends were two or three of the village boys. Except of course, Maisy Duckworth.

Maisy was not as bright as Martha, but she was of a similar mould; well developed in figure, good looking and never a regular to Reverend Brooks' assemblies on Sundays. On warm summer days, the two young women would be out and about looking for any boys who would spend a few pennies for their company. The village gossips would be tittle tattling over garden gates at the expense of Martha and Maisy. Their tongues would accuse the two girls of any wrongdoings that surfaced in Towton Meadows. Stealing milk, eggs from hen huts, drying clothes from washing lines. Leaving field gates open, so cattle, sheep or horses would escape. Nothing was impossible for the two victimised girls to be accused of. Yet to their amusement and to the frustration of the village gossips, Martha and Maisy revelled in their notoriety.

The final straw for Reverend Brooks of his losing battle to keep Martha out of mischief and turn her into a respectable member of the community, was to return to his tied cottage one evening an hour before he was due back and find the two girls enjoying each other's company in his double bed. Both were naked and lying head to toe against each other in a sexual embrace. It was all the more devastating because with Reverend Brooks were three middle aged women, who had accepted his invitation to enjoy tea and cakes and an hour of working on preparations for a forthcoming village garden party in the church grounds. The three shocked and embarrassed women made quick excuses and left.

The next morning Martha was told to leave Reverend Brooks' cottage. With a few possessions in a battered canvas bag, the clothes she stood up in and a couple of shillings, Martha was homeless for the second time in her young life. Spending that night in a barn on the edge of the village, with a few chickens, a couple of goats and a donkey for company, Martha slept a troubled sleep under a pair of hessian sacks laid on straw.

Three similar nights followed for Martha sleeping in the barn, but her friend Maisy visited on one night and stayed with her 'til the morning. They cuddled up for warmth and enjoyed an hour of passion, before falling asleep. On her fifth homeless night, Martha waited for her friend to come with promised food and drink, but Maisy never arrived. The following day, hungry, dirty, unloved and lonely, Martha packed her few belongings and left the barn. For the first time in years, she started crying. Towton Meadows had been her home for over seventeen years, but as she climbed a stile leading from the field where the barn stood, she looked up and down the lane to see if Maisy Duckworth was in sight. There was no Maisy, so heaving her bag up, she set off to leave Towton Meadows behind.

She hoped it was her old friend the Irish Tinker, Fimber O'Flynn. It wasn't but it was one of the village lads. Jack Spicer's cart was hauling a load of rotted horse manure. The stench from the manure hit Martha's nostrils even a hundred yards away. The broken and yellow teeth of the sneering young farm labourer sent a shudder through Martha's aching body. The thought that she had taken a few pennies from Jack Spicer a few days earlier, to let his grubby hands squeeze her ample bare breasts, revolted her. The cart drew nearer and Martha put a hand to her nose, stepping out of the way. To her dismay the old horse was pulled to a halt and the leering Spicer looked down at her.

"I heard the vicar kicked you out for snogging Maisy Duckworth in his bed," Spicer grinned.

"Go fuck yourself, Jack Spicer, because I would never let you fuck me," Martha retorted.

"I don't fuck lesbians, Martha Brooks, I'm particular where I put my willy," Spicer laughed.

"I heard it's only three inches long, so you couldn't if I wanted you to and my name's Martha Budd, not Martha Brooks."

"Who cares what you're called? Towton Meadows will be a better place without you around, or that other slut, Maisy Duckworth. She ran off yesterday with one of Cromwell's troopers. They're coming this way soon."

"You're lying, Jack Spicer, Maisy said nothing to me about seeing a trooper."

"His names Harry Jessop and he's joined up to fight for Cromwell. There's an army of them a few miles away. There's gonna be a big battle in a few days and Towton Meadows will be famous. I'm gonna join up as well and earn some extra money. I saw a lot of the Roundheads' horses pulling cannons just a couple of miles back. You'll be in luck though, 'cos those troopers are as randy as hell from what I heard and they'll be ready for a free shag when they get here."

Martha shook her head and turned away to continue along the lane. Jack Spicer laughed and watched as she made to leave. "Tell you what, Martha. How about letting me have the first shag, before that lot get their filthy hands on you? Tuppence and I get you up the back over a hay bale."

"Maisy told me she took tuppence off you a while back and you couldn't get a hard on, so what's new, Jack Spicer? It takes a man, not a boy with a limp willy that is only good for peeing out of," Martha laughed and walked away. Jack Spicer cursed a reply, but it fell on deaf ears as Martha continued laughing and waved an arm dismissively.

Spicer flipped the reins to move the horse along and turned to shout back at Martha.

"One day, Martha Brooks or Budd or whatever you're called, one day and I'll be the one laughing. And I hope one of Cromwell's soldiers gives you a dose of the clap. You see, Martha fucking Budd, if I'm not wrong. And the story around Towton Meadows is that you're a trainee witch and that old Irish tinker you're friendly with is your master. They burn people like you at the stake."

Martha heard his insult and waved her arm dismissively once more. Tears broke free again, were scuffed away and she took a deep sigh, heaved her bag up again and continued along the lane away from Towton Meadows. Sitting on a grass verge a mile from the village, her despondent mood changed as she caught a glimpse of another horse pulling a coloured covered cart. It was Fimber O'Flynn making one of his visits to Towton Meadows, to sell his trinkets and wares.

"A grand sight it is, lassie, for my old Irish eyes," Fimber smiled as he pulled the old piebald mare to a stop at the side of the grass verge. "You've been crying, I can tell. You tell old Fimber what's upset you and why you're carrying a clothes bag?" The tinker jumped down and put a comforting arm around Martha's slim shoulders.

"I was told to leave the village a few days ago. I slept in a barn at night and my friend Maisy came to bring me food, but she didn't come last night and I decided to leave. They hate me, Fimber, because I don't go to church and I'm friends with Maisy. I also got blamed when Reverend Brooks' wife died a few years ago. They said it was the devil in me that killed her. They say I'm a trainee witch and that you're my master. I'm not going back there."

"Then you come along with me, bonny lass. You know how to sell, my goods go quicker when you help me. We'll go into Towton Meadows and you do what you have always done, sell my wares, copper kettles, skipping ropes, pegs, wash tubs, dolls and brushes and brooms. You are now my apprentice and if they say I am your master, then so be it. You tell them that and be proud to be an apprentice tinker.

"Where do I sleep, Fimber? There is only one bunk," Martha asked curiously.

"I have a tent, bonny lass and I'll sleep in that. You can sleep in my bunk. In return, you can cook me some nice meals."

She started singing a song as the little cart trundled along the lane and Fimber joined in to add a little Irish spice to the melody. Fifteen minutes later and they entered Towton Meadows, to the astonishment of the villagers. Fingers pointed and acid tongues started wagging. Martha smiled and waved as blank faces stared. Fimber tipped his battered hat and winked at the women.

Some turned and hurriedly scuttled away to tell the tale.

Two hours later and Fimber O'Flynn had sold more of his wares than on any previous visit to the village. Martha had even sold a bag of pegs and some cooking oil to Reverend Brooks, who had wandered across the village after hearing the tinker's cart was tethered opposite the green. He had wanted to order Martha out of the village for a second time, but Fimber O'Flynn had simply put a hand on the austere faced vicar's shoulder and his attitude changed. He had felt the soft hand of the old tinker on his shoulder and with a glance into the old man's eyes, he suddenly forgot why he had needed to see his estranged adopted daughter. He had not even needed pegs or cooking oil.

As Fimber and Martha packed up ready to leave the village, they saw a commotion at the end of the main street. A couple of young boys came running and shouting. They were pointing backwards and breathless, gasped out that a lot of soldiers and horsemen were entering the village. People turned to watch and as sure as the boys had explained, there were indeed lots of soldiers and horsemen arriving in Towton Meadows.

Fimber O'Flynn tapped Martha on an arm as she, too, had turned to see what was happening at the far end of the main street.

"C'mon, lassie, let's move and move quickly and out the other end before that lot see us. I seen them before and they confiscate all the stuff on the cart."

A minute later and Fimber was ushering his mare along the village street, away from the soldiers. The mare pulled willingly on her harness, but she was too slow for a young cavalry officer who had spotted the fleeing cart and cantered his own horse to stop and interrogate the driver. The young officer grabbed the reins and ordered Fimber to pull up. The tinker cussed and shook his head disapprovingly. He glanced the youngster a cursory look. Martha held her breath and waited.

"Not so fast, mister," Lieutenant Hickory barked as he held the reins of Fimber O'Flynn's mare.

"I'm an innocent traveller and I have finished my business here and you have no right to stop me."

"I have every right, sir, because you might be an enemy spy and you will have to prove why you are here. Who, may I ask, is this young woman? She might be a spy as well, the Royalists have planted many of these attractive young women in towns and villages," Hickory insisted. As he spoke, another cavalry officer arrived and looked with suspicious eyes at the tinker and his cart. His eyes then wandered over the girl at the tinker's side. Martha smiled and puffed out her ample bosom.

Major William Trent nodded admiringly, then glanced at the old man at the girl's side. "I have seen you before, old man. I have a good memory and I saw your cart at Edgehill, near where we engaged the enemy a year ago. I saw you again on Seacroft Moor where we fought the enemy in Yorkshire. Then again at Adwalton Moor three months later. And now, tinker, here you are once more, this time at Newbury, with a battle against our enemy pending. I am wondering this is a bit too much of a coincidence, three battles where good men on both sides perished and you and your little cart were near each battlefield. We will take on the enemy again in a few days and you and your tinker's cart is once more, near a battlefield where good men will die. I see you are facing the opposite way to where my regiment is and you are leaving the village in haste. You are under arrest, old man and also, your very beautiful companion. I think you are both spies and the penalty for such abominable behaviour is death. Take them in charge, Lieutenant, and lock them up somewhere secure."

Shackled and locked in a shed behind the church, Martha was sobbing as she sat on the cold stone floor. A few feet away Fimber O'Flynn, also shackled, a bruise at the side of his face where a soldier had struck him, shuffled against his chains to get nearer to Martha.

"I'm sorry, Martha to have put you in this situation. The major was correct, I was at the battlefields that he mentioned, but not as a spy. I was on duty," Fimber said calmly.

"On duty, what do you mean?" Martha asked, looking bewildered.

"I have a debt to pay to someone and I have to travel to those sort of places where men die. I was young and foolish many, many years ago and I accepted money and a promise of a long life in exchange for doing what I do. I cannot get out of my debt, I wish I could, but I am cursed and if I refuse to do what I am ordered to do, I will suffer a terrible end to my wretched life."

"What about me, Fimber? I'm your friend. That major said we'll die for being spies. I'm not a spy," Martha said pitifully. "They can't believe we are. You're not a spy, are you? You're a tinker."

Fimber took a breath and slowly nodded. "I suppose I am, lassie, to be honest. For a long time. A long long time. I took the devil's money and he bought my soul. He owns me, lock stock and barrel, as the saying goes."

"What are you saying, Fimber? It doesn't make sense. The—the devil is not—not real. He's just a—well a creature of fiction. Reverend Brooks was always talking about him and that he only looks after very bad people— you know—people who have committed murder. You're not a murderer."

Again Fimber nodded and tried to reach a hand to the young woman, but the wrist chain held him back. Martha was crying again and looking terrified. Fimber sighed loudly.

"I haven't actually murdered anyone, lassie, but my information has caused the deaths of lots of innocent people over the years. A long time ago there was a terrible battle in Yorkshire, it was on a Palm Sunday. It was in 1462 during the War of the Roses, between the Yorkists and Lancastrians. Lord Lucifer ordered me to set up a trap for the poor Lancastrians. I won't go into detail, but I did what he asked and during a blinding snowstorm, the carnage was terrible. Thousands were slaughtered and a nearby stream ran red with blood for two days. I saw it all from a small hill and after the battle, I ran away to hide. For years I lived a normal life. I went over to Ireland to escape from him and I did. I was so happy to be rid of Lord Lucifer and for the terrible things I had done at his command. I honestly believed he had forgotten about me and that my debt was paid. A hundred years passed and my life was so blissful. I travelled the lanes throughout Ireland as a tinker and met lots of nice people. Well, mainly nice people, until one day, just outside a place called Cavan in the middle of Ireland, I fell foul of another tinker. He was a short man, stocky with large ears and a very big red nose. He had long straggly hair and his skin colour was—well, I could swear it was a pale green. He swore at me to get out of his area, saying it was his and his only and if I didn't leave immediately, he would put a tinkers curse on me. I had heard of such things over the years, but dismissed them as old wives' tales."

"Did you leave his area like he told you?" Martha asked as she listened with interest.

"Eventually, but not for a year. Then one night, it was October the twenty-fifth and there was a raging storm that blew trees down and toppled stone walls. Yet my little covered cart, the one I have now, remained upright and undamaged. Bolts of white lightning struck the sodden ground and the thunder was deafening. The storm raged for hours and then just before dawn, while it was still dark, it stopped. You could have heard a pin drop. There was a light breeze and then he appeared."

Martha stared wide eyed at the old tinker, her mouth open. "Lord Lucifer," she gasped.

"The one and only and by his side was the fat little green tinker who had ordered me from his piece of land. He was grinning and his teeth were yellow and pointed like the fangs of a wolf."

"The curse had come true?" Martha said as she shuffled on the stone floor.

"Yes, lassie. Lord Lucifer had found me. A hundred and one years I had been free. It was 1543 and once more I was in his debt. He banished me from Ireland and ordered me back to England. Every fifty years I have to do his bidding. It is 1643 now and I have done more terrible things this past year."

Martha's face was an ashen mask of disbelief. She scuffed more tears away and stared at her old friend, who looked miserable and beside himself with guilt. "Will the soldiers kill us, Fimber? I don't want to die like this, chained and frightened. Is what you did so bad, that death is the punishment?"

"They will put me to death, lassie, that is what happens to spies. I am so sorry that I have got you involved. Lord Lucifer walks amongst the dead on the battlefield and chooses those who he knows will sacrifice a place in heaven for an eternity of paradise and for that pleasure, will do his bidding whenever he wants. Like me. I am a slave to his whims and fancies. After this next battle I will be left alone for another fifty years. If I disobey again he drops that to twenty-five years.

"Disobey again and he uses me and other rebels like me, every day for eternity. For fleeing to Ireland as I did, my debt period was increased to a thousand years."

"How old are you, Fimber? You can't be as old as I think," Martha asked incredulously.

"I've lost count, young lassie, but it must be two hundred and forty or fifty years."

"That's not possible. People nowadays only live 'til they are about forty-five to fifty."

"If they are normal, perhaps, but I am not normal. My soul was taken so long ago and Lord Lucifer holds it in safe keeping," Fimber replied sagely.

"If I am put to death, will I be able to travel with you instead of going to heaven?"

"They will take you as soon as you have breathed your last breath, lassie. They have first choice over your soul. Lord Lucifer can only take the misfits who have turned their backs on the church or have done terrible deeds on earth. Have you done either of those?"

"I never went to church and I made Mrs Brooks die. I also put a curse on two girls at my school who bullied me. Mary Cox fell from a tree and broke her back and has never walked since. Joan Todd was kicked by a horse and had to have a leg amputated. She cut her wrists afterwards and died."

"Those could have been normal accidents, lassie, but you say you made Mrs Brooks die. How did you do that?" Fimber asked calmly.

"At night, she and Reverend Brooks made me say prayers before I went to sleep. I cheated and always asked for Mrs Brooks to die. Then she did. I wanted her to die, she was cruel and made me do things I didn't want to do. After they buried her, I went to the graveyard on some nights, lifted my skirts and peed on her grave. I hated her."

Before Fimber could answer, the door opened and Lieutenant Hickory entered the room, followed by a tall, well-dressed man and just behind, Jack Spicer and two plump middle-aged women, who Martha recognised as two of the three woman who had seen her in Reverend Brooks' bed with Maisy Duckworth. Jack Spicer pointed to Martha and nodded. Both the women pointed and nodded.

The well-dressed man stepped towards Martha and took a Bible from a bag he was carrying. He bent down and offered the Bible to Martha. The young woman hesitated and looked with terrified eyes at the man standing over her. He tapped the Bible.

"Take the Lord's book, young lady, and open it at any page. Place a hand on the pages and repeat what I say, do you understand?"

Martha glanced up at the man, then at Fimber, who had watched impassively. Their eyes fixed and Martha saw a glint of hope in the old tinker's eyes. For a few moments their eyes held and Martha felt a slight tremor filter through her nervous body. The other people in the room watched and waited.

The well-dressed man coughed gently and pushed the Bible a bit further towards Martha.

"Tell me you understand, Martha Brooks. That is your name, I'm told."

"I understand, mister, but my name is Martha Budd, not Brooks and who are you?" Martha replied politely, but her voice shaky.

My name is Thomas De La Rue and I have been summoned by the good folk of Towton Meadows to call upon you, young woman, to cleanse your spirit. You can be saved from a life of sin, blasphemy and degradation by simply swearing on the Good Book that you will change your ways and repent to the Lord. Go to church twice a week and stop your disgraceful and sinful ways. There are people in this village who accuse you of sorcery and witchcraft. Three of them are in this room and they are good honest people who have cast aside bad ways, attached themselves to the church and all that is good and banished evil from their thoughts. You will be given a chance tomorrow morning at nine, to take a test of truthfulness and servitude to the Lord. There will also be a test to determine your innocence of the charges I have stated. It is a tried and tested method that proves beyond any doubt whether you are truly a decent person, or if you are a sinner and deserve to be punished." Thomas De La Rue stepped away, looking at the old tinker. Fimber stared upwards at the man, but never showed any sign of emotion or fear. De La Rue looked to the lieutenant near the door, who had been joined by the major. The latter stepped closer to De La Rue.

"This is the man I told you about, sir. He claims to be a tinker, but I believe he is a Royalist spy, who I personally have seen on a few occasions loitering near the sites where we have engaged the enemy. My clear orders are to shoot any such individual we catch and nothing less. He denies such treacherous activity, but I am a god-fearing man and am not his judge, jury or executioner.

"So, I suggest we give him the same chance I understand you are offering the girl, who I strongly believe is also a Royalist spy. We will leave them this coming night to think of their plight and reconvene before nine in the morning, to witness eventualities. My men will be billeted just outside the village during the coming night. Lieutenant Hickory will make sure he has guards outside to prevent any escape. Good day, sir, and I will see you in the morn."

The major nodded to De La Rue and left the shed. The latter turned also to leave, with the two women and Jack Spicer, but Martha looked up and called out, in a strong, confident voice, "Jack Spicer, I put a curse on you, you snivelling, jumped up swine. I hope you die a painful death before this year is out."

Spicer turned and laughed, drawing a finger across his throat. De La Rue tutted and pushed Spicer and the two women from the shed. Lieutenant Hickory remained for a few seconds, checking that the shackles on Martha and the old tinker were still attached. "I'll send one of my men with some food and water. Get a good night's rest and God be merciful on you both. Goodnight."

It was warm and stuffy in the shed, even though it was mid-September. Martha's fastenings no longer hurt and she was able to relax, even though lying fully down was not possible. Fimber was quiet, reflecting on his and Martha's predicament. A couple of soldiers brought some dry mouldy bread, with a small wedge of cheese each and a tin of tepid water. Neither Martha nor Fimber took advantage of the poor food, both pushing it away, but Martha sipped some of the water.

"How do you feel, lassie? You've stopped crying and seem a lot better." Fimber asked.

"I'm fine now. I got a strange feeling inside of me. I'm no longer scared. Who was that tall man, do you know?"

"He's what they call a witch hunter general. Up and down England they have appeared from the woodwork, preaching and spouting deliverance and getting poor innocents to admit to sorcery and witchcraft. They get paid for every poor wretch that is found guilty and put to death. They burn some at the stake, stone to death others, or put others on trial on a ducking stool."

Martha stared at Fimber, her jaw dropped in shock. "What's a ducking stool?"

"A silly contraption, to be honest, lassie. Or sometimes they use a chair to fasten the poor wretch to. Bound hand and foot, then lowered into the water in the village pond. The whole village turn out to watch, even children. If they decide to put us both to death, it will probably be a stake hammered into the ground and both of us tied together. Although now that the Parliamentarian Army is here, we will probably be shot. I will be, anyway. I think you will be fine. They might show you mercy."

"If they put you to death, Fimber, you will at least be free of your debt. Lord Lucifer can't come after you anymore."

"It doesn't work like that, lassie. I'm his servant for at least another seven hundred years. I sold my soul for a pittance when

I was younger. I got a girl into trouble and I needed money to pay for a doctor to terminate her unborn. I touched evil that day many years ago. The girl died and I was destined to be a servant to Lord Lucifer for an eternity. There is no going back. What I did caused the deaths of two souls, one living and one unborn. I deserved my fate."

"You're a nice man, Fimber, it's so unfair. Can you not buy your soul back?" Martha asked.

"There isn't enough money to do that, lassie. At least I get fifty years to myself between the tasks I have to do for him. Time is all that I have left. I see many things and I never feel pain, or feel a warm sun on my back. I cannot take a scent of a wild rose, or of wild garlic. No wind stings my face. I never get hungry or thirsty. I can talk to the ravens and the crows. They treat me with contempt. I am a nobody, not human not even the undead. The undead can be finished with evil if they lose their head or have a wooden stake hammered into their cruel hearts. Not me. I wander the land and never get anywhere. The only thing I have that is real is my horse. Over the years I have had many and I earn enough from selling my wares to buy feed for my horse and to pay the blacksmith for the shoes."

Outside, night had taken hold and there was no light in the cold shed. Martha shivered as the chill crept over her body, but Fimber was not troubled. After a half hour, the door opened and a young soldier came in to collect the food plates. He turned to leave and noticed that Martha was huddled on the floor, her body shivering. He was no more than Martha's age and felt a twinge of sympathy for the young girl. He left the shed, but returned a few minutes later with an old, threadbare blanket. Carefully he handed it to the girl, his wary eyes and mind remembering that he had heard she was a young witch. He was happy being a strong youth, not the brainiest of people, but he did not want to be turned into a black cat or worse still, an ugly toad.

Martha eventually fell asleep, the sleep of a tormented, condemned person. A few feet away, Fimber O'Flynn sat hunched up, his eyes open, no sleep possible. He had no fear of the fate he would endure a few hours later. He was a spy of sorts, but not in the pay of the Royalists he had been accused of helping; his paymaster was the devil himself. Lord Lucifer would walk the bloody battlefield of Newbury and take his pick of the mortally wounded. There were always men or boys who would prefer a life of paradise in eternity, with a body not missing a limb or two, than struggling through life on earth, probably penniless and without hope. Lord Lucifer took the souls of these wretched beings and cast them into a bottomless pit. They were his and for eternity they would remain in the pit. Their original owners had no choice but to do as he asked and there was no escape. Lord Lucifer had never returned a soul to its original owner.

A bell ringer sounded out seven o'clock the following morning and Towton Meadows awoke, consumed with excitement. News had spread like fire the previous evening that the feared witch hunter general for their district had flushed out a Royalist spy and a young witch. Both were to be put to death at nine o'clock, unless of course the pair could escape justice by proving they were innocent. Bets were already being taken on which method of execution would befall the prisoners. The favourite for the old tinker, a known spy, was for him to be tied between two oxen and the beasts to be driven away, pulling his body in half. This gruesome torture always brought a hysterical cheer from the baying crowd as flesh, bone and innards were pulled apart.

The young witch faced either the burning stake or the ducking chair. The villagers were split half and half. The burning stake was the noisiest as the doomed prisoner, without fail, would scream to the heavens as the searing white and orange flames licked over the threshing, naked body for several long minutes.

The ducking chair was favoured by those hoping the prisoner would prove their innocence by surviving several plunges into the cold black water of the village pond. If they did survive the duckings, which started at thirty seconds' duration then increased steadily to five minutes, the prize was to confirm without doubt that he or she was innocent and be granted their freedom. No resident in memory could recall any prisoner ever surviving the dreaded ducking chair. Harlots, common thieves, homosexuals, witches and vagabonds had perished on the feared chair.

Little boys never up before seven were running and yelling as the village elders decided which method of torture and killing was to be used. After several minutes of deliberation and with the approval of Thomas De La Rue, it was agreed that the old Irish tinker, a confirmed Royalist spy, was to be burned at the stake. The girl now known as Martha Budd would be allowed to prove her innocence at being accused of witchcraft, by taking the ducking chair test. As usual, the condemned prisoner would be proven innocent if he or she was still alive after being submerged on the fearsome chair for several minutes. The good Lord would obviously look after his own and spare the wretched person's life. Innocence of the alleged crime, proved.

Within a half hour a tall piece of cut timber was carefully positioned on the village green and a stool placed at the base. Several tied pieces of kindling wood and dry branches were placed around the stake and oil poured over them. The tinker was to be executed first and two young soldiers from the Parliament regiment billeted outside the village, were dispatched to the church shed where he and the young witch were imprisoned.

Inside the shed, Fimber smiled at the terrified young woman. Martha tried to hide her fear and the old tinker knew how she was feeling. Their eyes met and once more Martha felt a strange sensation ripple through her trembling body.

"There will be no pain or suffering, lassie, I promise. I bargained with Lord Lucifer while you slept and he agreed to let you travel with me for as long as you want."

Martha scuffed tears away and looked again at Fimber O'Flynn. "You said he does nothing for nothing. What price did you pay?"

Fimber smiled and shrugged. "My free time has been reduced to twenty-five years. In return, you can travel time with me. If you would sell your soul, we are free to travel for fifty years between duties. If you do well at these duties, then he will consider extended our free time to a hundred years. He insists, though, that we have to do certain duties before he will consider moving us back to a hundred years. The first duty will be at this present time. He wants fresh souls now. He must have four souls, but one must be yours."

Martha nodded. "I will, Fimber. I will. He can have my soul today. I know who the other three souls belong too. How long do we have to send them to him?"

"By the next full moon. Twenty-one days," Fimber replied.

"When will you speak to him, to tell him I agree?"

Fimber laughed as he heard a key turning in the door lock. "He already knows, lassie. He will send a confirmation in a few minutes. It will go very dark and there will be thunder and a great flock of ravens will fly over Towton Meadows."

"What happens now, Fimber? When do we meet again?" Martha asked nervously as the door creaked open and two very young, nervous soldiers stooped under the door frame and looked across to the two condemned prisoners. Behind them, Lieutenant Hickory waited with his sabre drawn.

As one of the soldiers took off his ankle shackles, Fimber smiled at Martha, there was a twinkle in his eyes. "Don't let them see or hear you panicking, lassie. Choose your three souls and touch their owners on the head. You and I will meet again very soon, I promise."

Fimber was taken from the shed by the two soldiers and marched away towards the village green. Behind him walked the lieutenant and Reverend Brooks, who was saying prayers for the old tinker. As soon as the small group was spotted, a loud cheer rang out from the waiting crowd and then almost as quick, a deathly lull. A few minutes later and Fimber O'Flynn was tied securely to the rounded stake. Reverend Brooks did the sign of the cross and stepped away from the piled-up brushwood and kindling. A man with a hood over his head, waited with a burning torch. In a straight line, a column of Parliamentarian soldiers stood, ready to stop any troublemakers running forward.

Major Trent stood at the side of Lieutenant Hickory and had an embarrassed expression on his rugged, weather-beaten face. He respected men like the old tinker, who believed in what they did, but on this occasion had chosen the wrong side. He had wanted to use a firing squad to terminate the old man's life, but the witch hunter general, Thomas De La Rue, had papers to prove he was a retired colonel in the King's army and insisted it had to be death on a burning stake. Trent saluted the old tinker then pulled his horse around and left the macabre scene. A few moments later and the burning torch was used to set the fires burning. A loud whooping cheer sounded.

Stunned into an eerie silence, the packed crowd watched disbelievingly as the flames enveloped the old tinker, but there was no screaming or threshing about of the victim. Fimber O'Flynn watched the silent crowd with a wry smile on his face. The expectant crowd watched, waited, fidgeted but remained silent. Boys and girls started crying, women did likewise, but the old tinker still smiled. Minutes later the flames covered his body, the restraining pole collapsed in a flurry of black smoke and flying embers, the smoke cleared and it was all over. There was no charred body.

Now it was Martha Budd's turn and the same two young soldiers brought her out of the shed, her hands still shackled. As she took the hundred yard walk to the village pond, the same crowd of morbid onlookers that had witnessed the horrific burning scene on the village green, took their places to watch further entertainment. A familiar face to Martha appeared in the crowd and she stopped for a few moments. Her hands raised, she beckoned to Jack Spicer, who turned his grinning face around to see who it was Martha was pointing at. She called his name and someone in the crowd pushed him forward. He stumbled, collected himself and nervously stepped towards Martha Budd. Her shackled hands beckoned him. He trod carefully, but someone else pushed him forward. One of the soldiers pulled him to Martha, who was smiling sweetly.

"She wants a word with you, feller. Talk to her, it's the least you can do," the soldier snapped.

Spicer moved closer, his spotty, flushed face creased into a doubting mask. He was a couple of feet from the raised hands. They beckoned him closer.

"What d'ya want?" he said quietly.

"Just to touch you, Jack. It will be last thing I do before I die," Martha replied, her hands moving to his head. He blinked disbelievingly, but the crowd were heckling him to respond. He allowed the condemned girl's hands to touch his head. She was chained and unable to do him harm. Carefully Martha's hands caressed his unwashed hair and face. Then she withdrew and smiled again. This time her smile was touched with malice, there was fire-red colour in her eyes. He felt a cold shiver run through his body and then the first clap of thunder sounded. The crowd gasped in surprise; it had been a warm September morning.

The packed crowd followed Martha to the ducking stool that waited. Jack Spicer couldn't move. His body was frozen and another clap of thunder sounded. Martha turned to look back and smiled as she saw Jack Spicer staring upwards. He had not moved an inch since Martha Budd had touched him. Lord Lucifer was watching and knew another wretched soul would soon be his.

An oak spindle chair was carried forward by a youth, who planted it on the spot where the accused wretches would be fastened to it and unceremoniously lowered into the inky black cold water. As many had died on the chair in recent times since the witch hunters had arrived, as had perished in the flames on the stake. Today had been special, two prisoners instead of just the one. Unlike the burning stake, where the poor condemned person suffered a terrifyingly painful death, the ducking chair offered a chance of survival if they were pulled from the water alive, after several minutes of water torture. Of course, no one was ever alive.

Today's victim was a feisty young woman who had caused mayhem in Towton Meadows for several years, never attending church, having same sex fun, flaunting strict village laws and befriending a known traitor and Royalist spy. Worst of all, her bad behaviour to her adopted parents, the very respectable Reverend Joshua Brooks and his tormented wife Elizabeth. A lot of people especially some of the women, were pleased Martha Budd had got her comeuppance.

Another deathly hush fell amongst the watching crowd. Martha Budd was surprisingly almost unconcerned that in a few water-drenched minutes she would be dead. There was even the faintest of wry smiles on her beautiful young face. The two men who were to fasten her hands, body and feet to the spindle chair were gently eased to one side by Reverend Joshua Brooks who wanted to speak to his condemned adopted daughter for the last time. He held his Bible and looked solemnly at Martha with unloving eyes. He was about to speak to her but she smiled at him. "Let me touch you one more time, Father. I need to feel the warmth of your skin just once more on my hands."

Martha raised one of her hands towards him and he bowed his bald head. Martha gently smoothed her hand over the sweating skin of his scalp and held it there for several moments. Joshua Brooks had wanted to say a few last words, but they never came. He leaned back and tried to stand, but there was no strength in his legs. One of the men carefully helped him to his feet, but he remained still and from above, a thump and roll of thunder sounded. The sky darkened and for a few seconds no one in the crowd of onlookers moved or spoke.

Pushing his way through the transfixed crowd, Thomas De La Rue strode to the front and stopped in front of Martha. He too held a Bible and opened it in the middle, holding it out to the condemned young girl. Martha smiled at the witch hunter and took his gaze to her own. Pushing a hand to the Bible, Martha carefully closed the Holy Book and then reached to the man's face. He held tight and felt her soft warm hands run over his facial skin, then up to his forehead. She kissed two of her fingers and tapped them onto his forehead. His eyes widened and a cold shiver ran through his body. Martha smiled and nodded at the two men, waiting to fasten her to the chair.

A couple of minutes later and she was moved to the water's edge. The crowd watched in silence and held their breath. It was strange, because like the old tinker who had perished earlier at the stake, Martha did not protest or start screaming for mercy. There was no struggle, no sound, no panic. A stout pole fixed to the chair was heaved forward by three burly men, a ginney wheel held on a diagonal timber and a rope fastened to the ginney wheel held the chair firmly. All eyes were on the doomed young woman, but she still did not struggle or make a cry for help.

Then a tremendous clap of thunder echoed across the darkened skies and from nowhere, a large, screeching flock of hundreds of ravens swooped down to the frightened crowd. Children screamed and ran for cover, mothers tried to grab their terrified offspring, men ducked and fell over as they bumped into each other. The ravens turned and swooped again and pandemonium took over. Even the soldiers, watching the events from a distance, turned and ran away to find shelter or safety.

Amidst it all three lonely figures remained stock still, their bodies like pillars of stone, blood frozen and eyes staring upwards to the grey menacing sky. Lord Lucifer was watching with blood-red eyes. He had taken another soul this day and three more were pledged. He would take them one at a time. Then he would walk the Newbury battlefield and steal some more. His trusty servant, Fimber O'Flynn had done well and now he had another on his payroll. The young girl, Martha Budd. He looked across the black pond and saw the submerged ducking chair, held by two strong twines of rope fixed to a ginney wheel. Three men were pulling on the ropes to bring the chair and the captive to the surface. They had been under the water for over five minutes.

A mile from the village a little gaily painted cart pulled by a horse, trundled along a track with two people sitting on the driver's bench. They were laughing and sharing a joke. In the distance two miles away, a few thousand soldiers marched towards their common enemy. Another six hundred were mounted on war horses. Several larger horses pulled heavy cannon.

There would be only one victor this day in late September. Lord Lucifer licked his lips and wiped his excited blood-red eyes. Who won the impending battle was of no interest to him. He sighed and chuckled to himself. By midnight it would have been a very fruitful day.

Back in Towton Meadows, Major William Trent ordered his men to retrieve the ducking chair from the village keepers. He had decided it was an inhumane method of execution and wished he had insisted on the prisoners being shot by musket fire. The chair was put onto the back of a supply wagon to be taken back to his home, where he would make sure no poor wretch would never again have to be suffer death on its seat. Lieutenant Hickory was pleased at his major's decision to remove the chair to safe keeping, but wished he could have taken it back to his home. It was a fine chair of English oak and he could have remembered the young woman who he had admired and marvelled at her stunning beauty.

As the two officers walked back to their camp, a field scout came riding along the main street. "The Royalists, sir! They are three miles distant. Infantry, cavalry and cannon in tow," the rider called, almost breathless, pointing back the way he had travelled.

Major Trent waved the rider away and hurried back towards his waiting regiment, with Lieutenant Hickory at his heels. "At last, Lieutenant, we can give the Royalists another bloody nose. A great pity we had to witness the barbaric stupidity of what happened here this morning. How are your new men shaping?"

"Most are good fellows, sir and will do us proud this day, but there is one who has too much to say and not enough effort to match his mouth. We would be better without him, to be honest," Hickory replied as he gasped for breath while running.

"Then put him in the front line, Lieutenant, with the pikemen. And I mean right at the front. What's his name?" Trent asked, not breathing hard as the pair neared their encampment.

"One Jack Spicer, sir. A troublemaker and braggart."

"No great loss, then, huh. Easy come, easy go. Has he been paid yet?"

"No, sir. Not a penny." Hickory replied with the last of his breath.

"No problem, then. Fodder. Lose the misfits and save the best for last. Just make sure this Spicer fellow faces the musket fire and cannon before our best men do. Sacrifice the worst of the ones you've got, use up the enemies' firepower and make the kill with your best men. That, Lieutenant, is how battles are won; save the best for last."

Hickory stopped and leaned forward, hands on knees, gasping for breath. Trent laughed and reached his command, barking out orders. He had another battle to fight and win and after the debacle at the nearby village less than an hour earlier, he was in no mood to lose.

Martha hooked an arm into the elbow of the old tinker and looked up into the blue sky as the mare pulled the little cart along the track. "What happens now, Fimber, are we free?" she asked.

"Heck, no, lassie. We will never be free. There is a price to pay and believe me, we have to pay it. Fifty years we can roam the country and along the way we have to find poor souls for

Lord Lucifer. His appetite is enormous and we and others like us have to feed his insatiable greed for lost souls. Along the way, though, we can go where we want. Do what we want. No one can stop us. He will come for us again in fifty years' time and we have to obey his every command. There is no escape for us. He owns our souls and we have to do his bidding."

Martha said nothing for a few moments then turned to Fimber as they ambled along. "I will buy my soul back one day, Fimber. One day he will have to sell it back to me. You see."

Fimber tweaked the reins gently and nodded as he chewed on a sliver of a grass stalk. "Aye, lassie! Reckon you will at that. I think Lord Lucifer will one day meet his match in you."

Chapter Two
Marston Moor, Yorkshire

July 1644

Colonel William Trent had fought the first battle wearing his new rank colours, following his promotion after the battle of the civil war at Nantwich a few months earlier. He had fought for the Parliamentarian forces at Adwalton Moor, Seacroft, Edghill, Newbury, Nantwich and now, on this warm summer's day, at Marston Moor, a few miles from York. He had come through all the previous battles without a scratch, but today he had been seriously wounded. A cannon shot had exploded near his horse and red hot shrapnel had killed his faithful mount, torn off one of his legs and ripped into his upper body. The battle was over and hundreds of men from both sides had been killed. He lay on a makeshift bed at the side of the bloody battlefield and realised he had fought his last battle. He guessed he was going to die from his wounds and called to a young medical attendant, desperately helping other injured men.

"Young man, will you do me a favour?" Trent called softly.

The young medic stopped and turned to the critically injured officer. "Yes sir, if I can."

"Go to the officers' tents yonder and fetch me my spindle-back chair. Ask anyone over there and they know which chair it is. I'm Colonel Trent. Hurry please." The young medic looked surprised and caught a nod from a senior medic to do as he was bid.

A few minutes later the young medic returned, carrying the chair. He found Colonel Trent trying to slip off the bed.

Carefully he helped the officer onto the chair and stepped back. He knew the officer was dying and wondered why he had preferred to die on the chair rather than the bed.

Trent noticed the boy's concern and managed a faint laugh, but coughed up blood as he spoke.

"Don't be worried, young man, I have great affection for this chair. It belonged to a very beautiful young woman who also died sitting on it. Go back to helping other injured men and leave me. I have my chair and I'll die a happy man in a few minutes."

The young medic turned to leave the colonel, but pointed at the chair, now stained with the officer's blood. "I reckon the chair will always be yours, sir, and this young woman's you mentioned. I think anyone who owns it will die in it as well. Creepy it is, sir. God bless you, colonel, and I'm so sorry you got hurt today."

The following day, the dead and injured were being taken away to be either buried in mass graves or set aside for treatment in dozens of makeshift hospital tents. Both sides joined in the gruesome task; men who twenty-four hours earlier had been trying to kill each other, but now shared a common duty to bury the dead or treat the wounded. The night following the battle had been like any other after a fierce, bloody confrontation; screams and pitiful cries for help, from combatants who had been left where they fell.

Ravens, crows and others of their kind attacked the corpses at will, picking from the bloodied bodies whatever treats they had the strength to pull away. Even the mortally wounded men, beyond help for their injuries, used their last segments of strength to ward off the black scavengers. Eyes were scraped from sockets on dying bodies of fallen men, too weak to resist the attacks. Amidst all this carnage, a single figure stalked the crippled bodies of the near-dead.

Lord Lucifer was in his element. He had plundered dozens of feeble souls on the Marston Moor battlefield and his blood lust was still bubbling with excitement. His servants had served him well this day and as usual, he was begrudgingly grateful. Two of his servants watched from a distance, sitting on a little coloured cart, their eagle eyes surveying the appalling horror of the conflict.

"I wish I hadn't sold my soul to him," Martha remarked.

"Well, lassie you did and I'm afraid he will never let you buy it back. I thought the same after I gave in to him more than two hundred years ago, but I cannot see how I can sleep peacefully ever again. He is the most cunning creature that has ever walked the earth."

Martha sighed and continued looking across the expanse of open ground where the battle had been fought the day before. After a few more minutes she wiped her eyes and looked with more intensity at a couple of soldiers, who seemed to be arguing over a piece of timber. She stood up from her seat and shielded her eyes from the sun. Then she jumped down and took off across the field, skipping over dead bodies, tripping over discarded muskets and debris. Eventually, ignoring wolf whistles from other soldiers, she reached where the two men were pulling at what she had seen to be a spindle-backed chair, not just a piece of timber. The two soldiers, blood-soaked dirty shirts and trousers, tousled hair and muck-grained faces, stopped and looked at the young woman.

Martha noticed that they were from opposite sides and grinned. The Royalist soldier held on to the chair, but looked sheepishly at Martha. The other soldier held on like grim death to his part of the chair.

"Lads, that is my chair. Can I please have it back? It belonged to my granny," Martha said in her finest seductive voice.

"It's mine, miss. I saw it first. It's spoils of war," the Royalist remarked, not giving an inch.

"Bollocks, matey, it's mine. We won the battle yesterday so we get first choice." The other lad argued, gritting his teeth.

Martha moved closer and put out a hand to the Parliamentarian youth, looking at the Royalist youth in turn.

"He's right, you know. It is spoils of war, but only if you can prove it doesn't belong to somebody else, like me. Have either of you got proof that I don't own it?"

The two lads let go of the chair and glanced ruefully at Martha. They shook their heads in unison.

"So that settles it, lads, it is mine like I said, or should I say my sweet old granny's? She will be looking down on you both now and hoping you are both good honest Christian soldiers. You are, aren't you?" Martha smiled and looked to both the youths. Now, a nodding of heads in unison.

"Come here, each of you, and take a kiss from a grateful young girl." Martha teased. Neither of the youths moved, so Martha stepped to each and kissed them fully on their dirty faces. They blushed and allowed Martha to pick up the chair. As she turned away with her prize, the Parliamentarian youth called to her.

"One of our officers died on it, Miss. Colonel Trent. He had lost a leg and most of his belly, but he was found sitting on it last night. Covered in blood it was. Last night's rain washed most of it off, but you can still see some of his blood on the legs. Me and this kid here think it might now be cursed or haunted. I was just going to chop it up for one of our fires later on. So I suppose it's going back to a good home."

Martha smiled and nodded. "It is, I can assure you. I sat on it not too long ago and I'm so pleased I've got it back. It's part of me and always will be. Bye bye, lads and I hope neither of you get killed, but if you do, don't sell your souls. You'll regret it."

The two lads stared after the young woman and shrugged nonchalantly. They did not know each other's names but even though they had fought on opposite sides, there was no bad feeling between them. After watching the girl carry the chair away for a minute, they looked at each other, shook hands then turned away to resume their body collecting.

Martha returned to the cart with a wry smile on her face. She put the chair in the back of the cart, then Fimber put a hand down and pulled her up to the seat. He flipped the reins and the horse pulled away.

As the little cart trundled away from the deathly battlefield, a pair of blood-red eyes watched. Razor sharp yellow talons instead of finger nails raked at the dying bodies to release the tormented souls beneath the bloodied flesh. Lord Lucifer had persuaded a few of the dying soldiers to sell their souls for paradise in eternity and he was pleased with his day's work. He took a breath from his macabre work to watch the cart moving away. He had more work for the two occupants to undertake and smiled to himself. The young woman pleased him and he licked his scaly lips. She was his property and in the years ahead he would take her, as was his eternal right. He needed more offspring and the woman would provide him with such creatures. For now and hundreds of years ahead, he had work for her and the sometimes disobedient tinker she travelled with.

They had moved north, away from Marston Moor and the battlefield and pulled over on a lonely tree lined lane overlooking a wide expanse of open fields. The mare was calmly nibbling grass and Fimber had carried a bucket of water for her from a stream.

"Do you miss never being thirsty or hungry, Fimber?" Martha asked as she watched the mare enjoying her grass meal.

"Always, lassie. I sometimes believe I can smell food, like roast ham and cooked turnip. My mother was a good cook and her beef stews were to die for." This remark made them both laugh and it took a minute to get their senses back.

"I was five when my mother died of the pox. I never knew what it was like to have proper food. I learned to steal what I needed to eat and this got me through life. When I was taken in by Reverend Brooks and his wife, they often just gave me bread and water once a day. If I left even a crumb, I was locked in a dark cupboard for two days and nights. I hated them. They made me say the Lord's Prayer over and over again and if I missed a word, Mrs Brooks would beat me. I was glad when she died. I would sneak out at night and jump up and down on her grave. I hoped she could hear me as she rotted under the ground."

"Well you're free of them now, lassie and no need to steal food ever again. Stay with me and roam the highways and byways for as long as you want. If you get tired of me, just say and I will wish you well as you go on your way. Just one thing though, lassie. Why did you take the chair back? Doesn't it remind you of something terrible that happened to you?"

"That's why I wanted it back, Fimber. Because if I meet someone on our travels who I don't like, I will get them to sit on my chair. Like that major, who could have prevented me from being drowned on it. He walked away and left me. He sat on it and he died sitting on it. It has his and my blood on it and it can never be washed away."

"The funny thing is that I've found out all these years I've been in debt to Lord Lucifer, is that like me and you of course now with your chair, possessions like the chair and my little cart, never wear out. I change my horse every twenty years, but otherwise everything stays the same. Your chair will go through the ages, like my cart."

"Maybe I will always be young. Is that what happens to us? We never eat or drink or feel ill or feel cold or hot. We never grow old?"

"We, do, lassie, I'm afraid we do," Fimber said ruefully.

Martha shrugged and settled into the seat. The mare had been watered and fed, so they set off again as the early evening July sun started to drop to the west. Fimber had gone quiet and Martha looked at the old tinker, wondering what he was thinking. He smiled and patted her hands.

"I was not much older than you when I sold my soul. That was over two hundred years ago. You might have noticed that I'm getting older as the years roll on. We age, of course, as time passes, but much much slower than normal. In two hundred years' time, you will have aged like me. Like normal people, we slow down and that's when Lord Lucifer starts to replace us with younger souls. We lose our freedom as time passes and he dispenses with our services. We have to join all the lost and worn out souls to a place where the sun doesn't shine, where there is nothing to do but wait out a timeless eternity of misery and rejection. It is a permanent darkness and to hear the suffering of endless wailing and cries of torment. In two hundred years, that is where I will be. You will go there two hundred years later, lassie."

"Is there no escape from that place?" Martha asked.

"The place is called Hell, lassie and the answer is no. Unless—" Fimber's voice trailed off.

"Unless what?"

"You deceive him and play him at his game. He is cunning and he cheats. He will use all of his limitless powers to beat you down. Obviously he can't kill you, you are already dead, but he is the master of trickery and deception, but he was once beaten. No one knows who it was, but a long suffering soul who festers and rots in the bottomless dark pit, knows the story. It may be just a story, it might be false, but it could just be true. Think of that, lassie. There is a chance, but a chance so slim that it is futile to imagine its credibility."

"I want my soul back, Fimber, and I will get it back. If it takes me five hundred years, I will beat Lord Lucifer and be gone with him." Martha sighed contentedly and settled back on the seat. Fimber smiled and nodded as he flipped the reins to the mare.

Lord Lucifer cackled and scratched his half scaly, half fleshy skin. He had collected a dozen souls from the battlefield and put them in a leather pouch, hanging from his side. His work was done for the day and rose to his hoofed feet, sniffed contemptuously and grinned. So you think you can beat me, Martha Budd? Think you can outsmart Lord Lucifer? I let my guard down the last time I was challenged, but there will never be a second time. You will give me twenty offspring before I send you to the bottomless pit. There you will be at the very, very bottom. There you will remain in the slime, the sweat, the foul air and the cramped space, half the space I normally allow for worn out souls. And your travelling companion, the old tinker who feeds you all this rubbish? I will let Smegtooth, my fat little green Irish Boggimp take care of him. The Boggimp will be pleased to have the tinker as a peat slave for a hundred years after I have done with him. Then I'll throw his worn out soul into the bottomless pit, to await the arrival of his watery friend. Lord Lucifer stepped over discarded corpses on the battlefield to make his way to the lair, where he would stay the night. He patted the leather pouch to feel the frightened souls he had collected and laughed his cackling laugh. He had lots more battles in the years ahead to look forward too. Lots more souls to collect.

"There is a battle brewing over in Ireland some years ahead, that's where I will send the girl. Smegtooth the Boggimp will be pleased. More lovely juicy souls to be had." Lord Lucifer quickened his pace and left the battlefield as darkness fell. He wanted to get to his night lair and play with the souls before casting them down to his main lair, six hundred and sixty-six miles below ground.

"Ireland, that's where I'll send them." He laughed loudly and caused hundreds of ravens to squawk and screech into the night air. "The Boggimps can have them for a hundred years."

Chapter Three
The River Boyne

Ireland 1690

"I love Ireland, Fimber. It's so peaceful and idyllic and the fields are so green. It reminds me of Towton Meadows, back in England. That is of course not including the people, they were stuffy and awful. I'm glad I put a death curse on Reverend Brooks and that despicable witch hunter man who came to end my life. And that snotty little toe rag, Jack Spicer. Do you think they all died?" Martha picked up another daisy to finish making a daisy chain.

Fimber was lying on the lush grass chewing on a grass stalk. The sky was a deep blue and cotton wool clouds drifted overhead, chasing each other.

"Oh they did, lassie, they certainly did. That is one of the things you can do when you let Lord Lucifer take your soul. All three of them will have met an untimely end soon after. Mind you, it's another debt you owe Lord Lucifer. He writes them all up in his payment ledgers. He has twenty of them, all in alphabetical order. Eighteen for the regular letters and two for the irregular letters. Four letters in each. Obviously your name is in the B ledger. You are allowed six favours. You have three left."

"Then what, if I use up all six?" Martha asked cautiously, putting the daisy chain around her neck.

"It depends how he feels about you. I have heard of a cavernous chamber where the six users are sent. It is policed by his most trusted servants and the most violent and evil soul sellers. There is no escape from this horrendous chamber. When you arrive having used all six favours there is a list of torture berths. You can choose which torture berth you prefer to stay and work in for the next hundred years. Once in your torture berth you have no rest, no friends no peace, no mercy. My advice, lassie, is never never use up all six favours. Stay well inside the six. Remember, Lord Lucifer is a cheat, a cunning creature and a poor loser. He will try and persuade you to spend all your six favours."

Martha stared in shock at the old tinker and took a deep breath. "What choice is there in these chambers, what sort of things?"

"You really don't want to know, lassie. None are places where you ever want to enter. Just keep inside your six." Fimber sat up and shook his head slowly.

"Tell me, Fimber, I want to know," Martha pleaded.

"They are evil places. I have heard one is a large blood-covered stone ramp. Hundreds of poor souls spend a hundred years pushing gigantic boulders from the bottom to the top, slipping and sliding every exhausting step. No soul has ever made it to the top. They fall, scream and are crushed by the boulder as it hurtles back down the bloody slope. They try to stay on the slope to catch their breath, but the guards lash them with barbed whips and drag them to the bottom, to make them start all over again. A hundred years non-stop on the boulder slope," Fimber explained and put a comforting arm around Martha as she stared in horror.

"How many of these boulder slopes are there?"

"A thousand, lassie. So you can imagine just how big that particular torture chamber is. It is by no means the largest chamber. There are six hundred and sixty-six torture chambers, Every one as demonic and heinous as the others."

Martha wanted to shed tears but she couldn't. Such things never happened now. After a few moments she sighed and put a hand through her thick, luxuriant auburn hair. "Tell me another, Fimber. What others are there?"

The old tinker lay down again and pulled a leg over his other knee. He twiddled the grass stalk across his mouth and took a deep breath.

"Very well, lassie. I mentioned the blood-soaked slope. Well, the blood has to be collected and poured from the top. That is done by souls in the adjacent chamber. A high scaffold made of thorn bushes and bramble stalks twisted into large round pieces is fixed in place with barbed wire to a height of two hundred feet. Buckets of blood taken from every creature on the earth, including humans, is carried up the scaffold by these souls as they climb over the thorn branches, the bramble spikes and barbed wire. When they get to the top with whatever amount of blood is left in the bucket, it is poured over the boulder slope. There is no rest at the top, they then have to climb back down and in a fixed time, to prevent time wasting. If they drop the bucket, a year is added on to their sentence. Hundreds of these poor souls are climbing up and down the scaffold every minute of every day of every week, month and year.

"Remember, there are six hundred and sixty-six boulder slopes, so there is an equal number of scaffolds. For at least a hundred years, these wretches are drenched in all types of blood for all that time."

"So there are another six hundred and sixty-four torture chambers?" Martha gasped in total horror.

"Yes, lassie, every one as bad as the two I have mentioned, some even worse. There is not a soul in the torture chambers that has not regretted selling their soul to Lord Lucifer. As I told you some time ago, only one soul has ever escaped from his clutches. That was hundreds of years ago and he will never let it happen again."

"I will escape, Fimber, and I want you to escape as well." Martha lay down and looked up at the cotton wool clouds. She put a hand up to touch one of them and tried to feel the softness run through her slender fingers.

"The problem is, lassie, that after the first one escaped, Lord Lucifer declared that anyone else who tries to escape and fails, as lots have tried, will spend double time in the torture chambers. Two hundred years of horrific torture. It would take a very brave soul to attempt to escape. Don't try it, lassie."

Martha shrugged and smiled. "Well, Fimber, I have lots of time to think about it."

"Don't think about it, lassie, because now we have to earn our living, so to speak. There is a battle about to take place along this river and His Majesty requires our assistance to find the dying after the fighting has ended. He wants more souls and he wants the blood for his torture chambers."

"Who is fighting who, Fimber?"

"A feller called King Billy is at loggerheads with his father-in-law. One is a catholic and the other, I think that's King Billy, is one of the others. A protestant. The French are involved on one side and the Dutch and Germans on the other. Throw in some trained English soldiers and cavalry and a lot of Irish labourers with shovels, axes and big sticks and there's going to be a right old bash on yon river bank." Fimber sat up and pointed to the riverbank a hundred yards away.

"I saw a lot of ships out on the sea, are they involved, do you think?" Martha asked as she turned to look towards the coast.

"Aye, lassie, most certainly. They will have sailed across from England with King Billy's lot. The others, I think I heard it was a feller called James, who is another King, has hundreds of fighters hidden someplace over here. What the heck they are fighting about is a mystery to me, but Lord Lucifer knows everything a year in advance, as he always does. He sees everything and hears what he can't see."

As the pair sat and chatted, the mare tethered a few yards away let out a warning snort, to tell them that they had company. Both turned and glanced back towards their little cart. They blinked and stared in surprise at the sight of a short and stocky green-looking man, with a big belly and large pointed ears. Climbing all over their cart were more of the green characters, laughing, squealing loudly and pulling out some of Fimber and Martha's belongings, throwing them to the ground.

Martha was immediately up and running back to the cart, cursing and shouting. The first little green man was whacked out of the way and a second and third trampled on by the furious young woman as she dived at a green man holding a pair of her bloomers. Martha snatched the frilly underwear from him and delivered a stinging slap to his ugly face that sent him sprawling. Other fat little green characters dived for cover and clambered down, running away. Martha had climbed onto the cart, grabbed one of the squealing green men and booted him unceremoniously into the air. He bumped to the ground, gathered himself and like the others scrambled for cover.

The bigger of the green men was jumping up and down, waving his arms in the air. His green face had turned red and he did not look a happy bunny. He stomped towards a grinning Fimber and pointed with large, gnarled fingers at the old tinker. Fimber stood his ground as the larger, wart-faced green man prodded him in the chest.

"I told you the last time you trespassed on my land that you would be in trouble, tinker. I'm in charge over here and you have no right to be on my land. Your stupid fancy assistant with the big bosoms has assaulted my men and I'm going to report you to Lord Lucifer. I'll have you both slaving for me on the peat bogs for two hundred years. I'm Smegtooth, Chief of the Boggimps and I rule over here. Five hundred and sixty-seven years, ten months and eleven days I have ruled this land and no jumped up, broken down, washed out, snotty little tinker is going to cause me grief. I cause the grief and I say who stays." Smegtooth stopped prodding Fimber and glanced across to Martha, now guarding the cart and standing with hands on her hips. "She can stay though. How much do you want for her, before I send you to the peat bogs? Sell her to me and I'll drop your sentence to a hundred years."

Fimber laughed and shook his head sagely. "Ask her yourself, Smegtooth. She's got a tongue in her head."

Smegtooth puffed out his chest, popping a brass button from his yellowish tunic. His face had now changed back to green and his extra-long purple tongue swished out, with spittle to wash mud from his face. He rubbed a gnarled finger over his pointed yellow teeth in a vain attempt to clean them. His sighed deeply, pulled a hand through his long greasy hair and pulled his tunic down at the front. The tunic had spots of dried blood and egg stains on it. He marched across to where Martha was standing on the cart and smiled one of his vile, furtive smiles. Martha was sitting on the ducking chair now and her piercing brown eyes burned into the rat-like eyes of Smegtooth the Boggimp.

The fat Boggimp stopped a few feet from the cart and looked up at the beautiful young woman. Her eyes had never moved and they still burned with venom at the grinning Boggimp Chief. He held his gnarled hands together just below his belly, his pants held up with a thick buckled belt. He felt intimidated and somewhat foolish, but he was beside himself in admiration of Martha Budd, the young witch. Perhaps he hoped her thoughts toward him might be of a similar admiration for his splendid figure and handsome features.

"Er—I, er, was thinking you might be willing to, er, consider a marriage proposal. You are the most beautiful thing I have ever seen. We could have lots of little Boggimps. Ten maybe, or even twenty if you like. I was the sixteenth of twenty-three my mother had not long ago," Smegtooth stated as he crossed his legs nervously. "My name is Smegtooth the Terrible, but you can just call me Smegtooth if you like. I am the Chief of the Boggimps and you would become my Queen. We can marry on the next full moon, which is in five days' time and I will take you to my cave and we can start that night to make our first little Boggimp."

Martha looked down at the ugliest creature she had ever seen and smiled.

"How long ago did your mother have you, Mister Smegtooth?"

"Oh, not long, miss. Just over eight hundred years ago. A blip in the swing of things, as you will agree. Will you marry me and become my next wife?"

"Your next wife, sir? How many wives do you have?" Martha asked in amazement.

"Just one or two," Smegtooth replied, uncrossing his legs and switching them around.

"How many?

"Eight. Well, nine, to be honest. My first one just said she is leaving me in thirty years' time, but you could replace her and I will send her away immediately. My cave is big enough for all of you—er, my wives."

Martha smiled sweetly at the repulsive Boggimp, but retained her cool.

"I need to consider your marriage proposal, Mister Smegtooth, before I agree. Help me down, and also my chair. You look tired and you can sit on my chair while I go away for a few minutes to think it over."

Smegtooth jumped at Martha's suggestion and quickly helped her down and pulled the ducking chair to the ground. He tripped over it in his excitement and stumbled forward, to the amusement of his followers, who were watching everything with gleeful interest from various hiding places, but careful not to cause the young witch to attack them again. Smegtooth picked himself up, dusted down his already scruffy clothes and pulled the chair around. He waited for Martha to nod her approval.

"Take a seat, Mister Smegtooth, and give me a few minutes. I need to discuss your marriage proposal with my guardian Fimber O'Flynn."

Smegtooth plonked his fat body down and glared across to where the old tinker was leaning against his cart.

"Forget the tinker, my darling, he's going to the peat bogs to work his socks off for the next hundred years. When he's finished there we will have made at least twenty little Boggimps, and who knows, maybe thirty. You are going to make me a very happy Boggimp King."

Martha sighed, took a deep breath, then stepped towards the seated fat green man with the large pointed ears. She kissed two of her middle fingers and with bated breath, thankful that she could not smell his repulsive body, reached to his head and tapped the straggly, greasy hair covering his oily skin. Smegtooth leaned back in the chair and sighed with profound pleasure at the touch of her soft white hand. He was so in love with this beauty that he could have died with excitement. He closed his eyes and started to think of his forthcoming wedding night. He knew he was such a desirable creature, so handsome, so forceful and of the highest esteem, no damsel would ever turn him down. He started to think of names for all the little Boggimps that she would give him. He couldn't wait to tell Lord Lucifer of his good news. He would be rewarded with more land for his undoubted expertise and good womanising skills. As a wedding present, he hoped Lord Lucifer would allow him to walk the forthcoming battlefield, collecting souls for his master. It was something he had wanted to do for at least four hundred years after he had served his apprenticeship in demonic sciences. Pointing out the dying humans as the fools lay bleeding to death was boring; he wanted to move up a rung and become a soul picker.

Martha shuddered at the thought of being taken by Smegtooth as his bride. To think of bearing the little fat green monster with twenty or thirty little Smegtooths was too revolting a thought. No fool could ever be so desperate as to slip into bed with such a foul, despicable monster. She just hoped the powers that her ducking stool was bestowed with carried over the sea to Ireland. This was the first real test of the chair and of her own powers. If she really was a witch, then her execution on the ducking chair, had not been a tragic mistake.

When she walked back to where she had left Smegtooth the Terrible, sitting on her chair, she was surprised to see most of his helpers standing chattering to themselves and looking dumbfounded, pointing at the empty chair. As soon as they saw Martha reappear, they immediately took off back to their hiding places, not wanting to suffer her wrath. None wanted to be turned into frogs, toads or beetles. Martha walked cautiously to the ducking chair and realised there was no sign of Smegtooth the Terrible. She hesitated and looked carefully at the chair. Running down the spindles and down the carved legs was a thick, green, slimy liquid and on the ground beneath the chair, the broad leather-buckled belt the Boggimp King was wearing and a few brass buttons from his dirty tunic. Smegtooth had melted. The chair had claimed its third victim.

A white flash of lightning speared into the ground nearby and a few seconds later, a resounding clap of thunder erupted. From the bushes around the area, all of Smegtooth's followers broke their cover and ran for their lives, squealing loudly. The fearsome young witch had killed their leader and would surely come after them. In fact, she had not just killed him, she had melted him. More thunder and lightning darkened the surrounding countryside and Fimber looked upwards to the angry sky, as Martha skipped happily along, clapping her hands and laughing.

"He's real mad now, lassie. You wiped out, or should I say melted, one of his favourite assistants. Old Smegtooth ruled this part of Ireland with an iron fist. However, I'm pleased you did, because I was destined to be a peat digger for a hundred years and it's back-breaking work. Twenty-four hours a day, every day, standing up to your knees in filthy organic peat, bent over and filling sacks with the stuff. Our names will be going in the ledger books tonight when Lord Lucifer goes back to his lair. More black marks, I'm afraid. We'd better get off again and try to score a few good points. There's a battle tomorrow and we need to be in place before it starts."

With the chair safely back on the cart, Fimber and Martha headed towards the River Boyne. Martha was singing one of her songs, as she always did after something pleasant had happened. Fimber was unsettled though; he knew Lord Lucifer was watching and knew that once again he was in trouble. So too his capable young assistant. They had to look good the next day, do their job and not upset the master. Get their work done and hopefully they could move on again, until the next time, whenever that was.

At first light the next morning, on a hill overlooking the river Boyne, Martha watched as the two rival armies faced each other from opposite banks. To the northern side, the battle flags and banners were of the English and the Irish Orange Order fighters. Hundreds and hundreds of infantrymen and not a small amount of cavalry. Dozens of cannons were strategically positioned along the riverside, ready to blast the iron balls of death into the enemy ranks. It was the first day of July and a breeze wafted the English and Orange Order banners for all to see. These were King William's soldiers and cavalrymen, waiting for the orders to run or ride into battle. King Billy, as he was nicknamed, rode along the riverside with three or four of his senior officers, rallying his men and stirring up enthusiasm for the fight. The noise was almost deafening as soldiers clanged their shields with sharpened swords and infantrymen stood ready with their rifles. Pikemen raised the ten-foot- long weapons and waved them menacingly. It was the order of battle, intimidation and provocation. Rallying the troops.

On the south side of the river, the strength of the Irish Catholic army was larger in number, but not as well trained or experienced. King James the Second, father-in-law of this young upstart, William, watched as the leader of his army, a French nobleman and over two thousand five hundred mostly French soldiers, waited for their order to cross the river and attack the Protestant army. Added to the Catholic army were hundreds of local men, armed with only axes, pitch forks and sticks. No battle training, but determined to fight for their country and drive the invaders away back to the north.

From his vantage point, Lord Lucifer was beside himself with excitement and joy. He wanted a bloody battle and was not a bit concerned which side won the day and kept their colours. He wanted the River Boyne to run red with blood and he wanted his spotters and scouts to point out where the mortally wounded lay bleeding and butchered. He had his leather pouch at the ready and before nightfall, he wanted it brim full of souls he had bought, stolen or ripped from bodies with his razor sharp talons. He had lost his best ally in Smegtooth the Terrible, because of the dirty, underhanded, treacherous antics of a young witch the day before, but all was not lost. There were still souls to be had and he would return to his lair with a pouch full. The young upstart of a witch could wait, she was his for the future and he licked his lips at the thought of taking her, savagely and mercilessly, in the years ahead.

At the river, it was a bloodbath. The north siders, with the advantage of experience and better equipment, had repelled numerous assaults by James the Second's hired cavalry and dead horses and riders had either been taken by the current, or lay in the shallows in crumpled heaps. The Frenchmen fighting for the Catholics on the southern side had made some impact and fought their way across the river, but the Protestant fighters held their cool and drove the foreigners back. Heavy casualties were suffered by both armies, but after three hours of constant no-mercy fighting, it was the southern siders who broke and ran back. Musket fire dropped a lot of the retreating Catholics and by the end of four hours, the battle was won by King Billy's fighters.

It was a hard won victory for the more experienced combatants, but more than half of their men had been cut down and killed or were injured. King Billy waved a victorious sword in his hand, saluting his victorious fighters, but he was gallant enough to ride to the middle of the river and bow humbly to the beaten southern siders. James the Second had already left the battle area and was riding further to the south to lick his wounds. His son-in-law would later call for a meeting with him to discuss the Irish political and religious problems. It was in both their interests to resolve the politics of the situation, but what neither man would know was that in the years to come, it would get worse. Much worse.

At the end of that July day in 1690, the victorious Orangemen walked or rode away in high spirits. The many scores of ships anchored just off the coast, north of Dublin, would take battle weary fighters back to England, Holland or France and leave a divided country still in turmoil. No side actually won the Battle of the Boyne.

Two days later, the River Boyne had shed its blood and returned to a tranquil river, meandering through the warm Irish countryside. On both banks between where the battle had been fought, most of the two armies had departed, but a handful of people from both sides wandered around, trying to find any survivors of the fierce fighting. Hundreds had died, but most of these had been carted away in a variety of vehicles. Those who belonged to no one were buried in mass graves.

Half of the local untrained men, who had taken up arms to fight King Billy's army, had lost their lives and weeping mothers, sisters and daughters remained to pay their last respects where their loved ones had died. Little boys who dreamed of being soldiers or cavalrymen in a future battle, suddenly realised the futility of war, if their older brother, father or uncle had been killed in the riverside battle less than two days earlier. It suddenly seemed such a waste of a good life.

The little painted cart trundled away towards the north with two passengers, sitting silently, lost in their own thoughts. More death and bloodshed behind them, the scavengers still desperately picking through the leftovers. Hundreds of ravens feasting on the unburied remains.

One cursing red-eyed figure visiting the site for the second time, hoping to find one more lonely soul looking for a saviour. Lord Lucifer had had a good first day of pickings but at the end of the second day he had just four souls in his leather pouch. A lot of potential souls had been lost because his spotters and scouts had not done their jobs properly. The damned inconsiderate dying fighters had breathed their last breaths before he had got to them. He was mad, really mad. Someone would pay for his loss.

He glanced to the north and saw the tinker's cart trundling away. That pair of disobedient slaves he tolerated would pay for his losses on this battlefield. He would cut their free time from fifty years to thirty. Teach them a lesson. On top of their stupidity, he had also lost Smegtooth the Terrible. The young witch had outwitted the fat old Boggimp. He knew he would have to keep an evil eye on her. Martha Budd was a barrel load of trouble. He would have to rein her in before he had wanted to.

Smegtooth had wanted her to deliver him as many as thirty of the little Boggimp runts. Old fool, thinking he had the right to marry the young witch. Who would want a smelly, over the hill, podgy, green-skinned, has-been for a randy husband? Smegtooth deserved to be melted into green slime. Lucifer cackled and hogged his way from the battlefield, cursing as he stepped over a couple of rotting bodies.

"These two idiots probably had good souls and now they've gone to that place I hate to think of. The tinker and that young witch will pay. Twenty years' free time is all they deserve. Any more cock-ups and they drop to twenty. In fact, I think there is a battle in a couple of years' time over in Scotland. Two years' free time. Yeah, that will stuff them. Think about that tonight when I'm more relaxed and had a few drinks. No more cows' blood, though, back to human blood. I got enough here yesterday, knock it back before it goes off. Daft, using fresh blood for my torture chambers. Six pints of fresh human blood tonight and a good sleep. Think about those two itinerants tomorrow, but I will definitely send them to Scotland for the next battle."

Chapter Four
Western Scotland

Glencoe Valley 1692

"Why does he hate us so much?" Martha asked as she looked out at the desolate bleakness of the wilderness at Glencoe. It was mid-February and the rugged landscape was covered in a thin covering of snow. There was no one in sight and the only living creatures foolish enough to be outside in the near-freezing cold were some highland sheep, but even they were trying to find shelter from a blustery wind blowing from the east.

"He hates everything he can't have, lassie, or at least creatures like us who can still think for ourselves. He's trying to teach us a lesson for his poor collection of souls back over in Ireland two years ago. Not to mention you melting that old fool, Smegtooth of the Boggimps. That was pure genius, I must say. It will be a long time before he gets that out of his mind."

"I still shudder at the thought of that ugly wart-faced idiot thinking I would be his wife! His ninth wife at that. Can you imagine seeing him without his dirty clothes on? Wrinkled green skin and those horrendous gnarled fingers with claws at the ends? Uggh, disgusting. Where did he come from in the first place?"

"Well, it goes back hundreds of years, lassie. There are three tribes of smallish green people in Ireland and they are always at war with each other. They are ungodly fiends and in league with the devil himself. There are the Leprechauns, the Banshees and the Boggimps, all green in colour but of different shades. Three feet tall, stoutly built and hairy. Their teeth are like fangs and the hands, as you saw, with four fingers; long, crude and gnarled, with small talons or claws at the end. They can live to be a thousand years old, but because they are always fighting and killing each other, they probably only live to be a couple of hundred years old. They are cannibals as well, delighting in eating their victims. When Smegtooth said he had eight or nine wives, that is because he only has that many at any given time. He gets fed up with them after a while, kills and eats them, then finds a replacement, like you!"

Martha gasped and stared at the old tinker. "He would have eaten me!"

Fimber smiled and nodded ruefully. "Yep, in time, and roasted you for dinner. He invites his closest friends and on a night of the full moon, cooks his latest dinner, carves her up and serves the offerings up on wooden plates. Then, with goblets of blood, his ex-wife's blood, they get drunk after the meal, then fall into a drunken stupor. That, lassie, is a common occurrence for the male Boggimps." Fimber leaned back and stretched his legs out and glanced at Martha. If she could have turned whiter in the face she would have, but her ashen face was creased into a mask of disbelieving shock.

"They're downright evil, ugly little creeps. And that—that thing—wanted to marry me!"

"Well, he wanted you to bear up to thirty of his offspring before he killed and ate you, lassie. That would have been in about a hundred and fifty years' time."

Martha took a deep breath and shook her head. "I think being a witch and never dying again and living for a few hundred years and never feeling hot or cold, might not be so much fun after all."

Fimber laughed and pointed to the frozen landscape all around. "You would want to be out in all that frozen weather right now, lassie? I'm glad I'm not."

"Yeah, well, it has some advantages I suppose, but I do miss the smell of roast chicken every now and then, not to mention plum pudding."

"You better stop reminiscing, lassie, Lord Lucifer doesn't like his servants having a sense of humour. We have a job to do here tomorrow morning and he's still brooding over our poor performance at the River Boyne. We should be on our free time now, but he intends to punish us for what he claims we didn't do back in Ireland."

Martha looked out as the night took over from day. Apart from a few freezing and hungry sheep, the moorland was deserted. "Why are we here in the middle of nowhere, Fimber? There are no people to be seen. No large armies or suchlike."

"There will be in a few hours. Nothing big, mind you, but men will be killed and injured. Lord Lucifer knows just where and when it will happen. Whatever happens near here will be a tiddly little bit of nonsense, but there will be blood spilled and a few lost souls to be collected. "

"How does he know when and where a battle takes place? It's unreal," Martha asked, looking perplexed.

Fimber laughed and patted her knee. "Everything in our world is unreal, lassie. I thought you would have figured that out that by now. Look at you, still young and beautiful. When was it you were put to death, what year?"

Martha screwed her face up and shrugged, then said, "1643, I think."

"So if you were still alive, you would be how old? It's now 1692."

"I was eighteen when they took me, so—" She thought for a few moments, doing the sums. "If I was still alive, er, mid-sixties."

"So by now you would be dead, as people these days only get to about fifty, if they're lucky. So you see, lassie, we exist in an unreal world, and to answer your question, Lord Lucifer is very, very unreal. He has a meticulous brain, an unreal brain and he sees things years ahead. He possesses great power, an untold memory bank so he can remember the tiniest detail of every one of his soul servants, including you and me. The only one he fears is the great Almighty, God himself. Never underestimate him, he never forgets or forgives," Fimber stated.

"But one of us got away, you said."

"Hundreds and hundreds of years ago. He let his guard down and the soul—it was a woman's soul, escaped to freedom. Proper freedom."

"Who was it, do you know?" Martha asked.

"She was a warrior queen called Jacindra, the daughter of Boadicea, the leader of a Saxon tribe in ancient England. Very beautiful, very intelligent, very cunning. Fearsome and ruthless. It was said she escaped from a Roman prison and killed several guards as she made her way to freedom.

Starving after she escaped, she slaughtered two more Romans and dragged their bodies to a secret cave in the marshes and hid them. It was mid-winter and everything was frozen. She survived the winter by eating the flesh of her two victims. The winter ended and she broke her cover to travel back to her tribe, in what is now called Anglia in the east. Unfortunately, she met a couple of travellers and foolishly confided in them. They left her and made their way to a Roman fort a few miles away and for a few pieces of silver, betrayed her. A centurian and his men tracked her and eventually found her. In the fight during her recapture, four more Romans were killed and she was taken back in chains, flogged and then sentenced to death. They crucified her and left her close to death, on a rough wooden cross for all to see, as a warning of what happens to murderers and enemies of the Roman Empire. In the last few minutes of her life, before dawn one day, Lord Lucifer called and spoke to her. He left with her soul. They found her dead body in the morning with a smile on her beautiful face. Her tortured body was unmarked, yet she had received a hundred lashes before being nailed to the cross."

"He took her soul and then what?" Martha was desperate for more detail.

"The years passed and Jacindra became a model servant. Three hundred and thirty three years after she sold her soul, she fooled Lord Lucifer and escaped. No one knows how, where or what she did but it happened. He was in a blinding rage for weeks and destroyed a million souls in retaliation for being cheated. He made the torture chambers more severe and reduced free time to one year. He gives his most trusted soul keepers, the demonic brutes who run the torture chambers, free use of any soul that takes their fancy. In return, he gets total loyalty from these brutes and they report to him any souls who harbour bad feelings towards him, or talk of escaping."

"Does he hear and see everything we do?"

"No, not everything, lassie. The one thing he isn't, is a million per cent perfect. But he has hundreds of helpers with him all the time. Lost souls who are everywhere. Trustees, they're called. You and me can't see them most of the time, but I learned how to detect them some time ago. He knows now that I have learned how to flush out these trustees and that is why I get the chance to roam around like I do. I have to obey him, of course and do his bidding when he wants, but he knows I could make a dent in his armour if I really wanted. "

"Can you teach me what you know?" Martha asked hopefully.

"In time, lassie, maybe, but not before I am sure you can handle the knowledge I can pass over to you. As soon as I do that, Lord Lucifer will know what I have done and he will destroy my soul. A treasonable soul, as I will be, will suffer an agonising destruction ten times worse than the most painful death a human can suffer."

"Then I can't ask you to help me, Fimber. Forget I asked," Martha declared disconsolately.

Again the old tinker patted her hands. "No, lassie, I will. I'll go under and suffer whatever demise he inflicts on me, as long as you beat him like Jacindra did over a thousand years ago. If you do what she did, I will be a very happy but very dead old tinker."

Martha squeezed his hands and nodded with approval. "I'll beat him. I will beat him."

5.00 a.m. February 13th

Another flurry of snow had blown across Glencoe Moor and footsteps appeared on the whitened earth. A little hamlet a mile south of Loch Leven was asleep, as the silent assassins made their way to a motley little group of cottages. Just over a mile away to the east, another hamlet was sleeping as another group of assassins quietly trod the new snow, with murder in mind.

Invercoe and its neighbouring hamlet, Achaean had been cruelly targeted by soldiers of the Argyll regiment under the command of Captain Robert Campbell, to wipe out alleged outlaws who were loyal to the MacDonald clan. Rumours had been widespread that the MacDonald clan, or bandits as they had been branded by the authorities in Edinburgh, had looted and pillaged across a wide area of central and western Scotland. Farms had been raided, some burned to the ground, livestock stolen and women raped by the lawless intruders. Aides to King William had convinced him that the only way to stop the bandits and restore law and order, was to wipe them out once and for all. All able bodied men under seventy were to be killed.

At Ballachulish, the regiment's commander, Major Robert Duncanson, gave the final order to Captain Campbell, to carry out King William's instructions. Such an act of legal violence and retribution was frowned upon by some in the government, but the written order was approved, signed and handed to a messenger, to be taken to Robert Duncanson's headquarters, for him to immediately put together a raiding force of trained soldiers and for them to carry out the assassinations of the MacDonalds, under Captain Campbell. To that end, a company of a hundred and fifty specially selected soldiers were despatched to the hamlets near Loch Leven before daybreak, to kill the outlaw clan members.

The bloody massacres that followed on that freezing February morning wiped out a large number of the MacDonalds, most of them asleep in their beds. At least thirty-nine of the outlaws were shot or hacked to death and several who ran away were hunted down and mercilessly killed. It was conveniently reported to have been a fierce battle, to save embarrassment for the government, but the truth is, it was a cowardly, bloody massacre, approved by Duncanson, but initially put together by the king and his advisers. King William refused to accept the blame for the murders and insisted he had been misinformed of the troubles up in Scotland.

Within two weeks of the murders of their menfolk, at least forty-five women and children of the MacDonald clan died of exposure, because their simple homes had been burnt to the ground and they had had no means of finding shelter or food. Major Duncanson's assassins had murdered the men and then left the area as quickly as they had arrived. It was ten days before anyone informed the authorities that there might be helpless women and children abandoned near Glencoe.

Back in Edinburgh, the men responsible for the murders of so many of the MacDonald clan members and afterwards, the sad deaths of women and children, were ducking and diving and making themselves scarce. Robert Duncanson somehow managed to get himself promoted, King William returned to the relative peace and quiet of London and two or three members of the Scottish hierarchy received knighthoods or titles.

The little cart was pulled to a stop, a few yards from a burning cottage. The roof had collapsed and the walls were ready to cave in. It was just one of about ten similar crudely built dwellings that had been torched an hour earlier. Daylight had still not pushed darkness away, but the devastation was clearly visible to Fimber O'Flynn and his young companion, Martha Budd. They could see clearly, even without help from the dying embers of the fire that had ripped through the cottage. It was the same devastation a mile away at the next hamlet. Dead bodies and several badly injured clan members. The Argyll soldiers had disappeared into the night.

Bunched in a few small groups, distraught women and crying children stood around, huddled together for warmth and comfort. All around on the snow covered ground, now bloodstained, bodies of mutilated men and teenage boys lay. Some had been beheaded. Frightened dogs cowered, even these poor creatures unable to bark after witnessing the senseless murders of their masters.

As usual at such sites of atrocity, a cackling, red-eyed figure scavenged around the bodies of the near-dead victims. He prodded and poked and was seen to lean close to the bloodied mouths of the dying men. He held a leather pouch carefully in his wicked looking-clawed hands, but he had been unsuccessful in buying more than a couple of the souls. One had been a sixty-one-year-old man, who had been dying of the tetanus, before he had been pulled from his bed, dragged outside and clubbed to within an inch of his life. He was only too happy to sell his soul to Lord Lucifer for the promise of eternity in paradise.

Lord Lucifer raised his scaly body and cursed loudly. He looked across the bloody snow-covered ground and waved a dismissive arm at Fimber O'Flynn. He had expected more bodies at this place of freezing desolation and he needed to pass the blame. "Get gone you useless pair of imbeciles, before I destroy you both. Get gone north in this barren freezing country and await my instructions. I have a mind to send you across the raging seas to a wild lawless country where you can't escape. I know what she thinks, but she is sadly mistaken if she thinks I will let another mindless soul take back her freedom. She is mine and in time I will have my way with her. Keep her safe, tinker, or I will pulverise your feeble soul. Now get gone out of my sight, until I need you again."

Fimber flipped the reins and his mare willingly took the strain on her harness and pulled away.

Martha settled onto her seat and instinctively pulled a woollen shawl around her slim shoulders to ward off the cold, but realised she could not feel a chill any more. There was no pain in her condition, no sense of smell, or suffering the inevitable winter time coughs or bouts of influenza. If she had still been alive and able to breathe fresh air normally, these conditions would have been a regular nuisance. What she could not stop thinking of was the story of the Saxon woman, Jacindra. The only lost soul to have escaped from the terrible fanatical clutches of Lord Lucifer. Was she as good as Jacindra, as tough, as tenacious and clever as the Saxon Queen? What exactly had Jacindra done to rid herself of Lucifer?

Martha took a breath and looked across the wild, expansive moorland. She turned to Fimber and wondered what the old man was thinking. He was a thoughtful, knowledgeable character who did not seem to have a bad feeling about anyone or anything. He never tired of her plentiful questions and he was happy to share his time with her for however long it had to be.

"Fimber, we can't smell things, we can't feel pain as we once did, we can see in the dark and we never get hungry or thirsty and we don't feel the cold as it is now. It will be freezing out on the moors. Those women and children back there were blue and shivering in the cold, but the one thing we can do is lift things, like I pulled my chair from those awful Boggimps in Ireland. I could feel it just as I could have when I was alive. We have a sense of touch, we can see and hear. Is that what paradise is, to live for hundreds of years, without a care?"

The old tinker chuckled and shook his head.

"Paradise, lassie, is back where we came from. Not here, wandering the earth at the beck and call of you know who. Watching his heinous and despicable antics with the near-dead. Fifty years of life as we used to know it is much better than what we do now. Yes, it's a very short time of course, fifty or, if you're lucky, sixty years, but I know which I would have preferred, knowing what I know now. Having the ability to touch normal things is a good thing, like when I put a harness on the mare, or picking her feet up to scrape stones or mud from them, but this is not paradise, it is purgatory, mindless depredation and profanity. We chose this ungodly path and there is nothing we can do."

"How many of the six favours have you left?"

Fimber grinned ruefully. "Just one, lassie, and to me, that is like finding a cask of gold coins worth a king's ransom back on the real earth. I guard that one favour with every thought in my soulless head. He tries to test me to give it up, but I know he is keeping the worst torture berth for me."

"Is there a bad one, Fimber, the worst of them all?" Martha asked.

"Oh, yes, lassie. He always keeps two or three places spare in it. I know one is for me, should I ever be foolish enough to spend my last favour."

"Tell me. I want to know," Martha persisted.

Fimber sighed heavily and shook his head. "It is a chamber where you have a chance of redeeming your soul, to win back all six favours. It is the most evil, vile place you can imagine. To come out it and call yourself a winner, you have to be a soul with no conscience. There are many tests of strength and wisdom. One of the tests is to vanquish as many souls as are pitted against you. Once destroyed, these poor souls are committed to every torture chamber for six eternities. Six hundred and sixty-six torture berths for ever and ever. No respite, perpetual darkness, no friends, nothing but sheer terror and hard labour for ever. One of these souls you have to destroy could be mine. It could be of a child who was dying of the black plague and was cheated by Lord Lucifer into selling his or her soul, for a place in paradise. A young mother who was dying in child birth and sold her soul. Undead innocents who had no chance of enjoying a normal life. Could you do that, lassie, to win back your favours?"

Martha once more wished she could shed tears, but of course she could not. Her dead eyes drifted across the frozen moorland of Glencoe and then she bowed her head. Fimber reached across and once more patted her soft, clenched hands.

They headed north and as they did, the weather became colder and the terrain less hospitable. Mountains became more common and the tracks less accommodating. Fimber knew he had to go north with the little cart, but did not know where or when he had stop. It could be a few days of travel or a few years. Would the mare pulling the cart at that moment still be the one pulling the cart, when they reached their destination? He had no idea.

Chapter Five
Drummossie Moor, Culloden

April 1746

Rain had been falling for two days, the ground was saturated and the wheels of the gun carriages were constantly stuck in the mud. Heavy horses did their best, but no amount of whipping them or shouting and cursing helped. Field commanders were no better than the ranks, their shouted orders falling on deaf ears. For as far as the eye could see, thousands of weary troops, soaked to the skin were at the mercy of the wind and ceaseless rain.

The Duke of Cumberland, leader of the Hanovarian Army, sat in a large tent with a half dozen of his senior officers. On a table in the middle, a large parchment map of the surrounding terrain was unfolded and held down by whisky decanters. Presumed battle positions on the well-thumbed map had been drawn and hopefully positioned in the right places, by a team of strategists and advisors.

A young recently promoted major, hopeful of saying the right thing to his older colleagues, pointed a manicured finger to a position on the map. After ten minutes of deliberations and counter suggestions, the youngster, only twenty-five, had seen what his more experienced counterparts had overlooked. William Belford, English educated and with a refined English accent, though he had pure red Scottish blood in his veins, had nervously made a valid point.

The others agreeably nodded and the Duke of Cumberland stood, finished off a glass of malt and joined his men, staring at the map. Major Belford held his breath and waited for an expected rebuttal. Instead, the heavy hand of the Duke patted down on his slim shoulders.

"Why did you lot not see it? I was waiting to see if any of you spotted the obvious. Three cannons on that small hillock, a few feet apart and at different angles—" Cumberland hesitated and looked at Belford. "What would you say, Major, what difference in positions for the three guns?"

Belford put a hand to his mouth and coughed gently. The others watched him carefully. He tapped the position he had mentioned, confidently. "Five degree angles sir. Six at the most and elevation difference two degrees. That way the three shots will explode several yards apart, causing maximum damage to the Jacobites. I reckon—" he coughed again and felt the eyes staring at him, "Assuming they attack our positions in force and in lines five yards apart, our exploding charges will take down at least forty men at a time."

The other officers looked at Cumberland's deadpan, heavily whiskered face, then back to Belford's face, which bore a faint smile. He was enjoying his few moments of glory and continued confidently, his voice now louder.

"With three sets of cannon in groups of three, twenty-five yards apart, the same angles, fired at the same time, we can cause havoc and kill and maim going on a hundred and twenty, possibly even a hundred and fifty. What we need to do is put white markers in place, starting at a hundred yards' distance from our cannon, and those will give our gunners something to aim at. The Jacobite infantry will think they are just pieces of wood, small twigs sticking out of the ground; only our artillery will be able to see the white side. The dead bodies and wounded will clutter the heavy ground, making it difficult for the following ranks to proceed without hindrance. We have to reload quickly and watch for the markers, raising elevation another degree in height. In between reloading the cannon, our sharpshooters will be able to fire their muskets at the following, and might I say very frightened, infantry."

Cumberland looked with admiration at the young major, who had made his mark and knew it. A stuffy faced colonel, a tall thin man who had the colours of his home clan on the kilt he was wearing, huffed and took a drink from his glass. The other officers did the same. Belford resisted the temptation to pour himself a glass of malt. He had not been invited to share a decanter of whisky. Cumberland patted him again and pushed a glass towards him and a decanter. He nodded once at Belford. The youngster poured himself a small measure and took a drink. The liquid burned his throat and he coughed most of it out. The laugh of derision around the table, brought him back down to earth and he meekly stepped back a pace. This was a man's world and he still had a lot to learn of how to handle himself in that world.

Three miles away, the six thousand strong Jacobite army were camped beside a strong running stream, less well equipped than the Duke of Cumberland's army, but despite the foul weather, most were in high spirits. Their leader, James Edward Stuart, who had been saddled with the nickname 'Bonnie Prince Charlie', was in a confident mood as he had dinner with a gathering of his senior officers. He had travelled over some weeks earlier from France, his second home, to lead his Jacobites against the Hanovarian forces who he had vowed to put down to their last ignorant man. The boyish looking King, some would say effeminate, his cultured voice soft, laughed at jokes he did not find the least funny, but was wise enough to appear confident and approachable to his officers; one or two he had never met before. By ten the following morning, the two great armies were facing each other, in places less than eighty yards apart.

The ground was boggy, uneven, the worst possible battle positions that could have been chosen. Rival chanting, encouraged by hardened leaders from the ranks, desperate to gain advantage against the enemy. Drummossie Moor, near Culloden, was about to explode with the noise of battle. Men and boys, their hearts beating like drums, their nerves at breaking point, hoping they would walk back to loved ones when the last musket shot was fired, the last cannon sending its deadly missile into the enemy lines.

Major Belford, sitting on a Cleveland Bay mount, felt a ripple of excitement run through his taut body, watching with pride as cannons were placed at the positions he had suggested the evening before. He watched through a brass field glass, as the cannons in sets of three, were primed ready to fire. Twelve cannons, most never having been fired before in anger, ready and waiting. All battery commanders waiting for the order to send the red hot projectiles into the lines of enemy infantrymen.

Almost to the minute of eleven o'clock, a loud whistle sounded and the Jacobite infantrymen screamed out their battle cries and the battle had started. It was raining, the sky a brooding grey, a chill hanging in the air over the bleak moorland. Men and boys moved forward apprehensively, muskets held tight in nervous hands, bayonets fixed. To a man, they were drenched, clothes saturated, rainwater running down unprotected necks.

Belford had his sabre held high, his every movement carefully watched by the gunners, waiting for the swirling steel to drop in his gloved hand. He waited for nail-biting seconds to give the order. William Augustus, the Duke of Cumberland, watched from a distance with two of his senior officers, impatiently waiting for the young upstart Belford to start the government response. Lieutenant Colonels Robert Rich and John Ramsey pulled their horses around, desperately wanting the cannons to open fire.

Then the sabre dropped and the first three-pounders blasted. A couple of seconds later and the second set blasted, then the third and the fourth. Five seconds later eight Coehom mortars sent missiles high into the air. Ten more seconds and the three-pounders blasted again in sequence. The well trained Hanovarian gunners were moving quickly as they reloaded. The Coehom mortars sent another series of missiles high in the air, this time set an extra couple of degrees, to maximise the killing spread. Gun smoke swirled upwards, the smell of burnt powder and cordite stinging already sore nostrils.

The government infantry waited for the smoke to disperse before charging forward. Three hundred of the troops, mostly clansmen opposed to the Jacobite rebellion, held broadswords at the ready. Musket men had levelled their weapons in three organised lines, set two yards apart. Five hundred horse waited to both sides, sabres and lances drawn.

Cumberland had crossed fingers, hoping his confidence in Major Belford was assured. Colonel Henry Conway, sitting on his very calm Cleveland Bay, had no such doubts or worries.

He knew the young major had made his preparations to a fault. The gunners were reloading lightning quick and even ankle deep in mud, soaked to the skin, they had worked magic. At two hundred and fifty yards' distance, the three-pounders had wreaked havoc amongst the Jacobites. The mortars had added to the slaughter and the dead and dying were scattered everywhere, some bodies split into three or four pieces. Severed heads lay in the mud, bodies less limbs, men and boys screaming pitifully.

The carnage fifty yards ahead of the government troops was a sorry sight, but the gleaming broadswords of the clansmen were raised and ready to inflict more carnage. Musketry men had now fixed bayonets and waited for the clansmen to hurl themselves against fellow Scots, but of the despised Jacobite supporters.

A blood curdling roar sounded and three hundred clansmen raced forward, wielding razor-sharp broadswords. Even with energy-sapping mud clinging to their simple leather shoes, the colours of the different tartans worn by the clansmen stood out against the gorse and bracken of Drummossie Moor. They surged fearlessly into the almost frozen terrified Jacobites, cutting and slashing with their large broadswords.

One young Jacobite, a lad no more than seventeen, tripped as he ran back and fell face down in the mud. He clawed his way up, but stopped as he was on his knees and saw a large red-bearded clansman standing over him, a broadsword above his head. Walter Stirling looked up with wary eyes and saw the shiny metal weapon hovering a few feet above his rain-soaked head. The bearded clansman stared down at the downed youth and hesitated. He had just taken a head from another Jacobite with one mighty sweep of his sword, but this boy was no older than his own son. Gordon MacTavish sniffed contemptuously and spat on the ground at the side of the boy. He lowered his sword and ran after his friends, who were hacking and cutting their frenzied way through the retreating Jacobites.

Walter Stirling clambered up on trembling legs, using the sword he had carried into battle. He looked up to thank his maker, but the swipe of another broadsword caught him across the back just below his neck and he fell once more, face down in the bloody mud. The broadsword struck him again, severing his spine and he was unable to move as the slimy mud seeped into his mouth. He cried out to his mother, but he knew the words would never carry to her. He could not stop the mud trickling down his throat.

The Jacobite commanders watched in disbelief at the ferocity and accuracy of the government artillery. In less than ten minutes, more than four hundred of their fighters had been slaughtered. General Murray turned to look at Charles Stuart, the boyish monarch. The latter, flamboyantly dressed, was white faced and dumbstruck. Murray called to Stuart to give the order for their hired French cavalry to move forward, but the young pretender was unable to respond, sheer fright had taken over his body. Colonel John Sullivan rode to General Murray to persuade his commander to take over leadership. Murray hesitated, for fear of reprisals later, but as the sight of three hundred loyal government clansmen, hacking their way through disorientated and terrified Jacobites, he finally signalled for the French cavalry to join the fight.

The mud was worse for the horses and within five minutes of the French cavalry joining the fight, a quarter had perished as Major Belford's artillerymen had continued their slaughter of the enemy. Some would say later that a red mist was carried over the Culloden battlefield, this the blood of the slaughtered army of Bonnie Prince Charlie.

An hour and a half after the first three-pounders had dropped amongst the front ranks of Charles Stuart's Jacobites, almost sixteen hundred men and boys of his impoverished army lay dead or dying on Drummossie Moor, near Culloden. No more than fifty of Cumberland's troops had lost their lives.

On a small hillock covered in gorse, the rain still falling, Major William Belford sat on his shivering war horse, looking across Culloden Battlefield. He felt no pride at the sight of hundreds of the enemy lying in bloody, slaughtered heaps. His three-pounders and mortars had accounted for a third of the dead. Broadswords had butchered another third, almost two of the enemy for each of the ferocious clansmen. Pikemen and infantrymen had taken the rest. Lots of the Jacobites had deserted the battlefield. Most would be hunted down and hanged for desertion.

William Augustus rode over to his young, sad-faced artillery major, to shake his hand. A promotion would follow Belford from the battlefield. The doubting officers he had taken malt whisky with the previous evening rode to him to tender congratulations. He shook their hands, then turned his horse away and as he did, he caught a glimpse of a small painted cart a couple of hundred yards away. He wiped his wet face to look again, but the little cart had vanished. He pushed his horse forward into the mud and again glimpsed a strange figure in the distance, but this time nearer. He blinked and wiped his face again. This time he saw a tall figure, a man, and he thought at first sight it was reddish in colour and picking its way through the battlefield's, dead and dying. The rain was playing tricks with his vision, but as he stared once more through the rain and mist, which he could swear was reddish, the figure had also vanished.

"Where now, Fimber?" Martha asked as she turned from looking at the battlefield.

"Dunno yet, lassie, His Majesty will be happy enough now that he has rich pickings to choose from. He might leave us alone for a few years if we're lucky," The old tinker replied happily.

"How far north can we go in this country?"

"Not far, lassie, it gets wilder though. Not many people around. I came up here about a hundred years ago, hoping he would not find me, but he did. Sent me over to a little island off the coast, where a disease had broken out, to locate people who had been left to die. I had to put a mark on the doors of these cottages where someone was dying inside. He took souls of children as well as those of adults."

"How old is he?"

"Thousands and thousands. He has the souls of lots of nasty people who have lived."

"Like who?"

"Ivan the Terrible, Attila the Hun, Vlad the Impaler, King Herod and others."

"Have you met any of those people?"

"Just one, a real evil man. King John of England. He was a traitor to his people and had hundreds of poor innocents murdered, because they could not pay him the taxes he imposed. If they had they would have starved to death. He is in the torture chambers now for eternity. I met him just before he used up his sixth and last favour."

"Have you ever seen Lord Lucifer?"

"Aye, lassie, I have."

"What does he look like?"

"That's hard to say, because he can change appearance to suit his moods. He's always the same height though, a bit taller than the average man and lean in body, but he is an extraordinarily powerful creature. He can vanish before your eyes and reappear twenty feet from the ground, sitting on a ledge looking down at you, with those evil red eyes. He has a sense of smell stronger than a blood hound's. He can see just as clear at night as in broad daylight. He drinks only blood and any kind of blood; human, animal, reptile. He can hear sounds from great distances, so be very, very careful if you speak of him with derision. He can see things before something has happened. He never forgets anything."

"Can he father children?"

"Yes, lassie, he can and he does. His offspring are just as powerful and with almost the same dominant and destructive temperament. He sends them to walk amongst the real living humans, to feed him information and to take over the minds of the susceptible, so that atrocious evil can be committed. There is no compassion, no merciful thoughts in these creatures' minds. He breeds them to spread hatred and confusion. Like Lord Lucifer, they are indestructible and powerful. Just as their maker, they prowl the earth to seek evil and collect tormented souls."

"How many of them are there walking amongst the humans?"

"Too many, lassie. They're in every country of the world. They look normal, act normal and speak normal. They know who are children of Lucifer but never intermix. They cannot breed with each other, but they can with normal humans. So to answer your question, there are thousands and thousands of them loose on the lands all over the world."

"Could we make them out, if we were back among the humans?"

Fimber laughed and shook his head as he guided the mare along the track they were on, heading deep into the Highlands. "Only one of us can do that, lassie. Jacindra, the daughter of Queen Boadicea. Her quest on earth has been to seek out the children of Lucifer and destroy them. By gaining her freedom and taking back her soul, she has been granted the same indestructible powers that these creatures have. They can kill her and she them, but she has the advantage of once outwitting their maker and they fear she could repeat her cunning to destroy them. They stay clear of her for that reason, but as a group they could destroy Jacindra. For hundreds of years she has walked as a free woman amongst the humans and enjoyed the benefits of feeling the warmth of the sun, eating and drinking, being able to take in the scents that are in abundance in real life. In all intents and purpose, Jacindra is a normal woman, with the ability to bear children and has in fact done that. Her offspring are the opposite of Lord Lucifer's offspring. Their quest is that of Jacindra's. To rid the earth of the evil children of Lucifer. Many have perished from both sides."

Many miles to the south, a skulking figure hissed and cursed as he collected another pouch full of wretched souls from those wishing a life in paradise, instead of a lingering and painful death on the mud of Culloden and Drummossie Moor. The two armies had been long gone and in the aftermath of the battle, there were still some near-dead combatants, who had been left to rot on the bloody, rain-soaked ground. Their pitiful, agonised cries went unheeded and one by one they died where they lay, in mutilated heaps.

Lucifer had heard what Fimber O'Flynn had been telling his young friend and nodded to himself as he prowled the killing field of Culloden, collecting his souls. "One day, tinker, I'll take that last favour of yours and you will suffer more than anyone has ever suffered. But soon, I think I'll send the pair of you across the raging seas to a wild barren wilderness."

He was happy to have a full pouch of souls and turned to leave the battlefield to go back to his lair. He stepped over a couple more dead bodies and then heard the faintest of a laboured cry, from a mud-covered, broken body. He looked at the figure in the mud and licked his lips. There were very few near-dead bodies left, but he had found one in the mud. He scraped mud from the face of the dying figure and saw the youthful if harrowing face, with almost lifeless eyes staring up at him.

Young Walter Stirling was minutes from death, a death that had lingered for two days in the mud of Culloden, where he had lain after being brutally cut down by a broadsword. His spine was broken and he had lost half of his body's blood. He had called for his mother and his sweetheart a thousand times as he lay broken and bleeding. The pain from his mortal wounds had stopped after the first day, but he had lost the power to move. He had heard the sounds of other wounded fighters, screaming pitifully, but one by one they had fallen silent as death took them. Now, his watery eyes saw the reddened, scaly face of something grinning at him. He blinked and tried to focus, but there was mud in his eyes.

He had been a strong youth, tall for his age and a bit of a daredevil. Fear had not been a fault of Walter Stirling; he was never afraid of fighting for his honour or to support his brothers and sisters. He had joined the Jacobite Rebellion a year earlier and had fought fiercely at the battle of Prestonpans, near Edinburgh. In a fierce and deadly hand-to-hand fight, he had cut down three of the enemy fighters. Wounded after that frenzied two minutes of madness, he had fought his way through a throng of government foot soldiers, to assist two comrades who had been injured.

The reddish man was leering at him and speaking into an ear not submerged in the mud. He feebly nodded, after hearing the man promise him paradise and life for eternity. Then everything went black and he felt pain in his body, fingers or claws raking at his flesh and a ripple of white heat energy running through his broken body. He saw the smiling face of his sweetheart for a millionth of a second, a flash of light and red spots in front of his eyes.

Before his tormented brain succumbed to its last flicker of life, he heard the heinous cackle of something that was ungodly. Then nothing, the lights had gone out. He was being pulled away by strong hands, but he saw a crumpled bloody figure a few feet below, lying half submerged in the mud of Culloden.

Chapter Six
Mid Atlantic

1773

Charlie Boot threw the dice and scowled as his throw earned him just three points. He had needed four to win the pot of twelve shillings. A jubilant shout echoed across the deck, from a younger man, Bob Jennings, who quickly scooped up the mixed coins and was back-slapped by his best friend, Davey Dobbs. Jennings flipped a florin to his friend and clambered up from the deck. The pair started to walk away to resume duties after their half-hour break was over, but the gruff voice of Charlie Boot sounded. The two lads turned to look back.

"Dobbsy lent you two shillings, did he?" Boot called menacingly.

"Yeah, so what, Charlie?" Jennings replied as he jingled the remaining coins in a pocket of his baggy pants.

"So what? So what, smartarse, that's not the rule in the game of dice we were playing. You play with what you start with and everybody knows that. No borrowing allowed. I win on default, hand me the money." Charlie Boot, a big Devon man of over sixteen stones, demanded, pushing a large calloused hand forward.

"Go fuck yourself, Charlie. I won fair and square and you know it. That right, lads?" The smaller man looked to the other crew members who had been taking part in the dice game. Some nodded, some shrugged, and some shook their heads.

Charlie Boot was adamant and flicked the fingers of the hand he was holding out. "You cheated, Jenno, and you know it. Give me the money."

Bob Jennings laughed and shook his head. "Not fucking likely, Charlie. I've never heard of that rule about borrowing. I threw five and you threw three. I win. You lose."

Charlie Boot reached forward and grabbed Jennings by his shirt scruff, pulling him almost off his feet and raising a fist to the smaller man's face.

"I'll throw you to the sharks, you snotty nosed twat. The money's mine. You cheated and you're gonna give me the money. I'll dump you over the side in one minute if you refuse." Charlie Boot's voice was rising in anger. Everyone was watching the pair.

Bob Jennings pulled away, his face showing slight fear, looked around and bravely stood his ground. He shook his head and raised his arms in supplication. "There aren't any sharks near here, Charlie, and even if there was, I'm not giving you the money, I won it fairly and you know it. Any special rules have to be declared from the start."

Charlie Boot was about to grab Jennings again, but a soft voice called out from a few feet away. Eyes turned to look at the small Irish tinker who had been travelling on the tea clipper, with his young and very beautiful companion, Martha Budd. Martha was sitting on a wooden chair, at the side of a small covered cart the couple had paid for, to be carried on the clipper on the voyage to America. She had watched the incident unfold with bemused interest.

"The lad's right, Mister Boot," Fimber O'Flynn called softly. "I've played the game hundreds of times and any definitive rules have to be made known at the start. He won the money like he said, fair and square."

Charlie Boot snorted and shook his head. "Mind your own fucking business, old man and stay out of this. The winnings are mine and Jenno goes for a swim if he doesn't cough up."

Bob Jennings stepped to Fimber O'Flynn and shook his hand. "Thank you sir, I'm grateful for your support. Please take a florin for helping to settle this." He handed a florin to the old man.

Fimber shook his head, refusing the coin. "No, thank you, young man. I was just glad to help settle the dispute."

Charlie Boot pulled Bob Jennings out of the way and pushed Fimber backwards. The old tinker staggered backwards and toppled over in a heap. Martha dashed to him and gently helped her friend up, with the help of Bob Jennings. They carefully walked him to Martha's chair and sat him down.

Not finished with his ranting, Charlie Boot stomped across and grabbed Bob Jennings by his jacket front. "This isn't settled, Jennings, the old man knows sod all about the game. Now give me the money or you go over the side."

Other deckhands had followed Charlie Boot and tried to pull him away. He swung a fist and knocked one of them off his feet. The deckhand slid several feet along the wet deck, bumping his head on one of the wheels of the little cart. Charlie Boot wheeled around and grabbed Bob Jennings, but now a few of the other deckhands joined in and grappled the big man to the deck. Boots and fists were used in the following free-for-all, but ended when Bob Jennings friend, Davey Dobbs, staggered back and fell over the side.

Everybody ran to the gunwale siding and looked down to the swirling grey Atlantic.

Davey Dobbs was nowhere to be seen, he had been sucked under the dark cold waters. Bob Jennings had wanted to go in to find his friend, but strong hands pulled him back. He pulled away from the men and glared at a dumbstruck Charlie Boot, who still had anger in his eyes.

Bob Jennings walked to the big Devon man and pulled the coins from his pants pocket.

Charlie Boot had flopped down on Martha's wooden chair, angry eyes of the deckhands glaring at him. He raised his arms in supplication. Jennings stood over him and held his right palm upwards, with the coins in the middle.

"Take the money, Charlie. It's blood money and it's all yours. You wanted it and poor Davey Dobbs had to die for it." Bob Jennings tossed the coins at Charlie Boot, who flinched and stared white-faced at the former. "I hope you go to Hell, Charlie. Spend the money down there." Bob Jennings was pulled away and he turned with tears in his eyes.

Charlie Boot laughed, leaned down to pick up the coins and shouted after Bob Jennings, "It was your fault, Jennings. You cheated and caused Dobbs' death, not me." He had collected the coins and made to stand, but a gentle hand pushed him back to the chair.

Fimber O'Flynn was smiling at him. "Take a few moments to reflect on what happened, Mister Boot. Get your senses back and put your money away. It's over now, no need for recriminations. The young boy has gone and he might be in a better place, who knows?"

Charlie Boot looked up at the old tinker, shaking his head. "Not my fault, tinker. It was your fault for interfering. You should have minded your own business and kept quiet. It was my money and now I've got what's mine. Tough about Davey Dobbs, but that's how it goes."

Martha had moved closer and stared at Charlie Boot as he moved to stand up. He smiled at her with a mouth full of rotting teeth and pushed her away roughly. Martha stepped back and smiling, kissed two of her fingers, tapping them to the side of his grizzled cheek. Charlie Boot wiped his face and glared at the young woman.

"Women on ships are bad news and all you will be good for is a nice romp and a shag. Get out of my way, woman, I got to get back to work." Charlie Boot stomped away, laughing. Fimber watched him go and shook his head, then turned to look at Martha, who had retaken her seat on the chair.

"The kiss of death, eh?" he chuckled and lit an old clay pipe he had smoked from for years. Martha smiled.

"He deserves it. He is one very nasty man and I hope Lord Lucifer puts him in the worst of his torture chambers."

"Remind me not to get on your wrong side, lassie," Fimber chuckled.

The three-masted tea clipper had had an uneventful voyage from England, carrying a thirty-ton cargo of several cases of Ceylon tea, many boxes of cloth from Lancashire, barrels of Somerset cider, ammunition and weapons from Birmingham. Into the last few hundred miles from the coast of America, just north of Bermuda, the brave, well-travelled clipper ran into a raging Atlantic storm.

The seasoned crew had had an easy job of the various tasks on the decks of the Bristol built clipper *Tintagel*, but twenty-foot waves now pounded the rolling decks of the old ship. The frothing, seething mass of mountainous white waves struck with great velocity against the hull, sending shock waves through every plank of English oak the ship had been built with twenty years earlier.

Captain Wilbur Fawcett, a white-bearded, experienced mariner, had barked orders for an hour and with a severe sore throat, he pointed to the little cart that was strapped to the decks near the port side. He feared the straps would loosen and the tinker's cart washed overboard. Boatswain Jack Henry shouted to Charlie Boot and Bob Jennings to go and make sure the straps were secure. Jennings, one of *Tintagel's* best deckhands, obeyed and ran forward.

Charlie Boot, for ever a persistent malingerer, but the ships strongest man, cursed and hesitated. The savage sea was showing no mercy and the old clipper rolled heavily, but bravely withstood the cruel seas to send her down.

Jack Henry, a big man himself, was having none of Charlie Boot's protestations and pushed the belligerent deckhand after Bob Jennings. The latter had reached the old cart and grabbed one of the spindle wheels to avoid being swept overboard. He scrambled to the front wheels and with blinding seawater stinging his ruddy face, he slowly but carefully manoeuvred his saturated body between the wheels, checking the straps. Behind him, the large figure of Charlie Boot had arrived at the rear wheels, shouting insults at Jennings, but the words were driven away to oblivion.

Bob Jennings refastened a strap that had loosened to one of the front wheels, checked others and after a few minutes of work, perilously holding on to the cart like grim death, satisfied himself all was in order. He let go of a front wheel, grabbed for a steel spring under the carriage and turned to go back and help Charlie Boot. The big man was desperately trying to refix a strap, but was reluctant to use both hands to accomplish the task. Jennings realised the other man was struggling and decided to help him. He let go of the curved steel spring to scramble to Charlie Boot, but at that moment the ship was struck by a huge wave that sent the *Tintagel* rolling almost onto its side. Bob Jennings lost his grip, frantically tried to grab something, but was washed straight into Charlie Boot's prostrate body. Jennings hit the big man feet first with the full force of his thirteen stones body weight and dislodged the screaming terrified Charlie Boot, sending him crashing against the gunwales.

The *Tintagel* rolled back again and Charlie Boot's seventeen stones bodyweight had no chance against the ferocious, seething mass of white water. He was smashed mercilessly across the waterlogged deck as the ship rolled again, tried to grab hold of a loose rope, missed and screamed as his large body was tossed over the side like a rag doll.

Bob Jennings had broken a few ribs as he hit the rear cart wheels with a sickening thud, but managed to push his arms through one of the rear wheel spindles and hold on with every ounce of strength he could muster.

Three hours later, the battered *Tintagel* was through the raging storm and sailing on under cloudless blue skies. However, the brave old ship had been thrown miles off course, towards the south and had a damaged steering rudder. Several of its crew had been injured and besides, young Davey Dobbs and Charlie Boot, a third deckhand had perished.

Captain Wilbur Fawcett surveyed the damage to his battered ship and his despondent crew.

Morale was low and their fresh water had all but vanished. Barrels were smashed and they were over two hundred miles off course. The *Tintagel* had been heading for Boston, to the north, but now the great expanse of the Mexican Gulf beckoned. He had sailed the southern seas in the past and taken the *Tintagel* to British colonies in the Caribbean seas. His only reservation now was the lingering threat of pirate ships which plundered vessels in the tropical waters of the Caribbean.

Normally British, French or Spanish frigates patrolled the area, but they would usually only protect ships displaying the flags of their own countries. It had been known for Spanish warships to 'look the other way', for a bribe of a casket of gold coins or other valuables. Before he had taken over a British merchant ship, Captain Fawcett had been in the Royal Navy and a lieutenant on such a patrol vessel. He knew the waters of the Mexican Gulf very well and had seen action against pirate ships. Turned fifty now and looking forward to a comfortable retirement at Scarborough in his native Yorkshire, he had no wish to be confronted by a ship full of pirates, armed to the teeth.

On a calm sea, nearing the islands of the Bahamas, a favourite hunting ground for the pirate vessels, Fawcett instructed his second in command, Tom Sharpe, another ex-Royal Navy sailor, to break open some of the weapon crates in the hold. These were weapons that had been scheduled for delivery to the Loyalists in Massachusetts, but he felt justified in 'borrowing' some of the muskets and powder, if the *Tintagel* was threatened by pirates.

Tom Sharpe, a Londoner and with thirty years' experience on the high seas, including several years as a gunner on a Royal Navy warship, voiced his doubts to the white-bearded Yorkshireman. He had explained that a few muskets fired by untrained merchant seamen were no threat to a dozen four-pounder cannons, fired at close range.

The gritty, whiskered sea captain nodded nonchalantly and shrugged. "I know, Tom, but we have a beautiful young woman on board with her grandfather and if we are captured by pirates, she will be taken and subjected to God knows what ill-treatment. We must stand against these rogues and put up a fight."

"We'll all be killed, Captain and she'll still be taken. Let them have the cargo and hopefully they might let us sail on. The *Tintagel* is knackered after that storm, it's not worth blasting to Hell and wasting ammunition," Tom Sharpe replied and looked to Coxwain Jack Henry for support.

Jack Henry, a Bristol born seaman, sniffed, sniffed again and shook his head. "Well, I bin all over the seven seas since I was fourteen and I seen these miserable misfits a few times. It's a fact that the young lass will be kidnapped and hauled off to Port o' Spain, Georgetown or Montego Bay, raped a few times by some thieving, sadistic, lecherous pirate captain and then sold on as a white slave. But they might spare our lives if we don't put up a fight. On the other hand, I was on board a ship in the Indian Ocean a few years ago and we were stopped by a bunch of mixed white and African pirates. We surrendered without a fight, had our cargo stolen, then the black devils ran amok with machetes and spears and butchered almost the whole ship's crew. They took three French women away, confiscated our ship and sailed off. Me and two others had hidden in the hold and escaped a few days later after the pirates docked in Zanzibar."

"So you were three cowards, Mister Henry?" Captain Fawcett scowled.

"Put like that, Captain, you could say so, but we lived to fight another day. And we did. We slit the throats of a half dozen of the bastards, before we escaped."

Captain Fawcett straightened and sniffed. He nodded slowly at Jack Henry. "Very well, men. Then we must hide the young woman for her own safety. I suggest we get the boxes of weapons and powder on deck and if we encounter any pirates, we throw the lot overboard. "

"Good idea, Captain. I'll go get the stuff sorted," Jack Henry replied and left the cabin.

Tom Sharpe smiled and accepted a tot of rum from Captain Fawcett.

"You know, the girl is a real beauty, Captain. She and her grandfather are a bit strange, though."

"In what way, Tom?" Fawcett asked as he topped his glass up, but not that of Sharpe.

"Well, it's as if they don't sleep. We been at sea now for quite a while and I haven't seen or heard of them sleeping. Another thing is that they don't seem to relieve themselves."

Fawcett looked at Tom Sharpe with a look of disbelief. "They don't pee or do the other, is that what you mean?"

"Yeah. The old man could take a piss over the side at night, I suppose, but I can't see how the girl could. They never use a bucket for the other. Mind you, they don't eat much, or drink, for that matter. Bloody damn strange and weird."

"No reason to worry, Tom. They're normal, living, breathing human beings just like every man on this ship. Let's concentrate on getting the *Tintagel* to a safe harbour and let our travellers look after themselves. "

Tom Sharpe shrugged and walked to the door of the cabin. He stopped and looked back at Captain Fawcett.

"One other strange thing, Cap'n. Their cart was totally undamaged after all that seawater we took earlier. Not a scratch." \

Fawcett laughed and shook his head. "You're getting paranoid, Tom. This isn't a ghost ship we're on. Relax and go help Jack Henry get the weapons up on the deck. Make sure they're covered with a waterproof cover, just in case we don't meet any pirates."

Two Days Later

A clear azure blue sky spread across the horizon for miles in every direction. The *Tintagel* had sailed on a south westerly course for a day and a half, the damaged rudder having been temporarily repaired by three volunteer divers, who had accepted extra tots of rum to brave the waters in an area known to be frequented by sharks.

Only two ships had been encountered, both like themselves European merchantmen and one had passed over a couple of barrels of fresh water. An air of optimism was evident as the crew, most stripped to their baggy pants to brown their upper bodies, took advantage of the relaxed atmosphere. Martha had laughed and joked with several of the crew, even taking part in a tin whistle jig on the deck, before an appreciative audience of the mixed bunch of men.

Captain Fawcett himself had joined in under polite sufferance, as Martha took his hand to join in one of the jigs. Her swishing skirts and the occasional display of shapely legs drew wolf whistles from the younger deckhands. One sixteen-year-old lad, a freckled-faced, fair-haired youngster on his first voyage, had taken to the sweet natured, likeable but feisty girl and had declared his love for her. Martha had captivated him with her non-stop energy, flirtatious actions and soft, taunting voice.

Johnny Watson had slept in his hammock the previous night, thinking of how he could persuade the beautiful young woman, with abundant energy, an infectious laugh and dancing skills better than any girl he had ever seen, to leave the *Tintagel* when it made port and run away with him. His shipmate and friend Jim McAvoy, a red haired Scot, older and wiser, tried to convince him that such attractive girls were not for common, uneducated youths, who still had acne spots on their faces and were still virgins. Johnny Watson refused to accept his friend's advice. He had a lot to offer and even though he had just a few shillings to his name and could neither read or write, he knew how to use a scythe to cut grass and make it into hay and how to sheer a fat sheep and make the fleece into wool. He had what a girl needed and he wasn't a virgin. He had fondled fat Joanie Maynard's breasts under her clothes a couple of times and she had let him kiss her nipples. His pals back in Croxford in the depths of Dorset, had been green with envy.

The shrill call from the crow's nest thirty feet above the *Tintagel's* deck, made everybody stop and look upwards.

"Ship ahoy, mateys." Jimmy McAvoy was pointing towards the eastern horizon. Four sets of brass telescopes were quickly raised and viewed to starboard.

Tom Sharpe stared intently at the large dot that was a ship, a few miles distant across the flat expanse of sea. At his side, Captain Fawcett watched through his spy glass.

"Any idea, Tom?" Fawcett asked.

"In full sail, Cap'n, and heading our way," Tom Sharpe replied, wiping his eyes of sweat. "Will be a few minutes before we can make out who it is."

"Well, we can't outrun anything with our little tub at the moment. A full cargo and a damaged rudder. Best I think is to just plod on as we have been doing. Just hope it isn't flying a skull and cross bones."

Fawcett laughed at Tom Sharpe's joke. "Never seen one to be honest, Tom. Those we came across in the Navy were flying flags of convenience. Spanish naval types and such."

"Yeah, on the ones I saw as well. They always have the element of surprise, until you can see the whites of their thieving eyes."

"As soon as we got close and the buggers knew they couldn't escape, they surrendered."

On my ship, *HMS Scorpion,* one of the captains, Lewis Griffiths, a Welshman, shot first and asked questions later. He was feared the length and width of the Caribbean. Brilliant sea man."

"He retired then, back to Welsh Wales?"

"Oh, no, Tom. He died in Trinidad. He got a dose of the clap and it turned nasty. Put him six foot under in less than two weeks."

"Big price to pay for a bit of nooky. Was he married?"

"Five kids back home in South Wales. "

"Poor little beggars. The kids always suffer," Tom Sharpe said as he stared more intently at the other ship. "Yon ship has got every sail up, Cap'n, and on a course towards us. I've got a bad feeling."

Captain Fawcett said nothing in reply for a few seconds as he continued peering anxiously through his telescope. He lowered it and wiped perspiration from his forehead. "Me, too, Tom. We'll give it another twenty minutes, thirty minutes let's say, then make a decision."

"To dump the weapons and explosives?"

"I reckon so. No use in letting the stuff fall into the hands of villains."

"What about the young woman, Martha Budd? I reckon we should hide her away, sooner rather than later."

"Go tell her, Tom. And the best of luck, she's a feisty young madam, to say the least." Fawcett remarked with a wry grin. Sharpe nodded and left Captain Fawcett peering through his telescope.

Martha and Fimber were looking over the gunwales at the tiny speck of the approaching ship across the calm sea and were deep in conversation. The old tinker was still puffing at his clay pipe, as he watched carefully.

"You know, lassie, some of these fellers on this ship think we're a strange pair."

"I know. I've seen them staring at us a few times. Particulary the good-looking seaman from London. I think he's second in command, after the white haired one with the funny accent."

"Thomas Sharpe of Tilbury. I can read his eyes. He wants to ask us certain questions, but isn't sure what to make of us. The young lad from Dorset is sweet on you though. His eyes watch your every movement, whenever he comes near. He wants you to run away with him."

Martha gasped and stared in astonishment at the old tinker. "He doesn't, you're joking."

"No, I'm not, lassie. I see his thought waves. He's besotted with you."

"You've never said that before to me, that you can see what humans are thinking."

Fimber puffed sweet smoke out and grinned. "I've waited to tell you, lassie. It was one of the favours I asked of Lord Lucifer. One of my six."

"For how long?" Martha asked tremulously.

"About two hundred and forty years since. I was curious, but I wish I hadn't. I have just the one left now. Lord Lucifer wants it back, so he can send me to the torture chambers."

"I want to be able to do it, see what humans are thinking."

Fimber shrugged, shaking his head and pursing his lips. "Don't do it, lassie. You see things that are not nice and you lose another favour."

"Do I lose favours, every time I get someone to sit on my chair?"

"No, only when you make a death wish, like you did in 1645. You spoke to Lord Lucifer and asked for those three people to die. He arranged it and they died. The chair is yours and only you can use its power. You were put to death in it and even Lord Lucifer cannot interfere in its potent and deadly effectiveness. He would want to be able to use its power, but that would only be with your unquestionable permission. One of the very few things he has no control over."

"If I ask him will he give me the power to see what humans are thinking?"

Fimber sniffed and took a long pull on his pipe. "Yes, and he will want you to ask. You spend another favour. That would leave you with only two. Don't do it, lassie."

"But I want to be able to see what humans are thinking. I used to dream about it when I was living. I wanted to see what people were thinking of me, what naughty thoughts were going through boys' minds. Like the boy on this ship you told me about. I want to ask for it."

"Then you have to wait for a full moon and call to Lord Lucifer six hundred and sixty-six times at midnight. Take a big stick with you and beat yourself the same number of times. If you do not beat yourself severely, he will refuse your request and send you to a torture chamber for eternity. He has you watched by six hundred and sixty-six of his souls. If any of them disobey him, they too go to a torture chamber for eternity. There is no turning back once you have called to him. When your ordeal is finished, you are granted the power to read minds, but many who take the test, fail. The sheer brutality of the test is too demanding and they give in, they are not strong enough or have not the will power to see it through. While you feel no pain in your present state of the undead, you suffer terrible pain during the test. More pain and suffering than any you have experienced when you were alive. But afterwards, you have the power to read minds."

"Even Lord Lucifer's mind?"

Fimber sighed and slowly nodded. "Yes, lassie. But that is something you should never contemplate. He is a demon of the most heinous kind. He sinks to the deepest depths of depravity if he is faced with danger. If you take him on and lose and remember, in all the centuries he has prowled the earth, only once was he fooled. Jacindra escaped from Hell, but he vowed never to let it happen again. It never has. Let it be, lassie, it is no great joy to read minds. I regret it."

Martha smiled and turned around as she heard footsteps. It was Tom Sharpe and he approached warily. He sensed there was something not genuine, not factual or righteous about the odd couple. The girl was the most beautiful thing he had ever seen, but she was, strange. He touched a battered old hat he was wearing and forced a humble smile.

"The cap'n has sent me to tell you the ship on the horizon may be a pirate ship and if so—" he looked at Martha, "It's best if you take cover, hide and not let them see you."

Martha smiled and shook her head. "I am not afraid of any pirates, Mister Sharpe, so you good seamen look after yourselves and my friend and I will do the same."

"They will, er, not be too friendly to you, miss. They will—"

"Rape me," Martha interrupted blandly.

"They always rape the women, miss. Not just by one of them," Sharpe added.

"Then I will just have to lie back and think of England, Mister Sharpe."

Tom Sharpe shrugged and turned away with embarrassment. A wicked thought passed through his mind as he thought of the young woman and of his own sexual fantasies.

A half hour passed and it was established that the approaching vessel was indeed a pirate ship, of good size and with at least fifty cannon ready for use. Captain Fawcett gave the order for all the weapons cargo to be hitched over the side. Every pair of eyes of the eighteen-man crew of the *Tintagel*, looked with disdain at the large galleon that was steadily catching the old tea clipper.

On the bridge platform, Captain Fawcett and his two corporals, Tom Sharpe and Jack Henry, watched gloomily as the pirate ship approached.

"I wish I was on board the *Scorpion* right now, lads," Fawcett remarked tersely. "We would have sent that bloody abomination to the bottom of the sea."

"Well, Cap'n, all they're going to get today is fifty cases of tea, boxes of cloth, some West Country cider, a lot of boots and shoes and a couple of boxes of Bibles," Jack Henry said with a grin.

"Have all the lads stashed their valuables, Jack?" Fawcett asked, as he wiped sweat from his face.

"If you can count a few gold earrings, a couple of books of naughty girl drawings and a few pairs of Sunday best shoes, then yes, Cap'n," laughed Jack Henry.

"Very well, lads, then all we can do is wait for yon buggers to catch us and may God look after all on the *Tintagel* and the young lass and her grandfather. She was unwilling to seek a hiding place then, Tom?"

Tom Sharpe nodded ruefully. "Aye, Cap'n, she was defiant to a fault. I just can't stop thinking about them two though. Even the air around them is different. And she never calls the old man granddad or grandpa."

Captain Fawcett looked at Sharpe and shrugged. "They're a happy pair of souls though. Tom, and no trouble and they paid more than good money for the trip. Our main worry now are that lot of ungodly misfits on board yon galleon. The old man and his—well, good looking young friend, have to take their chances."

Two Hours Later

The three-masted Spanish built pirate galleon was drawn to the side of the *Tintagel* by grappling hooks spread along the port side of the old clipper. Heavily armed men were positioned at key points of the *Tintagel*, ready to board the old tea clipper. Other men holding muskets at the ready, were positioned to shoot any protesters on the *Tintagel*.

With no defiance shown by the *Tintagel* crew, the pirates quickly swung across on ropes and landed on the deck with comparative ease. Cutlasses drawn and primed pistols ready, at least thirty pirates in several modes of typical seafaring dress walked cautiously along the well-scrubbed boards, their experienced eyes taking in everything.

After a few minutes, two better dressed pirates emerged, both walking along a wide wooden board that had been put in place from the galleon. A third person walked calmly behind the two in front. The three, stepped onto the *Tintagel's* deck and quickly looked to all four corners. The boarded ship's crew were rounded up and pushed into line roughly, all searched for weapons and relieved of any.

Captain Fawcett was brought from the bridge platform and checked that he was not armed, along with Tom Sharpe and Jack Herny. Very little was spoken until, satisfied a total, bloodless take-over had been secured, a tall, long-haired pirate of the three who had walked across on the wooden board, gestured mockingly around *Tintagel's* deck.

Enrico Suarez laughed as he pointed along the deck towards the small covered cart, fastened to the gunwales. Three of the pirate crew stood guard, with pistols pointed at Fimber O'Flynn and Martha Budd, sitting quietly, with their feet dangling over the rear boards.

"You have sailed from England, Captain, on this beaten up old ship and you carry an old gypsy cart as cargo. I hope that in the holds there is something of value. Suarez waved an arm to some of his men, and they disappeared below decks to investigate. "I am Enrico Suarez, captain of the *Black Diamond* the most powerful man o'war in the Gulf of Mexico."

"Pirate ship, sir," Fawcett corrected indignantly. "You are the captain of a motley bunch of pirates."

Suarez, a sun-bronzed, handsome character of over six feet, his long dark hair fastened in a ponytail with a black ribbon tie, turned to his two companions. "Did you hear what the Englishman called us, Jose? A motley bunch of pirates. Meaning we are sea bandits. What do we do with those who insult us and call us names? Jose is my young brother and he has no sense of humour, Captain."

Jose Suarez stepped to his brother's side and quickly withdrew a sword he was carrying, raising it menacingly towards Fawcett. "I slit his throat, Enrico, and then cut off his head after the dog's blood has poured out. Then I have his body thrown to the sharks."

"And you, Françoise, my dearest." Enrico Suarez turned to the third and smaller of the three pirates. "This beautiful lady is my fiancée. She is French and no lover of the English. What would you do to such a bad mouthed Englishman?"

The French woman, slender in figure, wearing tight leather pants and high leather boots; full busted, with strawberry blonde hair set in ringlets and carrying two pistols in a broad leather belt, as well as a sword in one of her hands, smiled and stepped towards Captain Fawcett. She pushed her hand forward and pressed the tip of her sword to the front of Fawcett's breeches.

"I would see first if this English dog has enough English meat to please me and then if he has, I would bend over for him to see if he can satisfy me. If he can, I would let him live, but keep him as a slave. When I get tired of him, I, too, would slit his English throat."

Enrico Suarez laughed and gently pulled the French woman away. "So, Captain, it would seem you have little time to remain on this old monstrosity of a ship. I capture such vessels normally and take them back to my base, but I couldn't even sell this piece of dilapidated piece of woodworm. So I hope you are carrying cargo that I can take away and trade or sell."

"Kill me then, if you must, but spare my crew,'' Fawcett said calmly.

"Oh, very noble of you, Captain and very English. Don't worry though, I will spare the younger members of your crew to take them back and sell off as slaves. The older ones will go overboard and take their chances with the sharks."

"Take the cargo if you must, but please do not harm my crew, they are no threat to you," pleaded Captain Fawcett. As he spoke, a couple of the pirates returned to the deck from below and spoke quietly to Captain Suarez. The latter shook his head as he listened to his men, who were shrugging and shaking their heads agitatedly. Suarez dismissed them and turned back to a smiling Captain Fawcett.

"My men tell me that you are carrying some everyday items. Tea, cloth, boots, some Bibles, but they also say there are some traces of gunpowder and they found two or three balls of shot. That tells me you were carrying gunpowder and shot, also probably muskets, Captain. If so, where is it?"

Fawcett's face creased into a broad smile. "At the bottom of the ocean, Captain. As soon as we realised you were pirates, I ordered it over the side."

Suarez sighed heavily and called one of his men over. The man was large, scarred on his face and brutish looking, heavily tattooed. Suarez spoke to him and the man signalled to others standing a few yards away. Five walked over and one drew a large knife from his belt. They grabbed young John Watson, standing near Fawcett, and held him tight. The knifeman stepped to the terrified *Tintagel* youngster and sliced into his face, slicing a cut several inches long and to the cheek bone. Johnny Watson screamed in agonizing pain as blood oozed from the cut, was lifted off his feet and carried to the side of the decking.

Martha Budd screamed loudly and dashed forward as she saw what had happened to the *Tintagel* youth. Everybody stopped and looked at the young woman, who had pushed into the men holding the boy. Her hands pulled at the pirates, but they resisted her actions and tried to push her away. Martha held firm and pushed back.

A voice snapped out and the men, still holding the bleeding Johnny Watson, held back. The French woman marched forward and grabbed Martha, delivering a sharp slap to her face. Martha turned to the woman and with clenched fist, struck the woman square on the jaw. The woman dropped like a lead weight and crashed to the deck, flat on her back. There was a numbed silence as every pair of eyes watched the prostrate French woman. Groggily she clambered to her feet, blood trickling from her mouth. Her hand grabbed for one of her pistols, but another hand stopped her.

"Not yet, my darling. Save her for later," laughed Enrico Suarez as he gently pushed his woman back. The French woman hissed her anger at Martha, but stepped away, holding her face. Suarez waved a hand to the men still holding the boy, blood pumping from his slashed face and hoisted him up; then, without a thought, the screaming boy was hurled over the side. Martha dashed to the side and glanced down to where young Watson had entered the water. Blood-stained water swirled as the threshing figure of Johnny Watson surfaced after a few seconds. He desperately grabbed for something to hold on to, but the greasy sides of the *Tintagel* evaded his scratching fingers.

Everyone looked at the doomed, pathetic figure being carried away from the ship. Then an excited shout from one of the pirates and all eyes stared out into the calmness of the blue sea. The tell-tale, blacky grey fin caused a whoop of joy from most of the onlookers, as a sixteen-foot shark appeared to investigate the scent of blood, then a second and a third joined in the hunt. Young Johnny Watson screamed for the umpteenth time, but the one ton sharks moved in with deadly instinctive skill and commitment.

Martha turned away and left the pirates to savour their few minutes of gruesome enjoyment. Her undead eyes glared at Captain Suarez and then at his brother and the sulking, brooding figure of the French woman. Captain Suarez would tell his brother later that he was sure the English girl's eyes were a burning red, when she glared at him.

Suarez sniffed his contempt and smiled at Captain Fawcett. "That is the price you pay, Captain, for insulting my intelligence. Now I need the strong box you keep your money in on this old ship. I will take all the goods you have travelled across the Atlantic with and all your food and water, then take your young men on to the *Black Diamond*, as I said earlier. You and the rest of your crew can turn eastwards and go back to England in this old weather-beaten ship. I will give you a one hour start, then chase you and after getting within a hundred metres, I will use your ship as target practice. Before that, though, I intend to take your angry young woman across to the

Black Diamond and show her what a real man is made of. My brother can follow me and if she wants, my dear fiancée. She enjoys the pleasures of beautiful young women from time to time and your very beautiful young English lady owes Françoise an apology for assaulting her. I also like the little gypsy cart you have on board and I will give it to one of my sons back in Cadiz, when I return to Spain."

As soon as the *Tintagel's* cargo and the little cart had been moved over to the *Black Diamond*, the crew were sorted into men and boys. Of those left after the deaths of Johnny Watson, Davie Dobbs, Charlie Boot and Hughie Packham, Captain Suarez picked out seven of the younger men, to take away and sell as white slaves. He also kept Tom Sharpe, as he himself needed an experienced mariner to serve on the *Black Diamond.* The eight seamen he retained were put in the hold and shackled with chains. The remaining crew, with Captain Fawcett, were left aboard the old clipper, but with no provisions.

To his word, Captain Suarez gave the men on the *Tintagel* a one hour start, but then with plenty of daylight left, he set chase on the old tea clipper. As dusk crept in, the faster, full-sailed *Black Diamond* closed for the kill. At fifty yards distance, the big Spanish galleon move to a broadside position and let rip with every cannon. The old unarmed clipper had no chance and after twenty minutes of cold-blooded butchery from the *Black Diamond* gunners, the old ship was blown apart with the loss of all on board. Fimber O'Flynn went down with the ship, but he called to Martha before he sank beneath the waves. He still had to serve Lord Lucifer, so he would return, but he had no idea when and where he would be sent to finish paying off his debt. He could wait, he had waited for three hundred and fifty years.

Martha was tied and bound to her chair inside the little cart. Her thoughts were of Fimber, who had spoken to her for several minutes, in the soft educated voice she loved to hear. Her apprenticeship was over and it was time for her to go out by herself. A hundred and thirty years she had been taught by the old tinker and she had listened, watched and learnt the skills of the undead. Fimber had told her never to spend her remaining two favours. Lord Lucifer wanted them back. Martha wanted to beat him and follow Jacindra to a better life. If the daughter of

Queen Boadicea could beat Lord Lucifer, then Martha Budd would find a way to do it.

It was dark when they came for her. The big galleon was heading south west into the Caribbean, on a blanket level sea that was surprisingly calm. A Spanish flag of convenience flew from the stem, to avoid any suspicion from passing vessels. A British frigate had passed a half mile distant, but had paid no heed, their two countries at that time in a period of fragile peace. The British warships were more concerned about French vessels.

Martha was untied and offered a bowl of warm scented water to wash herself and an equally scented towel to dry herself. She waved the three pirates away, noticing that one was a coffee-skinned female, but as hard looking as her companions and probably just as deadly. When she had washed herself, Martha opened the door and called the young female inside. Not sure if the girl could speak English, Martha made signs to the chair and hoped her actions could be understood.

The coloured girl glared at Martha, but nodded. "I speak English, Missy. Why do want the chair removing?"

"Because I do, Missy. Don't argue with me or I'll strike you like I did that other woman," Martha hissed and indicated for the pirate girl to pick the chair up.

"Françoise Clementine will kill you, if she gets the chance. You made an enemy of her."

"That makes two of us then. I'll kill her when I get the chance. Now be careful with my chair, it goes wherever I go."

"Don't know why you want it now. In a few minutes you'll be naked and lying on a bed with your legs spread wide. Enrico Suarez wants you straight away," the girl sniggered.

"And then his brother and then Françoise Clementine, no doubt," Martha laughed.

The girl shook her head and hoisted the chair up. Martha was surprised at the pirate girl's strength. "They will all have you one by one at first and then all together, Missy, in the bed at the same time. Two three days it will go on, until we get into port and then you will be sold to the highest bidder."

"Have they fucked you?" Martha sniggered in return.

"Of course, and given me two children. We better go, Enrico is waiting, he hates being kept waiting."

"Where are your children? On board this galleon?"

"I sold them on. Two pieces of gold for each. They were girls and will be slaves for some rich white plantation owner when they reach eight or nine. Then they will finish up like me as soon as they are old enough. Raped and abused, then abandoned. "

"What's your name?"

"Sunday."

"That's a day, not a name," Martha replied flippantly.

"I had no proper name, so I call myself Sunday, the day I killed the white man who owned me. I was eight and he had just raped me. I stabbed him."

Captain Suarez's quarters were sumptuous. He had had it furnished to a high standard with velvet drapes, rosewood furniture, a bed with gold braided pillows and silk sheets.

Martha was escorted into the oak panelled room by Sunday, who had carried the chair for her. Two male pirates stood by the door.

Sunday put the chair down and looked at Martha before she left. "Don't argue with him, Missy. Do what he wants." Sunday's voice was just above a whisper. Martha smiled.

Martha watched the young woman leave and then pulled her chair towards the curved rear window glasses. Behind the galleon, the wake it was making was spreckled white and a mass of gulls were swooping to pluck out the small fish caught in the dispersed sea water. Martha sat in the chair, staring out of the windows.

A few minutes passed, then the door creaked open and Captain Suarez stepped in to his cabin. Martha did not look round. The tall pirate captain closed the cabin door and sighed heavily. He took a couple of paces, then started laughing.

"You brought your own chair. I'm impressed, it looks a fine piece of English oak. I'll keep it. It is a present, I assume."

"You want to fuck me, Captain, then you sit in my chair and I will sit onto your lap, so I can look out at the blue sea, while you enjoy yourself of my body," Martha replied curtly, still facing the windows.

Suarez laughed and quietly walked to where Martha was sitting. He put his hands on her shoulders and pressed gently.

"You English are so dominant, even in lovemaking, but if you prefer it that way, so be it. I will take your clothes off, though, I enjoy such treats before I make love."

Martha stood and turned the chair round, but remained on her feet. Suarez was gentle as he removed Martha's clothes, taking time to explore her ample breasts, before letting the cotton garments drop at her feet. He lowered his body to kiss her pubic region, then straightened and began taking his own clothes off. A minute later and he was naked. Martha had to admit that he had a fine, muscular, tanned body and an equally fine manhood. He reached down to fondle her breasts, sighed and closed his eyes, to embrace the sheer thrill of touching the firm, youthful twin mounds. After a minute of cupping her breasts, Suarez hesitated and looked down at the beautiful young woman. Martha looked up and her eyes caught his gaze. He was sure they had glinted red. He blinked, looked into her eyes again, but they were blue.

Martha stood and turned him to the chair, gently pushing him down. Suarez sighed with unadulterated pleasure as she climbed onto his lap, her back to him. His soft hands reached forward and cupped her swaying breasts, as he entered her body from behind.

Suarez moaned with delight as he thrust upward, every push releasing pent-up frustration, until the spasms of his orgasm erupted. Martha had looked out of the windows and counted sea birds as Suarez had taken her body. When he relaxed and settled back again, Martha grinned and kissed two of her fingers, then tapped them to his forehead, with a wry grin.

She stood and reached for her clothes, but Suarez gently reached for her again. "Leave those old clothes and throw them away. I have fine dresses of satin, silk or whatever pleases you, that I have taken from ships we have plundered. Blue, red, green or lemon silks trimmed with white lace. I will have some brought to you and you can sit at my table at dinner and be my lady, because you just kissed your fingers and touched me. I think you like me."

Martha smiled, but remained naked and looked at Suarez. "Oh, I like you, Captain, but the French woman likes you as well. My touch finger kiss was a goodbye kiss."

"Call me Enrico, and what is your name?"

"Martha Budd."

"A good English name, Martha. But Françoise is no problem to you, my dear. I need a new woman in my life and you must stay with me."

"And what of the French woman?"

"She will leave the *Black Diamond* at our next port of call. I took her from a French ship two years ago and she has proved useful, but it's time to say goodbye. Stay with me, Martha Budd, and I will make you a rich woman. I would like children, but Françoise cannot bear children. I will take you to Cadiz in southern Spain and build you a fine villa where you can have our children. What do you say?"

"And your brother, Jose? What of him? I was told you share your women."

"Jose will do as he is told. He is quick to temper and I am tired of being his guardian. He, like Françoise, needs to go his own way. We have had good times and taken a lot of riches, but I need a new challenge and a good woman."

"You have killed a lot of people on your way to riches."

"A lot, yes, but I am still a good man."

"You threw a young boy to the sharks, his name was John Watson. He was fond of me."

"If I had known that, Martha Budd, I would have thrown another of the crew overboard. The old man you were with. He was very old and I would have done him a favour. He had nothing left to live for."

Martha sighed and reached for a piece of clothing. Suarez pulled his clothes on and walked to the door. Sunday was waiting outside and humbly waited for Suarez to speak.

"Go and fetch a trunk of the best women's clothes, Sunday. Stay with Martha Budd and help her choose a nice dress, undergarments, stockings and slippers. You can look after her and make sure she has whatever she wants. Take her old clothes and get rid of them."

Sunday nodded and left.

An hour later and Sunday had helped Martha into clothes a queen would have owned.

Martha chose a dress of purple silk that made a soft swishing sound as she moved. The dress had trimmings of soft cream to the bodice and expensive white lace around the neckline and wrist cuffs. An ample cleavage showed, which Sunday looked at with envy. The shoes Martha chose were white, soft leather with tiny silver buckles on the top.

"I've never seen anyone so beautiful, Missy. Madam Clementine will be so jealous," Sunday remarked as she stepped back to admire Martha in her new clothes.

"I feel overdressed, Sunday. I've never worn such things in my life. I liked my older ones."

Sunday looked at the pile of discarded clothes Martha had worn and sighed.

"They are better than anything I have worn."

"Take them, Sunday. You have them, we are similar in size," Martha remarked.

"I can't, Missy. I've always worn boys' clothes. I would look, er—You know."

Martha giggled. "Like a young woman."

"Well, possibly."

"Not possibly, Sunday. Definitely. You have a nice figure and you're pretty underneath all that scuff."

"Dirt. I don't wash now. I am not a woman now. Men don't look at me and if they do, they just want me to drop my pants and take me."

"Then leave this ship and make another life somewhere."

"Where? I have nowhere to go. I lived rough and worked fifteen hours a day on plantations for just bad food and a filthy straw bed. I was raped three or four times a week by both the white owners and the other black slaves. I ran away but was captured by the British and then sold on to slave traders. Captain Suarez bought me three years ago, to let his men have treats while they were at sea. Most of the men on the *Black Diamond* have raped me. I learned how to fight and shoot a pistol. I am the best sharpshooter on this ship now and one of the best sword fighters. No one rapes me now. The last one who tried, I slit his throat from ear to ear."

"Can you get into the hold, where the men who were captured on my ship are held?" Martha asked.

"I suppose so, but why do you ask?"

"There is a man there called Tom Sharpe and two others who I know. A Scot called Jim McAvoy and an Englisman called Bob Jennings. They are tough men, who will know how to fight. The others are young lads but they will not be soft. If you can get them free, get them knives or something, they can take this ship from Captain Suarez."

"Captain Suarez is no fool, Missy. Even if I could get your friends free, he will recapture them and kill every one of them."

"Captain Suarez has little time left on this earth, Sunday," Martha grinned.

"He is a healthy man, Missy, and a good fighter and evil. If he suspects I helped free your men, he will skin me alive and drag me behind the *Black Diamond* until the sharks have ripped me apart. He does that a lot to people he dislikes."

"He is going to die, Sunday. Very soon."

"How? When?"

"I will be at his dinner table tonight. The French woman will also be at the table. She hates me for striking her. There will be green envy and hatred in her French eyes. I will let her know very subtly that the captain has had sex with me. If I was her, I would react with spit and venom."

"What if Jose is there as well? He adores his brother and will stop anyone harming him."

"Not if he finds out his brother is going to ditch him very soon."

"The captain said that?"

"He did. Time for Jose to fend for himself."

"Jose is weak, unlike Enrico. He would never survive on his own."

"Will you help me to free my friends to take over the *Black Diamond*?"

"If I can persuade the black members of the crew to help. It would be hard with so few to try," Sunday said quietly as she collected Martha's discarded clothes.

The look of sheer hatred on Françoise Clementine's face would have sunk a ship. The dinner table in Captain Suarez's cabin was stacked with food. The *Black Diamond* was anchored in a bay, a mile off a small palm tree covered island in the northern Caribbean. Silver trays of food kept arriving, until there was enough to feed twenty. A silver bowl in the centre of the table was similarly stacked high, with various tropical fruits. Goblets of the best wine were filled, as the four diners settled into plush, high-backed chairs.

Jose Suarez laughed loudly at a joke his brother Enrico had told a hundred times.

Françoise Clementine had heard it many times and nodded half approvingly. Martha tittered politely, but had not found it amusing. Both women were stunningly attractive, in dresses of unmitigated quality. Jose Suarez found it hard not to snatch sly glances at each of the women's ample cleavages. Enrico noticed his brother's attentions and winked at both women. Françoise, who had been bedded by both brothers on several occasions, kept a wary eye on her new rival. She had seen off a few other love rivals in her time on the *Black Diamond*, but this new one was extra specially beautiful and had a superb figure.

Conversation between the two women was stilted, but Françoise was determined to sit at the table and leave in two hours' time and join Enrico Suarez in his magnificent bed. The clumsy-fingered, foul breathed, feeble brained and sweaty Jose Suarez could bed the English girl, if she wasn't too particular about her bed partners.

"It was a good thing that my handsome Enrico sent that old beaten up ship we caught you on, to the bottom of the sea. You obviously are not used to sailing on gallant fine ships as the *Black Diamond* is. A lot of French workers and the best of Spanish materials were used in its construction. Not to mention the English crew gave up without a fight. Are you not a slight bit ashamed of them, for not fighting?" Françoise took a sip of her wine and smiled. Martha looked across the table and noticed the woman's face was bruised from where she had struck her. The grin on her face was noticed by the other three.

"Fight with what, you stupid French bitch? Bare hands and teeth against muskets, cannon and four times more men? Are you French always so stupid and why do we English always beat the shit out of you in a battle?"

The stunned silence after Martha's outburst lasted several seconds, until Enrico Suarez raised his glass to both women. "Bravo, bravo, ladies, a true fighting spirit from you both and if you were men, I think duelling pistols at dawn.

Françoise Clementine smirked and shook her head. "I could shoot her English head off from fifty paces, before she raised her pistol ten centimetres. The English are a boastful race and besides everything else, they are useless at making love. I have made you very happy, Enrico, in bed, so if this young madam thinks she can do better she is mistaken. And look at her at this table of fine food. She eats nothing or drinks nothing. The English cannot eat properly."

Martha smiled and looked to Enrico, sitting to her right. "I think you better tell her, Captain, that I made you very happy earlier today. You sat on my chair naked and took me from behind so manfully. You made me so happy and said you wanted me to have your children and you were taking me back to Cadiz, where you will build our villa. How many times have you fucked her, but she still hasn't given you a child?"

Françoise spilled wine from her goblet and shrieked with anger. Before the others could respond, she reached under her skirts and pulled out a pistol. She pulled the hammer back and lifted it, aiming at Martha's face. Martha smiled at her, but Françoise turned to her left and shot Enrico, point blank, in the head. He slammed back against the chair, toppling it over and fell dead in a heap. Next to her, Jose pulled out a pistol he carried and shot Françoise point blank. She was blown sideways, half her head disappearing in a pink haze of skin and bone.

The door flew open and three stunned faces stared into the room. All had pistols drawn and Martha quickly pointed at Jose, who was dumbstruck, still holding his pistol in a trembling hand.

"He shot the captain and the woman, kill him!" Martha shouted. Three pistols blasted and Jose was blown several feet from the table. Martha shoved her chair back and lifting her skirts, ran to the nearest pirate, who was staring wide-eyed into the cabin. Martha grabbed him and pushed his shaking body backwards. "Go get Sunday, tell her what's happened. Be quick."

Without a pause the man scuttled away and Martha turned to the other two pirates, both with open jaws. She pointed to the enormous amount of food.

"Get some of the food, fellers, before everybody else gets here. Go on. Nothing we can do for those three, they're dead. Eat your fill, lads." Martha hoped her English had been understood, but she had no need to fear. The two were joined by others who had heard the shots and come to investigate.

A minute later and the cabin was a scene of several pirates, all climbing over the table, grabbing as much of the feast as they could manage. Bottles of wine were opened and the cabin became a free-for-all.

Sunday had arrived and she was tempted to join the band of pirates, fighting for the food and drink. Martha pulled her away and took her out into the narrow corridor. She shoved a large chicken leg into the young woman's hand. "Take it, Sunday, there will be more later. Can we get to the hold now and set my friends free?"

Sunday was chomping greedily on the chicken, but she nodded and wiped a hand across her mouth. "They won't hurt me, will they, as soon as they're free?"

"They're English, Sunday. No, they won't, I promise."

"If you are lying, Missy, I will kill you," Sunday replied, biting off more of the roast chicken. "I spoke to some of my friends, the black ones, they are with me, but are afraid they will be treated just as bad as they were with Captain Suarez."

"On my honour, Sunday, they are good men, they are English." Martha pulled Sunday away, but let her chomp at more of the chicken. Martha lifted her troublesome skirts and ran after Sunday, who had freedom of movement in her long, dirty pants. Climbing down a ladder into the hold, Sunday saw two of the pirates who had been left to guard the prisoners. They had heard the commotion up top and had wanted to find out what had happened, but feared being skinned alive and fed to the sharks. Sunday explained what had happened, told them she had been sent to take over and without a moment's hesitation the two quickly ran, leaving their pistols and muskets. Hunger took over from fear.

Within a minute, the shackles had been removed from the English seamen and all were free, but Tom Sharpe was giving orders. With as many weapons they could muster, Tom Sharpe carefully led his small group up onto the deck. It was as if the ship had been abandoned.

Standing partly hidden, another small group waited, all carrying weapons. Sunday's black friends stepped out and looked to Sunday, their self-appointed leader. She had enjoyed the chicken and now rallied them out of hiding. Large black eyes stared at the Englishmen, especially the big man who seemed to be in charge. Fourteen in total, excluding Martha, who wished she had not given her old clothes to Sunday. Tom Sharpe put Sunday in charge of her friends and they crept quietly to the cabin towards the stern of the big galleon. Noises of laughter and loud voices, mostly excited voices, came from where most of the pirates were drinking and eating. Muskets, cutlasses and some pistols littered the floor as boisterous and hungry pirates took advantage of their good fortune.

Twenty minutes later and the *Black Diamond* had a new skipper. Tom Sharpe had won most of the pirates over. Those who could speak English had accepted the big Englishman's offer of a new life, sailing the seven seas. A few suspicious pirates, mainly Spanish and French, decided it was too big a chance to take, to trust an Englishman, and accepted a rowing boat to row over to the island a mile away.

The big galleon was re-named before it set sail again. Food and provisions had been purchased from a store on the island, rowed across to *Martha's Sunday* and with a refreshed and re-motivated crew, the sails were lowered and Captain Thomas Sharpe steered the ship westward, towards Jamaica, where a new cargo would be collected and shipped to England.

Martha had a new passenger with her as she saw the little cart put on to another ship in Montego Bay that would take her over to America. Girl Sunday, as Martha now called her, was thrilled to be joining her friend Martha Budd on the voyage across to America. She had heard that slavery was to be abolished in the country and with no home roots, no family to worry about or look after, a new life in the new country of America was her desire.

On the platform bridge of his new ship, Tom Sharpe looked back to Montego Bay as *Martha's Sunday* ploughed through the sea, heading for England with a full cargo of fruit, sugar cane and cotton. His second in command, Jim McAvoy, at the wheel, wondered what his new captain was thinking.

"Penny for your thoughts, Cap'n?" the Scot asked.

"That young woman who saved us from a certain death, Martha Budd. You know, Jim, it might sound silly, but I think she was a ghost."

Jim McAvoy laughed and nodded. "The best looking ghost I ever saw, Cap'n."

On the small, two-mast cargo schooner, heading northwards to America, Sunday looked at her friend, who appeared deep in thought as they leaned on a gunwale.

"Penny for your thoughts, Missy?" Sunday asked, as the pair watched the sea below them.

"Oh, Sunday, I was just hoping a certain character from my past, will leave me alone and another one will find me. I miss the second one so much, I knew him a long time."

Chapter Seven
Louisiana, America

Petite Anse Island
1773

Girl Sunday stepped ashore and took a deep breath as she breathed the fresh air of the small island a couple of miles from the Louisiana mainland. The schooner she and Martha had travelled on from Jamaica, was anchored in a small bay of Petite Anse Island and would stay there overnight, before taking on tons of salt extracted from the islands salt mines, the following day. The salt would then be taken to the mainland, unloaded and then a second load would be put on board to be taken to Jamaica, unloaded and reloaded with cotton and fruit.

It was an adventure for the two young women, who were thrilled to be on dry land for the first time in many weeks. Martha had disposed of her fine purple silk dress and now wore a plain cotton frock over her petticoats and small black leather ankle boots. Sunday had returned to wearing long striped pants and a man's red shirt and a black bandana, but these were now clean. She wore the high leather black boots that Françoise Clementine had worn on the *Black Diamond*. Tucked into a leather belt was a pearl handled dagger and on the other side, a flintlock pistol she had taken from the dead body of Captain Suarez. A small leather pouch she also carried, contained shot and powder.

"You still look like a pirate, Sunday," Martha grinned as the pair strolled along a boardwalk, to curious glances of men working along the harbour side. A few wolf whistles shrilled out and both laughed them away.

"I still am a pirate, Missy. I feel safer with the tools of my trade hanging from my belt. I'll slit the throat of any man who dares put an unwelcome hand on me. Those bad days are in the past. I can beat most men in a fight and I know how to fire a pistol."

"So I'm safe with you, am I?" Martha laughed.

"Sure am, Missy. You saved me from a living hell on the *Black Diamond*, so I am in your debt. You're my best friend and I'll look after you."

"Well, we have a new country to explore and a little cart to take us wherever we want. As soon as we buy a strong young horse after we get over to the mainland, we are on our way."

"Any ideas, Missy, where we're heading?"

"I spoke to Tom Sharpe before we left his new ship and he said there are a lot of British colonials in this new country. There is a town called Boston in the north and lots of British are up there. There are also lots of French in this part of America in the south. I don't speak French, so I think Boston sounds good."

"I speak French, Missy, not perfect but pretty good. I came from an island in the Caribbean, inhabited by the French. I was taken by a French pirate and sold to a plantation owner, who raped me when I was fourteen. I got pregnant and had my baby girl stolen for a couple of pieces of gold. A year later I was raped for the umpteenth time and made pregnant again. I was forced to sell another baby girl and not long after, I was beaten to a pulp by another man who raped me. I lost a baby I was carrying and now I can't have babies. I hate most men, they are savages. Captain Suarez bought me for a pittance from the British in Haiti a few years ago and he used me as a sex slave. The one good thing about the *Black Diamond* is I learned how to look after myself on that ship. I killed three men who tried to rape me. I cut the balls off one fat slob and pushed them into his slobbering mouth. He choked to death on his own balls. I was flogged within an inch of my life after that bit of fun, but no man as ever touched me since, unless I want him to. Thing is, no man wants me now, because they fear me."

"I know someone who would want to meet you, Sunday, but he is the most evil creature walking the earth. I met him once, a long long time ago and wish I hadn't. He chased me and my friend, an old Irish tinker, all over England, but I think I've escaped his clutches now."

"Was that the old man you were with on the *Tintagel* that the *Black Diamond* sent to the bottom of the sea?"

"Yes. He was called Fimber O'Flynn and he rescued me a long time ago and saved me."

"How long ago, Missy?" Sunday asked as the pair continued their stroll along the boardwalk.

Martha laughed and shook her head. "You would not believe me, Sunday. A long time ago."

"It can't be so long, you're still very young. How long?" Sunday asked as she stopped and took Martha's hand.

"One day I might tell you, Sunday. The time is not right yet." Martha gently squeezed Sunday's hand.

"I'm your friend, Missy. You're the best friend I have ever had. I would do anything for you, go anywhere with you. Why can't you tell me?"

"Like I said, Sunday, you would not believe me. I'll tell you one day, I promise."

"I never forget, Missy. I'll keep asking."

Martha turned to walk back to the schooner. As she walked, she could see Sunday's curious dark eyes watching her. The young pirate girl almost skipped along at her side. Martha smiled to herself, she knew Sunday was a friend for life, but how she was going to explain to her who she was, what she was?

Three Days Later
Abbeville, Louisiana

In excellent French, but unable to understand some of the Cajun slang spoken by a lot of the townsfolk, Sunday was able to barter for provisions she and Martha would require for their journey northward into the new land of America. Before she had left the *Black Diamond,* or the newly named *Martha's Sunday*, Sunday had taken an amount of gold, silver coins and precious jewels from a secret store in Captain Suarez's cabin.

Her crafty eyes had taken in the oak panelled walling in the cabin, as she lay naked on the bed, after Suarez had fallen into a drunken stupor after bedding her one day, soon after she had arrived on the *Black Diamond*.

Gold, silver and a variety of precious jewels nestled in a casket behind a secret panel that the crafty young black girl had discovered, after slipping from Suarez's bed to investigate. A day might come, she had reasoned, that one day she could take what she wanted, to escape and run away to start a new life. That day had arrived, after Suarez, his brother and mistress had been killed.

The French American store keeper, a tall, skinny man with a pock-marked face, uneven yellow teeth and greasy hair, had supplied the two young women with provisions, a couple of muskets and ammunition, clothes, rope, oats and horse feed. His lustful, wandering eyes had taken in the two young women, as he helped them load their little bow top cart.

Claude Gilbert watched with a wicked smile, as the cart was driven away, pulled by a stocky young coloured cob that Martha had chosen shrewdly. Her years with Fimber O'Flynn had taught her how to choose a suitable cart horse and the one pulling the cart was the best in a bunch that a local livery stable had had for sale.

A couple of miles north of Abbeville, Sunday called for Martha to pull up. The day was a sultry, cloudy but hot day and Sunday was thirsty. Her canteen was empty and she jumped down to refill it from one of the two water tubs strapped to the cart. Taking a long drink, Sunday then offered the canteen to Martha, but she shook her head.

"You need to drink, Missy," Sunday called, looking up at her friend.

"I'm fine. I'll take a drink later," Martha responded, feeling awkward for lying.

"Make sure you do, got to keep your strength up. Anyway, I think I'll test the muskets while we're stopped. Pass me one down, Missy."

Sunday took the musket and levelled it from her shoulders, then rolled it around in her hands. It was obvious to Martha as she watched her friend, that Sunday knew what she was doing. "Nice and balanced. Want to watch me shoot?"

Martha nodded and watched as Sunday put shot and powder into the new musket.

"Pick something for me to shoot at, about fifty yards away," Sunday called confidently.

"There's a tree over there, with a broken branch. How about that?" Martha had pointed to the tree and Sunday nodded.

"I'll take the broken part off." Sunday raised the musket that was almost as long as she was tall. Carefully she levelled it to her shoulder and looked with one eye closed along the gun metal barrel. Her slender first finger touched the brass trigger and held for a second. Then she squeezed and a split second later, the broken part of the branch was blown off. A squeal of joy erupted from Sunday and a clapping of hands from Martha.

"Impressed or not, Missy?" Sunday called excitedly.

"Very impressed, Sunday. Can you teach me to shoot like that?" Martha called.

"Of course I can, but it takes time. Pass me the other musket and I'll try that one."

A couple of minutes later and Sunday had loaded the second new musket. As with the first one, Sunday carefully rolled it around in her strong fingers and after a minute, nodded confidently. Then the sound of horses' hooves and Sunday, stopped her attention to the second musket and looked to where she had heard the sounds. Martha leaned sideways to also look backwards. For a few moments neither girl saw anything, then pushing through bushes, two horses came into view. Sunday wiped sweat from her brow and stared more intently at two figures riding the horses. Martha was staring at the two riders and suddenly recognised one as the owner of the store where they had bought provisions. The other man was similar in appearance, the same ruddy complexion, thin and with the same straggly, greasy hair. It was apparent to both young women that the men were brothers.

Sunday had lowered her musket and stood with the weapon on its butt end, a firm hand clutching the upper part of the barrel. The two pressed their horses forward until they were about twenty yards from Martha and Sunday, now turned fully, facing the two men.

"We heard a shot and came to investigate. Hope you aren't in any trouble, ladies," Claude Gilbert called out, his rat-like eyes staring mainly at Martha, sitting on the bow top cart. "Me and my brother, Roland, hope you are not lost or anything, there are some rogues in these parts. Two young women on their own need to be careful."

Sunday never took her eyes from Claude Gilbert and flexed her fingers on the musket barrel. "We're not lost, mister. We have just stopped for a rest and to try out these fine muskets we purchased from your store a couple of hours ago. We'll be a few minutes and then be on our way. You can travel on now, we aren't in trouble."

Claude Gilbert wiped a hand across his mouth and smiled, showing his yellow teeth. He nodded towards Martha on the cart. "I gotta be truthful, I rather took a fancy to you, mademoiselle, you are a real beauty and such beauty is rare in these parts. My brother likes Negro girls and you, mademoiselle," he turned to look at Sunday, "are also a beautiful woman. Perhaps my brother and I could stay a while to become acquainted with you both. You did not purchase any wine earlier, so we brought some bottles for us all to enjoy a drink. Show them, Roland."

Roland Gilbert reached to a saddle bag and took out a bottle of red wine, waving it around with a sardonic smile on his ruddy face. Sunday watched him and steadied herself, her heart beating fast with apprehension. The two brothers made to climb from their horses, but in a swift movement, Sunday raised the loaded musket and held it at shoulder height, pointed at Claude Gilbert.

"No, thanks, mister. We're fine on our own. You turn around and go back where you came from and leave me and my friend alone. If we need two men to pass time on, we'll choose our own."

Claude Gilbert settled back on his horse and started to laugh. "You don't scare me, lady, with that single shot musket. You probably don't know how to shoot properly, no woman I know has a clue how to shoot a heavy musket, especially a Negro woman, so put it down and be a bit more friendly to me and my brother. We only want to show you how a couple of Cajun men treat good looking women passing through Louisiana. You said some nice things back at my store and I took it to mean you were up for a bit of fun. I know a bit about women like you and we ain't gonna hurt you, no sire. We just want a bit of rumpy dumpy and then we'll be on our way. What d'ya say, ladies?"

Sunday smiled and turned slightly to look at Roland Gilbert, but the musket still levelled at the latter's brother. "So you like Negro women, do you? Have you ever shagged a Negro woman before?"

Roland shifted on his saddle and coughed to clear his throat. "No, not yet, but I sure would like to—"

"Shag me?" Sunday interrupted with a dry laugh.

Roland stared wide eyed at Sunday and shrugged. "Er, yeah. If you let me."

"Not today, mister, not even next week or next month. You're just about the ugliest man I have ever laid eyes on. Well, besides your stupid, smelly brother. So, like I said, turn around and go back. I'm very particular who I let shove his willy up me and you're not in the running. So go on and get gone, or I'll blow one of you off your horse."

Claude Gilbert shook his head and started to dismount, but Sunday screamed at him as he moved. "Get gone, mister! I've warned you."

"Like you just said, nigger woman, you can only shoot one of us. You're bluffing and I've just changed my mind. I want you and I'm gonna shag some sense into your black arse. My brother can shag the white woman. Then we'll swap over and Roland can shag you while I take care of your lovely friend."

Claude Gilbert was blown backwards off his horse, a ball shot embedded in his skull.

Roland Gilbert gasped in horror as some of his brother's blood splattered across to splash onto his startled face. He never saw the dagger as it thudded into his chest and knocked him from his horse. Both horses took off, leaving the brothers flat on their backs, one dead, the other near death. Sunday dashed to Roland Gilbert and pulled her dagger from his chest, then ran to the cart. She hoisted the musket up to Martha and climbed up beside her.

A minute later and the bow top cart was trundling along the track they had pulled off a while earlier. Martha was speechless as she held the reins. Sunday was wiping blood from her dagger and smiled as she put it back into her belt.

"I take it you didn't fancy either of those two repulsive brothers," Sunday chuckled.

"I could think of something a bit worse than repulsive, like nauseating, repellent or hideous," Martha replied, to an agreeable laugh from Sunday. "Did you ever see such a pair of ugly people? Those teeth and the ratlike eyes and the smell. I could smell his body from where I was sitting. The thought of having either of them two rejects on top of me. Captain Suarez was like Prince Charming in comparison."

Sunday looked at Martha and nodded. "He bedded you then, Missy?"

"No, he was sitting on my chair. I made sure he sat on it, while he took me."

"Why? Did it matter if he sat on it?"

"It does, Sunday. Very much so."

"It's just a chair, though, nothing more, nothing less. If you're going to get raped then you might as well take it in comfort. I just lie back and close my eyes and imagine I'm being shagged by a handsome witch doctor back in Africa, where my original family came from."

The bow top cart trundled on, with the young cob horse happily pulling his cart effortlessly. He was out on his own now and the two women who reined him were easy to please, especially the white one with the gentle hands. He knew she had travelled with horses before and for a long time. He hoped he had her for a master for the rest of his life. Out on the open road was far better than sharing a day with other hungry, bored horses, penned in small fenced areas and suffering bites or kicks from spiteful horses he shared his day with.

They had stopped just before dusk on a road that led to a town called Lafayette. Sunday had cooked a meal over a fire, grilling some fish she had plucked from a narrow river and with some beans and pieces of bread, she handed a plate of the delicious-smelling supper, to Martha. Sunday was ravenously hungry and with a bottle of the wine they had recovered earlier in the day from the Gilbert brothers, she set about her food and drink with a vengeance, polite ladylike manners cast aside.

Her plate empty, she stared in bewilderment at the plate of food Martha had not touched. She shook her head in disbelief. "You must be hungry, Missy. You don't eat or drink. What's the matter, is it my cooking? I know it was a bit rough and ready, but the fish and beans are so tasty. You have to eat something. You'll die otherwise."

Martha passed her plate of fish and beans to a still hungry Sunday, who quickly devoured the food and gulped down a mouthful of wine, wiping a hand across her lips. She put the empty tin plate down and shook her head.

"Tell me, Missy. What is it? There's something not right. Tell me, please."

Martha reached a hand out and looked at her bewildered friend. "I am so sorry, Sunday. I cannot explain what it is."

"Do you remember the red-haired seaman on the *Tintagel* that you sailed on? He was from Scotland?" Sunday asked as she drank more wine.

Martha nodded. "Jim McAvoy. I remember him. Why?"

"Well, I had a quick word with him before we parted and left the Englishmen on the *Black Diamond,* or *Martha's Sunday*, as it's called now. He said something funny. He told me that the big man, Tom Sharpe, the ship's new captain, said he thought you were—you were a ghost. The Scotsman laughed it off as nonsense and I haven't thought about it at all, until now. You don't eat, drink, or—or even go for a pee. It's been hot today and I sweat like any normal person, but you don't. Are you a ghost?"

Martha took a deep breath and put out a hand to her friend. Sunday took her hand and with her dark brown eyes, looked into the blue eyes of Martha. Tears broke free from Sunday's eyes and trickled slowly down her brown face. She scuffed them away and the look of despair showed in her face. Martha squeezed Sunday's hand gently.

"I've tried to tell you, Sunday, but how can I start? You can see me and you can touch me and feel my skin, but the truth is, I am not like you. I died a long long time ago and I foolishly sold my soul to—to this this man called Lord Lucifer. In return I am free to roam wherever I want, I see the same things as you and other people who are still alive. I age very, very slowly, unlike humans. I was born in 1625, in England, at a place called Towton Meadows. I was put to death, charged with being a witch, tied to the chair that I take everywhere and drowned in the village pond. Just before I died, Lord Lucifer offered me the chance of living for eternity in paradise. I accepted his offer."

Sunday stared in shock and shook her head slowly. "It's 1773 now, Missy. If you were born in 1625, then—then you are a hundred and—" Sunday paused, trying to work it out.

"A hundred and forty eight years old," Martha said calmly.

"You look no older than twenty." Sunday gasped.

"I was only eighteen when they killed me. Maybe I've aged a couple of years." Martha giggled and Sunday joined her.

"If I stuck a pin in you, would you feel it?" Sunday asked.

Martha shook her head and grinned. "No, we—others like me feel no pain normally, but there is one time when we do."

"When?"

"Not to say now, it doesn't matter. I have to think about something."

"The old man you were with on the other ship. Was—was he like you?"

"Yes. He is much older and he taught me all that I know. He was already dead when the ship went down. He is somewhere up here. I don't know where. We are chased by Lord Lucifer and are his slaves, we have to do things for him, not nice things. He wants me at some time to—give him creatures like I am—the undead. There are thousands of his little creatures prowling the earth. Fimber O'Flynn told me."

"The old man?"

"Yes. He knows a lot of things about the undead and Lord Lucifer. He is about four hundred years old. There is bad feeling between Fimber O'Flynn, me and Lord Lucifer. About seventy years ago in Ireland, I killed this absolutely evil green dwarf, called Smegtooth the Terrible. He was King of the Boggimps and I made him sit on my chair. You see, Sunday, everyone who sits on my chair dies a horrible death. I touch them on their heads with a finger kiss and they die. I did it to Captain Suarez after he fucked me, sitting on the chair."

Sunday's eyes widened and she smiled, "You crafty mare, you let him take you on the chair and then you touched his head. The kiss of death."

"If that's what it is, the kiss of death. Very simply, if someone upsets me, they die very soon afterwards."

"I could fancy that. But remind me not to sit on your chair," Sunday grinned.

"You wouldn't die unless I give you a finger kiss."

"Who was this green dwarf that you killed?"

"Well, if you think those two back there who you killed were ugly, Smegtooth was the most despicable creature you can ever imagine. He actually said he wanted me for his wife. His ninth wife and he wanted me to give him thirty little Boggimps. Thirty little wart-skinned, scaly little dwarfs, with green slime for blood. He sat on my chair, I finger kissed him and he melted."

The two fell about laughing and Martha put an arm around her friend. Sunday looked into the undead blue eyes and for a brief fraction of a second they glinted red. She sighed heavily, leaned forward and kissed Martha tenderly on the lips. Martha responded and embraced Sunday, but in an instant the young Negro woman pulled back and shook her head.

"I've never kissed another woman before. I'm so sorry, Missy, I was not thinking properly. It's a sin to engage in same sex passion."

Martha smiled and put her head forward, returning the kiss. They held for long moments and then relaxed, but held each other's hands.

"I have enjoyed same sex passion, Sunday. It was beautiful and so natural. It was one of the reasons I was put to death. Abnormal and disgusting, inhuman and heinous, that's what this silly man said to me just before they killed me."

"Did you give him a kiss of death?" Sunday asked.

Martha nodded and smiled. "I did. He, with two others the day I died, but it cost me dear."

"How? What do you mean?"

"Well, Lord Lucifer gives all the souls he takes, six favours. I asked for the three men to die and they did, but it used up three favours. Then I used another, so now I have just two left."

"Then what?"

"After using the sixth favour, Lucifer sends you to his torture chambers. In there you stay for eternity. As I said, we the undead feel no pain, and we don't, but in the torture chambers every soul condemned to that abominable existence does, and it is for ever and ever. Lucifer wants every favour back that he gives and to him it is a sport. He sees everything, hears everything and he never forgets anything. He has spies all over, the creatures he sires with the undead females like me. I am on his list and one day he will come for me."

"Can you escape? Hide someplace? We could go to the other side of the world, on a ship, I will help you, Missy."

"There is almost no escape, Sunday."

"Almost. You said almost."

"Yes, I did. The old tinker I was with, told me about this daughter of a warrior queen who lived hundreds and hundreds of years ago. He took her soul and she was one of his slaves for over three hundred years. The old man told me she, her name is Jacindra, tricked Lord Lucifer and she gained her freedom. He was beyond madness and reason and vowed it would never happen again. No soul has ever escaped since Jacindra did, over a thousand years ago. She wanders the earth with others she has given birth to and they seek out Lucifer's offspring to slaughter them. I want to be like Jacindra and escape and then give birth to my own children, who will take up the fight against Lord Lucifer's children."

"You can't fight though, missy. You're beautiful and womanly. Not like me. I have always had to fight."

"Teach me then, Sunday. I saw you throw that knife to kill one of those ugly brothers."

Sunday laughed, leaned forward and kissed Martha again. "It takes time, Missy, but I will teach you how to fight, if you show me how to enjoy same sex passion, like you said you did before they put you to death. I have been raped so many times by horrible, dirty men that I never want to let a man touch me again. I'll teach you how to fight, if you teach me how to enjoy love-making, with you."

Martha returned the kiss once more and looked into Sunday's brown eyes. "Very well, we will start the first lesson right now. It's getting dark now, we'll go inside and begin."

An hour later and the two young women lay in each other's arms, reflecting on the lovemaking they had enjoyed. Sunday sat up from the bed, scrambled to her bare feet and reached for a small bag on the floor, which she always slung around her slim shoulders. Emptying the contents onto the bed covers,

Martha stared at the selection of jewels and gold and silver pieces. The naked girls sat and looked at each other, Sunday beaming a broad grin.

"You've got a king's ransom there, Sunday. Where did you get it all?" Martha gasped and picked up a large ruby, set expertly on a thick gold necklace.

"From the *Black Diamond,* after you had Captain Suarez killed. When he used to bed me, I always looked around the cabin as he had his way with me. I spotted a place in the oak panels where I guessed he had a hidey hole."

"You little thief, madam. That would have got you a free seat on a ducking chair," Martha chuckled and rolled the precious jewel in her fingers. Sunday reached to her hand, took the ruby necklace and gently turned Martha's neck. Flipped up her long auburn hair, she fixed it in place, then reached for a looking mirror, handing it to her friend.

"It's so beautiful, Sunday. Something Cleopatra would have worn around her neck."

"Who?"

"An ancient queen in Egypt. She was fabulously rich," Martha replied, feeling the ruby with trembling fingers.

"It's yours, Missy. A present from me for doing what you just did to me, it was so pure."

"I enjoyed your touch as well, Sunday. So, so different and wonderful, than Reverend Brooks' lecherous hands."

"Who was he?"

"My adoptive father. He and his wife adopted me when I was a little girl. They did things to me all the time when I was growing up. I put death curses on them and they died."

Sunday leaned away from Martha and stared at her with wide eyes. "You can put death curses on people?"

Martha laughed, still admiring the ruby necklace in the hand mirror. "Of course. It's one of the things that you can do when you are of the undead. It uses up one of Lord Lucifer's six favours, though."

"I want to become undead, Missy. I want to stay with you for ever. Is it possible?"

Martha stopped looking in the mirror and turned to look at Sunday, shaking her head.

"Don't say that, Sunday. I would give anything to go back to being a normal human. I could have children, grandchildren, I could eat a meal, enjoy a drink of honey mead, I could even lift my skirts and take a pee in a grass meadow on a sunny day, teasing a young boy as he watched."

"Did you do that, Missy, tease boys when you were peeing?"

"Of course, it made them gawk with eyes that nearly popped out of their scruffy heads."

"Then you let them shag you?"

"Oh no, not every time. I would offer to hold their willies while they peed, pull their pants down then run away. To see the silly sods trying to run after you, with pants around their ankles was so funny. I had a friend called Maisy Duckworth and that's what we used to do. Get two lads in a field, pull their pants down and then run away and hide. They went bonkers, chasing around with their willies flopping about."

"You're evil, Missy. You put death curses on people and tease boys like that." Sunday smiled and kissed Martha's breasts. Martha chuckled and lay back, letting Sunday take her body again as she held her ruby necklace. They embraced and enjoyed another hour of passionate sex, before Sunday fell into a deep sleep. Martha turned on her side and watched as her friend slept peacefully. Sleep would never happen for Martha again, but she was content to watch the young part Negro woman sleeping as she held her close.

It was midnight and a full moon was high above the bow top cart. A wind rustled leaves in nearby trees and made Martha turn nervously on the bed. Sunday slept on, but Martha heard the husky voice in the background. The top half of the carts door creaked open and outside, the young tethered horse whinnied loudly in alarm.

Martha sat up and looked to the moonlit sky outside. The husky gravelled voice called out again and Martha listened. The leaves rustled again, more loudly this time and once again the young horse whinnied. The bow top cart shook slightly and the half door slammed into the jamb loudly. The noise woke Sunday, who sat bolt upright, shaking. Martha held her and pulled the girl close into protective arms.

"What was that, Missy, I heard a strange noise?" Sunday whispered softly. "I must have been dreaming."

"It was a message for me." Martha whispered back. "I have to go to the north."

"The north? When?" Sunday asked, rubbing her half asleep eyes.

"I have to be there in two years' time."

"Just you, not me?"

Martha kissed Sunday's head. "You can come with me if you want, Sunday, but I have been ordered there. I have to go and be there for April 1775. I have a job to do."

Chapter Eight
Two Months Later

A field at the side of the Mississippi River.
Martha and Sunday were camped at the edge of a copse of trees, waiting for a ferry barge to take them across the river into Mississippi. A high sun had taken the temperature into the eighties and their young horse – Martha had named him Watson, after the young lad on the *Tintagel* who had been killed by the sharks – was happily munching sweet meadow grass.

Sunday had been teaching Martha how to shoot and after a few weeks of practice on their trek north east, the latter had become extremely proficient. With three out of four hits on a target hung from a low branch, Martha was overjoyed and had reloaded her musket. Sunday had hit her target four times out of four and sat on Martha's chair, waiting to take her turn, holding her loaded musket propped up on its butt end.

"In another couple of months you will be as good as me, Missy," called Sunday.

"No chance, Sunday. I'm getting better, but you're a wizard at musket fire. You're shooting twenty yards further than me," Martha replied as she raised her musket to take her fifth shot.

"Squeeze gently, Missy and lower it just a bit to allow for this breeze," Sunday called.

"I'm going to aim at the target you've been using. I think I can hit it even though it's a bit further," Martha called and closed an eye, ready to take aim. Then the sound of horses sounded and she stopped to look around. Sunday had heard the horses and stood up, lifting her musket. The young women watched as eight horsemen appeared several yards further back, slowly moving towards them

For a few silent seconds Martha and Sunday watched the riders approaching. Martha's eyes, now red, stared intently and then she looked more closely at one of the men. She blinked and then she recognised the man in the scruffy clothes. At the same time, Sunday had spotted him and now carefully raised her musket. It was one of the brothers she had thrown her knife at several weeks earlier. Roland Gilbert pulled his horse up and spat a mouthful of black tobacco onto the grass. He pointed a raised hand towards Sunday. The others looked.

"That's the black bitch that killed my brother. Murdered him. Left me fer dead at the same time. We've finally caught up with the murdering bitch. Now we hang her from one of these trees, and the pretty one at the same time, if she tries to stop us." Roland Gilbert spoke gruffly in his Cajun accent and kicked his horse forward. The other men followed cautiously.

Her musket raised and aimed at Roland Gilbert's head, Sunday stepped away, from the chair and towards the leering man. A few feet away, Martha had turned and had her musket at the ready. A fat man at the side of Roland Gilbert, her chosen target.

Another rider moved from the group and pressed his horse to the side of Roland Gilbert, his hand up, indicating for his friends to stop. They obeyed and moved their horses in a straight line, a few feet apart from each other. This man pressed his horse a few feet further forward, his eyes darting between the two women. In the same Cajun accent, he nodded at Sunday.

"We've been tracking you for quite a while and finally caught up with you. Like my friend said, he claims you shot and killed his older brother, Claude Gilbert and for no apparent reason. We are going to take you back and put you on trial for murder and attempted murder. We have no grievance with you, young lady," he nodded at Martha, her musket still pointed at the fat man, who had a look of fear on his sweating face, "So I don't want you to interfere. My name is Pierre Lamonte and I promise you no harm. Your black friend, however, will come back with us, to face justice by a Cajun court. Do you understand, young lady?"

Sunday held her aim at Roland Gilbert, but answered for Martha, who looked blank.

"She doesn't understand French, Mister Lamonte, but I do and that evil slimy man who accuses me is a liar. Yes, I did shoot his equally slimy brother and threw a knife at him, but they followed us from a store where we bought provisions earlier in the day and were going to rape us both. I had no choice but to shoot his brother and throw my knife. Is that what Cajun men are capable of, accosting innocent women and trying to rape them?"

Lamonte dismounted, held his horse and turned to look at Roland Gilbert. "Is that true Roland? You and Claude followed these two young women with the idea of raping them?"

Gilbert shook his head and waved a hand. "She's lying, Pierre, lying out of her black ass. They made it clear at my brother's place, that they were up fer it. Flirted with both of us and with Jules. That right, Jules?" Gilbert turned to look at the fat man at his side. He nodded vigorously. "See, Pierre, she's lying. Let's hang the black bitch right now, save time taking her back. Hang the white bitch as well, she stood by and watched Claude get shot."

Lamonte, a handsome, slim, tall, sun bronzed man in his forties, waved a hand dismissively at Gilbert's suggestion. "We take her back. Leave the other one, she is innocent."

He started to walk towards Sunday, but she shouted at him to stop. He pulled his horse to a halt and pointed back to his men. "You shoot, young lady, and we shoot. You and your friend will die. I promise you a fair trial. You have nothing to fear in my custody."

Sunday put a finger to the musket's trigger and nodded towards Roland Gilbert. "Any one of you reach for a weapon and I'll blow his head off. The fat one at his side will also die," she glanced quickly at Martha. "Leave it to me, Missy. Don't shoot your musket. We will need the cart, I'm coming with you, for ever. I've made my mind up."

Martha glanced at Sunday and shook her head. "No, Sunday, don't. It's not worth it. I don't want you to do it. Please don't."

Roland Gilbert pressed his horse forward and reached for a pistol at his side. The fat man, Jules, did the same. The ball shot from Sunday's musket hit Roland Gilbert in his throat and he fell backwards. The knife struck Jules Tabor in his forehead and he slumped across his horse's neck, blood oozing from the deep wound. Both men fell and lay across each other on the ground, as the two horses spooked and raced off.

Five pistols blasted at Sunday and she dropped to her knees, then fell face forward, mortally wounded. Martha screamed and raced to her, scooping Sunday up in her arms. Pierre Lamonte let go of his horse and joined Martha at the side of the dying black girl.

Sunday had a smile on her face as the seconds ticked away the last moments of her young life. Pierre Lamonte didn't hear the husky, cackling voice a couple of feet away at the side of the dying girl. Martha heard it and saw the red, scaly figure kneeling, with clawed talons and a drooling mouth, next to Sunday's ear. If Martha had not been of the undead, she would have smelled the repugnant stench of Lord Lucifer as he took Sunday's soul, after offering her eternity in paradise. Martha wanted to cry as the red figure whooped joyously then left as quickly as he had arrived. No tears could trickle down Martha's face as she cradled the dead body of Sunday in her arms.

A stunned Pierre Lamonte took Sunday from Martha and lifted the dead girl up in strong arms. He straightened and carried Sunday back to the bow top cart and laid her body on a blanket at the foot of the steps. Martha had followed and looked down at her dead friend.

"You fool, Sunday. I told you not to do it. He has you now, just like me," Martha said and knelt down to kiss Sunday's head.

The Cajun man watched and tapped Martha on her shoulder. He spoke in broken English, but Martha understood his words. "She was brave, mademoiselle. But you told her not to shoot, so don't blame yourself. We will bury her before we go back. I'm so sorry, it was probably how your friend described it. The Gilbert brothers are dead and that is no great loss. I have never seen such skill with a musket and a knife. Particularly from a woman. Where were you travelling to, anyway? This is a dangerous country for women to be on their own." Lamonte took a seat on Martha's chair and looked at the young woman. Martha stared at him, and realised she could make him die. Kissing two of her fingers she stepped towards him, but quickly thought better and wiped them on her skirts.

"North, to Massachusetts. I have business there," she replied quietly.

Lamonte stared at her in amazement. "That's hundreds of miles, mademoiselle, and now by yourself. Even with your friend it would be hazardous, on your own, foolhardy. There are tribes of Indians along the way. Some friendly, some not so."

"Please bury my friend, and thank you for your advice, but my business is important."

Lamonte called to his men and they dismounted to collect Sunday's body for burial. It took a half hour, then the men climbed back onto their horses and turned away. Pierre Lamonte stood before Martha and gently kissed her twice on the cheeks. He climbed up into the saddle and looked down at Martha.

"Safe journey, mademoiselle. I'm truly sorry about your friend. Au revoir." Lamonte followed his men, turned and waved back at Martha. She waved in return and watched until they disappeared from sight. Several stones had been piled on the raised earth where Sunday had been buried and Martha looked down at the grave.

"You foolish woman, Sunday—whatever your name is. I told you not to sell your soul to Lord Lucifer and you ignored me. Why didn't you listen to me?"

"Because I want to travel with you, Missy, that's why," Sunday replied. "I have no one else and I want to protect you. I love you, Martha Budd and you had better be loving me."

Martha threw herself at Sunday and hugged her tightly. The pair whooped for joy and whirled each other around. After a minute of hectic embracing, they stopped and held hands, looking at each other.

"You got shot. Not once but five times," Martha laughed. "Did it hurt?"

"Did you hurt when those nasty people drowned you?" Sunday replied matter-of-factly.

"I suppose it did for a few seconds, but not for long."

"Same for me, Missy. Now I'm fine and still alive—" Sunday stopped and shook her head. Well, maybe not alive, but I feel fine. Am I one of the undead now?"

"Very much so, Sunday, and a servant to Lord Lucifer. I tried to stop you."

"I know, and I'm a bit mixed up, to be honest. I'm dead, but I can still see and I can hear. I could feel you just now when we hugged. It can't be so bad to be undead and I can live a long time—well, maybe not live, but can do things, like you."

"You're a fool, Sunday. I warned you. You belong to Lord Lucifer now and he will never let you go, not to heaven or anywhere. You get six favours and when they are done, you go to the torture chambers."

Sunday looked at her friend with expressionless dead eyes and shrugged. "He can go boil his head, Missy, if he thinks he can put me down. I've fought the best and I've beaten the best, he won't be any different." As the last words came out, there was a great gust of wind that almost blew the bow top over. The horse panicked and started whinnying loudly. Then streaks of white lightning thudded into the ground and a few moments later, great blasts of near-deafening thunder. More lightning streaked across a suddenly blackened sky, then even heavier thunder. Sunday stepped to Martha and put an arm around her waist.

"Have I annoyed him, do you think?" Sunday said, as more lightning and thunder erupted.

"He heard you, Sunday. That's his reply."

"I get the message," Sunday replied, looking up into the brooding dark sky.

"We better get across the river and move away. We've a long way to go," Martha replied and walked to gather the horse to be hitched up once more. Sunday was at her side, her eyes darting everywhere. Watson was shivering with fright and was glad to be handled by calming hands. He wanted to be away from the field he was in and miles put behind him. He had seen a tall figure standing across the field in the flashes of lightning. The figure had raised itself from the ground and reappeared some distance away, almost as quick as he could blink. He was also confused now. The dark-skinned human was different.

There was no smell from it now. He enjoyed the smell of these two-legged creatures, but this dark-skinned human was the same as the pale-skinned one, no smell and it moved differently. They moved as though they weighed nothing. He could feel their touch, but in his feeble equine brain, he knew things had changed.

The bow top was moving again and Martha could sense the young horse was only too willing to leave the lush grass meadow. He would object normally to being taken from sweet grass, but not this day. Watson pulled with renewed vigor and Martha did not need to use the whip on his rump. She turned to look at Sunday, who was holding her loaded musket in wary hands.

"You can't be killed now, you know," Martha laughed.

"He's looking at me, isn't he?" Sunday replied, nervously.

Martha laughed again and reached to squeeze Sunday's knee. "He sees everything, hears everything, but he leaves us alone until he wants us to do his bidding. It's nasty, despicable work, but we have to do it, or we go straight to the torture chambers."

"What are they like, Missy, have you seen torture chambers?" Sunday asked, her eyes still busy, watching everything they passed on the track leading to the river.

"No, and I don't want to. Fimber O'Flynn told me a bit about them and believe me, they are places I don't ever want to be in. Let's just get across this river, it's called the Mississippi and it's hundreds of miles long. Lord Lucifer will put us in the torture chambers if we don't get to this place called Massachusetts on time."

"Daft name, Missy. What's there anyway?"

"A battle, more than likely. Lots of dead or near-dead bodies."

"A battle! Between who?"

"Haven't a clue. He knows all about it and we've got to get there and do our job."

"Lots of dead then, poor sods. When do we get there, tomorrow, day after?"

"Don't be daft. It will take months, probably a year or two."

Sunday turned and stared at Martha, with disbelieving dead eyes. "A year? You kidding! You mean—" Sunday's voice trailed off. "Or two!"

"Yes, it hasn't taken place yet, but believe me, it will and there will be bodies everywhere. We have to point the near-dead ones out to him. He goes in and takes the souls from the dying, lies to them about going to paradise and living for ever. Like he did with you today."

Sunday sighed and shook her head. "I don't remember."

"We don't. I didn't, but at the time when I was drowning, I grabbed at anything to go to paradise and live longer. It's a hoax and he lies to us."

"Sod that for a game of soldiers. He lied to me."

Martha nodded and grinned. "Join the club, Sunday."

"You mentioned a warrior queen who escaped from him. Tell me again," Sunday asked.

"Jacindra. She was the daughter of Queen Boadicea of England. A famous warrior who killed lots of Romans. Jacindra killed a lot more and was tortured after being captured. Lord Lucifer took her soul just before she would have died. Fimber O'Flynn told me some things, but I think he kept some of it back. He doesn't want me to get caught trying to escape and then sent to the torture chambers."

As Martha spoke, the bow top had reached the banks of the Mississippi and other carts and wagons were waiting to be ferried across. Suddenly a tremendous sheet of lightning streaked across the skies and once more the darkness returned. Thunder rolled again and the ground shook, horses in the waiting carts and wagons jostled in fright, handlers desperately trying to remain in control. More lightning and thunder, brighter and louder this time and a few of the horses took off along the riverbank. Three or four carts were dragged into the river and swept away by the suddenly ferocious current. People were hurled from the carts and horses pulled under as the heavy carts submerged.

A hundred yards back from the river bank, Martha and Sunday's bow top remained untouched by the sudden thunderstorm; the cart held firm in the strong wind and Watson was surprisingly calm, as other horses nearby stamped the ground in fright. Then it was over as suddenly as it had started, daylight returned and it was as if nothing had happened, although a few carts and wagons had perished.

Martha edged Watson into line and pulled the bow top to a halt behind a larger canvas covered wagon pulled by two heavy horses. A young boy, of about seven or eight, sat at the back of the bigger wagon in front of Martha and Sunday's bow top, staring at the two young women. Sunday waved to the boy, but he just carried on staring with large, deep-set eyes.

Once more Sunday waved at him, but he carried on staring, his pale face never twitching a muscle. A woman appeared at the boy's side and spoke to him. He said something to her, then she pulled a tied back canvas flap shut, before glancing, tight mouthed, at the two young women.

"He never stopped staring at us both," Sunday remarked with amusement.

"I've seen that same stare before, a few times. Always children, mostly boys," Martha said quietly as she nudged Watson forward again in the queue.

"Why do they stare like that? It's not normal."

"We're not normal, Sunday. That's why they stare at people like us."

"Are you saying they know what we are?" Sunday looked confused.

"Yes. Exactly that. It's not common, but every now and then a child will see us for what we are. The undead. Ghosts."

"How—how can they? I couldn't when I was little. Could you?"

"Once. I saw my mother just after she died when I was a little girl. She came to me in such a perfect shape, no creases on her face, no stooped figure, perfect skin, no pock marks and so beautiful. She touched me so gently and ruffled my hair. She told me I would live for a long, long time and travel far and wide. Then she left me and I never saw her again. What she said was true."

"Yeah, your mother was right, but you are no longer alive."

"But I'll never know if she knew what would happen to me. Maybe she did, but decided not to tell me."

"We're two of a kind, Missy. I lost my mother when I was also little, she was killed in front of me and my little brother when we lived on Martineque, in the Caribbean. I just remember her being dragged into an alleyway by a gang of drunken French sailors and raped over and over by these devils. She died in my arms that night. Me and my brother hid in a large crate on the quayside and finished up on a ship going to Jamaica. That's where I learned to speak English. We were found soon after and sold as slaves. Luckily we stayed together for the next few years, but ended up working on a plantation in Jamaica. Then one day the owner's son and his friends tried to rape me, but I fought them off. They took my brother and sliced one of his ears off and threatened to do it to his other ear, unless I let them take me, one at a time. I lay there on the ground and vowed that one day I would kill white men when I was older and trained to fight."

"Where did you learn to fight?" Martha asked as the wagon in front moved forward and the canvas flap opened, the little boy's face staring. This time Martha waved and once more there was just the blank, intense stare from the boy.

"On a pirate galleon skippered by an Englishman. He had captured a British frigate he had been an officer on, but the captain of this ship, the *HMS Whitby* was a brutish tyrant who regularly had his men flogged. There was a mutiny and Jack Masterson took over command. Still flying the British ensign and before news of the mutiny got back to London, Jack Masterson sailed into Montego Bay with his crew of fellow mutineers. The men who would not sail with him were offloaded and he took on replacements. I disguised myself as a young half-caste man and signed up as a galley worker, to scrub pans and suchlike. My breasts had not fully developed then, so I was able to sail with the crew and for a year I got away with it. They taught me to shoot and fight. Then off the coast of Mexico one day our ship, now renamed the *Sea Wolf*, ran into a couple of Spanish warships. The *Sea Wolf* was a fifty gunner, so Jack Masterson decided to fight. For two hours there was this hell of a battle. We sank one of the Spanish galleons and crippled the other. Our ship was battered, still afloat, but we had lost a third of our crew.

We raided the crippled galleon and took off loads of booty, but on the way back to our secret base in the Bahamas, we ran into the *Black Diamond* and Captain Suarez. We had hardly any cannon shot left, so had no chance, especially with fewer men and some injured. In the battle with the Spanish, I had been injured and the men found out that I was a woman. Suarez saw me and took me on to the *Black Diamond*. I recovered and he used me as and when for sex, until he met Françoise Clementine. I still wanted to fight, so he made me one of his cutthroats. I became one of the '*Black Diamonds*' best fighters."

"I noticed back there, Sunday, just how good you are, especially throwing that dagger. It hit that fat man in the middle of his head." Martha flipped the reins gently and Watson pulled forward. The boy in the larger wagon in front was still transfixed with his demonic stare at Martha and Sunday.

Steadily the queue of carts and wagons reduced as the Mississippi ferry barges transported them across the river, one at a time, with two strong hand-pulled ropes, by two stout men and a third man using a long pole to the river bed. There was just the large wagon in front of the bow top now and Martha and Sunday were thrilled to be almost ready for the river crossing. Then a man jumped down from the front wagon and marched back to the bow top. Tall and thin, black clad, a black, wide-brimmed hat, a stiff gait, sallow cheeked and holding a large red Bible, he stopped at the side of the higher seat and stared up at the two young women.

He sniffed and pointed back along the track. "I suggest you both turn around and go back to where you came from. Your lair or whichever blasphemous den of evil you belong. This is a country with God's blessing and no place for wretched creatures such as you. Go and begone, you daughters of Satan." With that, the man turned, waved the Bible in the air and marched back to his wagon.

Martha and Sunday were speechless, but the latter had a wicked smile on her face and with the boy in front still staring, she put a thumb to her nose and wriggled her slender brown fingers at him. The woman reappeared and pulled the boy away, closing the canvas flap again. The wagon was pulled onto the next ferry barge and the guard rails secured. The three burly men on the ferry barge, started to do their jobs in guiding the log ferry across the river.

After about twenty yards, the skies darkened and once more, streaks of lightning flashed menacingly in all directions and a few seconds later, the loud, deafening thunder. From nowhere, a huge flock of ravens appeared and dived to the wagon being pulled across the river. Thousands of the ravens swooped and shrieked hideously, swooping down and then pulling away, to return moments later, attacking the two large horses. The terrified horses jostled and reared, then stamped down, pulling on the harness. The man with the large guide pole swished it rapidly at the birds to disperse them, but he lost his balance and toppled from the log barge. Ravens swooped at the two rope pullers and in turn, with blood pouring from stab wounds, they let go and dived into the river, to escape. Both horses, stabbed repeatedly by the razor sharp beaks of the ravens, broke free and ploughed into the moving waters of the Mississippi. The log barge was loose and at the mercy of the Mississippi. The wagon on top juddered, broke from the chocks holding the cart wheels, rolled forward and dropped over the side into the cold black swirling water. The screams of the people on the wagon carried for brief moments then died against the noise of the river and the ravens still swooping in great numbers against the drifting wagon. Then, as quickly as they had come, the ravens flew away. A last flash of lightning streaked down and then the final roll of thunder bellowed.

A strong sun beat down on the greenery of the Mississippi banks. People on the wagons and carts behind the roll-top mulled around in a daze at what had happened, many still looking out across the shallower stretch of the great river, where countless hundreds of such crossings had been made over the years. The doomed wagon had disappeared from sight, sucked under the water, but the two horses would miraculously survive and drag themselves from the water down river.

Martha and Sunday stood by their horse, Watson, feeding him carrots. They would have to wait for the return ferry barge, to take them across to Mississippi. Neither showed any emotion at the events that had taken place, the probable deaths of the family in the wagon that had been in front.

"The boy did know then, Missy?" Sunday remarked as she gave Watson her last carrot.

"Yes, he knew what we were. His father was obviously a Bible preacher. We get it from time to time."

"It's just children, then, who can tell?"

"Yes. Very few, but those that can, have a sort of sixth sense. In girls who grow up a few years, they are often cast as witches and killed. In England there are men called witch hunter generals and they travel the land, searching for such people. I suppose it's possible over here in America, there are the same people searching for witches, or the undead."

Sunday laughed, pulled out her knife and started throwing it against a practice board she had made.

Martha watched her friend hit her chosen spot on the board, almost every time. "You're good, Sunday," she said admiringly.

"This lad on the *Sea Wolf* taught me to throw. His best trick was to put an apple on somebody's head and throw the knife to split it in two. He took bets on it and always won, but he didn't have many takers for standing still with an apple on their heads. He would share his winnings with anyone who was daft enough or hard up enough to stand for him."

"I wouldn't. Did you?" Martha asked as she walked back to the cart seat.

"Yeah, after I knew how good he was, but I always chose the biggest apple." Sunday laughed as she joined Martha, ready to climb up again to the seat.

They heard a noise behind them. They turned, Sunday with the knife in her throwing hand. A couple of young men, neither older than twenty, stepped around the bow top and made their way towards the girls. Martha reached for a loaded pistol just behind the seat.

"Howdy, ladies." called one of the young men, a stocky fair-haired type, dressed in blue bib overalls. "You saw the rumpus up front, huh? All those crows or rooks or whatever they were, real bad, that family lost into the river. Real bad, huh?"

"Ravens, mister," called Sunday, still on the ground. "They were ravens."

"Yeah, ravens. Where you ladies heading? Bobby Joe here and me—I'm Caleb and we're a couple of wagons behind yours both." the stocky youth asked.

"Massachusetts," Martha called down from her seat. "We're going north on business."

"Hey up, Bobby boy, this one's English. That right, miss?" Caleb Thompson laughed.

"I'm English, yes," Martha replied politely.

"My grandfather was from England—Plymouth. You bin there, miss?" Bobby Joe Dixon called. He was taller than Caleb Thompson, with a boyish, freckled face and also wore blue bib overalls, but with repair patches neatly sown onto the knees.

"No, I have never been to Plymouth. Now lads, we have a long way to go and you probably have, so nice meeting you, but time to go," Martha replied.

"It will be a bit of time yet, before yon ferry barge is ready. How about me and Bobby Joe keep you company for a while?" Caleb grinned and took a step nearer. "I never had an English girl before. Bobby Joe ain't too particular about a bit of black, are you Bobby Joe?"

The knife thudded into a timber post, between two of Caleb Thompson's fat fingers. He pulled his hand away from where he had leaned on the post and stepped back quickly. The pistol in Martha's hand was aimed at his head, the trigger hammer cocked. Sunday walked to the post and pulled the knife out effortlessly.

Caleb was looking at his fat hand, counting the fingers. He was white-faced and shaking.

His taller friend had stepped back several paces and was staring in disbelief at a grinning Sunday. She held the knife towards his ashen, wide-eyed face.

"So you like a bit of black, eh, Bobby Joe?" Sunday said flirtily, pushing her ample breasts out. "Never shagged one of my sisters then, a nice juicy black girl?"

Bobby Joe Dixon shrugged, said nothing, turned and ran. Caleb Thompson was satisfied he had not lost any fingers and backed away cautiously. As soon as he was several yards away, he pointed a fat finger at Sunday, who was standing with her hands on hips, a broad smile on her brown face.

"You're bloody mad, the pair of you. We just wanted a bit of fun. I hope you both go the same way as those others, drowned and to the bottom of the Mississippi." Caleb remarked and walked backwards a few more steps, then turned and ran after his friend.

Sunday and Martha's laughter would have been heard for several carts and wagons back. Sunday climbed up to the seat and kissed her knife.

"Can you drown twice, Missy?" she asked as she settled back, "Or do go the same way as the preacher man and his family?"

"Don't think so. Not sure about you, though, Sunday. You got shot, remember. You might be able to drown."

Sunday thought for a few seconds then looked at Martha. "Given the choice, which way would you prefer to die? Being drowned, or shot like me?"

A voice called out from the river bank and a man was waving them forward. Martha flipped the reins and Watson obliged and pulled ahead. The ferry money was handed over as the bow top trundled carefully onto the large log platform. The cart fixed in place, chocks under the wheels, a couple of boys holding Watson calm, Martha smiled and squeezed Sunday's hands. "Neither. I'd tell Lord Lucifer to go to Hell."

"Aye, Missy. I suppose you're right, but I've never had so much fun in my life." The girls' laughter carried the bow top safely to the other side and a willing Watson pulled them from the ferry and into the state of Mississippi.

"Massachusetts, here we come," Martha called as she flipped the reins.

Chapter Nine
Boston, Massachusetts

June the fifteenth 1775
Two young red-coated British Infantrymen stopped the bow-cart as it trundled along a narrow track just outside Charlestown, on a peninsula near Boston. They had been posted on picket duty to stop travellers heading towards the hilly positions on the peninsula. Boston was under siege and British warships were anchored in the bay with cannon aimed at the village of Charlestown, where it was believed a large contingent of American colonialist fighters were billeted.

Private Arthur Pembleton and Lance Corporal Robert Pudsey were uncomfortable in the stiff red tunics the British wore. It was not a fiercely hot day, but it was warm and the two lads had been on duty for three hours. Their patience with locals wandering out and about to see what was happening on the peninsula was at breaking point. Their water flasks were almost empty and both thought they had been forgotten by their sergeants.

"Clear off, you two and get away from here," young Pudsey barked out as the bow top stopped. He looked up, wiped sweat from his brow and blinked rapidly. Two very attractive young women were looking down at him and his colleague, Arthur Pemberton. He was surprised that one was definitely white and the other a very coloured young woman. In this part of the world colours did not mix and did not travel together. Back in Lancashire, England, where he was from, there were very few black people. "Where you think you twos are going, anyway? This is a dangerous place to be in."

"Just out for a quiet jaunt with our little cart, to see what is going on," Sunday called down softly, hitching up a skirt she was wearing to afford the lads a few feet of shapely legs. The two young soldiers looked at her smooth brown legs with wide eyes. She leaned forward, dropping her shoulders and afforded the lads an eye-watering view of her ample cleavage below her white frilled top. Both lads licked their parched lips.

"Do you need a drink of water? You look thirsty," Martha called. The lads nodded. "Then take some water from our tubs at the side. Our horse won't mind, it's his water."

Both lads turned and accepted the offer, eagerly filling their canteens. After long quenching drinks, wiping their mouths, they returned to the front of the cart.

Arthur Pemberton looked at Martha and smiled. "You're from England, aren't you?"

"Yes, from Berkshire, a village called Towton Meadows. Have you been there?"

The lad shook his head. "Nah, miss. I never bin out of Oldham, where I come from, until I joined the army last year."

"Where is Oldham?" Martha asked.

"Up north, miss, Lancashire. Next door to Yorkshire."

"Oh, I've been to Yorkshire. I was up there some time ago, at a place called Marston Moor. There was a big battle there and it was awful. Lots of dead, I could have been sick at the sight of all those poor men cut to pieces."

Both lads looked at each other and then up to Martha. Suddenly Martha realised why they were staring at her so intensely. The battle of Marston Moor had been over a hundred years earlier. Sunday wasn't sure what had been spoken, but she guessed Martha had said something out of turn. She jumped in quickly.

"Hey, lads, tell me something. Why do you British wear red uniforms? The enemy can see you coming miles away."

Both young soldiers looked away from Martha and shrugged, looking now at Sunday. Pudsey shook his head and started laughing.

"Go tell that, miss, to the sods in London who run the army. We don't know why it is, to be honest. I heard someone say it's because of getting wounded and not to give the enemy a sight of your blood on your uniform."

Pemberton shook his head. "Nah, Bob, I heard it's because some idiot in London put an order in for tons of red cloth and until it's all used up, we have to wear red. Some bigwig officer complained and suggested we should wear brown or green uniforms in battle, to avoid giving the advantage to the enemy, but he was court-martialled for treason. Daft buggers down in London who run the country. We should have a separate country up north. Another civil war like the one—" His voice trailed away and he looked up at Martha again, with a glint of suspicion. Both girls knew what he was thinking, so Sunday chipped in again.

"So why are you over here then, in America?" she asked, spreading her legs slightly so that the young soldiers might sneak a look up her thighs. Both did and Sunday grinned.

"These colonialists over here, or the continental army they call themselves, are putting two fingers up to the British Government that America belongs to them now and not us," Lance Corporal Pudsey remarked positively. Arthur Pemberton nodded his agreement.

"So there's going to be a big fight, then?" Sunday continued, opening her thighs a little sneaky bit more. It had the desired effect and military attention was now totally on Sunday and her shapely brown legs.

"A bloody big do, miss, in the next few days from what we hear, Hey, you two aren't spies, are you? Because we'll have to shoot you if you are," the young lance corporal asked now, pulling his colleague away.

"Do we look like spies?" Sunday replied, reaching down to ruffle the lad's tousled hair and giving them both another glimpse of deep cleavage. "Besides, we're English and on your side, remember."

Pudsey smiled and nodded, stepped away and replaced his hat, which he had previously removed. He nodded at Pemberton and the young Oldham lad replaced his tall white hat.

"Well, you're English, miss, but you're not," Pudsey remarked, looking first at Martha and then at Sunday, "And anyway, spies are usually men in black clothes and wear top hats and carry walking sticks, we all know that, miss, but you two should go away now, or me and my pal might get into trouble. Away now, the pair of you," Pudsey called stiffly, waving his musket at them.

"Don't go any further, though. Turn around and go back," Pemberton called.

"Thanks for the water, though," Pudsey said and then looked up at the girls again. "You two are the best looking lasses we've seen while we've been over here. A pity if you are found to be spies and shot at dawn."

Sunday laughed, wobbled her breasts seductively and looked down at the two young soldiers. "Oh, believe us, lads, we're not spies, but even if we were, musket shot doesn't worry us. It would bounce off us, we're indestructible. Don't you two go getting shot though, keep your heads down and cheat a little bit. Take your red jackets off and put two fingers up at yon stupid officers for not doing so and here, take these." Sunday passed each of the lads a gold necklace with a silver cross on each. Both put them around their necks. "They might save you from getting killed."

Two Days Later
June the seventeenth 1775
Charlestown Peninsula, Boston.

In and around Boston, the American colonialists had upwards of fifteen thousand men on standby to engage the much smaller British forces. These consisted of trained fighters, but also a lot of inexperienced volunteers, including blacks who would gain their freedom from slavery for agreeing to fight against the red coated British. This military force of Americans would later be referred to as the 'Continental Army' in journals reporting on the battle near Boston.

The British force numbered no more than four thousand, but a more accurate figure would be about three thousand. There were however several British warships anchored in the waters around the peninsula, including the flagship of Admiral Sam Graves, the mighty *HMS Somerset*. On board these British warships were hundreds of experienced marines, who could, if need be, be sent ashore to assist the infantrymen in regiments under the command of Generals William Howe and Robert Piggot.

The Americans under the command of General Ward were unsure of the strength of the British and Ward was at loggerheads with another senior commander, Brigadier Putnam. Neither had spoken to each other for months and had left most of the everyday running of matters around Boston and on the Charlestown peninsula, to two able and experienced colonels, John Stark and William Prescott.

There was also unrest within the Boston region, with thousands of Loyalists, new Americans loyal to their British roots, who chose not to fight, but were anxious to retain their 'Britishness' in the new colonial territories of America. In the following years, after the wars between Britain and America ended, these thousands of loyalists would leave Massachusetts and go north to Canada to retain their loyalty to the British crown.

There were two or three small hills on the peninsula, Bunker Hill and Breeds Hill being two of the strategic points where both armies decided were places to be secured, in view of the advantage of overlooking the immediate waters around the growing city of Boston.

Neither hill was more than a hundred and thirty feet high, but by being in command of these hills it gave the occupying force a definite advantage to bombard the approaches to the mainland, by enemy ships. For some months, these two hills had been overlooked by both armies, but by mid-June, it became clear that whoever occupied the peninsula was in a definitely superior position to regulate activity and the approaches in and around Boston.

Had General Ward and Brigadier Putnam been in regular contact and had there been no ill feeling between the two most senior officers within the Boston section of the Continental Army of America, the impending conflict with the British may never have happened.

Fortunately, the Americans had two very experienced and conscientious officers in Colonel William Prescott and Colonel John Stark, who did talk to each other and were able to coordinate the defences of Boston and surrounds. They even did the unthinkable and worked their men during the dark hours. While the confident British slept, Stark and Prescott's men laboured during the night time and built defensive makeshift walls on the higher parts of Bunker and Breed's Hills. Had these low defensive walls not been erected during the night of the sixteenth and seventeenth of June, the battle the following day would have been over in a quarter of the time. As it was, the battles of Bunker Hill and Breed's Hill would have allowed the British to claim their objective on just one assault on each hill, with fewer losses.

It took three assaults up both hills to defeat the Americans, but the British losses were higher. Over two hundred British infantrymen were killed, to a hundred and fifty Americans.

A disaster following the battles of Bunker and Breed's Hills, was that a flagged message from the British on the peninsula was misunderstood by observers on the warships and Admiral Graves ordered his ships to bombard Charlestown village. The cannon fire lasted for an hour and the village was left in blazing ruins.

Victorious British troops who had valiantly taken both hills in the bloody fighting against the Americans, could only stand in numbed disbelief watching the destruction of Charlestown, just three miles away. The defeated Americans had left the peninsula before Charlestown was shelled to destruction, but retribution would be dealt to the occupying forces as the next few years passed.

Later That Day

It was not yet dusk, but the battle of Bunker Hill had been over some hours and with nightfall still an hour away, the dead and injured of both the British and American forces were being collected for burial or field hospitalization. A British officer who had been critically wounded on the second charge up Bunker Hill in the early afternoon, had given permission to allow a couple of young women to help with the clearing up. Their little bow top had been ordered away from the battle scene, but a half-caste woman had stood her ground and demanded to see the senior officer. Colonel James Abercrombie of the Twenty-Second Foot was lying propped up against a small boulder, two musket balls embedded in his body, one in his lungs and the blood was running almost black. A stuffy young lieutenant had ordered the two attractive young women from the hill, but Abercrombie had heard the half-caste girl arguing and had overruled the junior officer. Sunday knelt by his side and was holding a flask of water to his bloodied lips.

Martha joined her friend and knelt at the dying soldier's side. He looked into her eyes and tried to smile. Martha brushed some of his hair from his face and smiled at him.

"Don't give your soul away, sir. You might get asked for it, but refuse. I did a long time ago and I regret it. Go from here in a few minutes and don't look back, take your soul with you."

Abercrombie managed the smile and took Martha's hand. "Thank you, miss. I'll not give my soul away. Find as many of my men as you can and tell them the same."

"We'll try, sir. We'll try," Martha replied and saw the officer's eyes close and the smile remain on his bloodied face. Sunday lowered his head and gently rested it on the boulder.

The rush of wind blew straight in the girls' faces and they saw the red, scaly figure a few feet away. Lucifer's fierce red eyes glared at them and transfixed both for several moments. He raised his body and stood over the pair of terrified women for several seconds. Then he cackled his hideous laugh and stepped back a stride, his evil red eyes glaring with venom.

"You robbed me of his soul and you will be punished for that. I take a favour from each of you and for the next one hundred years, you will do as I bid, whenever I want. No more wandering the lands for years between tasks, you will both work more and do your duty. I know you, Martha Budd, want to try and escape and join that cheating, insolent and treacherous ungodly soul Jacindra, but you will not succeed. No soul will ever escape again. Get around this hill now and find me more souls. Find me six each and I will give you your favour back."

The fierce wind blew again and Lord Lucifer was gone. Martha and Sunday looked around the hill, but there was no sight of him. What they did see was a soldier cradling another in his arms. This soldier was not wearing a red tunic; the injured soldier was. The girls ran to the soldier in a bloodstained khaki shirt and realised he was one of the two they had seen on picket duty two days earlier. Arthur Pemberton was holding his friend Bob Pudsey's head to his chest. The latter was minutes from death, his chest pumping blood from a large hole where a piece of shrapnel had punctured his body. Martha and Sunday reached the two lads and squatted down at their sides.

Pemberton looked from his friend and wiped tears from his dirty face. "My mate's dying. He wouldn't take his tunic off, like you said, miss. He took a hit and I was at his side but it was Bob who got hit. I refused to put my tunic back on, because we were more or less sitting ducks. I'm on a charge for throwing mine away as we went up that bloody hill."

"You did right, soldier. Will you get into trouble?" Sunday asked as she reached forward to wipe tears, blood and dirt from his face.

"Loss of pay and some time in the stockade, that's if I walk away from this damn' place. I reckon we should leave this land and go home. They don't want us here. Just one thing, though, miss—" Pemberton looked at Martha. "Will you look after my mate? I know you two are—you know, not real. At least, not you, miss. I worked it out after what you said the other day."

Martha looked at Sunday and the two nodded slightly. Martha now reached to the young Lancastrian and smiled, taking his free hand. "He'll be fine, don't worry. He'll be going back to England." Martha reached to the dying soldier, kissed her fingers and touched his head. Robert Pudsey responded and his eyes flickered open. For the briefest of moments, the young corporal smiled and looked between the three at his side. Then he closed his eyes and died.

Sunday stared at Martha and looked around to see if they were being watched. She saw nothing other than the dead and dying on Bunker Hill. The fierce wind returned, blowing across the hill and the sinister red figure of Lord Lucifer was once more hovering over the two young women. He glared at them and the dead soldier. His yellow talons pointed at Robert Pudsey's dead body.

"If you cheated me again, I will send you both to the torture chambers," he shrieked.

"We did not, Lord Lucifer. We were about to point him out to you, but he died, we were just too late. If you had not stopped us a few moments ago to take a favour from each of us, we would have reached this almost-dead soldier in time,"

Sunday called out and looked into the venomous deep red eyes of the Devil. He hissed and spat green slime at the two young women, circled them, hovering a few feet from the ground, then with a snarl of fury, took off to collect more souls.

Arthur Pemberton had heard or seen nothing, other than feeling a slight breeze. He was still holding his dead friend's body, rocking back and forth, tears trickling down his face. He looked at Martha and smiled, wiping snot from his nose.

"Thanks, miss. I know you sent him on. I'm gonna bury him myself and put his cross and chain around his neck. He thought it a bit sissy to wear it, but he kissed it this morning first thing then put it in his pocket. I had mine on." The lad pulled his vest front down and displayed the one Sunday had given him. "I knew mine would keep me alive and I'm glad I threw my red jacket away, I don't care what they do to me. Can I just ask you both a question before you go?"

Both girls nodded.

"I think I know what you will ask," Martha said and reached to squeeze the young soldier's arm. "My name's Martha Budd. I died a hundred and fifty years ago in Towton Meadows, back in England. I drowned. Those who drowned me thought I was a witch. My friend Sunday only died a couple of years ago, in the south of this country. A place called Louisiana. She was shot five times. We both sold our souls to the Devil."

"You're right, miss, er, Martha. I was going to ask you that," Pemberton said.

"I know, I read your mind, soldier," Martha grinned.

"Arthur Pemberton, Miss, er, Martha. I'm real glad me and Bob met you both. When I get back to England I'm gonna find this Towton Meadows and have a grave stone for you erected in the churchyard there," Pemberton remarked and turned to look at Sunday, still kneeling at his side. "What about you, Miss, err, Sunday? Where do you come from? Not England, because you have an accent. You sound French."

Sunday laughed and scrambled up. "I suppose you could say I'm French, but I don't have a place I can call home. I think I was born on an island called Martinique, in the Caribbean."

Before Pemberton could say more, a barking shout stabbed out and the three turned to see the stuffy young lieutenant

Martha and Sunday had encountered earlier, stomping across the ground, brandishing a polished sabre that had never seen action.

"You, there, soldier. Get yourself up and find your tunic. Get it back on and join the burial gangs. Is that feller you're cuddling there a dead 'un?" the young lieutenant snapped.

"He's called Bob Pudsey and he was my best friend," Pemberton replied, gently putting his friend's body to the side, then standing up.

"And I'm 'sir', to you, soldier. A lieutenant in the King's Army and you address me as sir. Now get your tunic found and put it back on and drag that dead body over to yon pile, ready for burial." The lieutenant pointed to a pile of bodies being laid out for burial. Pemberton made to turn and walk, but the lieutenant grabbed his arm. "And who were you talking to just now? Your dead friend, or are you going mad?"

The young soldier looked around, but there was no sign of the two attractive young women he had been speaking with for several minutes. Martha and Sunday were a few feet away and smiled to themselves.

"Come on, Sunday. We've got to find some souls or we go to the torture chambers," Martha said ruefully and turned away.

"We could run away, Missy," chuckled Sunday.

"One day, Sunday. One day," Martha replied and hoped Lord Lucifer was not listening. Lucifer thought he heard a voice, but he was about to steal another soul and huffed in indignation, he was too busy to worry about trivial matters.

By nightfall the two girls had located a dozen souls between them and a begrudging Lord Lucifer gave the pair back the favours he had taken from them earlier. He hissed and cursed as he hovered above Martha and Sunday, made to leave, then turned and glowered at the two dumbstruck young women once more.

"You, Martha Budd, are becoming as irritating to me as that old tinker I let you travel with. I'm going to keep my eyes on you from now and keep you working. I was going to let you stay in this country for a hundred years, but I have a job for you both, back across the high seas, because your new friend speaks French and there will be rich pickings over there. In forty years' time a big battle will take place between the British and the French at a place called Waterloo. Thousands of stupid humans will perish on both sides and you two will be there to help me take souls. If you do well for me at Waterloo, I might let you come back over here to wander in your silly little cart."

Lucifer cackled and raised his red scaly body a few feet higher, ready to leave, but Martha called to him.

"Where is Fimber O'Flynn, what have you done with him?"

"That old and useless tinker is at the bottom of the sea and he will stay there until I need him again. He is covered in seaweed, barnacles and fish droppings and has a fish-like face now and webbed feet. He has one favour left and he will not part with it. If he gives it up, I will take him from the salty sea. It's his choice," Lucifer cackled and did a quick flight around the two girls, stirring up dust.

"You'll put him in a torture chamber if he sells you his remaining favour," Martha said in disgust.

"Then you give up a favour, Martha Budd, and I will consider taking him from the sea." Lucifer laughed loudly and swirled around again, stiffing up more dust.

"I don't trust you, Lord Lucifer. What guarantee have I got that you will bring Fimber O'Flynn from the sea if I give a favour back?"

"Choose your words carefully, Martha Budd, or I will send you back to Ireland to face the Boggimps again. Smegtooth the Terrible's offspring are always asking me to send you back. They want revenge for melting their father."

"He was an ugly, fat little green dwarf and I was so pleased he sat on my chair. He deserved to finish up as a slimy green puddle," Martha laughed.

"Give me the chair, Martha Budd, and I will release Fimber O'Flynn from the depths of the sea," Lucifer hissed and hovered above Martha's grinning face.

"Not while the moon stays round, Lord Lucifer. You can't take it from me, I know that much. It was made by humans and I died on it. Only I can allow anyone or anything to sit on it and I know you want it. Fimber O'Flynn told me all about the rules of such heavenly, blessed objects."

"Then keep your infernal chair, Martha Budd, and I'll send you wherever I please and to begin with you can go back to

Ireland and face the Boggimps, those green-blooded dwarfs will be very happy to see you again." Lucifer cackled hideously, raised his scaly form and was gone.

Sunday stared at Martha, wide eyed and bewildered. "Boggimps? Who in damnation are they?" she exclaimed.

"A lot of horrible, ugly wait-faced dwarfs who think they're the most beautiful creatures on the land. I melted their king, an ugly, fat, podgy creature with repulsive, dirty yellow pointed teeth."

"Not good looking, then," grinned Sunday.

"I've seen better looking toads," Martha added and shook her head disdainfully. "So we are ordered to Ireland now?"

"Yeah, and the Boggimps. Hundreds of them squealing and jumping around."

"I heard you tell Lord Lucifer about some rules of heavenly objects. What did you mean?" Sunday had taken the reins and was guiding Watson along on the cart.

"Oh it was something the old tinker mentioned. You see, I died on that wooden chair, put to death on it, an innocent not proven otherwise. By that, all my senses, my thoughts, memories and feelings passed into it. No living mortal, or any of us, the undead, can use its powers, just the poor soul who perished on it. The only way the chair's powers can be passed on is if the one blessed with the powers it commands, agreeably gives them away, and that has to be under a full moon at midnight in the open air and to obtain it, the receiver has to give something of equal value in return. If the receiver cheats in any way, he or she will suffer a thousand years of ill fortune, including a loss of half their original power."

"No wonder Lucifer wants the chair from you. It's not because he needs any more power, he has lots, it's because he doesn't want you to have the chair's energy."

"I know that, Sunday, and he will never get his fiendish hands on it," Martha stated. No sooner had she spoken than a great gust of wind blew across the land and rocked the bow top cart savagely from side to side. The girls had to hold tight to avoid being thrown off. For several minutes the wind blew, with Watson unable to make any headway pulling the bow top. The wind disappeared as quickly as it had arrived and Martha and Sunday relaxed their grips on the cart.

"I think he's a bit mad with you, Missy," Sunday remarked tremulously.

"He's always mad with me, Sunday. He was the same with Fimber O'Flynn. I could never understand why the old tinker suffered Lucifer's wrath all the time. I get his wrath now."

"Will he pick on me, do you think?"

"Who knows, Sunday? His moods change all the time. We can be left alone for years, then he's back and always snarling and spitting."

"So we've got to go to Ireland and face these Boggimps." Sunday frowned.

Martha nodded. "Buy a passage on a ship and go face the little terrors. Hide your undies though, the sods will root through all our clothes when we're not looking."

"Charming. I've spent a fortune on mine. Silk and lace and pink ribbons."

"Wait 'til you see one of them dancing up and down with a pair of your you-know-whats on their ugly green wart heads," Martha laughed as Sunday steered Watson along a track, taking them away from the peninsula.

"I suppose the men ones are not taken to undead human females? Molesting us humans, oops, undead human females, I mean?"

"They can and they will, given half a chance. Smegtooth the Terrible wanted me to give him thirty of the little green blobs."

Sunday pulled Watson to a stop and stared wide-eyed at Martha, who was grinning. "You are joking, Missy. They can do it with us?"

"Oh, yes. The old tinker told me. One of Lord Lucifer's favourite torture chambers is one where hundreds of the Boggimps are free to roam, rape and pillage with undead human females. Day after day, a hundred times a day. To the Boggimps, these chambers are a place of reward for the little green monsters. To them, this is paradise and they fight each other to be sent there for a hundred years of pleasure. They help to run the torture chambers to earn Impcreds. As soon as they have a thousand of these Impcreds they can join the queue to get in. The last time I heard, before Fimber O'Flynn was lost to the deep sea, he told me the queue was over sixty years long. The Boggimps just wait and wait to get in."

"I'll kill any little green blob that tries to touch me. I'll cut his thingy off," Sunday hissed with venom. "Ughh! A green wart-infested thingy inside me? No way!"

The bow top trundled on with Martha grinning and Sunday cursing and tutting.

Chapter Ten
Middle Ireland

The signpost, crudely lettered, gave the onlookers three choices at the crossroads they had arrived at. On the narrow, twisting road they had travelled, it carried on to 'Midget Marshes'. To the left it pointed to 'Gremlins Green'. To the right, 'Hobgob Hollows'.

"Well I think the Boggimps will live at Gremlins Green," Sunday remarked as the two girls observed the signpost. "They're green, aren't they?"

"Yeah, but what about Midget Marshes? They're also midgets," Martha replied, looking dubious.

"So we turn right to Hobgob Hollows then," Sunday compromised and flicked the reins at Watson. "Thirteen miles, it states. Or we turn around and go back and get a ship and return to America. That's my choice. I don't fancy fighting off hundreds of green blobs who want to wear my undies on their heads."

"And suffer Lord Lucifer's anger? He'll have our ship sunk and we'll finish up on the sea bed with the old tinker and look like fish in a few years' time." Martha replied.

"And I thought life was bad on the *Black Diamond* with Captain Suarez. I'd give all my jewels and gold back to sail the Caribbean again, plundering ships of loot." Sunday laughed.

"Not roaming the lands on this little cart?"

Sunday thought for a few moments and then nodded. "Yeah, Missy. Whatever trouble we've been in these last three years, I like what we do, other than what would I give to drink a few glasses of French wine and gobble a big roast turkey leg and gorge down a bunch of sweet grapes?"

"What about me? I've been doing this for over a hundred and fifty years and I'll be doing it for another hundred and fifty years. I try not to think of the no food part of it. At least we don't get hungry."

"And cold. I remember stowing away on a ship out of Montevideo and thought it would sail north to the Caribbean, but it went south to the bottom of South America. The ship almost sank in a great storm and it rained non-stop for days. I was in a life boat under a tattered canvas and I was drenched. I lived on mouldy food scraps that were thrown out for the sea birds. So not ever feeling cold is a real pleasure."

"So, what do we do, then? Turn around and go back, or try and find these horrible warty-skinned Boggimps and stay around Ireland until we are sent someplace else?" Martha said as Sunday shrugged, looking uncertain.

"Go on, Missy. Being one of the undead has its advantages. I just hope these little green monsters don't start their antics, or they'll be a lot less of them when we leave."

"I'm wondering who their king is now, after I melted Smegtooth the Terrible. I hope he's not as stupid and boastful as Smegtooth was."

"So, which way, Missy? You're in charge," Sunday grinned.

"Hobgob Hollows sounds good," Martha replied, pointing to the right.

"Hobgob Hollows it is. Unlucky thirteen miles though. Have you loaded our muskets and pistols?"

"Yep and polished my chair, in case I get the chance to melt a few of them down."

"How did you get this King Smegtooth to sit in the chair?" Sunday asked.

Martha laughed wickedly. "He had just proposed marriage to me and wanted to talk about a life with him and all his wives. I sat him down, it was like taking a toy from a baby."

"And he just melted?"

"After I gave him the kiss of death."

"He melted?"

"Dribble after dribble running down the chair to the ground and then a slimy green puddle on the ground."

Sunday started laughing and had a fit of the giggles. Martha joined in and even Watson turned his head to see what his two mistresses were up to. The little bow top trundled along the track towards Hobgob Hollows and the girls' laughter continued.

A few miles along, Sunday pulled Watson to a halt and jumped down to let the horse take a drink from a deep puddle and a nibble at the grass to either side of the track.

"Do you think they'll remember you, Missy? These Boggimps?" Sunday asked as she climbed up again and flipped the reins. Watson whinnied and obediently did as he was asked.

"Well it was about eighty years ago, so who knows? They live as long as we do, but some of them might be in the queue to work in Lord Lucifer's torture chambers."

"Mucky, lecherous little horrors." Sunday shivered. "A hundred times a day being groped and raped for eternity. Are you kidding me, Missy?"

"No. Fimber O'Flynn never lied to me. A lot of the six hundred and sixty-six chambers are given over to the Boggimps to rape the undead females Lord Lucifer has banished to those despicable places."

"And when you have no favours left, that's where you go?"

"Yeah. The torture chambers."

"Then I'm with you Missy. This warrior woman you mentioned, who escaped. What's her name?"

"Jacindra, daughter of Queen Boadicea. Why do you ask?"

"We find her and ask her what she did, how she got her freedom," Sunday replied and no sooner had she spoken than the skies darkened and the fierce wind returned, screaming and smashing against the bow top. Watson whinnied in fright and tried to break from his harness.

The howling wind increased and a stab of lightning hit the ground just a few feet from Watson. A tremendous roar of thunder erupted. The horse panicked, pulled at his harness violently and the leathers snapped. Watson ran from the twin poles and was away up the track, leaving the bow top rocking from side to side as the fierce wind bellowed.

Martha and Sunday held tight to their seat, until as suddenly as it started, the wind, thunder and lightning stopped. The sky returned to normal daylight and a bewildered Martha and Sunday scrambled down to the ground.

"We have to stop talking about escaping, Sunday. He hears everything we say," Martha said as she and Sunday looked up the track to see how far Watson had run. There was no sight of the horse as the girls stood with hands on hips.

"Poor Watson, I bet he wishes he had never seen us," Sunday said dejectedly.

"We need a dragon to pull the cart. They probably don't get as frightened," Martha said with a rueful grin.

"Are there such things, Missy?" Sunday asked as she started walking along the track.

"I heard there are still some in Wales. They live in caves off the coast."

"Where's Wales? I've never heard of it." Sunday asked.

"A small country stuck to the side of England. They grow leeks and daffodils. Funny people, with funny voices and speak a funny language that most of the people don't understand. It rains all the time."

"Sounds a fun place to live. I think I'd rather be warm in one of Lucifer's chambers," chuckled Sunday as the pair walked along the twisting track.

"I'll stick to living in the cart and travelling, as long as we don't have to pull it ourselves," Martha said as she peered anxiously ahead, hoping to see Watson nibbling grass by the roadside.

Thirty minutes later and they rounded a bend to see the horse tethered to a gatepost, waiting patiently to be collected. The girls had smiles on their faces as they walked to Watson, then stopped in their tracks as they saw a pile of carrots he was chomping at.

Looking around to every side of the track and into the field where the gate he was tethered, there was no sign of anyone. They approached Watson nervously, their curious eyes still darting around.

"Who found him, Missy, d'ya think?" Sunday asked pensively, as she patted the horse, happily eating his pile of carrots.

"Not a clue, Sunday. But he's unhurt and somebody found him and tied him up for us."

Sunday's hawklike eyes were still darting around but there was still no sign of anybody. Then she noticed a disturbance in the high grass, the thistles, the ragwort, brambles and the nettles. It was clear that someone or something had recently trodden through the thick overgrowth at the side of the track.

Leaving Watson tethered and happily munching his pile of carrots, Martha and Sunday investigated the disturbance. If they had not been of the undead, the thorns, spikes and stings from the nettles would have been intolerable, but they swept a way through the wild plants with their hands until they stopped in shock. A square of timber covered in moss, algae and trampled dead leaves was uncovered. The girls looked at each other in surprise and then at the square of timber, made up of short planks, about two feet in length. At one side, a half round metal latch was fixed, set into one of the planks.

"It looks like a trapdoor," Martha exclaimed, part nervously, part excited.

"It is a trapdoor, Missy, just like those on ships and someone used it recently."

"Or something," Martha added, joining Sunday in a concentrated stare at the wooden planks.

Both stepped back and looked around again, their eyes full of apprehension. Sunday, in her usual daredevil spirit, took a step forward again. She reached down to grasp the trapdoor handle, but as she did, a voice called out to her side.

"Best you don't do that," the voice called out.

Sunday immediately gasped in shock and stepped back, standing on Martha's feet. The pair glanced to where the voice came from and looked with astonished wide eyes. A small figure, no taller than two feet, brightly garbed in brown and green, with a small pointed hat, was peering at the girls with piercing dark eyes. And then, just to the side, another figure appeared, similarly garbed.

"Who are you two?" Sunday asked with as much politeness as she could muster.

"We live here. You were just about to trespass." The first figure said.

Martha stepped forward to Sunday's side and smiled. "Did you catch our horse? If you did, thank you."

"We caught your horse and gave him the carrots. He ran away, because he was frightened by the thunder and lightning. It was your fault, why the wind blew and the sky went dark."

"Why do you say that and what are—who are you?" Sunday asked concisely.

The second little figure stepped into the open and looked at Sunday with challenging eyes.

"You were going to say, what are we. Well, we are Blingos and if you had pulled that trapdoor open and climbed through, you would have entered Blingoburbia. We can only go through on the day of a full moon and not before eight o'clock in the morning and must be back before eight in the evening. And only in the four months that have thirty days."

Martha and Sunday looked at each other, then both started counting the months on their fingers. The first little Blingo laughed and called out, "April, June, September and November. Four months only in a year. Twenty-four hours in each year. One full day a year up here in the human world. That is the law in Blingoburbia and offenders are punished."

"I've never heard of Blingos," Martha stated nervously, hoping not to offend. The two little people chuckled and stepped onto the trapdoor.

"What about Goblins?" they replied in unison.

"Goblins?" Sunday said with a nod. "Yeah, I've heard of Goblins. Horrid little mischief makers, but they don't exist, like the Pixies and Elves."

Martha nudged Sunday and smiled sheepishly. "My friend is new to these things and doesn't understand yet."

Sunday glanced Martha a cursory look. "Understand what?"

"There are Goblins and Elves and Pixies and Boggimps," Martha said calmly. "And Leprechauns and Banshees, but I've not heard of Blingos."

The two little figures danced nimbly on the spot and laughed. "You're just as mistaken as all the other humans, or in your two cases, not humans, but the undead." The look of astonishment on Martha's and Sunday's faces made the two little people chuckle again. The other little man took a pocket watch out and nodded.

"You're lucky. It's ten minutes to eight and it's almost time for the two of us to go back. Before we go through the trapdoor again we'll explain about us Blingos and why we know you are both of the undead. First, there are no Goblins, because it's just the way both are spelt. Same letters but re-arranged. A fool of an old sorcerer called Wizadabra got it wrong over a thousand years go. He had drunk many goblets of turnip and beetroot wine before he wrote up his yearly ledgers, as is required by the powers to be, in Blingoburbia, which is below all the trapdoors on the ground, at rubbish tips in your Uptop world. So there are no Goblins, we are called—Blingos. Now, secondly, why we know you are of the undead. Very simply, it's because you can see and hear us. If you were still human you could not see a Blingo, unless you are a special one. During any of the twenty-four hours a year that the trapdoors are open, those of us that are not spreckled come 'Uptop' and root around, collecting stuff to be sent down to Blingoburbia. It's the month of April now and a full moon tonight, so that's why we're up here doing our work with all the others. They'll be here in a few moments.

Martha and Sunday looked around, but saw no other Blingos. Both of the little men chuckled and shook their heads in glee. The first one, who had spoken earlier, smiled at the two bewildered young women, standing with mouths open.

"At midnight on the night of the full moon and just for twenty-four seconds, the special humans and those of you of the undead who are chosen, can enter Blingoburbia and take orders and in return earn spreckle merits, but only if you have received the Mark of the SWAN. Without this mark you will never enter Blingoburbia."

"So this is the entrance to Blingoburbia?" Sunday asked, after looking around to see more of the little men, but none were in sight.

"Oh, this is just one. Over the world there are lots and lots. In hedgerows like this one and in rubbish tips. The special humans and those chosen from the undead, like you two, earn spreckle merits by looking after our entrances all over the world. After the trapdoors are closed our 'Uptop' helpers make sure the surrounding area is cleaned and put back in order."

"Who are the special humans you mention?" Martha asked.

"Those humans that can see the undead," the second little man replied and reached into a pocket and took out a small tin whistle. His companion did the same.

"You're small. How did you catch our horse and tie him up?" Sunday asked, still looking around to see if there were any more Blingos nearby.

"We aren't alone up here. There were about thirty of us who found your horse and we just climbed on each other's shoulders to reach him. It was not difficult."

"And you mentioned a name, Swan. What is that?" Martha asked, after she had scanned the area for a sign of any other of the little men.

"It's the first letters of Sorcerers, Wizard's and Necromance's Society. Swan. They rule over all non-human people who can speak. They are never to be disobeyed. Their symbol is a swan. The three Dabras—or Magus, to give them their proper name—can do the most powerful magic and sorcery. Disobey them and you will be punished severely. Now, I ask you a question. You mentioned the Boggimps, do you have any dealings with them?"

Sunday looked at Martha and both nodded slowly. "We have been sent to do work with them or whatever. It's a punishment," Martha said ruefully.

"So Lord Lucifer sent you here to Ireland?"

"Yes, for me, the second time."

"Are you the one who killed Smegtooth the Terrible about eighty years ago? We heard a very beautiful young woman ended his miserable existence."

Martha looked forlornly at the little man and humbly nodded. "That was me."

The whoops of joy and the sudden dance and skips by the two little men took both girls by surprise. They watched with relief as the jigs and skips and twirling, holding hands, by the two Blingos brought smiles to their faces. The jig and skipping stopped and the tin whistles they held were raised to lips and shrill sounds pierced the still air. From nowhere, a host of little men suddenly appeared and through the trapdoor now pulled open, they piled down into Blingoburbia. Forty, fifty, sixty, seventy, eighty and ninety-eight of the Blingos disappeared through the trapdoor, all carrying sacks full of items. The two, Martha and Sunday had been talking with sat on the edge of the black hole, their little legs dangling over the side. Both were grinning.

"Well, Martha and Sunday, we've got to go now. I'm called Jobsdone and this is Bossalot and we will report to our seniors that we have met you, Martha Budd, the woman who rid this land of Smegtooth the Terrible and your friend Sunday, who will be just as good a warrior of the undead. Come back here at midnight at the night of the full moon in June and we will talk again. Goodbye."

The trapdoor slammed shut and Martha and Sunday jumped back a stride. They stared wide-eyed at the wooden cover for a few seconds, then Sunday reached down to try the metal latch. She grasped it tight and pulled, but it was locked tight. Again she pulled, but had no luck. Then a voice sounded and the girls wheeled round to see a woman dressed in black, with a besom brush and a rake in her hands. They stepped further away to let the woman to the trapdoor. Without another word spoken the woman started to clear the area, raking and brushing and straightening all the trampled ground. The two girls moved away to take Watson back to the bow top. They stopped aghast at the sight of the little cart standing a few yards away, Watson still chomping at his carrots.

"How—" Sunday started and looked around. "How did it get here?"

"The Blingos brought it here. They just didn't want us to see them today apart from the two we met. I think we'll be seeing more of them, if I'm not mistaken."

"Well, I'm not sure, to be honest. Another lot of dwarf mischief makers and they live underground. How can they exist underground? How do they breathe, what do they eat, or are they undead like you and me and they don't eat?"

"Who knows, Sunday? But I have a strange feeling they are not to be feared, unlike the Boggimps. Which reminds me, we have to find them, or you know who will be threatening us with the torture chambers again."

"Ughh, don't remind me. If I slept I would be having nightmares thinking about the evil little green blobs. I can't wait to see them," Sunday sneered. Martha glanced a wary look at her.

"Joking, Missy. Just joking."

"Well, we have a little job to do before we can move. Watson snapped his leathers." Martha walked to the cart and for the second time in minutes she stared, astonished. All the leathers were neatly repaired. "They're better than before," she remarked happily.

"We need to get that Swan thing, so we can go down to that place," Sunday said.

"Blingoburbia and the Swan symbol. Why did they help us today? And how did they know our names? The one called Jobsdone mentioned Martha Budd. He knew you were called Sunday."

"Weird, Missy. And what was in those sacks the others carried. Did you see all of them just go straight down through the trapdoor? And where did they all come from? I kept looking all over, but not a sign. I thought my world on the *Black Diamond* was strange, but this undead thing freaks me and all these little people. How many are there, Missy?"

"Fimber O'Flynn mentioned quite a few different types. There are a gang of them here in Ireland called Leprechauns, who are deadly enemies of the Boggimps. There's the Banshees, who by all accounts have the ability to fly and change body forms. The female Banshees are dominant to the weaker male ones and you hear them before you see them. They have a high-pitched scream that terrifies their enemies. Over in England there are the Gnormkins, but usually called Gnomes, they're a peaceful bunch and no trouble. There are a warlike tribe called Smegmadites who are related to the Boggimps. Smegtooth, who I melted, was quarter Smegmadite, three quarters Boggimp. And there are the Trogladytes, led by Trogtrol, a fierce Hell Creature.

"So, we've got Boggimps, Banshees, Leprechauns, Smegmadytes and Trogladytes," Sunday said, shaking her head.

"That's not to mention the Blingos, who we have just met."

"Originally known as Goblins," Sunday laughed.

"Yeah, Goblins," Martha agreed, then her eyes narrowed. "Where are we heading for right now?"

"Hobgob Hollows."

"Hobgob Hollows. Back in England there were a tribe called Hobgoblins. Nasty creatures, real little savages. HobGob Hollows. Something tells me it's a place to do with Hobgoblins. I think we're going the wrong way, more likely Gremlins Green."

Sunday sat down and shook her head in bemusement. "If I had a magic wand, Missy, I'd wave it and ask to be sent back to a pirate ship and all the buck swashling, thieving and pillaging. Poor food, the dirty hands groping you and sea sickness."

"I wish as well, Sunday, but not possible. We took a chance and lost. We could ask this woman who is tidying up the trapdoor for the Blingos if she knows how to find the Boggimps."

Sunday jumped up and nodded. "Good idea, Missy, let's ask her."

Martha and Sunday turned from the cart to look for the woman, but there was no sign of her. They walked back to the area where the trapdoor was, but it was covered up again as if nothing had ever disturbed it. The thistles, nettles, ragwort and shrubs were all erect and prominent; not the faintest indication that they had ever been disturbed.

"Where did she go?" Martha said and looked around the area.

Sunday shrugged and did the same, her eyes searching. "Gone into thin air."

"Well, at least Wason has a full belly, he'll be content."

"I wish I had. Roast ham, parsnips, cranberry sauce, thick onion gravy and plum pudding and cream. A bottle of honey mead to wash it all down. And a sleep in a comfortable warm bed afterwards, with a scrubbed clean, shaved man at my side."

"I gave you a chicken leg on that pirate ship, if I remember."

"That was years ago, Missy, but it was absolutely delicious. I used to clean up after Captain Suarez and that toffee-nosed French woman on the *Black Diamond* had eaten a big meal. When no one was looking, I cleaned their plates of scraps they'd left. I licked the plates of all the juices. Finished off the wine from their glasses. I ate better than all the other crew, even if it was leftovers.

"Then you ate better than me. I had to steal most of the food I ate, until I was taken in by these two religious fanatics. Then it was mouldy bread and watery soup. Nothing else."

Sunday shook her head and gave Martha a hug. "And I thought you had had it good in England. You were worse off than me."

"So would I want to go back to that miserable life in Towton Meadows, I ask myself?"

"Would you, Missy?"

"And lose snuggling up in bed with you? Not in a month of Sundays, Sunday."

"If I could cry, I'd be slobbering now, Missy. That's the nicest thing anyone's ever said about me." Sunday squeezed Martha's shoulder and smiled. "Let's go and find Gremlin's Green."

"Well, we met these Blingo characters on the way to Hobgob Hollows and they don't appear to be nasty and horrid, so a bit of good fortune for us after taking the wrong way."

"And in two months' time we can come back and hopefully meet Jobsdone again. I wonder what it's like down in Blingoburbia?" Sunday said and flipped the reins and a carrot-full Watson pulled his bow top away along the twisty track to the crossroads a few miles back.

Chapter Eleven
Gremlins Green

Watson was scared as he pulled the bow top into Gremlins Green. The place was a motley mixture of shanty huts, mud-caked dwellings and rusty tin bunkers. Fires were lit everywhere and dirty metal cooking pots hung from tripods above the flames. Several short, stocky green figures crouched around the fires. Chattering loudly and poking fat, stubby clawed fingers into the cooking pots, the Boggimps of Gremlins Green were at home. Watson whinnied in fear as he saw the small, ugly, green-skinned figures suddenly staring at the bow top. The chattering stopped and every Boggimp, adult and infant turned to look at the intruders. The sudden silence was chilling.

Hundreds of yellow eyes watched as the cart rattled slowly forward, juddered and then stopped. Watson whinnied again, this time louder. Unlike Martha and Sunday, he could smell the obnoxious stench of the green-skinned dwarfs, with crude, hairy pointed ears.

"Mother of Blackbeard, they are ugly," gasped Sunday. "I've seen prettier hairy backsides on drunken pirates than this lot of shrunken misfits. This is punishment to beat any punishment."

"I had forgotten how ugly they are, but now it all comes back," Martha declared.

"From now on, Missy, I'm going to be a good girl and do as I'm told. No more getting Lord Lucifer annoyed."

"So escaping from his clutches is now unmentionable?"

"Totally. I want to go back to counting dying bodies on battlefields. We have to slave here for these horrible creatures for how long?"

"Probably twenty years, if we're lucky. Fifty if we're not," Martha replied. Sunday fell backwards into the back of the bow top with a loud, cursing scream. To all sides of the bow top, dozens of Boggimps scrambled up and ran for cover. Watson whinnied again and tried to turn around to go back, but Martha grabbed the reins to hold the terrified horse from bolting.

"I exaggerated, Sunday. Not fifty years, more like thirty if we're good souls."

The second scream was louder, high pitched, blood curdling and deathly. More Boggimps ran for cover. Martha looked into the back of the cart to see if Sunday was all right. Shapely, long brown legs were threshing in the air above Sunday's prostrate body.

"That's longer than I had lived before I was shot and killed," moaned Sunday in despair.

"It'll soon pass. Thirty years is just a blink of an eyelid in time for us now."

Sunday screamed again and jumped from the back of the cart. Without a pause she set off around the cart at high speed, kicking and waving her arms in the air, her screams becoming louder, hysterical, more high pitched. All around the Boggimp camp, short green figures had dived for cover at the sight of a crazy, tall, brown, undead woman, shrieking loudly, jumping and racing around like a mad dog.

Then she stopped and raised her head to the sky. The sound was raucous, wolflike and terrifying. The Boggimp camp was soon deserted. Not a green-skinned, pointy-eared creature in sight. Hundreds of red eyes and yellow eyes peering from hidey holes, but not a sight, smell or sound of a Boggimp.

Watson settled and breathed easier. Martha jumped down and tried to find Sunday, but her friend was charging around the Boggimp camp, snarling and spitting, knocking cooking pots over and stomping ferociously. Two-headed, red-eyed camp dogs, normally squabbling and fighting, had also disappeared. In less than five minutes, Sunday had achieved more than any of the Boggimps' enemies had achieved in hundreds of years, sending the little green monsters into hiding.

Eventually, a red-eyed Sunday walked to Martha and let out another raucous wolf howl. She followed this with an amazing back flip that stunned Martha. The two young women looked around the trashed camp, with disbelieving eyes.

"Did I do that?" Sunday exclaimed incredulously.

"The lot. The Boggimps took off like scalded cats. I think you made your mark," Martha laughed.

"How would those ugly, undersized green freaks react to be told they would have to serve as a slave for thirty years on a pirate ship, being shot at, flogged, starved, raped and soaked to the skin most times?"

"Well, if they come out of hiding you can tell them that. I've never seen so much panic take place. They fell over each other to escape. Time passes fairly well, though, you know."

"Don't start me off again, Missy. I've got to get my head around slaving here for thirty years alongside these slimy little creatures," Sunday scowled.

As they chatted, there was a movement at the far side of the deserted camp. One by one the Boggimps started to return. Cautiously, the green-skinned Boggimps trampled the trashed ground, returning to their selected places, nervous yellow eyes never leaving the tall brown undead woman. They had never seen an undead humanoid a brown colour before. They also recognised the other undead humanoid as the ruthless destroyer of King Smegtooth, eighty years earlier. Chattering between themselves, the Boggimps wondered why Lord Lucifer had dumped the two warrior women on their peaceful little enclave. It was so unfair; they were the most enviable, devil fearing, industrious and friendliest of the small non-human speaking tribes, as well as the best looking.

Their new king – and he had been serving his apprenticeship to kingmanship for almost eighty years – had to earn his crust. Plebtooth the Almost Terrible (he would become Terrible after a hundred years' apprenticeship) would have to exert his undoubted authority. It was time to make an example. Lord Lucifer had to stop using Gremlins Green as a dumping ground for disobedient undead humans. In one thousand eight hundred years he had sent no less than ninety-eight such ugly, undead specimens to Gremlins Green. These latest two grotesque creatures made it a hundred and enough was enough and to add insult to injury, they were different colours. At least the elegant Boggimps were all the same attractive green colour.

Plebtooth the Almost Terrible tentatively crept forward in front of about thirty Boggimps. The group made their way to where Martha and a still red-eyed Sunday waited by the bow top. Watson had his eyes turned to the group of green figures approaching his beloved cart. He wasn't sure whether to whinny, bolt or just lie down on his back, with his legs in the air. If had not been harnessed in, he would have done the latter.

A few yards from the bow top, Plebtooth stopped suddenly and the few following him bumped into each other. Martha stared at the leader and realised he was almost a clone of Smegtooth the Terrible. Same bulky green frame, large hairy pointy ears, a bulbous red nose and a fat belly, with a large buckled belt holding his striped pants up. A sprinkling of warts dotted his ugly face. He was larger than most of the other Boggimps.

"Er, I'm Plebtooth the Terrible. King of the Boggimp," he called nervously.

"Almost terrible," a softer, squeaky voice called from behind. "You're not a hundred per cent terrible yet, Plebtooth."

"I'm almost there, so shut up, woman," Plebtooth hissed at the frowning female Boggimp behind him. "You can stand up to your neck in the peat bogs for a hundred days."

"Yes, your most honourable and noble Majesty. Forgive me, sir, you only have another twenty years to go and I deserve to be punished for being so disrespectful. Perhaps you might have compassion on me and reduce my punishment somewhat."

"Very well, Gremstod. Ninety-nine days. Now, be quiet while I discuss business with these, er, two, er, things that our great Lord Lucifer has sent to us for re-training in the privileged reverence to the duties of the undead."

Gremstod bowed her head shamefully and nodded. "You are so kind, sir. I am so grateful for your mercy. I don't know how I can repay you."

"Simple, you give me two more beautiful, bouncy little Boggimp infants. I've only got twenty-three from you so far. Be ready for me after your ninety-nine days in the peat bogs."

Gremstod made a little whoop of joy and a merry skip. "I will be so good and obliging to you, sir, and thank you."

Plebtooth turned to her and scowled. "Good. Now be quiet, woman and let me get on with my duties. I have to report to Lord Lucifer at midnight, otherwise he'll send more of these disobedient undead humans to Gremlins Green."

Sunday had heard the conversation and took a couple of steps towards Plebtooth, her eyes flashing a deep red in anger. All the Boggimps behind Plebtooth took two quick steps back.

Plebtooth gasped in fright and took three steps back, trampling those immediately behind him. After the squeals had died down, Plebtooth lay on his back on top of three of his followers. He stared up with terrified yellow eyes at the burning red eyes of Sunday, glaring down at him.

"You dirty little green whatsit! I heard you just now. You've got twenty-three kids and now you want her to give you two more, are you mad or just greedy? Who feeds all of them?" Sunday growled.

Plebtooth scrambled up and shook himself down. "We have a non-ending supply of grubs beetles and worms in the peat bogs, we pick them out and cook them in our pots. That's what our women were doing when you two arrived to disturb the peace."

Sunday shook her head in disbelief. "Worms and beetles! You eat worms and beetles?"

Plebtooth looked at Sunday with amusement. "Well, we wrap them in dried cow dung beforehand to make a pasty, then they're cooked over a fire. To flavour the pasties we pour nettle and dock weed juice over them. That keeps our green skin in the lovely colour we are lucky to have. Not like you undead humans and—well, not you because you're the colour of cow dung, but her over there—the one who melted King Smegtooth—" Plebtooth's voice trailed off as he pointed to Martha. "She's that awful sickly pasty colour."

Sunday huffed and glared at Plebtooth. "I am not the colour of cow stuff. I'm a nice golden brown and you, Mister Plebtooth and your tribe are disgusting. Animals and birds eat beetles and worms and grubs. And it's barbaric to make one of your own stand for ninety-nine days up to her neck in peat bog, with worms and beetles crawling all over her."

Plebtooth laughed and nodded at his followers. They all started laughing. Martha had walked across and like Sunday, looked confused.

"Why are they all laughing?" Martha asked.

"I don't know, Missy." Sunday shrugged.

"We're laughing because you said animals eat worms and beetles. Well, what do you think we are?" Plebtooth looked around at his Boggimps and they all started squeaking and jumping up and down in fits of laughter. "We're animals, just like that creature that pulls your cart. The difference is, we can speak and we're very intelligent. We are favoured with attractive bodies and good looks. And when Gremstod takes her place in the peat bog for ninety-nine days, she gets to eat her fill of juicy worms, crispy beetles and sugary grubs. As many as she can eat. When she comes out, she will have doubled her weight and will be ready to come to my lair so we can make two cuddly little Boggimps."

"It's still a punishment though, just for interrupting you." Sunday looked alarmed.

"You don't understand, do you?" Gremstod called from behind Plebtooth. "We women have to stand up to our necks in peat bog so we can get the vitamins and nutrients for making little Boggimps. Forty days is required for each little Boggimp. Then our men pee down our throats and it mixes with the beetles and worms in our bodies to procreate and in ten years' time, out pops a little cuddly green Boggimp or two. We have to have at least thirty before we are able to go into the peat bogs for ever. We dissolve and become the peat bog. It's a privilege, not a punishment. Soon you will find out."

Plebtooth glanced Gremstod a cursory look and she bowed her head once again in supplication. Sunday had heard and glanced at Plebtootb. "Find what out?"

"Didn't Lord Lucifer tell you?" Plebtooth said almost innocently.

"Tell us what? No, he didn't tell us anything other than to come to Ireland and do some dutiful work for you Boggimps," Martha replied, as a melody of tittering and laughter erupted from the nearby Boggimps. Sunday and Martha knew the answer was not going to be something to their advantage.

"You are to spend all your time in the deepest peat bogs, up to your necks in it. You have to collect worms, beetles and grubs to pass on for us Boggimps to cook and eat. You will be allowed out one day every week to go into the meadows to collect—" Plebtooth didn't finish what he was saying. Sunday screamed hysterically, louder than the last time and did a backflip, then set off at a rapid pace around the camp, knocking terrified Boggimps off their big feet. They ran in all directions, bumping into each other, knocking cooking pots off again that had just been picked up. In less than thirty seconds a thousand Boggimps had disappeared. The camp was once more deserted.

Watson wanted to lie down on his back and lift his legs into the air. He was the only normal creature around.

Sunday was charging around, flailing her arms and jumping over the camp fires. After ten minutes of screeching, stampeding and howling, she slowed and returned to where Martha was standing.

"I can't do it, Missy. Twenty, thirty and even fifty years standing up to my neck in a peat bog. Collecting wriggly worms and big black beetles for them despicable fat green blobs to scoff. All so they can have more little green blobs. And did you hear what the ugly fat green-skinned men do, they pee down their throats, to, what was that word beginning with a 'p'?"

"Procreate," Martha replied.

"Yeah, that. Is that a posh word for 'having a baby'?"

"It is."

"Ughh. Unbelievable. Disgusting. We've got to escape, Missy."

Martha shrugged and put a finger to her lips. "Be careful, Sunday. Careless talk. We have no choice but to do what Plebtooth said. It's still better than some of the things that take place in his torture chambers. We're at least out in the open air."

"Up to my scrawny neck in thick, worm-infested peat bog for years and years," Sunday declared morosely.

"Well, there is something good about it, Sunday."

"Something good! What's that? That I haven't to stand on my head?"

"No, not that. We don't have to eat worms and beetles." Martha chuckled. "We don't get hungry."

"Oh, I forgot about that. Whoopee! But I stand for years and years in peat that has been dissolved from Boggimps that have procreated thirty little green blobs."

"We have one little problem to sort, though," Martha remarked.

"Just one? I can think of a hundred," Sunday scowled.

"Poor old Watson. He's real, remember. We'll have to find him a home."

"The Blingos. They know how to handle him. When did that one say we could meet up again?"

"Full moon in June, near midnight. That trapdoor again," Martha replied.

"Do you think they'd let us stay in… what was that place?"

"Blingoburbia. And no, we can't."

"Why not? We're good undead females. I promise to behave myself. No tantrums or anything. No swearing, no wolf howls, no shooting anybody," Sunday said.

"We need to have the SWAN symbol to be allowed in."

"Curses of Blackbeard. I forgot. How do we get it?"

"We'll ask," Martha said.

"Suppose we just refuse to go in the peat bog? Do other jobs in this place of madness instead. They're scared stiff of me. I could threaten them by saying I'm going to cut their pointy ears off. Stand them in a line and put apples, small apples on their heads and throw my knife. Accidently on purpose just a few inches lower. You could make them sit on your chair like that king you melted. It would be like making them walk the plank."

Martha looked puzzled. "A plank!"

"On pirate ships, some poor sods who burped or farted loudly or refused an order, like slopping out the—you know—"

Martha looked puzzled again. "Slopping out?"

"Slopping out, Missy. Pee and the brown stuff. Tipping it over the side."

"Oh, yes. That. And what happened when they walked the plank?"

"Curses of Blackbeard, Missy. With the tip of a sword up their raggy backsides, they dropped off the end. The sharks ate them." Sunday laughed.

"Oh. Honest?"

"Aye, Missy. At least one every trip. We all looked forward to it. Not doing it, watching the poor wretches drop off the end. The sharks were waiting with knives and forks in their fins."

"You jest, Sunday and it's not nice. I thought I was bad."

"Like me, Missy, you made a bad choice. That's all. But fifty years standing up to our necks in horrible peat muck is not fair. Not to mention having to spend a full day every week picking up cow muck. And they eat it afterwards!"

"Well, at least we don't have to," Martha said with satisfaction. Sunday nodded in agreement.

A half hour later and most of the Boggimps had returned. Martha and Sunday had released Watson from his harness and put him in a field. Plebtooth approached the young women with four of his helpers. One, a more than fat Boggimp female with the ugliest face of any of the tribe. She scowled at Martha and Sunday and was picking food from her pointed yellow teeth with a pin. Her yellow eyes looking the two girls up and down menacingly.

"This is one of my sisters, Gertlump," Plebtooth said, pulling the skulking Boggimp forward. "She will take you to your positions and give you each a bag to put the worms and beetles in. You have to fill four bags each a day. If you don't, a year will be added to your time. However, if you fill twenty bags each a day, a year will be knocked off your time. The other three are also my sisters. Gertgrog, Gertbone and Gertplug. They do all the counting and passing you the bags. No cheating by putting any peat in the bags to fill them up. If there is less than ninety-nine and three quarters per cent of worms and beetles in any bag, a year will be added to your time. Now off you go and enjoy your time at Gremlins Green. Your thirty year sentence will soon pass."

It was warm and sticky in the peat bogs. As far as could be seen, the flat peat beds stretched out in every direction, hundreds of Boggimp heads sticking out, the women doing their duty to become fertile bodies to produce little Boggimps. Occasionally one would disappear below the clumpy brawny-black surface as she finally dissolved. Bubbles would appear, with a haze of heat rising into the still air from the spot. A shrill whoop of joy then erupted from all the other Boggimps, as they congratulated the latest one to dissolve and make way for a younger one to take her long awaited place in the peat bogs.

Hundreds of sacks filled with beetles, worms, grubs and maggots, lay at the bog edges, ready to be collected by the younger Boggimps. Piles of empty bags waiting to be taken and filled.

Martha and Sunday stood in wide-eyed and disbelieving desperation, staring at the gruesome landscape.

"Missy, I can't put a foot in that horrible bubbling mess. Look at them, they're enjoying it. Ugly green heads bobbing up and down, bringing those disgusting things up and putting them in the sacks. Then back under again to grab more of the stuff," Sunday said in revulsion. Martha was speechless.

The fat Boggimp, Gertlump, pushed Sunday to the edge and hissed grumpily, "Get in and stop complaining. We do it for love and comfort. You two will soon learn how rewarding it is, so be thankful for getting the chance to do something every little Boggimp dreams of.

"You've both jumped the queue and I'm going to complain when I see Lord Lucifer."

Sunday turned and glared at Gertlump. She glowered down at the startled Boggimp. "Then get in there yourself, you ugly old wart-faced demon. You can have my place with pleasure."

Gertlump stepped back and looked for support from her three sisters. Gertplug, Gertbone and Gertgrog had moved out of harm's way. On her own, grumpy Gertlump took a deep gulp and looked up into the savage red eyes of the dark-skinned undead human female. Work had stopped in the peat bogs and hundreds of mud caked green faces looked on. Gertlump was in charge and began to wish she had dissolved and sunk in a big puddle of peat.

"Get in and—behave yourself, or I'll—I'll have to put you in myself and add a year to your sentence," she stammered haplessly.

Sunday put her hands on hips and started laughing. "Oh, yeah, you fat ugly little green blob? You and whose army?"

"I have authority here and you have to obey my orders," Gertlump replied nervously.

"And what about our horse, what happens to him while we stew in this peat bog?" Martha asked.

Gertlump sniggered and her yellow eyes glinted. A long purple tongue slithered out of her mouth and licked around her lips. "We'll eat it. We have it as a dessert after we've eaten our pasties. It will feed us for weeks."

She sailed through the air effortlessly, as Sunday grabbed Gertlump's sweaty green body and heaved it thirty feet into the peat bogs. The thump and splash Gertlump made as she disappeared under the murky, steamy surface, made dozens of frightened Boggimps scramble for their lives. Her three sisters had vanished and once again, Martha and Sunday were on their own at Gremlins Green.

"I think you've upset them, Sunday," Martha said as she looked around in amusement. "But I think the thirty years will now be forty."

"They'll have to find me first," Sunday growled.

"We can go see the Blingos at the full moon and ask for help. They might do if we plead for their help," Martha suggested.

"What do we do in the meantime?"

"Take a guess."

"I can't, Missy. I daren't guess, because I know the answer."

"Just a few weeks. Grin and bear it."

"Up to my neck in that bubbling imbroglio."

"What's that?"

"In foreign language it's a quagmire, Missy, but with beetles and worms and other nasties."

"Close your eyes, Sunday, and think of how bad it was on the *Black Diamond*."

"Missy, I'd scrub the decks on that pirate ship twenty-four hours every day, rather than stand up to my neck in that sludge. But you're right. I'll give it a few weeks, then beg those Blingos up the lane for shelter underground."

The loud scream even frightened Martha as Sunday took off in a fit of anguish and raced to the edge of the peat bogs, did a forward flip on her hands and landed with a loud squelch and a thump in the steaming peat. Ladylike to the end, Martha followed in trepidation and slowly, gingerly, prodded a foot into the peat bog.

A few minutes later and the two were up to their necks at the deepest part of the peat bog.

Dozens of yellow eyes were watching. A few seconds later and a tied bundle of sacks thumped at the side of the bewildered girls. Gertlump's gruff voice called from the edge, where she had scrambled from the bog.

"Get working, you two, and fill those sacks. Try and sneak out and Cerberus Junior will get you and take you down to Hell. His father, Cerberus Senior, will tear you apart down there. I'm going to enjoy eating some of your horse after he gets fat eating the grass in a few weeks. I'll save a few bones for you, so you can make trinkets as a reminder of him." The raucous laugh carried across to where the girls were standing.

Sunday made to turn and get to Gertlump, but Martha pulled her back.

"Leave her, Sunday, we're in enough trouble. We'll get Watson away from Gremlins Green. Somehow."

"Sooner rather than later, Missy, because I'm going to cut that hideous slimy tongue of hers from her hideous warty face."

"We'll get Watson away, I promise, even if I have to use one of my last two favours," Martha replied.

"I'll use all but one of mine, Missy, if need be. The thought of our little horse being eaten by these horrible Boggimps is too much to think about."

"She's watching us, Sunday. We best get started on filling these sacks."

"Ughh. Come back, Captain Suarez and make me walk the plank," Sunday quipped and thrust her head under the peat bog.

Chapter Twelve
Two Months Later

Gremlins Green was quiet. The Boggimps were in their lairs, snoring their heads off. Even the two-headed dogs were slumbering. Cerberus Junior, the king dog, was prowling the camp, but he was on the far side of the great number of shanty dwellings, as Sunday and Martha crept from the peat bogs, careful not to disturb the sleeping female Boggimps taking their daily two-hour nap either side of midnight.

Dripping wet peat and mud, with worms and beetles dropping from their bodies, the two young women squelched along a worn track to a field where Watson was fenced in. He was fast asleep as the girls found him. He stirred and looked at the two figures silhouetted against the full moon. His terrified whinny echoed around the camp; Sunday and Martha threw themselves to the ground. Watson was not sure who had disturbed his sleep and whinnied again. Martha and Sunday remained still, hoping Cerberus Junior had not heard the whinny. Their hopes faded as the terrifying roar split the still darkness and grew louder as the ferocious two-headed dog raced across the Boggimp camp.

Watson was on his four legs now and stared across the moonlit field. He saw the huge dog bounding forward, whinnied and threw himself down, legs in the air. He hoped the beast would not see him; it wasn't his fault he had upset the savage dog. These two undead females had done that. He didn't fancy the idea of being a two-legged horse.

Ceberus Junior cast his red eyes across the field. He knew there was a horse in the field and had been waiting for

Plebtooth the Almost Terrible to give him the order to kill the stupid creature. He couldn't understand why such inferior creatures pulled wooden carts all over the land. They were an insult to the animal kingdom. Slaves to the undead humans.

In the moonlight he picked out the trembling, raised legs of the horse. He licked his lips and stretched both huge jaws, licking saliva from both. The red eyes searched the field and he was just about to turn away, when he saw a slight movement on the ground. The four eyes focused and he blinked rapidly. He saw two prone figures lying near the terrified horse.

Heads down, haunches up, he started to move menacingly into the field. Watson saw and heard him. Four legs started to tread the night air desperately. He could get up and run and take his chance. The petrifying thought of being a one-legged little horse was not appealing.

Sunday's sharp, penetrating eyes saw the huge crouching figure approaching slowly. The low cruel growl increased, and Watson saw the figure moving across his field. He now wondered how he would survive without legs stuck to his body. He was rabbit fodder.

The knife was in Sunday's steady hand as she climbed to her feet. Cerberus Junior saw the glint of razor sharp steel a few yards ahead. This was unusual, he had never been faced with a threat to his all-powerful sleek body before. Both jaws opened and saliva dripped to the grassy ground underneath huge clawed feet. The fangs twitched, the heads remained low, the arched body quivering with flowing adrenalin.

Martha also climbed up now and pulled Sunday's knife hand back. Two fingers touched her lips and then her hand moved to the steel blade in Sunday's hand. She pressed the fingers to the knife blade for a second, as Sunday nodded with a grin.

Cerberus Junior stopped and stared at the two standing figures. Unlike the rotting, abhorrent stench of the Boggimps that he could smell a hundred yards away, there was no scent from either of the two figures. He now knew they were of the undead and he hesitated. His four red eyes watched the glinting blade, held by the taller of the two figures. He had never been beaten in combat through his six hundred and sixty-six years of privileged life and this night would be no different. His father, the three-headed Cerberus Senior, had guarded the gates of Hell for more almost three times that figure and only ever been matched once in combat. That devilish combatant had escaped being dragged back into Hell. Lord Lucifer had gone wild with rage. He had threatened to bring back Mordant and Cyberacid, the twin fire dragons who had guarded Hell for over a thousand years, but had become lazy and out of favour.

A young two-headed Cerberus Senior had wandered forth, a snarling, powerful, long-fanged creature and had sent the two dragons away with tails between their legs. Hundreds of years later, he had sired an equally ferocious pup in Cerberus Junior and this youngster had been snapped up by Smegtooth the Terrible, to guard the Boggimp peatlands. No creature, undead or otherwise, had ever beaten the youngster in over six hundred years.

Sunday held the knife firmly and stepped away from Martha. Her red eyes fixed onto the slobbering twin jaws, now open and displaying the cruel, razor sharp fangs. To her side, Watson whinnied loudly in fear and guessed he had to accept he was very soon going to be legless and even headless. Why had these two undeaders chosen him back in America where he had been safe?

Martha reached to Sunday's knife hand and tapped it gently. "It has the kiss of death on it now, Sunday. Use it without fear. It will work, I promise."

"I know, Missy. I'm not frightened of a dog, even with two heads." Sunday moved forward and hunched her taut body. Her eyes were fixed solidly on the similar red eyes of the hound from Hell. Cerberus Junior was not now as confident. He stopped and looked at the undead human figure twenty yards away. This figure was actually moving towards him.

Nothing had ever stood before him before, with fearless eyes. They always turned and ran. He skulked sideways a few feet to give him a few moments of thinking time.

Sunday matched him step for step and it had become a question of which was the hunter and which the hunted? Cerberus Junior stopped edging and turned face on to Sunday. He growled a warning, but it had no effect on the undead human. He stopped again and crouched lower. Both sets of jaws ran with saliva and the growl was louder. Sunday raised the knife and steadied herself. Cerberus Junior knew he was threatened and dug his clawed feet into the grass. A fearless Sunday stepped closer a stride. Cerberus Junior waited, his eyes watching the gleaming knife.

Across the full white moon, flying figures swept past. Hundreds of ravens, sent by Lord Lucifer to add support to his two-headed demon. Sunday saw them and grinned. She guessed the tall, red-scaled, cloven-footed Lucifer was worried. Cerberus Junior began to lift his huge muscular body, ready to attack, but Sunday was ready. With a rush forward, she screamed a blood-curdling roar, ran several steps and with Cerberus Junior ready to pounce, her split second advantage held. With forward flips, she soared over a started Cerberus Junior, his twin jaws snapping at the flying figure flashing by, missing by inches. Her run had taken in four flips and she landed several yards behind the hound and turned to face him once again.

He had turned as well and snarled belligerently as he faced the undead human again. Sunday flipped the fingers of her free hand to invite him forward. Cerberus Junior was wild with rage and responded. He let out a roaring snarl and lunged. Sunday watched and with split second timing, avoided the twin jaws once again, by forward flipping again over his twisting body. Landing a few feet away she turned, knife raised and leapt at the twin heads. The knife stabbed into one of the four eyes and Cerberus Junior squealed in pain. He swung his injured heads sideways and caught Sunday's body, knocking her to the ground.

On her back, Sunday was quick and lifted the knife upwards. Cerberus Junior lunged again, but the knife was thrust upwards between his front legs. He screamed with pain and fury, trying to avoid another thrust of the knife, but it caught him behind his head, Sunday burying it deep into the flesh. Cerberus Junior scrambled up and escaped another stabbing thrust. Sunday was on her feet and turning to face the maddened hound, but he swung a front leg and knocked her off her feet.

Blood was pouring from the perished eye and the two body wounds, but Cerberus Junior was more enraged and dived at his grounded adversary. Sunday rolled over to face him, as he lunged at her body. The knife plunged deep into his underside and as he withdrew for a few precious moments, it give Sunday a half chance to gain her feet. Cerberus Junior was pointing away from Sunday so she dived at his back, her long legs wrapping tight around his convulsing body. He tried to shake her off, but Sunday had grabbed the scruff of his thick neck and then reached forward to slash at the throat of one of his heads. The blade was drawn left to right and blood poured from the wide slash. With one mighty heave as his body writhed, Sunday was thrown off and landed several feet away, but she had dropped the knife.

Cerberus Junior dropped his two heads, blood pouring, and heaved breath into his large body. He saw the knife on the grass, nearer to him than Sunday and realised the undead human was now at his mercy. He was severely injured, but he still had strength to renew his assault. With one eye blinded, he set the other three firmly on Sunday, with no less thought than to rip her head off. He moved forward again, his jaws drooling with bloodied saliva.

Then he charged and caught Sunday square on and crushed her to the ground. Her hands reached upwards to try and stop the raking fangs, tearing at her face and head. She knew that if her head was torn off, Lord Lucifer would be rid of her for ever. With no head, she would go straight to his torture chambers.

The scream from Martha made Cerberus Junior momentarily stop and look around. The knife had been snatched up and Martha dived onto his back. She thrust the knife forward to the undamaged throat and ripped it viciously across the hairy skin. It sank inches deep and sliced a ten-inch gash, to release a torrent of hell hound blood. Cerberus Junior howled in stricken pain, but the blade slashed again and tore into the side of his body. A mighty heave of his body and Martha was thrown off, landing several feet away.

Sunday rolled to her side and quickly found her feet, rushed to a stunned Martha and snatched the knife from her hand. Her wolf scream screeched into the night as the full moon awarded her a clear sight of the massive hell hound. Sunday rushed at him, grabbed his twisting heads and plunged the six inch blade into another of the eyes, pulled it out and brought the blade down onto the skull. This time the blade was wedged into the bone and would not move as Sunday tried to pull it out. Cerberus Junior was defeated and had neither the strength nor the will to carry on. He staggered back from the two undead humans, shook his wounded body, lowered his heads, then backed further away, let out a terrible screaming howl, turned and ran.

Martha took Sunday into her arms and squeezed her tightly. They embraced in the moonlight for several seconds, both covered in blood. Sunday dropped her head to Martha's shoulder and wished that for the first time in her life, she could cry. Then they saw movements all around them. Hundreds of the Boggimps had emerged from their lairs to investigate the noise that Cerberus Junior and Sunday had made in the bloody fight.

Plebtooth the Almost Terrible stepped through his sleepy-eyed followers and approached the two bewildered undead. He was wearing a long striped nightgown that touched the grass and had a nightcap on. He looked stunned, his green-skinned, warty face, creased into an embarrassed smile. He stopped a few feet from the girls, head slightly bowed, and coughed to clear his throat.

"You've defeated Cerberus Junior and Lord Lucifer's anger will have no respite. You are not allowed to leave the peat bogs, but you did and you've beaten our protector. Cerberus Junior has guarded Gremlins Green for hundreds of years and now we will be punished. You must return to the peat bogs immediately and stay there for the remainder of your sentence."

Sunday stepped forward and every Boggimp stepped back two strides. Sunday walked to Plebtooth and prodded him in the chest. He stepped back and tripped over the long nightgown, tumbling to the ground. Gertlump helped him back to his feet and glared at Sunday.

"You're in big trouble now, brown-skinned one. I hope Lord Lucifer adds twenty years to your sentence. You deserve it for hurting Cerberus Junior. We will have to find him and nurse him back to strength. Get back into the peat bogs where you belong."

Sunday reached forward and grabbed Gertlump by one of her long, pointy ears. The Boggimp matron squealed, but she was lifted from the ground and taken to the edge of the peat bogs. With a mighty kick, Gertlump was booted twenty feet into the murky depths. Every Boggimp turned and ran, for fear of following the obnoxious matron. Only Plebtrooth remained and he had begun to tremble. He was standing in front of Martha and Sunday and his eyes were looking behind them. The cackling, hideous voice made the two girls turn. A bloody knife landed on the grass in front of Sunday.

"Pick it up. I believe it's yours," Lord Lucifer was hovering a few feet from the ground. "You will need it for where I am going to send you."

"Send her to the torture chambers, Your Majesty," the squeaky voice called from the edge of the peat bogs. All eyes turned and in the moonlight, the sludgy, peat-covered body of Gertlump appeared, desperately wiping the sludge from her grubby nightdress. Lucifer glowered at the disgruntled Boggimp matron and raised an arm and stabbed it towards her. In a flash, her body was lifted from the ground and catapulted two hundred yards into the darkening expanse of the peat bogs. A distant splash sounded and Lucifer cackled again.

"I hate grumblings from my servants. I don't need to be told what to do. I, and only I, decide what happens to any of you creatures. You do my bidding and you don't disobey. You two," Lucifer pointed down to Sunday and Martha. "You are causing me a lot of trouble. You, Martha Budd, should have left your brown-skinned friend to fight to the death just now. You interrupted the fight and joined in. Without your interference, Cerberus Junior would have ripped her head off. Instead, you meddled and now Cerberus Junior is dead."

"He wasn't dead, he ran away," Sunday called, looking up into Lucifer's red eyes.

"He is now. He was weak, unlike his father, the great Cerberus. I took your knife out of his skull and cut his heart out. Now, pick it up and keep it safe. It is the knife that killed one of the hounds from Hell. You will need it."

"Why will I?" Sunday challenged defiantly, picking the knife up.

"Because you will take his place here at Gremlins Green. You will stay here and guard the place for eternity, as you have proved you are a great warrior. That is, unless you give up all but one of your favours. You still have six. I want five of them back."

Martha stepped forward and shook her head. "That's not fair. Sunday fought your hell hound and beat him, before I picked up the knife."

Lucifer cackled again and swept around the three figures below him. Plebtooth shivered, but Sunday and Martha held firm.

"Don't argue with me, Martha Budd, or I will send you straight to the torture chambers. She gives up five favours or she stays at Gremlins Green to guard the Boggimps. They have enemies and she has proven tonight that she is a great warrior. It's her choice."

Sunday glared at Lucifer, who was still hovering, and smiled. "You can have four favours back. You might get the fifth, but never my last one."

Lucifer raised his body again and circled the three below. From above and with the full moon behind, a great flock of ravens swooped towards the ground, pulling away at the last moment. Plebtooth turned and ran. Martha and Sunday stood their ground.

"So be it, then," Lucifer hissed and glowered at the two girls. "You, Sunday Brown, have two favours left and you, Martha Budd, still have two. I will have all four from you both soon and then you are mine, all mine."

Lucifer vanished and the two girls looked around. Gremlins Green was once more deserted. Sunday was smiling. Martha looked surprised.

"Why do you look so pleased?" Martha asked.

"I finally have a second name. Sunday Brown. Worth losing four favours."

"You might regret it, Sunday Brown."

"Who knows, Missy? But I feel a proper person now, even if I am dead."

"Only four favours left between us. We have to be careful," Martha remarked, looking around warily. "So what now? Back up to our necks in the peat bog, or up the lane to the trapdoor and Blingoburbia?"

Sunday put the knife back into her belt and started walking. Watson looked up, still trembling and lying on his back, but still with four legs in the air. He was hoping no one had noticed him. He was happy having four legs still stuck to his body.

Sunday looked back and waved Martha to follow. "Come on, Missy. We'll come back for Watson later. He's happy munching grass, he doesn't understand what's happening. Lucky him."

Watson scrambled up and gave his woolly coat a vigorous shaking. He snorted and shook his head. He knew more than the two undeads knew. He didn't have to stand for years and years up to his neck in smelly, steaming peat. Oh no. He was a horse and he loved pulling his little cart around, up hill and down dale. Sweet meadow grass, a drink of clean water from a nice bubbling stream and lots of carrots. Four legs also came in handy. No, sir. He was a very happy little cart horse.

Chapter Thirteen
Entrance to Blingoburbia

A bright full moon lit up the area near the trapdoor where Martha and Sunday had seen the Blingos two months earlier. It was a couple of minutes before midnight, but the plants and grasses were not disturbed and Sunday had had no luck trying to find the trapdoor. She looked around the area with impatience.

"No sign of it Missy, nothing. It's vanished," Sunday grumbled, looking bewildered.

"It can't have vanished, this is the place," Martha replied, equally bewildered.

"How long have we got before you know who finds out we've left Gremlins Green?"

"Fimber O'Flynn told me the nights of the full moon are his busiest times. All his ungodly creatures are out and about. He is involved with them for an hour or two."

"What kind of ungodly creatures?" Sunday asked.

"Vampires, Werewolves, evil Warlocks, Hobgoblins and suchlike."

"Not Blingos, then."

"No. I think from what we were told by Jobsdone they're not of the Goblin fraternity. That sorcerer he mentioned, Wizadabra, spelled their name wrong. There are Goblins, or Hobgoblins, but they're evil little creatures and these Blingos are not evil."

Sunday was still looking around the area, prodding with her feet and pulling at ragwort stalks and bramble bushes.

"Nothing, not a sign," she shrugged. "I think we're at the wrong place, let's go on a bit further."

Martha was certain it was the same place, but followed Sunday a few yards along the lane. They walked slowly, twenty or so yards, looking at the undergrowth, then saw a dark clothed figure walking by. As they were about to call out, a voice sounded from several yards back.

"Martha Budd and Sunday Brown, where are you going?"

The girls turned in shock and looked back. The little figure was standing with hands on hips, with a wry grin on his cheerful face. He waved them back. They ran quickly.

"We were here just moments ago. We couldn't find the trapdoor, but we just saw someone pass us on the lane," Martha said looking confused.

"Our up top helper. She clears the trapdoor then returns later to cover it. Nobody will ever find our entrances unless they have been sprinkled with spreckle dust. We have Uptop helpers all over the world. They are rewarded in time by taking the Mark of the SWAN. They are then invited down to Blingoburbia. You two can become Uptop helpers for us, if you are accepted, as long as you have not been demonic while on earth as human beings. We've checked and neither of you were bad humans. However, you both let Lucifer take your souls. You were very foolish and for your foolishness, you have to serve Lucifer for ever. Unless of course you enter Blingoburbia as approved helpers for ever."

"How soon can that be?" Sunday asked. "I hate what I have to do as an undeader."

Jobsdone laughed and held his arms wide. "How long is a piece of string, as the humans say? It depends on you, Sunday Brown."

"How do you know I'm called Brown?" Sunday asked, looking puzzled.

Jobsdone laughed again and smiled. "We know more than you can ever imagine. In Blingoburbia we have three Great Dabras. I mentioned Wizadabra the last time we talked; he is the oldest of the three and then there is Magicadabra and our youngest master of mystery, Sorcerdabra. Between them, they see all and everything. They are the three Great Dabras. It is them and Missiquin who approve new entrants to our queendom."

"Do you mean kingdom?" Martha asked.

"No. Blingoburbia is ruled by Missiquin," Jobsdone replied. "Mrs. Queen in human language. Missiquin is our leader. The three Dabras sit with her around the great round table, with four other senior Blingos. They are all powerful and decide on the yesses and the nos of our lives in Blingoburbia. They are very impressed in the way you defeated Cerberus Junior tonight. He has killed and eaten a lot of our people up top in the years he has guarded Gremlins Green. You have scored many spreckle dust points in what you did tonight. The news of your great victory will spread throughout Blingoburbia. Wherever you travel up top you will both be held in high esteem, by all the peoples of Blingoburbia."

"So when can we be sprinkled with spreckle dust?" Sunday asked impatiently.

"Soon, Sunday Brown. Soon. The eight rulers of Blingoburbia have two meetings at the great round table on the eighth day of August at eight minutes to eight in the morning and eight minutes to eight in the evening. These two meetings last exactly eight minutes. A lot of business in Blingoburbia is dominated by the number eight. All the non-rulers have eight digits in their names. I am called Jobsdone and my name has eight letters. This trapdoor opened at eight seconds to midnight. It shuts again at eight seconds past midnight."

Sunday and Martha looked at each other; they were both thinking the same. Jobsdone grinned and nodded.

"Yes, I know what you are thinking. More than sixteen seconds have passed since we started talking. That is because this is up top. Below the trapdoor, time changes. In Blingoburbia a lot of things are different," Jobsdone remarked and pulled out a pocket watch. "I have to go back in a few moments. In two months' time it will be the eighth month of the year. Come back near midnight on the night of the full moon and I will come up to see you both again. The eight rulers will have had their two meetings, read my papers on you both and will decide whether you can be spreckled."

Sunday shook her head and looked appealingly at Jobsdone. "That means we have to stay at Gremlins Green and go into the peat bogs again. It's despicable and disgusting."

Jobsdone sighed and shook his head. "It has to be, Sunday Brown. I don't make the rules, I just do what is expected of me. Two months will soon pass."

"Just one thing before you go, Jobsdone. We're taller than you. How would we fit in if we are allowed to enter Blingoburbia?" Martha asked.

"The spreckle dust takes care of that, Martha Budd. As soon as you pass through the trapdoor, you shrink to the size of a Blingo. It doesn't hurt at all. You never notice the change. When you pass into the up top again, you become your normal size."

"What if it washes off? Then what?" Sunday asked.

"Unless you disobey rules or do something you shouldn't, it stays on you for ever. You don't see it and you can't feel it. The penalty for doing wrong is a sixty-four year sentence. You are banished from coming and going for all those years. Remember though, that once you are spreckled you still cannot enter Blingoburbia. You will be able to find all of our entrances all over the world, but you must agree to do up top work for us. Covering the up tops after the trapdoors are shut. Finding things in the up top that we need."

"Those sacks we saw your people carrying the last time?" Martha asked.

"Yes. The sacks were filled with lots of things we need. Nothing stolen, just things that are free and plentiful up here but not found in Blingoburbia. It is how we survive. We make lots of stuff from them. Tools, plates, clothes, shoes and even food. All sorts. That is why we need up top people to help. In return we help you. You become a member of the SWAN and you will be able to identify other members of the society," Jobsdone replied and stepped to the side of the open trapdoor, looking at his watch.

"How long do we have to be a helper up here?" Sunday asked politely, unusual for her.

"Sunday Brown, you are for ever impatient. A long time. Meanwhile you have to carry on serving Lucifer. There is nothing we can do to help you just yet, although there was once, a long time ago, another undead warrior who escaped Lucifer's clutches. Like you, she was impatient, but she worked out how to beat him. We helped her, I believe. After she was spreckled and by helping us, she learned how to do what she did to escape. That is all I know. The answer is in Blingoburbia. Be patient, Sunday Brown, and you will one day learn how to beat Lucifer. You should go back now, before he realises you are missing. Goodbye and I'll see you in two months' time." Jobsdone disappeared through the trapdoor and it banged shut. A few moments later and the black clothed woman appeared to do her covering up work. Sunday and Martha stepped away and knew it was no use asking her questions. They turned to walk back to Gremlins Green.

When they arrived back at the peat bogs the Boggimps were snoozing again, as another ten minutes of their two-hour sleep time was left. It was calm and the light from the moon swept across the flat landscape, hundreds of green heads not moving, just sticking out of the bogs.

"We best get back in." Martha suggested. "This lot are fast asleep again as if nothing has happened."

"I want to climb on to their heads and hop from one to the other," laughed Sunday mischievously.

"You can't. Gertlump will complain again, especially if you land on her head."

Sunday grinned and did a flip forward and landed neatly on one of the sleeping heads.

Then she took off, hopping from one to the next. Within a minute she was a hundred yards out and merrily enjoying herself. Not a whimper from any of the mistreated Boggimps, who were oblivious to their heads being used as stepping stones. Martha watched and couldn't help but laugh at the sight of Sunday, skipping from one head to the next. Sunday looked across to Martha and waved for her to do the same. Martha shook her head and dubiously stepped into the peat bog. A minute later and she had reached the deepest parts and was up to her neck in mud, sludge, peat and worms.

Finally, Sunday was back and up to her neck in the peat bog. She sighed and scooped up a hand full of the thick warm mixture, wriggling with fat worms. She looked at Martha.

"Missy, I have to say this. It was a bad day for me when you boarded the *Black Diamond*."

The Eighth Day of August

At eight seconds to midnight, the trapdoor to Blingoburbia creaked open and a pair of twinkling dark eyes looked out of the blackness. Jobsdone held a parchment tied with a ribbon and two small bottles of a silvery mixture. He stepped out into the moonlight and saw the two figures standing a few feet away.

"Martha Budd and Sunday Brown. A good evening to you both. You found the trapdoor this time?"

Both girls looked around to see if the dark clothed woman was still nearby, but as before, there was no sign of her. She had been a few yards away only seconds before Jobsdone appeared, but not now.

"We saw your uptop helper clearing the area. She's gone now." Martha replied.

"That is because you are not spreckled," laughed Jobsdone. As he spoke another Blingo appeared, holding a leather book, edged with gold leaf. It was Bossalot, who they had seen before.

"Bossalot will write your names in his ledger and tonight's date, then you take the first oath of servitude to Missiquin and Blingoburbia."

"Then what? We are accepted and get the Mark of the SWAN?" Sunday asked.

Both Jobsdone and Bossalot shook their heads.

"No, not tonight, Sunday Brown," Bossalot replied matter-of-factly. "You agree to be up top helpers for an unspecified period of time. How long depends on your assistance up here. I write your names down, put the date in and then you are spreckled with Blingoburbia dust. If the silver dust settles and does not fall off, you are accepted as an up top helper."

"What if the silver dust falls off?" Martha asked.

"Then you are hiding something from us and no longer welcome to train as an up top helper. You could be a messenger from Lucifer. He tries to get some of his offspring and servants into Blingoburbia, but the silver spreckle dust is a truth dust and is never beaten. Lucifer has tried for centuries to obtain some of the spreckle dust for his ungodly and sinister motives, but the three Dabras beat him every time. If there is a hundred millionth of a per cent of falsehood in your claim for entry to Blingoburbia, it will be detected. It has never failed. On the midnight hour of the full moon, the spreckle dust mixes with falling moondust and their combined power is without challenge," Jobsdone explained.

"Are you both pure of mind, Martha Budd and Sunday Brown? Not sent here by Lucifer or any of his brood?" Bossalot asked firmly and held his open ledger in front of the pair.

"I am pure of mind and not sent by Lucifer," replied Martha.

"I am pure of mind and not sent by Lucifer," added Sunday.

"Then I will write your names into the ledger and date the entry. Remove your clothes, kneel down, bow your heads and Jobsdone will sprinkle silver spreckle dust over you. Do not move for eight seconds so the spreckle dust can do its job," Bossalot said as he began writing in the ledger.

Without hesitation both girls removed their clothes and did what was asked. Jobsdone took over and moved to where Martha was kneeling, unscrewed the bottle cap and carefully showered the silvery spreckle dust over her head and body. He did the same to Sunday and stepped away to let the dust settle on their bodies. They counted to eight, watching with bated breath that the spreckle dust did not fall off. Bossalot and Jobsdone did a little jig then clapped their hands, their dark eyes twinkling. Jobsdone looked at the girls.

"Congratulations, young ladies, you were telling the truth. Now you need this parchment and on it are places where there are trapdoors to Blingoburbia. We know that Lucifer sends you both all over the place to do his despicable tasks, so at present you can't do up top work near Gremlins Green, but when you leave that horrendous place and go on your way again, you will see on the parchment where you can find entrances to Blingoburbia."

Martha unrolled the parchment and blinked in surprise. There was no writing on the thick buff-coloured paper. She handed it to Sunday, but it was handed back quickly. Sunday sniffed and frowned, then whispered to Martha.

"Missy, I can't read, but it hasn't any writing on."

Bossalot smiled and shook his head, he had heard Sunday. "It always appears blank, but when Jobsdone and me go back and the trapdoor closes, the writings will appear. Invisible ink is used and only those up toppers who are spreckled can read the writings, just in case it is lost and found by others not approved to read it. Keep it in a safe place and use it when you leave here. There is one creature who would like to get hold of it. Make sure he doesn't or you will be punished by the three Dabras."

"Lucifer," Martha and Sunday said in unison.

"Exactly," Bossalt replied. "He has managed to get his evil hands on two of them in the centuries that have passed. He sent his hell hounds and his offspring demons through the trapdoors and they wiped out huge colonies of our people. We had to have new trapdoors relocated, but he is desperate to get another parchment. Guard it safely."

"We will, don't worry," Martha assured him.

"Good fortune, then, Martha Budd and Sunday Brown. One day we will meet in Blingoburbia," Jobsdone said and looked at his pocket watch. "Seven seconds past midnight. Goodbye for now."

On the eighth second, the trapdoor closed and Martha and Sunday stepped away. They were about to leave when they saw the dark clothed woman appear. She smiled at the pair and stepped closer.

"Welcome to our world. I can speak to you now," she said in a husky voice. "I can show you what to do."

Martha's and Sunday's mouths were open in surprise. The woman bent forward and touched the undergrowth, talking quietly. "Talk to the plants, the bushes and the trees. They hear everything and will do what you ask. It takes eight seconds only to get the trapdoors covered again."

True to what the woman had said, within seconds the trapdoors were totally covered in thick undergrowth. Tangled weeds, bramble shoots, nettles and ragwort. It was again impossible to detect any disturbance.

"Who are you?" Martha asked politely.

"My name is Mary McGillycuddy and I have been an Uptopper since the year 1642. I was accused of being a witch by some English soldiers and they burnt me at a stake."

Martha looked at the woman sympathetically. "So was I, but they drowned me fastened to a chair. I was just a free young lass in my village, but never a witch. Was you a witch?"

"No. I did have some healing powers, by being able to put my warm hands on their heads and talking to them softly, but I was not a witch. I did this for one of the English officers who had a fever and he recovered. Two days later he had me burnt at the stake."

"Did Lord Lucifer get your soul?" Sunday asked.

"Yes. As the flames burnt my body and I was moments from death, in excruciating pain, he appeared at my side. He promised me a life in paradise for ever and so I agreed to sell my soul. I was sent to Gremlins Green soon after, to slave for King Smegtooth the Terrible. I was in the peat bogs for years, like you two are now. Then, after thirty years, King Smegtooth persuaded me to share his bed and would take me from the peat bogs, if I gave him baby Boggimps."

Martha and Sunday were almost dumbstruck and their mouths opened again in horror.

"You didn't, did you?" Sunday asked.

"I did. I had six of them for him. Then one of the young female Boggimps, a horrible bossy creature called Gertlump, pushed her way into his favours and he dumped me back to the peat bogs. After thirty-six more years in the peat bogs I ran away one night of the full moon and found my way here. Jobsdone and Bossalot saw me and took mercy. I'm hoping one day to be able to go down into Blingoburbia."

"How long have you been an Uptopper?" Sunday asked wonderingly.

Mary thought for a few moments, then shrugged. "Over seventy years. I like it and it beat having had to do another sixty odd years in the peat bogs. Especially being bullied by Gertlump all the time. She hates all undead humans like us."

Martha and Sunday exchanged glances and nodded.

"We've met Gertlump," Martha said disapprovingly.

"I'm going to have a word with her," Sunday laughed wickedly. Martha shook her head.

"Good luck then. You must go back now or you will be in trouble," Mary said thoughtfully. With a wave, Mary McGillycuddy turned and walked into the dark night, soon lost to sight of Martha and Sunday.

"Did you hear that, Missy? Sixty-six years in those horrible bogs. I'd die."

This remark brought a giggle from Martha and Sunday realised what she had said and joined in. They stopped and looked along the lane that led to Gremlins Green. Sighing, both shook their heads.

They reached the peat bogs before the Boggimps had awoken from their two-hour sleep. As usual, hundreds of the green, long-eared heads were sticking out of the mire. Just as they were about to take the dreaded step into the peat bog, Martha noticed that the bow top cart had been moved to the edge. A variety of their clothes had been rummaged through and some were discarded on the grassy ground. Lying on its side, Martha's chair had been pushed over.

"I bet they've run off with our underclothes. The men Boggimps did it to me the last time," Martha said wearily.

"If I find any of the mucky little perverts wearing mine, I'll slice their pointy ears off," Sunday hissed as she started collecting the discarded clothes, "And your chair is filthy. They've had it in the peat bogs."

Martha picked the chair up and as Sunday had noticed, it was covered in mud, sludge and peat. "Not damaged, though. I'll clean it later. Best we get back into the peat, before this lot wake up. No time for head hopping, Sunday."

"What about ear lopping, have I time to lop a few off with my knife?" Sunday grinned.

"No. We'll be in enough trouble as it is, if Gertlump finds us not in place when she wakes up."

"Can I just lop her ears off then?" Sunday pleaded.

"No, Sunday. What do you think she'll be like if she wakes up in a few minutes to find she has no ears?"

"One ear then, just one. Please?"

"No. She's bad enough now. Minus an ear or two, she'd be worse than Lord Lucifer."

"Very well, but I will cut the ears off any Boggimp pervert I catch wearing my underclothes. You were jesting about them wearing yours, weren't you?"

"No, I wasn't. I caught them jumping around all over the cart, with mine on their heads."

"You never wore them again, I hope. I mean, frilly lace things we have, to be worn on those warty green heads. Ughh. I'd have to throw all mine away."

"Not long ago, Sunday, women didn't wear anything down there. I didn't," Martha laughed as she stepped into the peat bog.

"That's why I wore men's pants on the pirate ships. The mucky sods couldn't take crafty looks up your skirts." Sunday started giggling. "Hey, Missy, do you think Jobsdone and Bossalot have little peckers and got stiff seeing us both naked, just now?"

"Probably. I was thinking the same." Martha now started giggling and the pair collapsed into a fit of hysterics.

The Following Day

Gertlump the Boggimp matron had been promoted by Plebtooth the Almost Terrible to do her supervising duties standing out of the peat bogs. Her barking orders rattled across the flat but lumpy surface and her underlings obediently increased their work output, terrified to object. The Boggimp matron had even claimed Martha's chair to sit on while she bellowed her orders across the peat bogs.

Sunday Brown kept looking across the hundred yards surface, her angry eyes watching the long pointed green ears on Gertlump's head. Martha knew what she was thinking and knew it was only a matter of time before Sunday set off to cut Gertlump's ears from her head.

"Where are you going, Missy?" Sunday asked as she noticed Martha trudging away.

"To tell that old faggot to get off my chair," Martha called back.

"Can I come and cut her ears off?" Sunday called. There were shrieks of alarm from the Boggimps working nearby.

Sunday pulled her knife out and there was a sudden mad panic as the terrified workers scrambled away, in fear of their lives.

"Stay there, Sunday. I'm going to put my chair back in the cart, I don't want Gertlump sitting on it. I'll threaten to melt her if she doesn't get off it."

"Melt her in any case, Missy, she deserves it. I'm fed up of hearing her shouting orders."

"If l do, we'll have to serve another fifty years in the peat bogs. Do you want that to happen?" Martha called.

There was a silence as Sunday mused it over in her mind.

"How long if I cut her ears off instead?"

"Probably thirty years."

"Okay, Missy. What's another twenty years? Melt her."

Martha trudged on towards where Gertlump was now standing on the chair, still shouting orders. After several sludgy minutes, Martha trudged from the peat bog, covered head to toe in the sticky warm peat substance. Gertlump saw her and waved her short, green-skinned arms.

"Get back, you. I didn't say you could come out," screeched Gertlump.

"I don't mind you sitting on my chair, but you'll damage it with your big feet," Martha called as she trod towards the belligerent Boggimp matron. As soon as Martha was just a couple of yards from Gertlump, the latter suddenly flopped down to sit in the chair. A big smile creased her face as she believed she had gained an advantage. A look of smugness and Gertlump started waving Martha back to the peat bogs.

"There, I've sat down now, so get your ugly, skinny body back to that different coloured one who thinks she's clever having Cerberus Junior killed. But I've got news for you, pasty faced one. We're having Mordant and Cyberacid, the fire dragons, sent to look after Gremlins Green. They're the two most feared creatures Lord Lucifer has under his command. Three times deadlier than Cerberus Junior's father, the great Cerberus. You two ugly, undead humans will suffer if you step out of line. I'll have them destroy you and reduce your silly thin long bodies to ashes. Now get back where you belong, or I'll have another year added to your sentence."

Martha humbly bowed her body and nodded in agreement to Gertlump's demand. She turned to walk away, but stopped and looked at the smug Gertlump. The Boggimp matron huffed and pointed to the peat bogs again.

"Just before I go back and start once more, Miss Gertlump, I want to show you something you will like. Your workers told me you would like it. I found it in the peat."

Gertlump's face changed from a scowling frown to a wary smile and she showed her yellow pointed teeth. She had the prettiest teeth of all the female Boggimps. It was a smile that sent the Boggimp men into fits of hysteria at her seductive powers.

"It better be something good, pasty face," she snapped.

Martha stepped towards her and held her left hand out, slender fingers upturned and clenched. Getlump knew from experience over the years that these undead humans always grovelled for favour. This pale-faced ugly one was no different. Her greedy yellow eyes were almost glued to Martha's clenched fingers. Martha opened her fingers and on her palm, was a glinting red ruby on a gold chain. Gertlump almost fell forward off the chair as she saw the precious red jewel. She immediately reached a stubby green hand towards the ruby, but Martha snapped her fingers shut.

Gertlump glared at Martha.

"Give me it. I want it, pasty face, and I'll knock a week off your sentence."

"It's yours, Miss Gertlump, but let me put it around your neck. You will look so desirable and beautiful."

Gertlump huffed again and shuffled on the chair impatiently. She had never seen such a priceless jewel before. "Very well, pasty face, but I have delicate skin, so don't fiddle too much while you put it on."

"I will be very careful, Miss Gertlump, I promise. Relax and I'll slip it around your beautiful neck," Martha replied, a glint of evil in her reddened eyes. Gertlump settled back and put her head majestically up a few inches. Martha stepped behind Gertlump and lifted her hand. There was a delay of a few moments as Martha unfastened the chain clip. The gold chain was fastened in place and Gertlump sighed with pleasure. The two-fingered kiss touched her head and Martha grinned mischievously and stepped away from the chair. A few moments later and there was a sudden flash of lightning, followed by a trembling roar of thunder. Then the skies darkened.

Gertlump tried to feel the ruby, but all she could feel was the gold chain. Her stubby fingers frantically pulled at the necklace, but there was no ruby to touch. Her yellow eyes stabbed into the red eyes of Martha and she realised she had been tricked.

"Give me the ruby, you insolent toad. You brought it for me and I want it, not just a gold chain. I want the ruby. It's mine. Give it to me."

"Enjoy yourself on my chair, you ugly, fat little dwarf. You have just a few moments left before you become a green puddle. Remember King Smegtooth? He ended up a puddle of green slime on the ground. Well, that's what you will be in a few minutes. A slimy green puddle," Martha laughed.

Gertlump tried to stand, but her body had become rubbery, soft and loose. Martha smiled and walked back to her chair. Carefully she moved her hands to Gertlump's neck and deftly unhooked the chain. She lowered it to the Boggimp matron's face and drew it along the softening green flesh. With a tormenting chuckle, Martha gave Gertlump a final smile, turned and began to walk away. She stopped after a few steps and looked back. A dribble of green slime was running down her chair and had begun to form a puddle on the ground.

"Oh, dear, Miss Gertlump, I do believe you're sweating just a little," Martha laughed and turned away, but saw a tall figure a few feet away, dripping mud and peat.

"You crafty little mare, you've melted Gertlump," Sunday chuckled. "I would have helped you if you had asked."

"You did, in a way, Sunday," Martha replied and handed Sunday the ruby necklace. "I borrowed it from your hidey hole in the cart. Gertlump was smitten with it."

"And of course, she received the kiss of death."

"Of course. It works every time."

"Remind me never to upset you and then sit in your chair," Sunday grinned.

"You're already dead."

"Umm, don't remind me."

The girls walked back to the chair and smiled. Gertlump had vanished. Just a large green puddle on the ground. They stepped around the puddle, avoiding the green slime, and retrieved the chair.

"Back to my favourite hobby now," Sunday remarked after they had returned the chair and the necklace to the cart.

"What's that?" Martha asked.

"Collecting fat wriggly worms for the Boggimps."

"Just another few years to go, it'll soon pass."

"You know, Missy, if we were on a pirate ship now, I'd make you walk the plank for that daft remark, it wasn't funny."

"Calm down, Sunday, it's only in your mind. Think of nice things instead of the awful peat bogs and the Boggimps here at Gremlins Green."

"Like now being spreckled. One of the chosen ones and still having to wait years to be rid of you know who. I wish the nice things would happen sooner rather than later."

"You keep forgetting, Sunday. You can't wish your time away. You don't have time anymore, just eternity in paradise."

"Oh yeah, I forgot. Paradise. Forty or fifty years up to my neck in a peat bog collecting worms. Come back, Captain Suarez, I forgive you for raping me and making me eat food with weevils in it." Martha looked at Sunday, her eyes narrowed.

"Weevils?"

"You don't want to know, Missy. Believe me."

"Something bad then?"

"Bad. Horrible. Disgusting."

"Worse than worm grabbing at Gremlins Green?"

Sunday paused and sniffed. "Let me think about that and I'll tell you in fifty years' time which was the worst. Eating weevils on a pirate ship for years, or worm grabbing for fifty years."

At midnight, the moon still glowing bright in the dark sky and all the Boggimps asleep either in their lairs or in the peat bogs, a lonely figure was standing at the edge.

Sunday noticed the arm waving and prodded Martha, who had just resurfaced with a handful of worms. The pair looked across the dark and flat, but bumpy, peat beds and realised it was Mary McGillycuddy waving at them. They did not need persuading to trudge to where Mary was standing. When they reached her, Mary held a hand out to each of them. The girls took her hands, looking surprised. Mary put a finger to her lips.

"I have a message for you from Jobsdone. He told me that the eight elders of Blingoburbia have had a round table meeting and your time to get approval for the SWAN mark has been cut to fifty years. On the full moon in August 1826 you will receive your mark."

"Another fifty years and we've already been spreckled," moaned Sunday.

"Well, I've been spreckled for seventy years," Mary replied, "But I'm not a warrior like you two. Ridding Gremlins Green of Cerberus Junior has infuriated rival tribes of the Blingos. They know that Ergosnatas, the vile Hobgoblin king, has spoken to Lord Lucifer and is demanding that you are both sent to Hobgob Hollows to be put on trial for treachery. Plebtooth the Almost Terrible has complained that you have killed Gertlump, his chief peat bog matron and you must stand trial for murder, and Chief Trogtrol of the Trogladyte tribe wants you banished to Lucifer's torture chambers for rebellious behaviour by the undeaders.

"Even Queen Miasmawench of the Leprechauns wants you to be deported from Ireland. You have become the number one enemies of all the small non-human speaking peoples, except of course the Blingos."

"So we're famous, then," laughed Sunday.

"In Blingoburbia your names have spread throughout the under nations. There are requests from far flung places for you both to rid the Uptops of Lucifer's demon protectors," Mary added.

"So what do we have to do now?" Martha asked.

"Do Lord Lucifer's bidding for a little longer. Don't give him reason to send you to his torture chambers. Don't give up your last favour. He will try to take it from you by any means he can."

"He can hear us, can't he, talking now?" Martha said thoughtfully.

"Not to another Uptopper who has been spreckled and is holding your hand. He hears nothing of what we are saying now. But he will get suspicious if he never hears you talking, so let him hear things occasionally. Jobsdone forgot to tell you about holding hands. He has been chastised for it by the three Dabras."

Sunday started giggling and Mary and Martha looked at her in amusement.

"He probably forgot because we had to take our clothes off to be spreckled. He and Bossalot were all eyes. Typical men, even if they are little," Sunday laughed.

"They are normal in that way, but it is forbidden for them to have sex with an Uptopper. The punishment is severe. Banishment from Blingoburbia. Also for a spreckled Uptopper if you are caught. Offenders are de-spreckled and never allowed back. That has been the rule for centuries. In the olden days it was allowed, but not now. Diseases from up top were brought into Blingoburbia and thousands died. Even before you are allowed into Blingoburbia, you have to be thoroughly checked by the three Dabras. They can detect any type of ailment or infection."

Both Sunday and Martha looked surprised. Mary McGillycuddy nodded and shrugged.

"If you're clean, you have nothing to worry about," she added.

"But we're dead, not alive. How can they tell?" Martha asked, looking doubtful.

"Remember the three Dabras are very knowledgeable. Even if two of them don't have an answer, the third one will. That's why there is more than one in the—"

"SS," Martha said.

"Senior Sorcerers. The three Dabras."

"I remember now. Jobsdone mentioned them," Martha remembered.

"I have to go now. Remember about holding hands when you are talking," Mary said.

"One thing before you go, Mary. Will you look after Watson and his cart?" Martha asked.

Mary nodded and smiled. "I will ask Jobsdone to spreckle your horse on a night of the full moon. He will be safe then and will live to be a hundred. How old is he now?"

"He was very young when we bought him in America three years ago, so he will be about six years now," Martha replied.

"Then he will live well into the next century after he is spreckled. I will make sure your cart and horse are safe." She let go of their hands and within a few moments she had vanished. Sunday and Martha looked around, but Mary McGillycuddy was nowhere to be seen. Martha turned and looked back at the bottomless pit of the peat bogs.

"Hate to say this, but it's back to the peat bogs for you and me," Martha said woefully.

"Then where? I have a feeling it won't be somewhere nice," Sunday frowned.

"Can you think of anywhere that is as despicable as Gremlins Green? Anywhere must be nicer," Martha replied as she walked to the edge of the peat lands.

"The Caribbean Sea on a fine sunny day would be nice, with a merchant ship stocked full of gold and silver and good food and ready for pillaging," Sunday said as she trudged after Martha. She laughed as she saw the green-headed Boggimps, still fast asleep, up to their necks in peat. Her good humour faded as soon as she herself was upto her neck in the mire.

Chapter Fourteen
Thirty-Eight Years Later

March 1814

Mordent and Cyberacid, the large fire dragons, flew over the peat bogs, swooping menacingly at the worm and beetle pickers below them. Only Martha and Sunday did not move. Every one of the hundreds of Boggimps had dived below the surface, for fear of being breathed on by the two feisty dragons. The dragons were playing games and enjoyed their twice daily skirmishes, flying over the peat bogs, frightening the green-headed, pointy-eared creatures. Just once, they hoped the two Undeaders would go under as well, but they never did.

"One day I'm going to catch either of them two obnoxious serpents and cut their tails off," Sunday cursed as she finished filling another bag of worms and beetles.

"Take you a long time, Sunday. The tails are about eight feet around, not to mention probably as tough as a tree trunk," Martha laughed.

The dragons swooped one more time, narrowly missing the girls' heads with their clawed feet, then uplifted and soared away as quickly as they had arrived. Sunday shook her head and watched until Mordent and Cyberacid disappeared from sight.

"We could sneak upon them one night at their cave and do the dirty deed. You're as good as me now with a knife, Missy. You take one, I'll do the other. Give His Majesty something to think about."

Before Martha could answer, there was swift rush of wind and from nowhere, a gigantic flock of ravens swooped from a darkening sky. A bolt of lightning thudded into the peat bogs and a number of Boggimps were sucked upwards, squealing their heads off and deposited a hundred yards distant, with loud splashes. A crack of thunder followed and Martha and Sunday waited.

"He heard you," Martha said grimly.

"Ooops. I forgot to hold your hand," grinned Sunday.

"He's coming, I can feel his presence."

"So you can, Martha Budd," Lucifer cackled as he hovered a few feet above the peat bogs. "My dragons will tear your souls to shreds if you were foolish enough to try and cut their tails off. However, I have a job for you. It's time to earn your places in paradise. There is going to be a great battle in the United Kingdom of the Netherlands. A place called Waterloo. It will take place next year in June, so you have just over a year to get there. Thousands will die, so it will be rich pickings. I was going to send two other of my experienced servants, but you two have been idle for a long time, so the job is yours. Get there and do my bidding. You owe me a debt of gratitude for not letting Plebtooth the Terrible, Ergosnatas, Miasmawench and my other leaders, send you to trial for treachery and murder. I am a forgiving master so make sure you work well. Fail me, Martha Budd and Sunday Brown, and I will let those rulers have your souls. Now get gone."

The ravens swooped once more, another bolt of lightning hit the peat bogs and dozens more Boggimps were sucked out and catapulted across the mire. Some finished up with just their big feet sticking out. The thunder growled and the feet disappeared.

Sunday looked at Martha and smiled. "Waterloo. Never heard of it, have you?"

Martha shook her head. "No. Haven't heard of this place called Netherlands either."

"Kingdom of the Netherlands, sounds fancy. But we get away from Gremlins Green and worm picking."

"What about Watson, we haven't driven him for years and years," Sunday asked. "Will he be like us, undead?"

"No, he was spreckled not killed like you and me. The Blingos have looked after him all these years. He was given extra life to a hundred years old. He still has years left before he dies."

"Lucky him. I wish I could have lived to be a hundred. Instead I've been in those horrible peat bogs for nearly forty years. I'm around sixty years old now. I don't look bad for my age though, do I? Nothing on my body has gone south yet."

"Wait 'til you get to my age. I'm about a hundred and ninety," laughed Martha.

"That's old, Missy, but I hope I look as good as you when I'm going on two hundred years old."

"Don't worry, Sunday, you will. But between now and then we have to get to this place called Waterloo. Get our cart hitched up to good old Watson and find a ship."

"Some more flirting then, eh, Missy? Show a bit of leg, a bit of cleavage and watch the fellers drool over us, fancying their chances for a bit of slap and tickle. Free passage to this place we've got to go to. Better than what we've been doing for nearly forty years. I'm going to pick and choose. No dirty, smelly-breathed drunken pirates. Had enough of them in the past. Not now. Miss Sunday Brown is going to be particular who beds her. You excluded, Missy, I'm yours whenever you want. I loved our romps before we were sent to Gremlins Green."

"Me, too, Sunday. Now we can get on the road again."

"So, Waterloo, wherever it is, here we come," Sunday said with satisfaction and wrapped her slender arms around Martha's upper body. Martha responded and the two embraced for long moments.

Fifteen Months Later

Quatre Bras Crossroads. Ten Miles South East of Brussels.

June the fifteenth 1815

The long column of almost non-ending French Infantry passed by the little bow top in apparently good spirits, just over a mile from the strategic crossroads at Quatre Bras. Most were in smart dark blue uniforms and pale breeches. Mounted officers marshalled them along on well-bred cavalry horses, pruned to perfection. Clean, well-oiled muskets were held across firm shoulders of the young infantrymen, half of whom had never seen battle before. They were excited, marching in rows of four by four, anxious to put their basic training into the reality of warfare. Five thousand young Frenchmen, marching to expected glory to reinforce a larger contingent of their countrymen, who had arrived at Quatre Bras several hours earlier.

Somewhere ahead, their commanding officer, Marshal Ney, a close friend of Napoleon Bonaparte, waited with his senior officers and over ten thousand men, to engage the allied armies of the Dutch, the Prussians and the British. Another three thousand men of Napoleon's Imperial Guard, were held in reserve should Marshal Neys' army encounter any trouble. It wasn't expected. Plans had been carefully and meticulously pondered over in the previous days. Napoleon himself, back from exile a few months earlier, waited three miles away with a large army of almost fifty-five thousand men and almost three hundred cannons.

He had ordered Marshal Ney to hold the crossroads and surrounds, to stop any retreating allied troops escaping after a larger battle that was imminent, to be fought near Wavre, a small village, the following day. Locals had named an adjacent area of land about three square miles as Waterloo, but records could not qualify why the name had been chosen. It was, however, strategically important to both the invading French and the people of the Kingdom of the Netherlands. It would later be part of Belgium and act as a buffer between France and the Netherlands and on to Prussia. The British were anxious to protect trade routes through Western Europe to the countries in the east. Napoleon Bonaparte wanted to increase the French Empire into Northern Europe and eastwards into the main body of Europe. A final, decisive war against the French by the allies, was unavoidable. The small area of land called Waterloo was the chosen battleground.

A young captain of the French Dragoons saw the small cart and rode to it, with a curious look on his moustache suntanned face. He pulled off his plumed hat and bowed graciously to the two young women driving the cart, pulled by a stocky coloured cob. Martha and Sunday watched him approach. He smiled warmly and pointed backwards.

"I suggest, mademoiselles, that you hastily go back some distance. You are in peril should you remain hereabouts. It is not safe here," he said politely in educated French. "I further suggest you travel some three kilometres distance; at least three kilometres."

"Who are you going to fight?" Sunday called in her native tongue, her eyes roving admiringly around his brightly uniformed body.

"Did I say we are going to fight? Perhaps you know more than me," he replied curtly.

"Well, there's an awful lot of you just out for a midday stroll," Sunday laughed.

The young captain swung his horse sideways and shook his head.

"Mademoiselle, you are not from France. I detect a Caribbean accent, St Lucia or Martinique perhaps, but I have to strongly advise you to go back. I will escort you myself to a place of safety."

"What's your name?" Sunday cheekily asked.

"I am Captain Philippe De Lacey of the Second Dragoons and I will ask your name in return."

"Sunday Le Brown. And I'm from Martinique."

De Lacey looked at Martha, who was trying to avoid speaking. "And you, mademoiselle? Your name, please?"

Martha hesitated and stared at the young captain. She guessed he had asked her name and took a breath.

"Martha Budd," she said softly, hoping she had acquired at least a notion of a French accent in the years of listening to Sunday. The young officer pulled his excited horse around and then looked at Martha closely. Before he could say anything else, Sunday pointed at his attractive uniform of green with wide red lapels and white crossed straps.

"I love handsome men in uniform, Captain. Are you married? If not, will you marry me?"

"I am not married, mademoiselle, but you jest with me. I would have a hard time keeping other men away from such a beautiful woman. You and Miss Budd. You are in the wrong place for me to ask an evening's pleasure of your company. I do insist, though, that you go back. I will escort you myself some way back. Please turn around and follow me."

Martha turned Watson and the bow top was soon plodding back along the track they had travelled earlier. They had only travelled a quarter of a mile when another rider appeared at a fast canter. He pulled up by the side of the captain and they exchanged words. De Lacey pulled his fine, almost black horse around and spoke quickly to the two young women.

"Mademoiselles, I have been ordered back by my commander, but this young dragoon will escort you the rest of the way. But I would like to invite you both to dinner this evening at an inn not far from here. I will ask one of my fellow officers to join me. Will you agree?"

Sunday almost fell off the cart and nodded with a flush of excitement. Martha looked at her in amazement.

"Where is the inn, Captain? We will be there without fail," Sunday exploded.

"It is called La Lune D'argent, and at seven this coming night."

"The Silver Moon," Sunday replied.

"In English, yes. I'm impressed. The dragoon will show you," De Lacey replied, smiled and turned away and quickly put his mount to a canter.

Martha flipped Watson on to follow the even younger French horse soldier and turned to Sunday, sitting with a wide grin.

"Thanks, Sunday Brown. If the captain's friend is fat, ugly and smelly, I get yon officer after dinner."

"We flip a coin, Missy. I've had my fill of fat, ugly and smelly men. And how many fat, ugly and smelly Frenchmen have you seen?" Sunday laughed, feeling excited.

"Those brothers back in Louisiana were French, for two," Martha replied haughtily.

"Oh, yeah. Those two. Okay, we flip a coin then. Heads I win, tails you lose,"

Martha laughed and gently slapped Sunday's arm. "Nice try, Sunday. I get Captain De Lacey for your cheek."

"I hope he can't get an erection," Sunday grinned.

"You're brassy, Sunday Brown. Suppose they can't speak English? My French is not that good."

"It's not bad. Besides, a lot of Frenchmen speak English. Stop worrying. If he can't get an erection, can I have yours after you've done with him?"

"You dirty mare. That's not done."

"You can watch if you want."

Martha started giggling and soon the pair were in fits of laughter. The young dragoon rider turned and looked at them in amusement. He hoped they were not laughing at him. He was new to horse riding, only just out of the Saumer Military Riding School and hoped he was not looking awkward in the saddle. Sunday saw his concern and called out to the youngster.

"We are laughing at your bum, you have a lovely bum and you look desirable. Are you a virgin? My friend would like to take it from you."

The young dragoon shuffled uneasily in the saddle and it disturbed his horse. It did a light rear-up and he desperately pulled on the reins, but it then did a buck and the lad lost his balance, but luckily remained in the saddle. Sunday and Martha stopped laughing.

"What did you say to him? Something about his bum?" Martha asked.

"Told him he had a nice one, was he a virgin and that you fancied him."

Martha stared wide eyed at Sunday and slapped her again, this time harder.

"You little liar. I do not. I'm going to tell him," Martha replied and looked at the young soldier, who was smiling at her. In awkward French she called out to him and he stared back with a look of disbelief on his face, then lost control of the horse and it bolted. Horse and rider sped off, with the young dragoon crying hysterically for the spooked horse to stop.

Sunday was staring at Martha, her mouth wide open.

Martha stared back. "What? Why are you looking at me like that?"

"Missy, you just told him you want to have his baby and does he have a big willy?"

Martha gasped in horror and looked stunned. "I didn't! Please tell me I didn't."

"Okay, not your exact words. You actually said you wanted six babies with him."

Martha looked ahead in shock and noticed the young dragoon had finally fallen from his horse. A group of laughing infantrymen were helping him to his feet. The horse had vanished.

"I didn't tell him that, I didn't," Martha pleaded sorrowfully.

Sunday sighed and nodded. "It gets worse, Missy."

"Worse!" gasped Martha. "How could it be worse?"

"You told him you would like it up your bum."

Martha flopped back into the cart with a high pitched scream. Now Watson panicked and tried to bolt, but Sunday grabbed his reins. Martha scrambled up and peeped over the seat from the back of the cart.

"Where is he? Is he angry?"

Sunday looked at Martha. "Angry? He's up ahead and looking a little bit—well, I'd say a bit pleased with himself. A few of the French soldiers are looking this way and have big grins on their mucky faces. I can't guess why, Missy."

"Let's turn around and go back," Martha said despairingly.

"They've started singing, Missy. The young lad is being back slapped and they're shaking his hand. We'll have to wait 'til he comes back to show us where the Silver Moon Inn is," Sunday remarked.

"I feel so embarrassed, Sunday."

"I'll explain to him that you're English and got your words wrong."

"Is that wise? Maybe they're going to fight the English and think we're spies. They'll shoot us." No sooner had Martha spoken than she realised what she had said and started laughing, joined again by Sunday.

The French Infantry still trooping by gave them smiles and some whistled, but fierce-looking sergeants pushed them along.

A few minutes later and a red-faced young dragoon reappeared nervously riding his horse. Sunday had a word with him and for a moment he looked disappointed, then cheered up and smiled. He said a few words to Sunday and they nodded agreeably, then shared a joke. He waved them on to follow.

"What did you say to him?" Martha asked nervously, as they continued on the road.

"I explained you were a bit simple and I was your slave. He was sorry for me and said I should run away to freedom. He also said he didn't have a big willy, so it was for the best because he thought, as you were so beautiful, you would prefer a man with—you know."

Martha turned to look at Sunday. "A big willy?"

"I would. I always did."

"I'm not bothered about the size, as long as it works. He looked cute, especially when he galloped away back there."

"Galloped! He was hanging on for grim death. He got thrown off."

"Was he hurt?"

"Just his pride. He did say that his captain is from a rich family back in France. I'll give you a diamond from my loot if I can have him tonight." Martha held a hand out.

Sunday dived into the back and returned holding her bag of jewels. She picked out a diamond and handed it over.

Martha sighed contentedly. "Never been rich. I hope it's real."

"Well, if Captain Suarez was good at anything, he knew about diamonds. It's real and I bed Captain De Lacey tonight." Sunday replied.

"Well, I've been thinking about what you said. If yours can't get an erection and mine can, then after I've done with him, you can have him."

"Honest? You don't mind?" Sunday exclaimed.

"Not at all, but it'll cost you another diamond."

"You're evil, Missy."

"I'm of the undead, remember and we had better start holding hands or you know who will be jealous."

"We're in our own time and we're not talking about him."

Martha shook her head and looked at Sunday. The latter quickly pushed a hand out. "Will he be jealous of us, do you think?"

"He told Fimber O'Flynn that one day he will take me so I can have his offspring. You as well probably, sometime in the future."

Sunday said nothing for a few moments then started laughing, but holding Martha's hand.

"Do you think he's got a big willy?" she asked.

"Probably. It'll be long and red though, with scales on. Might hurt a bit."

"Mmmm, you're right, Missy. Think I'll stick to smaller pink or brown ones."

After a couple of miles, the French troops had disappeared and the road ahead was empty. The young dragoon rider turned his horse and pointed to his right. There were a few stone buildings about two hundred yards distant, settled at the side of some elm and oak trees.

He pulled nearer the bow top and removed his hat. For the first time his face was fully visible and the two girls realised he was quite youthful and good looking. He had the beginnings of a moustache, but not as plentiful in growth as the one Captain De Lacey sported. He nodded at the girls and a smile was more aimed at Martha. He bowed gratuitously and started to back his horse away.

"What's your name?" Sunday called.

"Second Lieutenant Roger Fontenay of the Tenth Dragoons, mademoiselle. I bid you farewell and good luck," he replied in French. He looked across to Martha and touched his hat and spoke in very good English. "And good luck to you, mademoiselle. I think you are not a buffoon, but a very beautiful English lady who I would have loved to have six babies with."

Lieutenant Fontenay spurred his horse away and was soon at canter to catch up with the troops heading towards Quatre Bras.

They watched until he was out of sight, then Martha dug Sunday in her side and scowled. "A buffoon. You called me a buffoon."

"I couldn't think of anything else. He probably doesn't know what a buffoon is," Sunday replied, looking embarrassed.

"A man who speaks at least two languages fluently, is bright enough to know what a buffoon is. That's two diamonds I want if I let you follow me tonight."

"That's robbery."

"That's the price, Sunday Brown."

"I hope mine does get an erection, or to get myself taken care of tonight, that'll have cost me three diamonds. And that will have been the most expensive bit of love-making in history. For three diamonds he better have the biggest willy I have ever taken," Sunday complained.

"We might have a problem tonight," Martha remarked.

"I won't, Missy. I'm so sex starved I'm not fussy. Any way he wants, he can do it. On top, underneath or doggy style."

"Not that, Sunday. What if they want to eat?"

Sunday's face suddenly changed to a mask of horror. "Oh, curses of Blackbeard. I never thought about eating."

"Let's hope they don't want to eat." Martha replied thoughtfully.

Later That Day.

There was laughter from a group of French officers, enjoying drinks outside the La Lune D'argent in off-duty uniforms, but still looking resplendent in their regimental dress. The bow top trundled to a halt and all eyes turned to look at the two glamorous young women sitting on the driving seat. A magnificent two-horse carriage, pulling up outside an opera house or a restaurant in Paris, would have looked more normal, but the hardy coloured cob pulling the old bow top was passed over. The two young women on board were stunning, in brightly coloured dresses of silk and lace. A pin could have been heard to drop, as the officers stared in awe at Martha and Sunday.

Sunday would have started to climb down, but Martha gently pulled her back. There was movement from the dumbstruck Frenchmen as two tall officers stepped through and made their way to the bow top. Envious eyes watched as Captain Philippe De Lacey and his close friend, Major Vidal Sabinet, carefully helped the girls down. It was a first for both Martha and Sunday, but they played their parts to perfection.

The other officers parted to allow the two couples walk into the inn. A pin could have still been heard falling as they passed by wide-eyed onlookers. Inside it was warm, even though it was mid-June, the air was damp with the imminent threat of rain. A roaring log fire burned in the grate and a nearby table was reserved, set for dinner with silver utensils and a tall silver candelabrum. Five red candles burned.

Martha winked at Sunday as the two officers hesitated at choosing their lady guest for the evening. Martha took the initiative and allowed Major Sabinet to help her sit down. There was a slight look of surprise on De Lacey's handsome face, but he still smiled warmly as he pulled Sunday's chair back.

Major Sabinet, a six footer, late twenties, but arguably more good looking than the younger De Lacey, with piercing brown eyes and a curled moustache that tweaked upwards at the side of his nose, took his seat and then gently kissed one of Martha's white gloved hands. He started speaking in French, but a soft cough from De Lacey, caused him to smile sheepishly and he reverted to a good class of English. He introduced himself and confirmed Martha's name. A portly, middle aged man emerged at the table with menu cards.

Major Sabinet paused and took a card from the man and handed it to Martha. Suddenly he realised it was in French and looked embarrassed. Across the table Sunday laughed and spoke calmly in French, with as clear an accent as she could muster.

"My friend can read French, but not speak it like you and I can."

The major nodded with a smile and touched Martha's hand. "So no snails or frog legs, mademoiselle." he said in English, laughing.

"Martha. You can call me Martha, but I have to say that I am not really very hungry. I have been somewhat sick earlier of my nervousness in meeting you tonight. But please, take a meal yourself and I am happy to sit and chat while you eat."

Curious glances were exchanged between the two men and further surprise when Sunday also declared she was not hungry.

"Is it our dashing good looks and rank in our emperor's mighty army that unnerves you both?" De Lacey laughed as he tried to understand why the two beautiful women were not eating.

"Not at all, Captain, you are both dashingly good looking, but I couldn't eat anything this evening because of my delight in coming here to see you. We are both very nervous," Martha replied. Sunday was nodding in agreement.

"Then we will not eat, and please, call me Philippe," De Lacey responded politely.

Major Sabinet took Martha's hand and squeezed gently. "I think that is why English ladies are not as plump in later years as French women. They are good cooks and as a result they eat too much. You English are less adventurous with food, I hear. In the long run, a good, thing I think." He looked into Martha's eyes and for a very brief moment he thought they had glinted red.

"You speak excellent English, Major Sabinet," Martha said politely.

"Vidal, please. And I will call you Martha, a very good English name. I spent a year at a college in London where I improved my English. What part of England are you from?"

"Berkshire, in the south. A village called Towton Meadows, but I left there many years ago when I was eighteen," Martha replied and immediately realised what she had said. Sunday glanced across and also saw a look of disbelief on both men's faces.

"Martha is very, very English. They exaggerate so much. I met her two years ago, just after she had left England," Sunday explained and saw both men smiling and nodding.

As they spoke, the middle aged man arrived with bottles of wine for the table, but looked surprised as no food was required. He sighed and shrugged, tutting to himself as he walked back to his kitchen. Martha realised the two officers had expected to eat, but their manner was remarkably considerate and she touched Captain Sabinet's hands.

"Thank you for being so understanding, Vidal. I hope you are not too disappointed."

"Not at all, Martha. Your company here tonight is a real welcome change from why Philippe and myself are in Belgium. Food is unimportant, I assure you. Your presence is far more important than a rich meal washed down with several glasses of wine."

"Where in France are you from?" Martha asked.

"I am from a small village near Angers, a short walk from the river Loire. It's very beautiful and idyllic. Perhaps, Martha, after we finish here in Belgium, you might visit me at my parents' home. My father is the local mayor. We have a large house overlooking the river, with grounds of many acres and several horses. I learnt to ride there. I always wanted to join the cavalry when I left school. A dream came true when I did it.

"Are you in the same group as Philippe, whatever you call them?" Martha asked. Vidal Sabinet started laughing and shook his head.

"No, no, my dear. He is in the Dragoons, a lesser regiment. I am in the Carabiniers. Only the best horsemen get in the Carabiniers. We ride black horses, the best in the world. Dragoons ride bays or liver chestnuts, they are not as strong as black horses."

Across the table, De Lacey was laughing at his friend. "Forgive Vidal's boasting, Mademoiselles, but the Carabiniers are older men and as so are usually overweight and that is why they have to ride the bigger black horses. We Dragoons and my colleagues in the Lancers ride the faster, more versatile horses. Vidal was himself a trooper, way back. I think it was about a hundred years ago and he was a drummer boy in the greys. That is correct, eh, Vidal?" Sabinet laughed good humouredly at De Lacey's mild teasing and started pouring glasses of wine. Once again Martha and Sunday exchanged nervous glances. Sabinet smiled and looked at Martha. "Red or white, Martha? I prefer red, but you as English might prefer the sweeter white wine. A sweet wine for – if I might be so bold to say – a very beautiful young lady."

"Thank you, Vidal. White would be fine." Martha agreed, wondering how she could avoid drinking the wine. Sabinet poured Martha a glass of wine then smiled at Sunday.

"And white for you? Can I call you Sunday? And I must say it is hard to decide which of you ladies is the more beautiful," Sabinet said thoughtfully.

"Red for me, Major. I prefer red, like you. I was brought up on it," Sunday replied and like Martha, wondered how she too could avoid drinking. At her side, Captain De Lacey poured himself a glass of white wine, to avoid Martha becoming the odd one out. De Lacey and Sabinet raised their glasses to the two young women, who each responded by clinking their glasses with the two officers. Sabinet and DeLacy each took long gulps, but Martha and Sunday just touched their lips to the rim of their glasses.

Over the next hour the girls poured wine from their glasses into a flower vase on the table, when the two men excused themselves to relieve calls of nature. There was no stilted conversation between the four as the warm room softened any nerves. The innkeeper came across and dropped extra logs onto the ebbing fire and caused a sudden flurry of small red hot embers to fly out and settle on De Lacey's jacket sleeves, but also on both Sunday's and Martha's bare lower arms.

A loud curse from De Lacey, who instantly scuffed the embers from his sleeves, a cry of regret from the innkeeper for his actions, but astonishment on the face of Major Sabinet at the apparent lack of pain from the two young women as they simply wiped the hot embers from their skin. There were no burn marks on either. Sabinet stared at Sunday and Martha, was about to make a comment, but a call suddenly rang out and everyone in the room looked to where the voice had sounded. Through a swirl of smoke from the log fire and the tobacco being smoked, four soldiers stepped into the room and a hush befell the place.

"Everyone stand for His Excellency, Emperor Napoleon. Stand now," a large sergeant major of the imperial guard called out. There was a momentary hesitation, then chairs were pushed back and the room exploded into loud hand clapping and whooping shouts of high spirited applause.

Major Sabinet and Captain De Lacey stood and the latter nodded at the girls and flicked his head upwards. Martha and Sunday agreeably stood and De Lacey smiled. It took a few minutes for the applause to calm, then through the shroud of smoke, a diminutive figure clad in a grey top coat calmly walked towards the crackling log fire to warm his hands. Nervous bodyguards, much taller than Bonaparte, followed him, but held back a few strides. Two other men in senior uniform were with Napoleon. One a tall muscular man, with short black hair slightly tousled and a long moustache that grew below his lower lip, a dark blue uniform and white breeches, knee high leather boots, a stride behind Napoleon; the other slightly smaller, a crop of dark hair and the uniform of a Cuirassier Cavalry General, had a pale face and looked ill.

Napoleon reached the blazing fire and put his chubby but small hands out to the flames. He held the position for a few moments then turned to nod at the taller officer behind him. The man looked at the sergeant major near the door and the rasping voice boomed out.

Everyone resumed their seats and the room became vibrant again.

Bonaparte turned from the fire and saw the two officers and two young women at the nearest table. Sabinet and De Lacey made to stand again, but Bonaparte raised a hand indicating for his officers to remain seated. His dark eyes took in the two very attractive young women, nervously staring up at him. He looked to Major Sabinet and smiled.

"I have seen you before, Major. Remind me," Napoleon said calmly. Sabinet cleared his throat, his heart racing and he nodded.

"I was at both Bautzen and Lutzen in Saxony, sir. Last year at Champaubert," Sabinet replied.

"Ah, yes. Lutzen in Saxony." Napoleon turned to the officer at his side. "You were at Lutzen, General Goyet, is that correct?"

Brigadier General Claude Goyet nodded and smiled at Sabinet.

"I was, sir. And I remember the major from there. But he was a captain in the Carabiniers at the Battle of Lutzen. I promoted him after the battle for his gallantry on the day. He successfully, somewhat foolhardy though, took on and killed the crew of a gun battery after one particular charge. That correct, Major Sabinet.?" Goyet said brusquely.

"Yes, sir. And if I remember, you were injured on the day," Sabinet replied.

Goyet sniffed and smiled. "And you yourself, Major, if I also remember. Shrapnel cuts."

Napoleon nodded and glanced at De Lacey. "One of my dragoons, Captain."

"Captain Philippe De Lacey of the Second Dragoons, sir," De Lacey replied, his heart also racing, his neck running with sweat down his back.

Bonaparte's eyes drifted slightly sideways to Martha and Sunday, staring wide-eyed at him. Dwarfed by the tall brigadier general at his side, Napoleon returned his attention to De Lacey.

"I think you were also at Champaubert last year, Captain, if my memory serves me correct?"

"Yes, sir. My regiment was there." De Lacey answered. Napoleon smiled.

The other officer with Napoleon looked at De Lacey and started rubbing his chin. General Francois Kellerman's memory was jogged. He also smiled.

"And I remember a young lieutenant who was at Brienne before the battle at Lutzen, two years ago. I think that was you, Captain. Am I correct? I never forget my officers' faces."

De Lacey nodded humbly. "I was, General. I was in the attack when we took the chateau back from the Prussians."

Napoleon took a heavy sigh and nodded. "And now you and the major are here at Quatre Bras with these two very beautiful young ladies. Please introduce me, if you would."

De Lacey took a breath, stood and looked at the two bewildered young women. He reached down and gently touched Sunday's shoulder. Her dark eyes flickered.

"My partner for the evening, sir. Sunday—"

"Sunday Brown, sir," Sunday added with a slight bow of her head, looking into the equally dark eyes of Napoleon. Napoleon nodded and smiled. He turned to Major Sabinet.

Again Sabinet coughed to clear his throat and stood up. He looked down at Martha and wished he knew her second name. De Lacey had told him earlier, but he had momentarily forgotten. Martha saved him and looked up at Napoleon.

"Martha Budd, sir," Martha said politely and calmly.

Napoleon smiled and nodded. "And where are you from, mademoiselle?"

"Sweden, sir," Martha replied. Eyes stared at her in shock, but Napoleon's eyes blinked in surprise. He extended a hand to Martha. She took it and he bowed his head and kissed her hand. Napoleon looked around and wondered what to say. Sunday jumped in and looked bright eyed at Napoleon.

"My friend cannot speak French, sir. Do you speak her language?" Sunday asked, her fingers crossed.

Napoleon swallowed and slowly shook his head. "I know a few words in Swedish, but not enough to converse with your friend, mademoiselle. Please tell her she – and you – are two very beautiful young women and I wish I was taking dinner with you both. I wish you well, but I have matters to attend and bid you farewell. Enjoy your evening with Major Sabinet and Captain De Lacey, but please, do not keep them up late, they are needed, refreshed and fit for duty, tomorrow. I will see to it that your rooms at this inn are paid for and good luck. I suggest that in the morning you both travel far away from Quatre Bras. Perhaps we might meet again. Good night."

General Guyot stepped back to let Napoleon walk away, but gave Sabinet and De Lacey cursory looks, before he followed Napoleon. General Kellerman patted De Lacey on a shoulder, smiled and followed Goyet and Napoleon. The Imperial Guards followed and the inn was once more back to reality.

The two younger officers breathed a sigh of relief. There was a buzz from the packed, smoky room and most eyes turned to look at the two nervous young women. Then, a whoop of applause and a clapping of hands. Glasses were raised to the two cavalry officers and tables banged with ale tankards.

The innkeeper scuttled across and smiled at the four sitting at the table. He looked at Major Sabinet, who he guessed was the senior of the two officers.

"I'm told you will require two rooms tonight, sir," he said quietly, looking around furtively as he spoke. Sabinet took a breath, then turned to look at Martha. She smiled and nodded. She guessed what the man had said. As soon as De Lacey and Sunday had agreed, the innkeeper scuttled back to his station. A minute passed and then a busty middle aged woman appeared with a beaming smile. Her eyes glanced from Martha to Sunday and then settled on Major Sabinet.

"I will have your rooms ready in fifteen minutes. Shall I leave a bottle of champagne in each, sirs?"

Major Sabinet looked at De Lacey and he nodded.

"Why not, Vidal? We might not see another night. Our luck has held so far, but who knows? An English musket ball or two might end it tomorrow."

The innkeeper's wife scuttled away, grinning to herself. She tried to imagine which of the two handsome young officers she would welcome in her bed that night, given a wish. Given a second wish, she would take the other one the following night.

She envied the two young women. There was a time, many years ago, when she was as beautiful as them. Well, almost.

The oil light flickered in the room and cast eerie shadows along the walls. There was sufficient light for Martha to see the naked body of Vidal Sabinet as he finally discarded his clothes, tidily across a chair. He had even picked up his high leather boots after an also naked Martha had helped him pull them off. Most men with a fine erection would have dived straight into bed and left clothes and boots in a pile on the floor.

"You're very tidy, Major Sabinet. I'm impressed," Martha declared as the nervous cavalryman climbed into the bed beside her.

"Too many years in the army and regulations makes you tidy," Sabinet replied as an exploring, cold hand reached to his manhood.

"Huh? Your hand is cold, Martha, but welcome down there."

"Cold hands, warm heart, Major. That's what we say in England."

Sabinet laughed and reached to Martha's ample breasts and started fondling them. "We say the same in France. Do you want some champagne? I'll open it."

"Not yet. I need you, before I need a drink. You're very hard, Major and I reckon you are ready to make love."

"I need a drink first, Martha, to steady my nerves. I'm more scared at this moment than facing a row of enemy cannon. Do you mind?"

"No, if that will settle your nerves. Be quick, don't lose that fine erection," Martha laughed and lay back with a sigh.

Sabinet climbed from the bed and reached for the champagne bottle. His fingers deftly tweaked the cork and it popped out with a bang that made Martha jump. He poured a glassful and drank it quickly. Martha watched him, but grinned as his penis stiffly waved up and down, but remained erect.

Embarrassed, Sabinet climbed back into bed and immediately burped. Martha laughed more because this intelligent, brave, well-groomed cavalry officer was no different to most men, but also because the major was fairly well endowed. She thought of Captain De Lacey's manhood and wondered if Sunday was at that moment as content as she was.

Major Sabinet was gentle and considerate as he made love with Martha. It lasted for a half hour and for both it was fulfilling. Afterwards they lay together, chatting and drinking champagne, or Sabinet was, Martha carefully pouring her drink under the bed, out of sight. Sabinet was smoking a cheroot and had an arm around Martha.

"Have you ever seen this Duke who leads the English, Martha?" he asked.

"No, I haven't heard of him. Who is he?" Martha replied as her head nestled on his chest. Sabinet blew smoke out and looked at Martha.

"You haven't heard of the Duke of Wellington? He is famous in your country and dare I say, in France. He is as famous in your country as Napoleon is in my country. He fought many battles in Spain and Portugal against our French armies. I have to admit, he won more than he lost. Where have you been, dear girl?" Sabinet laughed, but with no sarcasm.

"I lived in Ireland for many years. I wasn't in England."

"What were you doing in Ireland? I've heard the Irish hate the English even though you speak the same language."

"I—I was —in a convent," Martha lied.

"You were a nun?"

"I—er, yes. A nun."

"You make love so well, Martha, for a nun, or one who was a nun. It's unbelievable and so beautiful. Why did you leave the convent?"

"I wanted to travel. I met Sunday and we teamed up."

Sabinet sipped more champagne and then took a pull on his cheroot. "Sunday is black, or rather, she has Negro heritage. Where did you meet her? Surely not in Ireland?"

"I took a boat from Ireland to America and met her in Louisiana. She wanted to see Europe so we came here."

"Two very beautiful young women, one French one English. A powerful combination. Perhaps we men should take that as an example instead of always fighting each other."

"Is there going to be a battle at Waterloo?" Martha asked as Sabinet had become erect again, his hands exploring once more. He stopped his exploring and looked at Martha closely.

"How did you get that name, Waterloo, Martha?"

"Gossip. I just heard, that's all," Martha lied again.

"You are a strange woman, Martha Budd. You and your friend. You arrive here in Belgium just as the French Armies are to make combat with the Allied Armies of England, Holland and Prussia. You mention Waterloo. It is a tiny, tiny area of Belgium. You haven't heard of the Duke of Wellington, you were a nun in Ireland. You are a woman of mystery, Martha Budd, but you make love with a passion that surprises me. Are you real, Martha Budd?"

Martha pulled Sabinet close and wrapped her legs around his writhing body. He entered her again and his thrusts were more aggressive this second time. It didn't last as long and after a couple of minutes he lay back, panting for breath.

"No more questions, Martha. I have my thoughts and suspicions, but you are the most desirable woman I have made love with. If I survive the next battle or the one after that, I would like you to visit me in France, at my parents' house overlooking the Loire River. I would like to make love with you on a grassy bank overlooking the river on a warm sunny day. Something tells me you won't come, but I hope you do."

Martha kissed Sabinet and lay once more in his arms. "I'm not real, to be honest, Vidal. I am just a woman travelling the land with my best friend and an old horse and an old bow top cart. We come, we go. That's all there is to it."

"Then take my best wishes with you, Martha Budd and tomorrow and the day after and the day after that, I will think of you as I ride my horses against the enemy guns and muskets. Tomorrow we take them on just up the road at Quatre Bras."

"Is that also called Waterloo?" Martha asked.

"No, Martha. It's a sort of crossroads that leads to the place called Waterloo. If you are a spy I should have you shot, but something tells me a musket ball would bounce off you. I know you are not an Allied spy."

"A lot will die, I suppose, on both sides?"

"Hundreds, even thousands. It is sheer madness, but I am a French cavalry officer and I have to follow orders. The two men with Napoleon here tonight, Generals Kellerman and Goyet, have ridden in many battles over the past fifteen years. They have seen friends killed, fifteen-year-old drummer boys bayoneted, favourite horses destroyed. War is obscene and a travesty, but it goes on and will carry on after everybody living today is dead. Quatre Bras or Waterloo might be where I die. I might never see the River Loire again, but I have to admit I enjoy the thrill of a cavalry charge. But with you, tonight, Martha Budd, was a bigger thrill."

Martha kissed him again and looked into his blue eyes. Their eyes fixed and he saw the quick glint of red in hers, but as quick as it had appeared it vanished. They climbed from the bed and dressed. Sabinet was particular in making sure his breeches, blue tunic and additions were all neatly in place. Martha helped him on with his polished high boots and stepped back to admire the major before they left the room. She knew that after their night of love-making, they would never see each other again, but in her troubled mind was the picture of them making love on a grassy bank of the Loire River.

He stopped her at the door, picked up one of her hands and kissed it for long moments. He straightened and kissed her on the forehead. A quick thought of why her skin was so cold, but he guessed she was still nervous. He smiled and gave her a salute, clicking his boot heels together to make a sharp cracking sound.

"Major François Vidal Sabinet of the First Carabiniers of the French Imperial Army salutes you, mademoiselle. I will ride against the enemy tomorrow with my heart as yours and carry a memory of our night together in a corner of my heart for as long as I draw breath."

Driving the bow top away from the La Lune D'argent after Martha and Sunday had said their goodbyes to Sabinet and De Lacey, the two young women looked unhappy. Sunday was unusually quiet, until Martha took her hand and squeezed gently, but held on.

"You look like I feel, Sunday."

"And how's that, Missy?"

"Sad, dejected, miserable, for starters," Martha replied.

"Try lovesick, Missy."

Martha turned and stared. "Lovesick. You only just had a couple of hours with him."

"He was fabulous with me. So gentlemanly, caring, romantic."

"Big, medium, little or tiny willy?" Martha tried to be amusing. It failed.

"Just good. His hands were so soft. He kissed me all over my body, even my feet. I have never had a man do that to me. They have always abused me, raped me, had a quick shag over a barrel, or against a wall up an alley and beggared off, usually without paying. Captain De Lacey was just perfect. He was so hard and long lasting. He had a lovely hairy chest right down to his willy. He wasn't big, but he knew how to please me." Sunday held Martha's hand tight and sighed. "I hate Lord Lucifer, Missy. I could make him walk the plank and see him gobbled up by the sharks. He's vile, evil and I'm determined to escape more than ever. I want to go back to Ireland and join the Blingos."

"They're all over, Sunday, not just in Ireland. Jobsdone said the trapdoors are in all countries. We can't go yet, he said we have to prove ourselves up here first. 1826 he said we can get the SWAN mark. We get that, then make our plans to escape from Lord Lucifer. I want to find Fimber O'Flynn and rescue him. Even join Jacindra and fight Lucifer's evil little hell creatures. We have to do his bidding for a while."

"At this place called Waterloo?"

"Quatre Bras tomorrow. Major Sabinet said they are fighting at this place up the road and hundreds, thousands will die. He said fifteen-year-old drummer boys are killed with bayonets at these terrible battles. Just boys. We think we are badly done by. At least we can roam freely."

"Or have to stand up to our necks for thirty-odd years in peat bogs," Sunday replied dryly.

Quatre Bras
June the sixteenth
1815

William, the Prince of Orange's Dutch troops had taken up defensive positions at three garrisoned farm houses, with support by Prussian troops sent by General Blucher, who was defending positions a few miles away at Ligny. From early morning the Allied troops had arrived at Quatre Bras, to the surprise of the French Army, led by Marshal Ney.

Napoleon Bonaparte had handed over leadership to Marshal Ney at the crossroads at Quatre Bras, while he personally coordinated the attack at Ligny. Michel Ney was his second in command and had an impeccable record in his military career.

The three farm houses, Le Haye Sainte, Papelotte and Hougoumonte had been visited by Wellington and his scouts days earlier and were considered structurally defensive enough to impede Napoleon's massed troops on their way to invade Brussels, a few miles to the north.

Wellington and thousands of his British troops were defending the village of Wavre, a few miles north east of Quatre Bras. He had also put two thousand soldiers, including the 27th Regiment at a small hamlet a mile from Quatre Bras, called Mont Saint Jean, to stand by in case reinforcements were needed at either Wavre or Quatre Bras.

Unknown to Wellington and his generals, Napoleon had had scouts monitor the area around Mont Saint Jean and around four thousand French troops, artillery and cavalry were hidden and held in reserve to take the hamlet if Allied troops took over.

Throughout the morning from the north, the Dutch troops commanded by Major General Jean Victor Rebecque, had set up rows of six and nine-pounder cannon to the front of Papelotte farm house and surrounds. Two thousand riflemen were positioned nearby in rows three deep, scattered along a line stretching two hundred metres. Supporting the Dutch were Prussian troops commanded by General August Gneisenau, sent by Marshall Blucher to bolster the defensive positions at the three farm houses. Blucher's main army was a few miles to the south east at Ligny, preparing to take on almost thirty thousand French infantry, artillery and cavalry.

Napoleon's Imperial Guard, including his Empress Dragoons numbering ten thousand or thereabouts, were positioned between Quatre Bras and Ligny to reinforce either position.

Napoleon's brother, Jerome Bonaparte, would assist General Bouduin with the Guard and the Dragoons. Later, in the battle for Quatre Bras, Bouduin would become the most senior French officer to be killed on this day.

Just after one o'clock in the afternoon, under a brooding grey sky and with the temperature in mid-June more like a mid-March day, the French batteries opened fire from the south. They had forty cannon, compared to over sixty of the Dutch and Prussians, but the French artillery units were seasoned professionals compared to the mostly raw-recruited Dutch gunners and within the hour, hundreds of the allied troops lay dead.

It was a similar tale for General Rebecque's infantry units. A lot of the Dutch riflemen were inexperienced youngsters, or older men who had weeks earlier been farm workers, but had gone south to join the Coalition Forces to fight the invading French Armies of Napoleon. They had received basic training from the British, but most had never seen battle before. The Prussians, however, were more experienced than the Dutch, but rival commanders between the two armies had personality differences and communications between them broke down.

Marshal Ley took advantage of the situation and pressed on to take the three garrisoned farm houses. Ley was an old fox and an accomplished battle commander. He held his heavy cavalry, the carabiniers and his light cavalry, the Dragoons, back to allow his cannons to continue wreaking havoc. The French artillery captains were well trained, experienced in battle and decisive. Not so the coalition artillery unit captains. The French would reload their nine-pounders vital seconds faster than the enemy gunners. It was a decisive advantage.

After an hour and half, almost a third of the coalition force was either dead or wounded. At La Haye Sainte farmhouse, Marshal Ley, observing from a small hill to the rear, decided his artillery had achieved its aim to 'soften up' the Dutch and ordered his heavy cavalry to charge. The large black horses with body armour swept forward, spurred on by confident and screaming riders. It was devastating. The young allied riflemen, some with no ammunition left because the untrained suppliers had not been quick enough to pass around musket ball and powder, broke ranks and fled.

Razor-sharp sabres wielded by the French Carabiniers were merciless. One after another, the riflemen fell as they tried to run for cover. If one dropped to his knees but did not collapse, a following cavalryman completed the job. Some of the carabiniers were trained to attack enemy cannon, frighten off the terrified gunners and then rope the guns and drag them away with their bigger horses. It was one of the bravest moves on a battlefield, but then only the bravest and strongest riders were used.

After dragging one six-pounder cannon away with his horse, Loire, Major Vidal Sabinet took a stray musket shot in one of his thighs. Bouncing behind the back legs of Loire, the cannon bucked and twisted along the grassy field, until Sabinet was out of danger from taking musket shot again.

Blood pouring from the wound, Sabinet dismounted and first checked to see if Loire had taken any shot. The big sweating horse was uninjured and Sabinet patted him fondly.

Enthusiastic young troopers disentangled the cannon, while another young trooper took Loire away and left Sabinet to be treated for his wound.

A smiling young captain of the Second Dragoons watched from his smaller horse as Sabinet's breeches were cut away by a field medic. Captain Philippe De Lacey couldn't help making a joke of the incident.

"Bet you wish it was the English lass taking off your breeches, Vidal," De Lacey grinned.

"You'd win the bet, Philippe. I couldn't help but think of her as I just charged that cannon." Sabinet replied as he lay on the damp grass, wincing in pain as the medic prodded into the wound with tweezers to find the ball shot. He looked up at De Lacey and shook his head. "You know, Philippe, this might sound really daft, but I think Martha Budd is not of this world." De Lacey sat on his horse and looked down at Sabinet with narrowed eyes. "What do you mean, not of this world?"

Sabinet cursed as a red hot stab of pain made him jump. "Something she said early on at the table and then, later." He looked at the young medic who was doing his job, but also listening. "You know, later, later on."

De Lacey laughed. "Oh, you mean between the bed sheets."

The medic's hands faltered as he found the ball shot, but missed with the tweezers.

Sabinet cursed again and scowled up at his friend. "Shut up, you illiterate cretin. I'll have you on a charge for insolence." Sabinet hissed with pain as the medic pulled the ball shot out. He waved the medic away. "Thanks, thanks. Go away now and find me some more breeches. Carabinier's breeches, not lancer's or dragoon's."

"I think I know what you mean, Vidal. The coloured girl, Sunday; I had the same thoughts. Something unreal."

"They couldn't be – you know – ghosts?"

De Lacey reached down to take Sabinet's hand and pull him to his feet. He looked around to make sure no one was near. "We'd get shot if anyone heard us, you know. We're fighting a battle and we're talking like idiots."

Sabinet limped to the side of De Lacey's horse and rested a hand on its body. "Martha was so cold. Not in herself, she was so – so damn good in bed, but her skin, it felt different."

"Same for me with the Negro girl. Bloody marvellous for a romp, but like you've just said, different."

"Ghosts, Philippe. Do you think they are ghosts?" Sabinet said as he winced from a stab of pain in his leg.

De Lacey would have replied, but a young lieutenant rode over and called to him. De Lacey's Dragoons were needed to ride against another of the farmhouses, to back up the heavy cavalry. Dragoons General Picquet was gathering his officers for a briefing.

"Got to go, Vidal. Picquet is not well pleased you and I met Napoleon and Kellerman last night. He feels left out," De Lacey laughed and turned his eager young mount.

"Away then, my young friend and ride well. Don't get shot like I did, it hurts." Sabinet called as he stepped away from De Lacey's horse.

The lieutenant held his horse and reached a hand down to Sabinet. "A lift, Major Sabinet?"

Sabinet waved the lad away with a smile. "I'll limp back, Lieutenant. Is Loire being cooled down after his charge?"

"Yes, sir, he's well and eating a few oats."

"Good. I need a drink and then I'll be ready to continue."

"Er, no, sir. General Guiton wants you to rest for the remainder of the day. He says you need two days before you ride again. I have a bottle of the best claret waiting for you."

"Lieutenant Gerrarde, you're a saint. Get gone, lad and make me proud."

Two miles away, sitting on their bow top, Martha and Sunday could hear the cannon fire in the distance. The sky was a dull grey, rain was imminent and a stiff breeze was developing.

"Do you think Captain De Lacey and Major Sabinet are involved in that lot, Missy?" Sunday asked gloomily as she held Martha's hand.

"Probably. It's why they are here. I hate all this fighting. I've seen so much of it over the years. England, Ireland, America. It never stops. Now here, wherever we are, France, Belgium," Martha replied as she gently drove Watson on.

"I hope they are safe and don't get hurt. Captain De Lacey told me a bit about his early life. He was an orphan and ran away from the children's home he was at. It was in a poor area of Paris and the nuns beat him almost every day. He was made to stand on a chair for hours on end. They made him bathe in ice cold water, because he couldn't remember long verses from the Bible. He joined a circus and became a stunt rider on horses. His circus were entertaining in a town called Nantes and a couple of army officers spotted him. He joined up and was sent to a cavalry school at Saumer in the East of France. He had no money, no decent clothes and his boot soles were loose from the uppers. Most of the other cadets were from wealthy families and a few made fun of him, but he became the best rider in his class. I love him, Missy."

"You have to forget him, Sunday. You have no choice."

Sunday let go of Martha's hand and shook her head. "I don't care what Lord Lucifer thinks. I want to go back and wait for him. I love him and I know he would love me. We were both orphans, we have a reason to love each other." No sooner had Sunday finished, than the breeze that was blowing, became a fierce wind and struck the bow top savagely. The already dark sky blackened and there was a mighty flash of lightning that made Watson whinney, then the tremendous roar of thunder that could have made the ground tremble.

The hideous cackling laugh started and Watson began to raise and drop his head repeatedly in fright. Lucifer hovered above the bow top and glowered at the two girls. He swept once around the cart, then stopped and hovered just a few feet above Watson's rear end.

"So, Sunday Brown, you want to go to your knight in shining armour. You have no gratitude to me for allowing you and Martha Budd to wander freely across the lands. I leave you alone for years and never trouble you, even though, Sunday, you killed Cerberus Junior. I hear that you talk to the Blingos and have thoughts of leaving my protection. You want to be marked with the sign of the SWAN. Treachery and blasphemy of the highest degree. Well, you will pay a high price for your skullduggery, Sunday Brown. And you too, Martha Budd, for being so callous and inconsiderate in holding hands with each other, because you are spreckled and I can't hear you when you talk about me. I know your game. Well, you both have two favours left and I want one each from you this day. If you refuse, I will send your gallant cavalry officers to their deaths before the last drop of blood is spilled on this battlefield and on the battlefield of Waterloo in two days' time."

Sunday withdrew her knife and started to reach forward, but Martha pulled her back.

Lucifer cackled and blatantly spread his enormous red scaled wings and flapped them threateningly. Watson reared and whinnied pitifully. Sunday tried to free Martha's restraining hands, but the latter held tight.

"Let me go, Missy. I want to kill him and I will," snarled Sunday defiantly.

"Hold her tight, Martha Budd, because I would take her two remaining favours and send her straight to my torture chambers. There is a very evil and brutish Boggimp working there called Gertlump and she would be delighted to see either of you again. She is now a master of torture methods. She loves her demonic work and is one of my top torturers."

"I'll talk to her, Lord Lucifer. She is upset. Let us do our job at Waterloo in two days' time. We'll point out lots of souls for you." Martha pleaded.

The next cackle was louder and longer. Lucifer swept once more around the bow top and made Watson drop to the ground in sheer terror. Lucifer hovered once more and cackled again.

"You will be at Waterloo in two days' time like I ordered and now, for your insolence, you will both work for me at Quatre Bras, up the road. A double duty of pleasure. And I want a favour each back from you, or your two gallant horsemen will die in extreme pain before the sun sets in two days' time."

Sunday now broke free and hurled herself at Lucifer, knife in hand. Her free hand grabbed at Lucifer's body, but he was quick, very quick and lifted his body several feet higher. Sunday finished up on the ground in a heap, behind Watson's rear legs. The cackle was again louder and deafening. Lucifer lowered himself and snarled at Sunday.

"If your knife had touched my body, you would now be on your way to meet Gertlump once again, Sunday Brown. But I am generous now because I get twice your help here in this land. A battlefield of wretched souls today and more in two days' time. Now, I want a favour back from you each, or I put a death curse on your foolish lovers. I will take one today at Quatre Bras and the other in two days' time at the battlefield of Waterloo."

Martha helped Sunday back onto the bow top and dusted her friend down. Lucifer hovered and waited impatiently. The girls talked for a few moments, then both nodded. Lucifer spread his wings and cackled.

"Say it, Martha Budd and Sunday Brown. You give up a favour each. Then you have one left, like that miserable old tinker Fimber O'Flynn, rotting at the bottom of the sea."

"I give up a favour," Martha said and looked sorrowfully at Sunday.

"I give up a favour," Sunday reluctantly agreed

"So be it. Now you only have one each. One day I will take them from you both and send you to Gertlump. In the end you all give it up. Always to help some other wretched being. Foolish loyalties which I can never understand."

Sunday glared at Lucifer and pointed at him. "I'll get the Mark of the SWAN, you evil devil and then I'll kill you. With the SWAN mark your powers are limited. I will cut your black heart out and feed it to the pigs."

Lucifer flapped his scaly wings and glared at Sunday menacingly. He swirled around in a rage and then cackled. "For your insolence, threat and stupidity, Sunday Brown, I will still put a death curse on one of the horsemen. One will die in pain either today or in two days' time." With those words, Lucifer was gone.

Sunday screamed and waved the knife in her hand. "One day, you red-scaled, cloven-hoofed devil, I will kill you."

Martha sighed and shook her head in despair, but took Sunday's free hand. "You fool, Sunday. You fool."

"I couldn't help it, Missy. He's so vile and despicable. I never thought he could be so evil," Sunday replied wearily.

"He's the devil. It's what he does."

"Will he have one of them killed?"

"He will. Which one, who knows."

"Do you love Major Sabinet, Missy?"

"I know why you are asking, Sunday, and no. I can't love a man now. Whether it's Captain De Lacey or Major Sabinet, it's out of our hands. What we can do is try and find them and hope they don't ride against the other side. We have to go to Quatre Bras."

Chapter Fifteen
Marshal Ney's Command Tent

Half a Mile from Quatre Bras Crossroads.
The sixty-five-year-old Marshall, Napoleon's second in command of the Imperial Army, looked up as the two attractive young women entered the tent, accompanied by a stuffy infantry lieutenant. Standing with Marshal Ney were five more senior officers. Quick words were spoken, then Michel Ney looked up from a large map on his table and cast inquisitive eyes over the two young women. His eyes lingered awhile longer on the tall, part Negro woman. Sunday smiled back at him. He nodded slightly.

"Mademoiselles, it is pleasing to see two such beautiful women at this hour and in the middle of a battle engagement, but the captain tells me you enquire about two of my officers. Major Sabinet of the carabiniers and Captain De Lacey of the Second Dragoons. Why is that?"

Sunday took a step forward and coughed to clear her throat. "They are in grave danger, sir. My friend and I both had premonitions last night that one or both would be killed today. We beg you to hold them back from your battle."

There was a dry laugh from one of the officers around the table and Marshal Ney looked at him. General Kellerman shook his head and looked from Martha and Sunday. "Sir, these are the two young women who were at the La Lune D'argent last night with Major Sabinet and the young dragoon's captain whose name eludes me at this moment."

"Captain Philippe De Lacey." Sunday said quickly.

Ney looked at Sunday and smiled. "I remember a young lieutenant of that name who fought bravely at the Chateau le Brienne on a miserable cold day a couple of years ago. Is he the one, young lady?"

"Yes, sir," Sunday replied.

"You speak excellent French, young lady, but you are not from France." Ney remarked.

"I'm from Martinique."

"Ah, yes. One of our islands in the West Indies. You're a long way from home."

"I was a slave, sir. I escaped and came over here."

"And you met this young dragoon's captain at the La Lune D'argent last evening and fell madly in love with him. Am I right or am I right?" Ney suggested and earned a round of laughter from his officers.

Sunday shuffled awkwardly and looked embarrassed. "Yes. I love him. Can you stop him riding into battle? Please don't let him be killed."

Marshal Ney looked at Kellerman and shrugged. "What do you say, General Kellerman? They are under your command, your cavalry officers. Will you spare them?"

All eyes turned to Kellerman who sniffed, took a drink from a brandy glass and slowly shook his head. He looked from both young women, but his eyes settled on Martha, who had not spoken.

"I guess then that you, mademoiselle, are in love with my other cavalry officer, Major Sabinet?"

Martha hesitated; she had only recognised three of the General's words. Sunday looked at Kellerman and spoke for Martha.

"My friend is—"

"Swedish," Kellerman interrupted with a wily grin. "I remember her telling His Excellency, Napoleon, that she is from Sweden. But I think your friend is English, mademoiselle. I further suggest that you are both probably spies for the Coalition Forces. It's not beyond the possibility." Kellerman looked at Marshal Ney, who was looking amused. "Sir, I suggest we hold these two young women on suspicion of spying for the Prince of Orange and Lord Wellington's forces."

Marshal Ney rubbed his chin and thought for a few moments. He took a deep breath and shook his head. "No, General. I actually believe the girls' tale. I spoke with Napoleon a few hours ago and he mentioned he, you and General Guyot visited the inn last night. He mentioned the girls who stand before us now and he had their little cart searched while they were inside with your two officers. Nothing of any interest was found, other than a splendid old oak chair that I'm told was made in England. No papers, nothing that could possibly be of use to Wellington. Two old American-made muskets and a quantity of ballshot and powder, a necessary requisite for two young females travelling on their own. A tank full of, er, ladies' clothes and a raggy old coloured cob who has seen better days. Surprisingly, though, no food or drink. Not even a moldy crumb of bread. Strange, I thought, but I don't think they are spies. Wellington is a man of principles and not known to use women as spies. So I suggest the lieutenant who brought them here, escorts them away from Quatre Bras to safety."

Kellerman looked annoyed, but reluctantly nodded. He nodded at the stuffy lieutenant, who also looked annoyed. Just as Martha and Sunday were being taken out of the command tent, Kellerman called out.

"Er, mademoiselles. Major Sabinet took part in a charge earlier today against the enemy and was injured. He is not in danger of dying, but will not be riding again for two days. He is in a hospital tent at the moment. He himself killed two enemy gunners and captured a cannon that will be put to use against the enemy in due course. Captain De Lacey is at this moment in action with the Second Dragoons against the enemy. The last I heard, he was still alive."

A disgruntled Lieutenant Roland LeMesurier of the Ninth Dragoons escorted the bow top away from Quatre Bras. He was an older cavalryman and had been overlooked for promotion by at least three senior officers in years past. He had briefly been a major during the Peninsular War in Spain, but heavy drinking, laziness towards his horses' welfare and fleeing during a skirmish against a British cavalry unit, had seen him luckily avoiding being shot for desertion of duty, but demoted to lieutenant and transferred from the Third Dragoons to the Ninth.

As soon as he was out of sight of other troops, he reached into a saddle bag and took out a bottle of cognac, taking a mouthful and drinking quickly. He pushed the bottle back and pulled his horse to a halt. Martha, who was reining Watson, pulled the bow top also to a halt.

LeMesurier turned his horse sharply, making it wince with pain as the steel bit nipped its mouth. He pointed towards a copse of trees.

"Over there, you pair of treacherous British spies. You should have been shot back there.

That useless slob Marshal Ney is too soft. Kellerman is no better. We used to have good officers in charge twenty years ago, now they're pompous, overpaid and lazy. I should be in Bonaparte's Imperial guard, not the stupid sons of wealthy Paris barristers and politicians.

Anyone with half a brain would see that you two sleazy women of the night are in the pay of the Prussians and the Brits." He pulled out a loaded pistol from a holster and waved it at the two dumbstruck young women. "Get down and strip off your fancy skirts. I'm gonna give you a bit of French meat, before you go reporting back to the British. You first, black woman. I've never fucked a black woman before. Spanish, Portuguese and Russian, but not black. Tie your pretty English whore up first, then get yourself ready for Major Roland LeMesurier of the Third Dragoons. I'm a major, not a pathetic wind and piss lieutenant of a lower regiment."

With a loaded pistol brandished in their faces, Sunday obeyed his instructions and tied Martha's wrists to one of the cart wheels. LeMesurier unbuttoned his breeches and flicked the pistol at Sunday. She knew what it meant; she had been raped by pirates and cutthroats brandishing pistols. Such men had no scruples. They wanted a fuck and some would kill to have their way with an unwilling partner. In the past she had succumbed to such advances, but now it was different. She was already dead.

As she started to lift her skirts, Sunday pointed to the back of the cart. "There's a chair up there, Lieutenant. If you're going to rape me, at least let me be comfortable. I'll bend over the seat and you can take me doggy style."

LeMesurier sniffed and gave it a thought, his breeches resting on the top of his high boots, his penis erect. "Go on then, whore, but no funny business. Get the chair."

Sunday winked at Martha as she climbed onto the cart, pulled the chair back and lowered it to the ground. Turning it around, Sunday began to lift her skirts, but turned and looked at the lieutenant. "My friend is cleaner at the moment, Lieutenant. I'm bleeding down here. Take her first and if you really want to fuck a black woman, then if you still can, I'll bend over."

LeMesurier sighed and brought Sunday's hand to his stiffness. Sunday obliged and ran her hand a few times up and down. LeMesurier moaned with pleasure, then pushed Sunday away. "Go get her then and be quick. Get her to tie you first."

A couple of minutes later and Martha stood before Lieutenant LeMesurier, her skirts raised.

She had not tied Sunday's wrists properly and he had not checked.

"Do you understand English, Lieutenant?" Martha asked.

"I understand your language, English woman. Why?"

"Sit down, Lieutenant, and I'll sit on you," Martha suggested.

"No funny business like I said, or I'll blow your head off," LeMesurier growled and flopped onto Martha's chair, the pistol in his hand. Martha did as she was asked and carefully lowered her body onto the stiffened penis. It was quick and lasted no more than a half minute. Martha climbed off and smiled at LeMesurier. She touched two fingers to her lips, then to LeMesurier's face.

He sniffed contemptuously and laughed. "A sheep would have been better, but a fuck's a fuck and why the finger kiss, English woman?"

"Because I've never been fucked by an old man before. Are you happy now and can we go?" Martha asked as she straightened her skirts, then stepped to the side.

The knife thudded deep into his chest and he briefly stared wide-eyed at Martha, his brain immediately telling him he was about to die. He mumbled incoherently, then his head slumped forward. Sunday dashed across, pulled her knife from his chest, then hauled his dying body from the chair, dumping him on the ground. She grabbed a handful of hair and pulled his head upwards. His eyes rolled but he had just enough life left to hear the words.

"Do you want to live, Lieutenant, and go to paradise, live to be five hundred?"

His head nodded as he coughed up blood. Sunday looked around and waited. A moment later and Lucifer was there, his talons clawing at the body of the near-dead French cavalry officer. Sunday pulled away as Lucifer took over.

"You owe me that favour. We did our job," Sunday remarked as she stepped away. Lucifer cackled and shook his head as he took the soul from LeMesurier's body, then pushed the corpse roughly away. He pushed the soul into the leather pouch and cackled.

"Get gone, Sunday Brown, and do your work. There are men dead and dying not far away and one soul will not earn you a favour back. In two days' time there will be another battlefield full of dying men and I want their souls and I will have them. Disobey me and you and Martha Budd will be guests of Gertlump." In less than a heartbeat, Lucifer was gone.

As Sunday dejectedly walked away, Martha reached a hand out, but Sunday shook her head. "Not at this moment, Missy. I don't care if he hears just now. I'm going to kill him and he can hear me if he wants. He can be killed, I know it."

"Don't lose your last favour, Sunday. He will do anything to get his hands on it. Take my hand and listen," Martha said and put a hand out. Sunday smiled and took it.

"Keep your temper until we get the Mark of the SWAN. I think it will have special powers. Fimber O'Flynn knows about it, I'm sure."

"He's at the bottom of the sea. How can he help?"

"I'm not sure, Sunday, but if anyone knows he will. At least your captain is still alive and Major Sabinet is out of the battle. Let's wait until the battle at Quatre Bras is over, then we'll find some souls."

"I was glad we got Lieutenant LeMesurier's soul, but there are good men here."

"I know that, but look at you and me. We are free to roam most times. We've had some good times in this so-called paradise."

"Gremlins Green comes to mind."

"All right. That place was horrible, but let's bide our time. After these two battles we must become good Uptoppers and earn our place in Blingoburbia. I want to get Fimber O'Flynn from the sea bed and the three Dabras will know how I can do it."

Sunday squeezed Martha's hand. "I agree then, Missy. I'll try and avoid trouble with Lord Lucifer. Get him some souls and then become good Uptoppers. Do you think we'll become SWANS in time?"

"I hope so, it's just a long time though 'til we receive the SWAN mark."

"Do you think any of the three Dabras see or hear what we are saying?" Sunday asked.

"Good question, Sunday, but I'm not sure. Probably, though. There are three of them and only one of Lucifer."

"Just Lucifer. What if there are three of his sort?"

"Not worth thinking about. Three Lucifer types and I'll willingly go to see Gertlump and say sorry for melting her," Martha laughed.

"Oh yeah, and that ugly little green-skinned demon will forgive you."

Sunday started giggling and Martha looked at her in amusement. "What's funny?"

"Did you see her sailing through the air about a hundred yards and plopping head first into the peat bogs after Lucifer waved his hand at her? Not once but twice. I could have peed myself if l wasn't dead."

"And a thousand big feet sticking out of the peat bogs and waving about after all that lightning and thunder and those two dragons diving at them."

The giggles echoed through the air and Watson turned his head to see why the two were laughing. It was a long time since he had heard them laugh.

Later That Day.

The battle for Quatre Bras had raged for several hours. At first the might of the experienced French troops had been decisive. William, the Prince of Orange's Dutch troops had been overwhelmed by the accuracy of the French artillery. The French had arguably the best artillery leaders in Napoleon's massive army. Captain Barbaux was beyond fault on the day. He moved between his guns with mercurial efficiency, sometimes jumping down from a horse to assist the gunners in reloading or carrying cannister and shot. His men had had extensive battle experience and knew every nut, bolt and inch of the howitzers or cannon.

The farmhouse at Le Hay Sainte had taken a merciless battering for three hours in the early afternoon. Barbaux's opposite number, Captain Heinrich Kuhlmann, was younger and less experienced, but not lacking in courage. He had more guns than Barbaux, but not the experienced men to use them. That was until at around five in the afternoon, when the field marshal arrived to take command of the farmhouse garrisons. Le Haye Sainte was already almost lost to the French, but the British field marshall had brought better guns and gun crews from the hamlet of Mont Saint Jean, that he had lost to the much larger French forces. There was a long ridge running between La Haye Sainte and the other farmhouses. The French commander, General Bouduin, had disregarded the ridge as of little consequence for strategic purposes, but Wellington thought better.

He was informed by his battle commander at the farmhouses, Major General Peregrine Maitland, that more than a half of his regiment's numbers had been killed or wounded in the day. The Twenty-Seventh Regiment and the Fifth Brigade of the West Riding Foot had taken heavy casualties. Even his experienced elite troops of the First Foot Guards had suffered heavy losses.

Wellington, though, had a slice of luck on his side. He was a crafty old campaigner and knew the value of using skilled sharpshooters to advantage, particularly on slightly elevated positions. He also had General John Byng at his side. Byng was an 'old school' soldier and totally battle hardened. Losing the hamlet of Mont Sainte Jean in the afternoon to superior enemy numbers had niggled Wellington. He immediately set about placing his experienced riflemen or sharpshooters on the long ridge near Hougoumont, Gemioncourt and Papelotte farmhouses.

It had high grass and was ideal for the battle hardened sharpshooters and also the best marksmen from his Thirty-Third Foot Regiment. He also brought in skilled marksmen from the Fourteenth Foot Yorkshire Regiment. Hundreds of skilled riflemen lay hidden in the long grass. Another stroke of luck was that Wellington had a rival artillery leader to the Frenchman, Captain Barbaux. Artillery Captain Charles Frederick Sandham had been with Wellington on previous campaigns and was keen to take charge of the howitzers and guns at Hougoumont and Papelotte. On instructions from Dutch General Jean Victor Rebicque, Captain Kuhlmann was ordered by Major Van der Smissen, to give assistance to the British gunners. Kuhlmann willingly passed over command of his tired gunners to Sandham.

By six o'clock, the course of the battle at Quatre Bras had changed. Two thousand Prussian troops had arrived, led by General Bulow to support the Dutch and British. France's Marshal Ney had failed to follow up his troops' early advantages at the farmhouses, General Bouduin had tired infantry soldiers and General Kellerman had over-used his cavalry. A certain victory by the French had looked ominous in the late afternoon.

They had lost fewer troops than the Coalition Forces; the different cavalry regiments had pushed the enemy back, but arguably the best military commander in Europe, was now in charge of the Coalition Army. Wellington was in command.

Frederick Sandham and Jacob Kuhlmann, the artillery leaders were now working with renewed spirit. Their howitzers had begun to turn the tide. During a furious non-ending barrage of cannister and ball shot, General Bouduin was killed amongst the French troops. Marshal Ney gave orders for Kellerman's cavalry to take the fight once more to the battered Coalition Forces still holding two of the garrisoned farmhouses.

Wellington's hidden sharpshooters and riflemen were ready and waiting in the long grass.

Four hundred nervous, but eagle-eyed troopers in three long rows, had long-barrelled muskets loaded, primed and ready. The first row had bayonets fixed.

A clear, loud shout screamed out and a curved, glinting sabre was raised high and a thousand horse moved forward to charge the guns at Hougoumont and Papelotte. La Haye Sainte had already fallen to the French and hundreds of Coalition prisoners taken. Marshal Ney was jubilant that this late afternoon charge of his cavalry would crush the almost exhausted resistance by the Dutch, Prussians and British.

His artillery had blasted the three farmhouses for another half hour and dozens more of the enemy had been killed or wounded. Salvo after salvo was sent at the beleaguered farmhouses, but they held. The guns stopped and General Kellerman watched from behind as the front line of his armoured cuirasses and the following line of carabinier heavy cavalry started their charge. Generals Picquet and Guiton were adrift of Kellerman with their colonels a few yards distant to each side. Regimental drummers on grey horses were between the colonels and the three generals. The youngest drummer was a fifteen-year-old boy.

At the front of the advancing line, captains led their squadrons, each commanding two companies. Before the front horses were spurred forward in to the final charge, a major moved through the squadrons, followed by riders holding the colours of the different regiments. Colonels and generals stayed behind the line.

The large black horses of the front line of armoured cuirasses and carabiniers started to gain momentum. Behind them came the light cavalry of the dragoons and then the lancers. These two horse regiments were the ones that usually inflicted most damage, after the heavy horse cavalry had initially broken the front line of the enemies' defence. These horses were lighter and more versatile than the bigger horses that would draw back so the usually bigger and stronger riders could take abandoned enemy guns. Fleeing artillery gunners would be cut down by the lancers and the dragoons.

Captain Philippe De Lacey was excited. He had ridden well at Brienne and Champaubert a year earlier. At the latter battle he had gained promotion to captain for his bravery. On his willing bay horse, Vardan, he felt the thrill of the charge developing. Vardan was one of two horses De Lacey used. He had found Vardan neglected and abandoned in a field near Amiens, two winters earlier. He had guessed his age at five or six by inspecting his teeth. The farmer who owned the field had demanded two thousand francs for the ill-treated young horse, but a defiant and angry De Lacey, with three equally angered companions to hand, walked him away after paying a hundred and a threat to remove the stubborn farmer's teeth.

Weeks of training and feeding took Vardan to full health and eventually one of the best and most fearless horses in the regiment. He was treading the field effortlessly now, as he walked forward with hundreds of similar excited horses to his right and left. He trusted his new owner and wanted to break free and charge. He had done it before and this one was no less exciting. It was better than freezing and starving in a lonely field.

A thousand horses were now advancing on the battle-weary defenders at the row of stone farmhouses. Roofs had part collapsed and thick walls were fractured by repeated cannon shot.

Hundreds lay dead all the way along the front of the battered farmhouses, to the sides and on the fields at the front.

Sandham and Kuhlmann's cannon were ready to fire. The long threatening line of advancing French cavalry was getting closer. Nerves were taut and bodies running with sweat. Most of the younger inexperienced gunners wanted to release the red hot cannon shot. Mistakes had been made all day by the Coalition gunners; cannon barrels set at either too low or too higher projectures. Van der Smissen, Sandham and Kuhlmann had run themselves ragged hour after hour to correct the firing heights. Exhausted, black-faced, legs like lead weights and hands blistered, they could only wait now and hope their men's nerves held.

A young corporal lost his nerve and disobeyed an order to hold. There was a chain reaction along the line and cannon after cannon opened up. The charge started and sabres were drawn. Panic stricken, the exhausted artillery gunners fumbled the reloading.

Grass divots were ripped out and thrown backwards as the cavalry horses charged. Behind the cavalry, hundreds of infantry, who had walked safely under cover, now ran screaming at the top of their voices, holding rifles with fixed bayonets.

Before the cavalry reached their targets, Captain Barbaux's artillery units opened fire again, sending salvo after salvo at the Coalition defences. Wellington would scoff at such random and wanton tomfoolery, but the French had used such tactical cannon fire in previous campaigns. As suddenly as it had recommenced, the cannon fire stopped, but it had gained valuable time for the heavy cavalry running down the enemy's big guns. Napoleon's generals were tactical experts at the use of artillery to support a cavalry charge. Some shot would accidentally hit their own men and horses, but in the main it created chaos amongst the enemy, already terrified at the sight of a mass cavalry charge, especially with young inexperienced troops.

Captain De Lacey on a thundering Vardan, was in high spirits. His magnificent horse aside, his prized possession, the glinting curved sabre, longer than the sabres used by the British, was held firmly. His green uniform with red epaulettes and broad white crossed chest bands, a black shako helmet with black plume, arguably the best of dress in all of the French Army, his second favourite. One of his best friends, Lieutenant Roland Fontenay of the Tenth Dragoons, three years younger at twenty, was riding abreast of him. It was Fontenay's first cavalry charge. De Lacey had told the young Caen-born Fontenay to stay at his side, although he should have been further back in the squadron. After the charge, one of the colonels would reprimand him for bringing Fontenay forward. Fontenay of course would say he did it by his own choosing. Both would receive extra duties and a fine.

Unknown to the French, two Dutch Cavalry regiments had been sent forward by Wellington to attack the flanks of Kellerman's mounted troops, as they would fall back after being hit by the rifle volleys from the sharpshooters on the ridges and other troops hidden in ditches. Lieutenant Colonel Van Merlen would lead his Fifth Dutch Dragoons and the First and Sixth Dutch Hussars.

Welshman Lieutenant General Thomas Picton would support Van Merlen's cavalry, with units from the Twelfth and Eighteenth Dragoons and the Seventh British Hussars. Picton was favoured by Wellington for his plain speaking and aggressive attitude in a combat situation, but had to accept that the establishment in London was not well pleased that the Welshman had a criminal record. Years earlier, he had been a high ranking official in Trinidad and had been arrested for the sexual abuse and torture of one of his house maids. He was acquitted, but sent back to Britain in disgrace. He rejoined the British Army and rose through the ranks.

On the ridges near the farmhouses and concealed in ditches, Colonel Van Ramdohr of the Dutch Infantry and Colonel Halketts of the British Infantry awaited the oncoming French Cavalry.

Soldiers of the Duke of York's Regiment, marksmen from the British Sixtieth and Ninety-Fifth Rifles, the Dutch Lunebergers and the Brunswickers held their breaths. Trigger fingers were itching, hands sweating.

Colonel Van Ramdohr waited to give the signal to his concealed marksmen. At a hundred yards he gave the order to shoot and the first line of riflemen immediately raised themselves from the long grass and fired. Then Halketts shouted his order and the second line fired a volley. While the first and second lines reloaded, the third line stood and fired at will. They were all shooting from an angle to either their left or right as the carabiniers and cuirasses charged the coalition howitzers and cannon.

It was devastating. The front horses were struck and catapulted forward, throwing riders head first into the melee of rifle shot. Following lines were hit and within a few minutes the scene was a bloodbath. Completely taken by surprise, Kellerman's ranks were confused and disorientated. Some of the French Cavalry had been hit at no less than thirty yards' distance. Men and horses were mercilessly cut down. Those troopers able to regain their feet were immediately shot by Van Ramdohr's jubilant sharpshooters.

Wellington now instructed his Scottish infantry regiment, the Forty-Second Highlanders, to charge the following French Infantry. The kilted fighters swarmed across the fields, shouting and screaming their war cries. The French were bewildered at skirted men brandishing claymores and others charging with their bayonet-fixed Baker rifles. Most of the French fled, but more experienced, braver ones held and confronted the Scotsmen. They received no mercy.

In retreat, the remaining French Cavalry tried to regroup, but from both sides they were now faced with the cavalry of Van Merlen and Picton. Dutch and British Dragoons and Hussars rode forward, sabres at the ready. It was a hot late afternoon and the dust and dirt thrown up by the hundreds of horses caused further confusion amongst the French. They rallied to the trumpeters calling them back, but loose horses impeded the retreat and the front cavalry, who had escaped the Coalition rifles, were hit from both sides by the enemy cavalry.

Lieutenant Fontenay had fallen from his horse, was bleeding from two musket wounds and had a broken left arm, hanging loosely at his side. He was frightened, but bravely stood his ground facing a hussar riding him down. He held his sabre at the ready, but the Englishman was not to be cheated. Fontenay lunged as the young ensign rode him down. The straight sabre slashed and Fontenay dropped to his knees and fell face forward. The ensign winced as the pain from Fontenay's sabre stabbed in to his senses. His thigh had been cut deep, but he had his eager eyes on another French rider.

De Lacey had seen his friend go down and pulled Vardan around to reach him. The musket shot cracked into his chest and pitched him from Vardan's saddle. De Lacey gasped for breath as he struggled to his feet. He picked up his prized sabre and hobbled the few yards to his injured friend. A young English rider of the Twelfth Dragoons saw the wounded Frenchman and lunged with his borrowed sabre. De Lacey miraculously avoided the thrust and made one himself. Thomas Cherrywood from Hampshire took the long curved sabre in his ribs, but held his reins and was able to ride off. He would die later of the wound. De Lacey's eyes were focused on the bent-over figure of Roger Fontenay. He had the strength to ward off another swipe of English steel from a British Dragoon and stumbled the few paces to Fontenay. As he reached his friend, a swipe of Dutch steel caught him across his shoulder. He still held his beloved sabre and staggered a couple of steps, then fell alongside Fontenay, his uninjured arm across the latter's upper body. For one of the Frenchmen, his battle was over.

A Dutch Hussar charging after the retreating French, took his horse forward and leaped over the two grounded green-jacketed cavalry men. He shouted a whoop of joy at his achievement and raced after a fleeing blue-jacketed carabinier, carrying the colours of his regiment. He never felt the steel tip of a French Lancer's weapon enter his back, an inch to the side of his spine. The Dutchman's battle was over. He would never see Utrecht again.

At nine thirty that sultry evening, the first whisps of the approaching night descended on the battlefield of Quatre Bras. There had been no outright victor. Between them, the French, the Dutch, the Prussians and the British had lost over eight thousand men and boys. The oldest casualty had been a seventy-year-old Belgian man who had fought at the sides of his two sons. The youngest, a fifteen-year-old French drummer boy, had been bayoneted by a Prussian Infantry soldier, determined to take his drum as a souvenir. The jubilant souvenir hunter was himself taken down by a Prussian officer, who had seen the defenceless French boy killed by one of his own men. The officer collected the drum and passed it to a French officer of the Sixth Lancers. They saluted each other and rode back to their own lines.

At camp that night, refusing food, Napoleon, who had defeated the Prussians at Ligny that same day, stamped around his command tent. Marshal Ney had arrived with his senior officers from Quatre Bras and had to take the ranting and ravings of Bonaparte, without too much reply.

Bonaparte's younger brother, Jerome, kept quiet. He knew that Marshal Ney had not lost the battle, even though he had not won. He had great respect for Ney's military experience and would not take sides. As a general, he himself had not foreseen the mistake in not occupying the Quatre Bras crossroads earlier that day. The Dutch had taken the area and dug in. He and Marshal Ney were at fault together. Generals Grouchy, Kellerman, Picquet, Guiton, Durotte, Pires and other senior officers stood shame-faced. Napoleon lambasted his commanders and asked if any of them had seen Marshal Bouduin. A younger colonel standing to the rear, coughed to clear his throat and spoke out. Several sets of eyes blazed at him.

"Your excellency, Marshal Bouduin fell at Hougoumont during an attack to take it from the British." The colonel stepped back and bowed his head. There was a silence and no one dared to speak out.

"We lost a marshal, a bloody good marshal," Napoleon blasted.

"The Coalition lost more men at Quatre Bras I'm led to believe, Napoleon," his brother said quietly. "Our field observers are usually fairly accurate."

"Did they lose a marshal as we did today?" Napoleon snapped at his brother. Jerome did not reply. "Gather all of your field officers and prepare to march within thirty-six hours. We take Brussels in two days and send the British back across the channel. The Prussians, who I beat today, will be licking their wounds and will not be able to rally enough troops to join Wellington's Army. I want eighty thousand men ready to march the day after tomorrow. There must be another twenty thousand walking wounded who can hold a musket. Get them together and in the mood to fight. Get the horses fed and watered. I want at least ten thousand horses ready to be used. General Kellerman, General Pires, see to it that the cavalry is ready in thirty-six hours. Goodnight, gentlemen. Get some sleep."

The command tent emptied and Napoleon was left with his brother and Marshal Ney.

The three men enjoyed drinks and discussed the past twenty-four hours' developments. None of the three would have any idea that in two days' time they would fight their last battle. For Napoleon, he would leave the battlefield at Waterloo, to be one of the all-time greats in military history, but rejected by the country he loved. He would be dead in six years' time, exiled to a remote island in a southern ocean. His youngest brother, Jerome, would suffer less loss of dignity, but his titles would be taken from him. He would no longer be the king of the small German province of Westphalia. He would reach old age. Marshal Michel Ney, born on France's border with Germany, fluent in both French and German, a veteran of over thirty battles, would die sooner, much sooner. Before the year was out, he would be shot by firing squad on a trumped-up charge of treason. He would be forty-six.

The politicians and bureaucrats in Paris would have got rid of the two most powerful military commanders in France. Louis XVI would be back on his throne and the upstart Jerome Bonaparte would fall from grace but be allowed to live on. He would die at seventy-five.

Some years later, the people of France would insist that both Napoleon Bonaparte and Marshal Michel Ney be removed from plain graves and be placed in marble tombs in two of the cathedrals in Paris. The people who judged and sentenced them would die forgotten men, but Napoleon Bonaparte and Michel Ney would live on in the folklore of French history.

At Quatre Bras, local people had swooped on the aftermath of the battle, looting and scavenging. As is agreed by the warring sides after a battle, a number of troops were ordered to patrol the area and possibly find wounded combatants, who might be saved from a lingering death. Among those wandering the bloody battlefield were two young women, quietly picking their way among the dead and dying.

Sunday had stopped working and was taking a rest, but a call from Martha, a few yards away, made her look across. She picked herself up and wandered to where Martha was kneeling at the side of another couple of bodies. As soon as she looked down, her eyes saw why Martha had called her over.

"Oh, no! Not my captain," gasped Sunday as she dropped to her knees.

Martha had Captain De Lacey's head cradled in her arms. A faint flicker of life showed in the critically wounded soldier's face. Sunday took over from Martha, who moved to another soldier lying next to De Lacey. She recognized him as the young, fresh-faced cavalry lieutenant who had taken them to the La Lune D'argent Inn the evening before. He was dead. Martha crossed his arms over his bloodied body.

Sunday stroked De Lacey's hair from his face and kissed him on the forehead. He had felt the movement at the side of his head and opened his eyes. He saw the saddened brown face staring at him. His arm twitched and he pulled it upwards slowly. He still held his beloved sabre.

"Take my sabre, Sunday," he called weakly.

"You'll need it, Philippe. You're not going to die."

"No, my lovely. I was waiting for you. I knew you would find me."

Sunday's eyes narrowed and De Lacey managed a feeble smile. He had lost a lot of blood, was near to death, but he knew Sunday would come to him.

"You're not going to die, I won't let you," Sunday said softly, supporting his head.

"I want to come with you. Take me, please. I know about you. I know." De Lacey's voice became weaker and his eyes were losing strength, they had started to glaze.

"I can't take you, Philippe. It's—it's bad. I should never have come this way. Go in peace, my darling. I love you." Sunday kissed him again.

De Lacey pushed his hand to Sunday's, the sabre offered. "Take it, Sunday. Take my sabre."

Sunday took the sabre from his hand, placing it carefully at her side. She looked into his fading eyes. They flickered and closed, opened for a few moments, then closed for the last time. Sunday's head fell to his chest. Then she raised her head and lifted it to the night sky. The loud call was long, piercing, harrowing. Heads nearby turned and eyes stared in terror.

A harsh wind blew across the fields and thousands of ravens swooped as lightning stabbed into the blood-red field. As the thunder crashed, scavengers stood, turned and ran. The killing fields were soon deserted and the cloaked red figure descended and swirled around the dead bodies of De Lacey and Fontenay.

Sunday stared red-eyed at Lucifer, holding De Lacey's sabre in her hand. He hovered and his voice snarled venomously.

"I told you once before, Sunday Brown, never to touch my body with steel. You would do me harm, but I am your lord and master and untouchable by such lesser creatures as you. Strike at me and I'll take your last favour and commit you to my torture chambers for eternity. Gertlump waits for you. Here, on this beautiful field of death, you do my bidding. It has been a good day for soul stealing. Get back to your work, before I send you to the Boggimps. I steal souls and you steal sabres. You are no different to me. Get back to work and be at the next battlefield in two days' time. As I speak, these fools who kill each other are planning more death and destruction. Bad for them, good for me. The next time you hold a steel blade to me, make sure you use it. I want your last favour back."

Sunday gripped the sabre firmly and fixed her vengeful red eyes on Lucifer's. He cackled and lifted higher in the air, swooped around in a full circle then vanished. Martha moved to her heartbroken friend and put an arm around her shoulders.

"You were unselfish, Sunday, with the captain. He knew what we are. I'm glad you let him go, he didn't deserve to become one of Lord Lucifer's slaves. I'm proud of you."

Sunday reached a hand out and Martha took it gently. "Kiss the blade of the sabre, Missy. I want it to hold your kiss of death, because one day I will kill Lord Lucifer with the captain's sabre."

Martha nodded and reached down and touched the bloody wounds on De Laceys body. With her fingers dripping blood, she kissed them, then touched the blade with the captain's blood and slowly drew them along the blade. Passing the sabre back to Sunday, she nodded and tapped it, but held on to her friend's hand.

"You as well, Sunday. Touch Captain De Lacey's wounds, with some of his blood. Do as I did, then put your kiss of death on the blade and it will be held for a thousand years. You will be invincible with it in your hands."

Sunday knelt at the side of Captain De Lacey's body and put two fingers to one of the bloody wounds, withdrew still-warm blood and put it to her mouth and swallowed. She gently took more blood and carefully wiped it along the blade.

"Are you sure, Missy, I will be invincible with it?" Sunday asked and kissed De Lacey again before standing up.

"Not a hundred per cent, Sunday, but a long time ago, Fimber O'Flynn told me such swords or sabres were used by the immortals in combat. The blood of a recently killed warrior was rubbed on the blade by the holder who had touched the blood of the warrior. It gave the sword bearer powers beyond what would be normal."

"Captain De Lacey was a true warrior, we know that. So I'll use it one day to kill Lucifer and then his evil offspring,"

Sunday said confidently. "I'll find this Jacindra and together we'll find these creatures and wipe them out. Rid the earth of evil."

"Well, I've got my killing chair and now you have your sabre," Martha laughed. "We should be able to get rid of a lot of evil between us."

Sunday looked around and stared into the dark. "We weren't holding hands, Missy."

"He'll be too busy getting his souls right now. Best we say no more and carry on with our jobs," Martha replied.

Two Days Later,
Waterloo Battlefield
June the eighteenth 1815 7.30pm

Hundreds of dead horses were littered everywhere. Cavalry horses, artillery gun carriage horses and supply wagon horses. The bodies of thousands of red-coated soldiers, thousands of blue-coated soldiers and greens and greys. Broken bodies, limbs parted from their bodies and headless corpses in the mud of the battlefield. Torrential rain the night before the battle had rendered the surrounding land to almost a quagmire. Napoleon's battery howitzers and guns had become stuck in the muddy fields of Waterloo. The big horses pulling the guns had floundered. Napoleon had made a massive blunder. Marshals Ney and Grouchy had tried to persuade him to place his heavy guns ready to face Wellington's guns soon after dawn.

Napoleon had decided to wait until late morning, hoping the ground dried out. It was a warm day, but the waterlogged ground stayed sodden.

Another blunder Napoleon made was to divert more than twenty thousand of his battle-hardened troops to take the town of Wavre from Marshal Blucher's Prussian Army. Wavre was just a few kilometres from Waterloo and having decisively defeated Blucher at Ligny two days earlier, Napoleon wanted to crush him once more. He had over seventy thousand troops at Waterloo and had expected his Wavre troops to rejoin him by midday. A more cunning Duke of Wellington and the mud of Waterloo had other ideas.

Wellington and his battle-weary commanders mustered around sixty thousand troops to hold Waterloo against the invading French army. Napoleon wanted to capture Brussels to further his ambitions to become Emperor of Europe. He had to smash through the British and Dutch troops at Waterloo to take the road to the Belgian capital. Gerhard Von Blucher's tired Prussian troops at Wavre were to be his nemesis.

Most of Wellington's one hundred and fifty cannon were in place on the high ground facing south. The ground was damp, but drier. To the south on flatter, lower ground it was wet and the French Artillery horses were getting bogged down in the mud. Two hundred and fifty cannon were struggling to gain correct positions. The advantage the French gunners had was more experience than the British and Dutch gunners. Another advantage the French held was their superb cavalry regiments. They had seen far more action in recent years than the enemy cavalry. Yet even well trained cavalry horses required firm footing to perform at their best. Waterloo was not going to allow these brave horses to be ridden to glory on this day.

The salvos started around one o'clock in the afternoon. For an hour the howitzers and cannons of both sides blasted the red hot shot and cannister at the enemy. Hundreds of men were killed or wounded around the small area of the Waterloo battlefield. By two thirty Napoleon was hoping his twenty-five thousand Wavre troops would arrive after defeating the Prussians. They didn't come. Marshal Blucher had held Wavre and prevented the French from rushing to rejoin their colleagues at Waterloo. It gave Wellington a slight advantage.

By mid-afternoon the bloody battle at Waterloo was on an even keel. Neither side had the advantage now. Wellington's less experienced troops were struggling. The one hundred advantage in howitzer and cannon numbers the French had was telling. The muddy conditions where Napoleon's gunners were working prevented them gaining a decisive advantage. Manoeuvring the heavy guns was back-breaking for the men and the artillery horses were becoming stressed.

Confidence within Wellington's troops was starting to buzz. By late afternoon it was becoming apparent that the French reinforcements from Wavre were not going to arrive on time. What did happen was that Blucher's Prussians from

Wavre did make the short trek to Waterloo. It was a deciding factor in the Battle of Waterloo.

As Wellington's senior commanders took pleasure in the change of fortune, moods changed and confidence increased. One officer in particular, Major General William Ponsonby, who commanded the Union Horse Regiment, a brave veteran of the Peninsular Wars, had overrun a group of French Infantry with his men and was returning to his own battle lines, but got stuck in the mud as he rode back. Three French Lancers on lighter horses spotted the general and ran him down, before his own men could ride back and save him. The Irishman died in the mud of Waterloo.

Under heavy fire and unable to collect their dead general, the British Cavalrymen pulled away to ride to safety, but spotted two enemy heavy cavalry riders of the Carabinier First Squadron returning to their battle lines. Major Vidal Sabinet was carrying a wound he had received at Quatre Bras and was struggling to steer his heavy black charger back to safety. The wound had not healed and had split stitches in his leg. His mount, Loire, was a strong and brave horse, but the mud was energy sapping. Sabinet saw the approaching Scots Grey riders and called to his partner, Lieutenant Claude Bisson, to turn and face the six British riders.

Sabres drawn, Sabinet and Bisson waited in the mud. Loire was exhausted, but obeyed his major faultlessly. Bisson was terror-struck and tried to press his horse from the mud, but could only make a half turn and being left handed, he was on the wrong side of enemy riders to his right side. Loire had made a full turn and gave Sabinet the best position he could.

Bisson was felled immediately by a sergeant of the Scots Greys and died as he hit the mud. Sabinet waited and faced the nearest of the enemy riders. He parried a sabre thrust by one of the Scottish riders and swiftly put his curved sabre into the heart of the Scot. He swung his sabre again and caught a young lieutenant of the Sixth Inniskilling across an upper arm. He thrust again and seriously wounded another enemy rider. It was the last strike Sabinet would ever make. He fell in a crumpled heap to the mud of the Waterloo battlefield. Loire knew his beloved master had perished and reared up on his hind legs.

Loire's reins were grabbed by one of the Scottish riders and the distraught horse was pulled away. The captured black French horse with the mud-covered burnished copper armour would be a prized trophy for horseman James McGregor when he relaxed later that day, after the battle.

Major Vidal Sabinet lay part covered on the muddy floor of Waterloo. He was paralysed from two sabre wounds to his body, one to the left, the other to his right. He had enough strength remaining to turn his head from the mud and not choke to death. He could not feel the rest of his injured body.

The battle was lost for Napoleon Bonaparte. The muddy conditions had been one of his biggest problems and the loss of a quarter of his army to the failed attempt to push the Prussians from Wavre. Had the Coalition Force not had a commander as brilliant a strategist as Wellington, the outcome at Waterloo might have saved Napoleon. As it was, he had finally met his match and his military career ended on the muddy killing fields of Waterloo.

By eight in the evening he had departed the field. His army was in disarray, there had been many desertions and the French had taken massive casualties. And so the Coalition, to a slightly lesser degree, but these losses were shared between the three main armies. Waterloo had no overwhelming victor, but there were four losers; the French, the British, the Dutch and the Prussians. Napoleon would not fight another battle.

The bow top cart trundled to a halt and Martha and Sunday reluctantly climbed down. The scavengers were all over, pulling clothes and boots from the dead soldiers. Troops who had been ordered to guard the battlefield while the dead and injured were collected, fought a losing battle to keep the thieves away. Frenchmen toiled alongside British, Dutch and Prussian, to collect dead comrades and take them to mass grave sites. A few hours earlier they would have been deadly enemies; now those feelings had passed. It was time to reflect on the futility of the savagery of war.

By midnight the battlefield was near deserted. Only a handful of people still wandered around. The exhausted troops had departed, to return the next day to resume collecting the fallen. Martha and Sunday sat on the bow top seat, ready to drive on. They were sick of seeing Lucifer collecting stolen souls and filling his pouches.

They were holding hands as they surveyed the muddy battlefield. Sunday was still thinking of Captain De Lacey

"I'm glad I didn't give him away to that despicable red swine," she said sadly.

"I'm glad you didn't. He didn't deserve to be killed here and then suffer again at the hands of Lord Lucifer," Martha replied as she gently squeezed Sunday's hand.

"Do you think Major Sabinet survived the battle?" Sunday asked.

"I hope so. That snobby general who accused us of being spies said he had been injured earlier that day, but was not going to die. He probably didn't take part in this battle at Waterloo. He asked me to visit his home overlooking this river. He called one of his horses after the river, Loire. It's a black horse and he's ridden it in a few battles. He said he wanted to make love to me on a sunny day, on the grass overlooking the river."

"That's romantic, Missy. I wish we weren't dead and could do things like that. Do you?"

"Very much. Mind you, I'd be a two hundred-year-old woman now and I think Major Sabinet would be a bit disappointed. My tits would be saggy."

The giggles lasted long moments and even Lucifer turned his head to look across the dark battlefield.

"Arrgh!! Have your laughs, Martha Budd and Sunday Brown. You will do my bidding again in the years ahead. I'll have the favour back you owe me. Get gone now and be done, I've got pouches full of souls and I don't need you for a few years."

Martha flicked the reins and faithful old Watson pulled away. Twin oil lamps dangling from hooks threw out some light against the darkness, but added to the eeriness of the scene all around them. They had been trundling along for a few minutes, then out of the dark, a horse appeared running across their path. Both stared after the horse, shiny black, as it carefully slowed as if to seek out something on the ground. It whinnied, then stopped and lowered its head to an object lying in the thick mud.

Martha pulled Watson to a halt and focused her eyes on the horse. Sunday also watched the animal as it snorted and then started pawing the muddy field with a front hoof.

"Must have escaped from somewhere. Probably one of the cavalry horses that was used on this terrible battlefield," Martha remarked, then flipped the reins again. Watson made a whinny and then snorted, but carried on along the track.

Fifty yards back, Loire, now rid of his copper armour, stopped striking the ground and pushed his nose to the side of Major Sabinet's face. He blew warm air at his master and then tucked his legs underneath his body and settled down beside him. Major Sabinet still lay where he had fallen in the late afternoon. He was minutes from death and smiled at his faithful horse. A few minutes earlier he had heard giggles away to his right and guessed it was two young women sharing a joke. He thought of the English girl he had made love with just two nights earlier. She had giggled a few times as they had held each other in the warm bed. He knew she was different, a passing spirit on her way to heaven. Perhaps he would meet her again and they could sit on a cloud and look down at the Loire River below. Would he be allowed to make love to her on the river bank on a warm summer's day?

Sabinet wanted to reach out and give his horse a last final pat to his muscular black body. There was no strength in his arms, but he could see the magnificent black horse from the one eye that was above the mud level. There was no pain in his body now. Then he saw the figure to his right. Tall and wearing the green jacket of a dragoon, with the bright red lapels; the knee high leather boots and the familiar shako hat with the black plume. A hand reached down and gently eased his broken body from the mud. Now he could use his arm and he took the soldier's hand and let himself be pulled up to his feet.

Loire scrambled to his feet and watched as his master took a last admiring look at him.

"Away now, my friend, and run back to the field at the side of the river where we come from," Major Sabinet said softly as he followed his friend, Captain De Lacey.

The black horse shook his body of mud and whinnied into the midnight air. He watched the two figures above him as they drifted upwards and then vanished. The broken figure still lay in the mud, but the wonderful scent he had breathed of it in years past, had also gone. He struck the ground again with a front hoof several times, then turned and ran. He knew the way back.

The following morning, Martha and Sunday were on a road heading west. Hundreds of troops of various regiments were also on the road: some mounted; some with heavy horses pulling field guns; hundreds walking in bedraggled columns. A few waved at the two young women on the bow top cart, others just plodded on, heads bowed, muskets slung over a shoulder.

"We need to read the parchment Jobsdone gave us when we were in Ireland. We have to find trapdoors and become Uptoppers once more," Martha said.

"I know, Missy. Let's get away from here first and find a quiet place. I've never been to England, so take me there. I want to see what it's like," Sunday replied.

"It rains most of the time, but it's green, with lots of trees and a lot of houses have straw roofs," Martha laughed.

"What about battles? I'm fed up of battles."

"Oh, there are battles. The English invented them."

Chapter Sixteen
England

August 1815

A warm late summer sun was lingering laboriously just above the tree tops, skirting a lane leading to Towton Meadows. The River Thames flowed peaceably past the river bank, as Martha settled Watson in a field for the oncoming night. When she got back to the bow top, Sunday was sitting on a patch of grass, holding her stomach, head bowed to her knees.

"If you weren't dead, Sunday, I'd say you look a bit troubled," Martha remarked.

"I am dead and I am troubled, Missy. I have a funny feeling inside my stomach."

"That's not possible. You are dead and like me and others like me, and you, we don't get stomach trouble."

"Well, Missy, I have a funny feeling and I've had it most of the day."

"What sort of funny feeling?"

"Like being pregnant."

"Pregnant!" gasped Martha incredulously. "Not possible."

"Ever been pregnant, Missy?"

Martha shrugged and shook her head. "No."

"I have, twice. And I think I'm pregnant," Sunday replied matter-of-factly.

"Impossible. We just don't get pregnant. You know that."

"I know. You know, and I totally believed we didn't, but I think I'm pregnant."

"How? Who by?" Martha asked, then stared wide eyed at Sunday. "Not—"

"Captain De Lacey," Sunday nodded calmly.

"Just not possible. He was alive, but you were dead and still are."

"Remember after that battle and we found him injured, lying next to his friend?"

"Yeah, the young lieutenant who thought you had said you wanted to have his babies.

"Six babies. He almost fell off his horse," Martha laughed.

"Right. Well, he gave me his sabre and we both kissed it and rubbed some of his blood on the blade. We put the kiss of death on it."

"I remember."

"Well, I swallowed some of Captain De Lacey's blood."

"I saw you," Martha agreed. "It can't have—can't have made you pregnant."

"It has done, Missy. We made love three times the previous night. Swallowing some of his blood the next day and it mixing with—you know—made me pregnant. I'm having his baby."

Martha settled back and stared at Sunday, who had the faintest of smiles on her face. The two shook their heads and said nothing for a few moments. Martha reached to Sunday and took one of her hands.

"I know who can tell us, if you are," Martha said confidently.

"Who?"

"The three Dabras in Blingoburbia."

"But, Missy, we're in England. The Blingos are in Ireland."

"They're all over the world, Sunday. On the parchment Jobsdone gave us, there were locations everywhere. Including right here in Berkshire."

Sunday lifted her head and stood up. She walked to the gate to the field and looked up and down the lane. Martha joined her and pointed to a spot forty or fifty yards along.

"There, where rubbish is being scattered. Rubbish tips and thick undergrowth is where the trapdoors are. What date is it today?"

"The seventh of August."

"So, tomorrow is the eighth and the trapdoors can be opened. We'll be here at eight prompt in the morning. Let's make sure there's a trapdoor here."

They carefully started pulling at the rubbish scattered around. Densely trampled and thick, it was a place where locals had deposited spoil and waste for years. No one with a sense of smell would contemplate disturbing the ground. After ten minutes, they found the trapdoor.

"I bet it pongs," Sunday remarked. "Glad I can't smell it."

"Me too. But we found it. Now we cover it up properly."

They walked back to the bow top, but stopped at the gate and looked across the field.

Three rough-looking youths and two girls were standing by their cart. Two men were inside, rummaging through the interior. Cautiously, Martha and Sunday walked to their bow top.

A teenage youth saw the two young women and called to his companions. One of the men in the bow top, stocky and with gold rings in each ear and a long scar running down one cheek, grinned and waited. He held Sunday's sabre in his hand. The others turned to face the approaching young women. The second man in the bow top held one of the muskets. On the ground, Martha's chair had been thrown down, and the trunk containing their clothes. It was open and the two girls were giggling as they rummaged inside.

"Get down, mister and put that sabre back and tell your friend to do the same," Sunday called, standing a few yards back.

The stocky man started laughing and started waving the sabre in one of his hands.

"Hear that, lads? The darkie woman can speak our language," he said in a thick Irish brogue.

"I won't ask you again, mister. Put the things back and get down," Sunday demanded.

The teenage youth started laughing and took a step towards Sunday. "Do I get first chance to shag her, uncle Mickey?"

"'Course you don't, young Benny. Me and your dad get first helpings," Michael Flannery laughed and stood on the edge of the cart. The second man with the musket moved to the side of his brother.

"After me and Mickey shag the two of 'em, young Benny, you can choose which one you want. Your cousins can have a go as well, if they want," Joe Flannery remarked in a similar Irish brogue and raised the musket to his shoulder. "What if I put a ball into the darkie's head, Mickey?"

"And you like shagging dead women, eh?" Michael Flannery scoffed.

Sunday glowered at the two brothers and shook her head. "Get off the cart, you stupid dimwits, or I'll kill you."

Michael Flannery stopped waving the sabre and tossed it towards Sunday. It stuck in the ground a few feet in front of her.

"Go on then, darkie. Pick it up and try. I'll slice your tits off with it before you can get six feet nearer."

"I'll ask you one more time, Mickey, and then I'll kill you," Sunday threatened. "Get off the cart, get your misfit clan with you and go."

All the Flannerys started laughing and one of the girls, a pretty, black-haired youngster of late teens, with a full figure, held out one of the frocks from the trunk.

"After you've sliced her black tits off, Uncle Michael, can I have this frock, before you sell all this stuff?"

Flannery looked at his niece and nodded. "Course you can, sweetheart. And get one out for your cousin." He returned his dark eyes to Sunday and pointed at the sabre. "Now then, darkie, are yer gonna make a grab for the sword?"

"It's a sabre and no, I don't need to," Sunday replied.

"Why's that, darkie?"

Sunday reached behind and withdrew her knife from the back of her pants. "Because, Mickey, I have this."

The knife thudded into the wooden boards between Flannery's feet. He looked down in shock at the knife that was embedded in the timber. The others stared and in the few moments of stunned silence, Sunday ran to the sabre and pulled it from the ground. Michael Flannery stared wild eyed at her.

Martha had walked forward and quickly eased the knife from the footboard and passed it to Sunday. She handed the sabre to Martha.

Side by side, Martha and Sunday faced the Flannery brothers. The two Irishmen looked down at the two young women, their eyes never leaving the sabre and the knife. Sunday was grinning.

"Now then, Mickey, are you going to get down from our cart, or do you want my knife sticking out of your Irish head? You are Irish, I assume?"

Martha had turned to face the three teenagers, but they were all dumbstruck and nervous. The sabre in the woman's hand had a long curved blade and at a guess, they had decided she knew how to use it. One by one, they backed away a few feet.

Mickey Flannery and his brother jumped from the cart, both sets of dark eyes watching the knife in Sunday's hand. Martha smiled and waved the sabre at her chair, lying on its side.

Looking at Mickey Flannery, the bigger of the two brothers, she tapped the chair with the sabre.

"Pick my chair up, mister and sit in it, if you please, and your brother can hand my friend the musket."

Joe Flannery looked at his brother, who nodded. He passed the musket to Sunday, who had the knife in her hand ready to throw. Sunday carefully lowered the musket to the ground, then smiled at Michael Flannery.

"Sit down, Mickey and relax. Take the weight off your feet."

"I'm happy standing," Flannery replied.

Sunday raised the knife. Flannery flopped into the chair.

"Now, my friend has something to say to you." Sunday flicked her head at Martha. The latter walked to the brutish Irishman and smiled sweetly.

"We don't take kindly to people rooting through our little cart or threatening to cut our tits off, so here's what you do. You apologise to my friend for saying that to her."

Flannery looked up at Martha but his eyes glanced at the knife in Sunday's hand. He knew her first throw had not been luck; he guessed the black woman was better than lucky.

"Michael Flannery doesn't apologise to a darkie. I'm an Irish gypsy and we don't back down. She's got one throw left with that knife and then my family will kill the pair of you."

Martha raised the sabre and prodded the end of the blade to his groin area. He pulled back in the chair and took a breath. Martha jabbed him again and this time he winced.

"You lose your balls, Mister Flannery. I think you're a feller who needs them every now and then. Am I right?"

Flannery scowled and wiped sweat from his face. "You don't scare me, whoever you are. Irish gypsies fear no one."

The sabre swished twice and a cross was etched into his ruddy cheeks, blood spurting out. Flannery shrieked in pain and gripped the sides of the chair. The other Flannerys gasped loudly, both girls dropping the frocks they had taken from the chest.

Martha smiled and raised the sabre again. Flannery put his hands up and screamed, "I'm sorry! I'm sorry."

"Get up, Mister Flannery, get your misfits and go. Don't trouble us again, or you die."

Flannery pushed his bulk from the chair and walked away. He signalled his family and with dark eyes staring hatred, they skulked away.

Sunday was grinning and looked narrow-eyed at Martha. "No kiss of death? And what about that sabre cut? Impressive," she laughed.

"I wanted to cut his balls off, to be honest."

"Why didn't you?"

"Because those kids were looking. They're unlucky to have fathers like those two."

"Yeah, I agree, but I think that will not be the last time we see the Flannerys. We best get a long way from here after tomorrow. I bet you're a mad woman with a sabre in your hand."

"I expected to see the knife in his head, not between his feet," Martha laughed.

"Just as good, Missy. They stop and think. Was it luck or was it pure class?"

"I think you'd better start carrying two knives in future. Just in case."

Sunday reached to her boot and pulled a thin-bladed knife from inside. Martha shook her head. Sunday put an arm around her shoulders and grinned.

"Always have, Missy. That's why I wear high boots mostly. I learnt that on the pirate ships. Throw a good warning shot and then pull out the second knife. You can hear their brains working. If the second knife fails to stop them, pull out the third knife. That always stops them." Sunday pulled a similar thin-bladed knife from the inside of her other boot. She laughed and shook her head. "Now I'm dead, I don't feel the nuisance of having them inside my boots."

"When we met our soldiers in the Silver Moon, you had boots on under your frock, I wondered why. You had the knives with you," Martha remarked wonderingly.

"Of course. Hell of a job stripping and pulling my boots off quietly and carefully. I pretended to be shy and went behind a curtain to strip," Sunday laughed.

"You, shy? Not the Sunday Brown who I know."

"I made up for it later. I think he went away that night feeling well satisfied, I know I was."

"And now—" Martha took Sunday's hand. "You're carrying his child. I can't believe it and we better not let Lord Lucifer hear of it."

"Or me, but I think I am. I must be. I have a body and if I say so myself, a good womanly body. Men always wanted it and most times when I didn't want their grubby flesh next to mine. With Captain De Lacey I felt wanted, clean and feminine."

"Before Major Sabinet, I felt like you. I hated men touching my body. Not far from here, at Towton Meadows, I had that despicable preacher and his wife abusing me regularly. I hated them and later they suffered for what they did to me. With you, Sunday, I always feel good."

"Same for me, Missy, but it was different with the captain. No man has ever made love to me like he did. I tasted his blood and I know it helped to make me pregnant. I'm dead, I understand that, but I'm going to have a baby. Nothing will stop me. Not even he who is the most evil creature walking the earth."

The Next Day
A Few Seconds Before Eight in the Morning.

They had scraped the trapdoor surface clean and waited patiently a few feet away. The morning was dry and warm. A few white clouds drifted across a blue sky and birdsong was vibrant. A couple of rabbits scurried quickly across the wooden trapdoor and disappeared into thick undergrowth. Martha and Sunday watched with hopeful eyes. There was a scrabbling sound from the trapdoor, a slight banging and thumping, then the door started to open and twinkling eyes could be seen in the narrow gap. The gap widened and then a full, beaming face looked out.

The door was pushed up and over. Several little figures emerged, scrambling upwards, all carrying empty sacks. They disappeared into the undergrowth as Martha and Sunday watched in fascination and smiled. A few seconds and two more little figures appeared. The mischievous eyes twinkled and carefully ran over the two transfixed Uptoppers.

"Martha Budd and Sunday Brown, no less. Welcome to Blingoburbia. We were expecting you. I'm Enufsaid and the keeper of this entrance, which is number one million and thirteen. This is Lafsalot, my apprentice," Enufsaid put an arm around the slim shoulders of a younger-looking Blingo, with a happy smile on his boyish face. "He has another thirty-six years to go to become a qualified Uptop entrance guardian, but he is learning well. My cousins Jobsdone and Bossalot have told me all about you both. You rid Gremlins Green of King Smegtooth the Terrible and Gertlump of the Boggimps and the fearsome two-headed Cerberus Junior. Missiquin is looking forward to meeting you, as well as our three Dabras. Everyone in Blingoburbia has heard of you and are hoping you will be their Uptop helpers. In eleven years' time you are to be awarded the Mark of the SWAN. Right now, though, how can we help you?"

Martha took Sunday's hand, looking at Enufsaid. "Sunday needs to see the three Dabras for a test. We were hoping they would see her."

Enufsaid looked at Sunday and read her mind. He was surprised, but looked concerned.

"I see. That's unusual, but not exactly miraculous. There was another I have heard about, before my time, but with a similar concern. And I see you're holding hands and very wise. While you are talking to Entrance Guardians it is not necessary, as our bodies release energy that allows you Uptoppers to speak without being overheard. So I guess, Sunday, you want to know if you are pregnant?"

"I'm certain I am, but it would be nice to know for definite," Sunday replied.

"I can arrange that for you. However, only you can come into Blingoburbia, because Martha has not received the Mark of the SWAN yet and it's just you with the concern. One of the three Dabras – as we call them, will see you. As you are spreckled, Sunday Brown, your body will start to decrease in size as soon as your feet pass through the opening. On returning to the Uptop it will return to your normal size as you start to pass through again. Lafsalot will take you to the Dabra's chambers, then he will bring you back."

"How long will I be gone?" Sunday asked.

"A few minutes in Uptop time, Martha will be safe with me and I can show her what we do up here. Go now, Sunday Brown and we will see you in a few minutes."

Lafsalot took Sunday's hand as he stepped into the entrance, the latter looking concerned.

The trapdoor closed and Martha stared at it for a few moments, until Enufsaid smiled and indicated to her to help him cover the entrance. In a few seconds it was covered once more. Enufsaid found a safe place to sit, hidden by shrubs and bushes. Martha joined him and sat at his side. He stretched his little legs out and smiled.

"She will be safe in our world, don't worry. Eleven years will soon pass and then you will both be Uptop SWANS. You will be able to come and go from Blingoburbia on your own, but only on the eighth day of August and between eight in the morning to eight in the evening. On the night of a full moon the entrance is open for sixteen seconds at midnight, but only myself and Lafsalot pass through. The same at every entrance all over the Uptop world."

"You mentioned another Uptopper who was helped many years ago. Was that a warrior woman called Jacindra?" Martha asked.

Enufsaid nodded, then a few moments later shook his head. "Yes, that was her name, but it was many centuries ago, even I was not born then. She still wanders the Uptop with her offspring to destroy Lucifer's offspring. Every one hundred years, on a night of the full moon, she returns to Blingoburbia to be re-spreckled, so she is always protected. Her powers are immense, but she and her offspring can be killed and a lot do get killed, by Lucifer's offspring. They fight with swords and knives, but a blow to the head can get them killed. Either losing their heads or taking two stabs into the brain through both eyes. Both are fatal."

"Jacindra is an immortal, is that so?"

"Yes. She has done excellent work on the Uptop for many centuries. She comes this way every now and then. There are always some of her children with her, also immortals. They look like normal people and act normal, but they are not normal and their powers are the equal of Lucifer's offspring. Only Jacindra is the equal of Lucifer and the other devils in power and strength."

Martha looked at Enufsaid in surprise. "Other devils! There are others?"

"Oh yes. They are brothers, but only one at a time in the Uptop world. Lucifer is the one who appears now. His brothers are Abaddon, Leviathan, Drebmif, Belial, Beelzebub and Mephistopheles. Their father is Satan. He is the overlord of Hell. The ruler of all the ungodly demons. There is a long standing tale, that one son of Satan, the seventh and youngest, escaped his father's clutches to try and become just and honourable, decent and respectful of the Uptoppers' world and religions. Satan bestowed the same powers on this seventh son, but he refused to do his father's bidding and set off to try and restore the goodness and trust of the immortals that had been vanquished by the rulers of Hell. The immortal you mentioned, Jacindra, she met this seventh son during his term as the Uptop ruler and he helped her escape. It was in the period of time when the next son of Satan takes over his six hundred and sixty-six year spell as Uptop ruler. The next takeover of duty by one of his sons is in just a few years' time."

"Do you know when?" Martha asked.

Enufsaid rubbed his chin and pondered for a few moments. "Very soon, I believe. It is always on the night of a full moon. Not a place to be near when it happens. Every ungodly demonic creature crawls or flies from its lair to attend the ceremony. The offspring of all the immortals and demons clash in mighty battles during the following hours. It is a bloodbath. It's the one night in six hundred and sixty-six years when all the entrances to Blingoburbia remain locked and hidden."

Enufsaid stood and shook himself then waved Martha to follow him. She followed and they were soon lost amidst the undergrowth.

Lafsalot skipped along a path going slightly downhill, as a wide-eyed Sunday tried to take in all the sights and sounds of Blingoburbia. Hundreds of the little people were happily engaged in various types of work duties. Some were pushing wheelbarrows loaded with produce or materials; others simply carrying bundles or small sacks. Curious eyes stared at the brown-skinned Uptopper as she walked quickly along the winding path. Millions of glow worms were visible on the side walls, placed every few inches. They emitted bright light that provided clear vision all around.

After what to Sunday seemed a couple of hours, they reached a resting point and two Blingos in different coloured attire handed them drinks. It was warm and Lafsalot accepted a beaker of drink and swallowed. He wiped his mouth and smiled at a bewildered Sunday.

For the first time since she had died and sold her soul, her mouth was dry.

"Drink it, Sunday Brown. You're in Blingoburbia and things are different. Your body needs fluid." Lafsalot smiled.

Sunday was thirsty and the feeling inside her body was different. The Blingos watched her in fascination. Slowly she put the beaker to her lips and took a sip. It was fruity and tasted nice. Enufsaid nodded and his eyes twinkled. Sunday took a longer sip, then realised she could feel the fluid tingling in her throat. The whole beakerful was gulped and Sunday unashamedly wiped her mouth with the back of her hand, then licked her lips. A second beakerful was consumed and Sunday felt refreshed.

"That was delicious. The first drink I've had in years and years," she remarked.

"Everything here is different. While you are Blingoburbia you are normal, just like us and of course, the same size. You can eat and drink as you would have done before in the Uptop," Lafsalot replied and started walking again. Sunday followed and quickly caught up with him.

Her eyes wandered everywhere. Hundreds and hundreds of the little people could be seen, all purposefully doing work on a variety of jobs. It was light as it would be on a normal day above ground and a slight warm breeze tingled Sunday's face.

After another hour, they came to a large cavern, hewn out of the rock. More drinks were taken and for the first time in her undead years, she tasted food. The bread was soft and crusty and the warm soup tasty. From a bowl of fruit she chose a large, fat red plum. The juices trickled down her chin and once more she wiped her mouth with the back of her hand.

Cheery-faced Blingos watched with curiosity as Sunday took another large plum and showed it no mercy.

"We go down now, Sunday Brown. The lift carriage takes us further into our queendom. There are tunnels in all directions which lead to all our provinces. We use waterfalls to work the mechanism, just like there are in the Uptop lands at the side of your buildings near a river or stream. There are seats in the carriage because it is a long journey to the Dabra's chambers. Today Sorceradabra is on duty, he awaits your presence. Relax and enjoy the journey."

They had travelled downward an hour in the carriage, then transferred to a vertical carriage, again propelled by steady flowing water. After another hour they reached the chambers of the three Dabras. Sunday had tried to imagine what any of the three looked like and was surprised to be welcomed into a brightly lit chamber, by a solemn-faced, white, long haired Blingo, garbed in a long cloak of finely woven cream coloured cloth, held in a red waist sash. The room was stocked with glass jars on numerous shelves, containing various coloured substances. Copper pots and dishes were on tables. A book shelf against a wall held several leather bound books.

Sunday's roving eyes wondered where the large black cooking pot, hung above a fire, was located. Where was the large black cat that usually sat near the pot? Sorceradabra looked with interest at the brown-skinned young woman and smiled.

"You are expecting an iron cooking pot in which we boil unfortunate, dare I say, souls."

"It crossed my mind," Sunday replied.

"Fear not, Sunday Brown, we only cook food in our cooking pots and they are only small vessels. However, I have heard that you want to learn whether you are carrying a baby in your body. I can tell you in moments if you are. Please stand in front of me and I will touch your lower body and see."

Sunday stepped towards him and took a breath. Very gently, Sorceradabra placed his hands on her stomach and moved them around a few inches, pressing gently. He started nodding and looked into Sunday's dark eyes.

"You are indeed carrying a child, Sunday Brown, a man child."

"A boy? You mean I will be having a boy?"

"Yes. A boy."

"Vardan. I will call him Vardan. His father had a war horse called Vardan. He will be the greatest warrior of his time."

"He will be half human, half spirit. Bring him to the Dabra Chambers after he is born and he will be blessed by each of the three Magus. On his eighth birthday, bring him again and he will receive a second blessing. On his twenty-fourth birthday, when he has reached full maturity, send him to us and he will receive the Mark of the SWAN that gives him immortality. He can then go out in the Uptop world to combat Satan's children."

Sunday smiled and humbly bowed to the old sorcerer. He put a hand forward and placed it on her head. A flow of heat passed through his fingers and into her head. For a few moments everything inside her body went numb, then it changed and a feeling of warmth flooded through every nerve, muscle, tissue and bone within her trembling figure.

"Take a deep breath, Sunday Brown, and be revitalized. You are still of the undead, but from now you can take comfort in the senses you had before Lucifer took your soul. You will have taste, smell, hunger and thirst back, but also pain. You will have greater strength, hearing and sight. Near your time to give birth, wait until the night of a full moon and have Vardan out in the open air, standing in the shallow water of a river that flows to the sea. As soon as he takes his first breath, lower him into the water until the water covers his head."

Sorceradabra took his hand from Sunday's head and reached to a table and picked up a small bottle. He handed it to Sunday. "Take the bottle, Sunday Brown and keep it safe. It contains spreckle-dust, to be loosened over Vardan's body with falling moondust that is in the air on that night. Do it as soon as he settles after taking him from the water. As he grows he will be able to stay under water for long periods of time. He will be able to go the depths of the deepest seas. Now it is time for you to go back to the Uptop."

"Thank you, sir. Thank you for the bottle of spreckle-dust," Sunday said and bowed her head again.

"Thank you, Sunday Brown, for the work you do above and for ridding the Uptop of Cerberus Junior and Smegtooth the Terrible. We may need your help again for such deeds in the years ahead."

"And Vardan."

"And Vardan's help as well, when he is fully grown."

Sunday almost skipped out of the chambers and saw Lafsalot waiting for her. He caught her smile and grinned.

"You look pleased," he remarked.

"I am. I can eat again and drink and do things I haven't been able to do for many, many years. And I am going to have a little boy. He's going to be a warrior when he is fully grown and his name will be Vardan."

"There are others like him. I've heard they are fearless and they hunt down Satan's brood. But there are dangers."

"Like what?"

"Very often they have to fight all of the Hell-Demons, the Vampires, Werewolves, Warlocks, Hobgoblins and others. Often they are greatly outnumbered. We hear tales of many battles between the immortals and the Hell-Demons. Not something I would want to do."

"Vardan will be special. In twenty-four years' time, he will go out on his own and he will take my sabre with him, it was his father's and used in battle. With it he can't be beaten. It has his father's blood on the blade."

"I will remember his name. Vardan, slayer of Hell-Demons, but now we have to go back to the entrance, we have a long journey." Lafsalot took Sundays hand and walked her away.

The trapdoor opened and Lafsalot pushed his way through the small opening. Sunday followed and blinked as the bright sun hit her eyes. She had returned to her normal height and for the first time since she sold her soul to Lord Lucifer, she could feel the sun's warmth on her body. She threw her head back and let her long hair fall behind, enjoying the tingling sensation of sunshine on her face.

"You look as if you can feel the sun," Martha remarked as she saw her friend's movements. "And you weren't as long as I thought you would be."

"I can, Missy. I can feel the sun on my skin. And I must have been gone for a few hours. It was a long way to get to see Sorceradabra, one of the Dabras,"

"Minutes, Sunday. No more than fifteen minutes. Twenty at the most," Martha replied. Before Sunday could answer, Lafsalot did what he was named for; he started laughing.

"Time is different in the Uptop world. Lots of things are different," he said.

"My young friend is right," Enufsaid added, as he appeared at Martha's side. "Time moves at a different pace in Blingoburbia. And if Sunday Brown can feel the sun, it means that she has been blessed by one of the Dabras. Still an undead Uptopper, but with some of the feelings back that she enjoyed before selling her soul to the devil."

Sunday reached to Martha and took her hand. "This hasn't changed, Missy. We still have to hold hands up here if you know who is spoken about. And I'm hungry. I could eat a whole roasted chicken and a bowl full of vegetables. I used to love carrots."

Martha stared at Sunday with wide eyes. "Hungry!"

"Yeah. I'm ravenous. I haven't eaten for years."

Now Enufsaid joined Lafsalot in laughing. "I said things are different, especially for you, Sunday Brown. Don't be jealous though, Martha Budd. You never have to feel hungry or thirsty again, so there are advantages for you. However there is still work to do up here, before we Blingos return to our homes. Sacks to fill and items to collect. You can help and then tidy up after we have gone back. An Uptopper's work is never finished."

To the second, the trapdoor closed and the two girls looked at each other. It was on the dot of eight in the evening and once more they were alone. The sun was still showering the greenery and tree tops with a warm, light breezy heat and Sunday stretched her aching limbs. Martha watched in fascination; stretching her arms and legs was something she had not done in almost two hundred years.

"I'm jealous. I wish I had feeling in my body again," she whispered softly, taking Sunday's hand. "I started before you and now you've got most of yours back."

"I need a pee, Missy. Some things haven't changed, unfortunately," Sunday grinned.

"Well, at least that makes me feel a bit happier," Martha laughed.

Sunday took her call of nature as Martha watched with a wry grin.

"Tonight you might get a – you know – a thrill."

"You'd better make me get one, Missy. I'll share it with you."

They started giggling and sat down on the grass after they had covered the trapdoor. An embrace and kisses followed as they lay together on their backs, looking up into the evening sky. Sunday turned, kissed Martha for long moments on her lips, raised herself to her elbow and stroked Martha's long auburn hair, taking her hand at the same time.

"I'll look after you, Missy, you know. You taught me all I know and I'll be in your debt for ever and ever. Maybe I'd be long dead now anyway, even if hadn't become an undeader.

"Murdered, probably by some thieving, groping, filthy pirate. Or made to walk the plank and get eaten by the sharks. Or captured by a French or British ship and hanged after being raped by half the crew. It's not been so bad. I'm pregnant again and having a boy. I'm calling him Vardan after Philippe's cavalry horse. He told me as I lay in his arms the night before the battle, after we had made love three times, that he rescued his horse from a weed-covered field and he was starved and his ribs were showing. He took him away and brought him back to good health. Vardan took him into battle a few times and was one of the bravest cavalry horses in the French army. I can see them both charging across the ground, Vardan at full gallop and Philippe with his sabre held, ready to strike." Sunday gripped Martha's hand as the latter gently wiped a tear away as it trickled down her friend's brown face.

"I'm giving the sabre to Vardan when he's twenty-four and fully grown. It has his father's blood on the blade and he will seek out the devil's creatures and kill them. He will be the fiercest immortal warrior of them all. I want him to stand at Jacindra's side as they slay the hell creatures."

"What was Blingoburbia like?" Martha asked.

"Very bright and warm. Lots and lots of Blingos all over the place, happily working at different tasks. They make all sorts of things from the stuff they collect in the sacks that they take through the trapdoors. Clocks, baskets, ladders, rope, clothes, boots and shoes and all sorts of things. Tunnels everywhere, leading miles and miles underground. Bridges over streams and water-powered carriages lowered and lifted by ropes. Little houses perched on the rocky sides, all reached by ladders. Even flower baskets hanging outside. Millions and millions of glow worms providing the light. Cooking pots everywhere and as I returned after meeting Sorceradabra and getting blessed in his chambers, these scrumptious smells of food."

"He confirmed you are having a baby?" Martha asked.

"He did. He put his warm hand on my stomach and told me I was going to have a baby boy. Then he put a hand on my head and this warm surge rippled through my body. He told me I would be able to smell things again and get hungry and thirsty, but I would feel pain as well. When I give birth to Vardan I have to stand in a river that runs to the sea, then hold him under for a few moments, put spreckle-dust over his body and when he is older, he will be able to go deep into the water. The deepest parts of any sea. I was wondering about your friend who was on the *Black Diamond* with you."

"Fimber O'Flynn."

"That's him. Lord Lucifer sent him to the bottom of the sea, where he still is."

"One day I'll get him back."

"Vardan will get him, Missy. Sorceradabra told me that by the time he's twenty-four he will be fully grown and immortal. He can go deep into the ocean. He'll bring Fimber back."

Martha embraced Sunday again and held her tight. "I can't imagine ever seeing him again. He took me in after I sold my soul, that horrid day in Towton Meadows. I always thought there was something strange about him, but to think of him rotting at the bottom of the sea is unbearable."

"You'll see him again, Missy, I promise," Sunday remarked and settled down again.

"Tomorrow we'll go through Towton Meadows and if it's still standing, I'll show you the cottage where I lived, or should I say existed," Martha said as they lay in each other's arms.

"I know it's morbid, but will you show me the pond where you were murdered?" Sunday asked matter-of-factly.

"That is morbid, but to be honest, I'd like to see it myself. I used to catch tadpoles when I was little, from the pond. I learnt to swim in it and one day the rector's wife caught me with two boys after we had been playing in the water. We had no clothes on and I was taking care of the boys with my hand, when the old witch caught me. She dragged me back through the village stark naked and beat me black and blue with a stick. I couldn't sit down for days."

"You killed her, didn't you?"

"I helped her on her way, I suppose. I hated her and the rector. They used me as a slave and he raped me a lot, but she let him. Saved her from being groped by him. He was smelly, thin and ugly. I gave him the kiss of death, just before they killed me on the chair."

"You were a little witch then, eh Missy?" Sunday laughed.

"Yeah, I suppose I was. I gave three of my favours away that day. The rector, this witch hunter feller and a snotty youth who fancied me. Jack Spicer. He was vile and had the most horrendous yellow teeth. He paid me a few pennies one day to let him have it with me, so I waited 'til he pulled his pants down and then I ran. I can still see him hopping about with his pants down to his ankles, trying to catch me. I stopped after fifty yards and pulled my skirts up to let him see my fanny, then I ran on, with him screaming after me."

The girls rolled over in fits of laughter and for Sunday, she started crying with tears running down her face. Martha scuffed the tears from Sunday's face and sighed. Sunday kissed her.

"I know, Missy. I can shed tears again, not that I ever did. Hard faced I was and made hard by the men who abused me."

"You have to sleep now, Sunday, another thing you can probably do once more. I'll keep watch and wake you after dawn, then we'll set off again."

Sunday embraced Martha snugly and kissed her again, but this time in a long kiss to her lips. She finished the kiss and looked at her friend.

"I love you, Missy, and I want you to help me be a mother to Vardan. He will have two mothers."

"I'll look after him as though he was my own. Go now and sleep." Martha gently pushed Sunday away and watched her friend as she climbed into the bow top. Martha looked on as Sunday settled onto the bed and after a couple of minutes fell asleep.

At first light the next morning, Sunday awoke and looked around for Martha. A light drizzle was falling, but it was cool and the fresh damp air tingled her face, a feeling she had not had for many years. A yawn followed and once more she felt the pleasure of a working body function. Her eyes searched the immediate area around the bow top and she realised her vision was stronger. She could clearly see birds in a blackthorn hedge more than a hundred yards away. A twig snapped behind her and she turned to look. Martha was leading Watson by his rope in the field, more than sixty yards back. Sunday waved and her nose twitched; she could smell Watson's body scent through the drizzle.

"You were sleeping like a baby, all curled up and cosy," Martha remarked as she climbed up to sit at Sunday's side. They embraced and Sunday was smiling.

"I had a dream, can you believe it, Missy?"

"What about?"

"Your friend Fimber O'Flynn, would you believe. He spoke to me and—and he told me to tell you not to waste your time finding him. He is being punished for doing bad things and doesn't want to do anything bad again. He said to leave him where he is."

"He's only being unselfish, Sunday. He's the nicest person I ever met. He's not bad."

"I saw him, Missy. He—he is covered in awful fishy things and his head—his head is wide and flat. He looks like a type of shark I saw when I sailed the seas. They're called hammerheads."

"Don't fib to me, Sunday, Fimber O'Flynn is decent and a gentleman. He is not bad and he can't look like a shark."

Sunday reached for Martha's hand and squeezed gently. "I'm not fibbing, Missy. I'd never do such a thing to you. I saw him in the dream, just like I explained."

"I'm sorry for doubting you, Sunday, but will you help me to get him back?"

"Of course I will. I know where he went down. We'll find him. Vardan will find him."

Chapter Seventeen
Towton Meadows

Watson was tethered in a field and happily munching grass as a warm sun took over from the earlier drizzle. The bow top was pushed into a corner of the field, shielded by high hedges and Sunday was enjoying the first breakfast she had had in years. Sitting in her chair, Martha watched her friend eating boiled eggs and crusty bread, washed down with fresh milk they had taken from a cow in the next field.

On the grass, Sunday looked up at Martha as she polished off the last of the three eggs she had boiled. "I feel awful, eating like this, Missy, but I'm feeding two now."

"I enjoyed watching you eat. I don't mind. You need food now, but yeah, I wish I could join you. Cooked rabbit or chicken comes to mind."

"Swap milk for red wine and that breakfast would have been bliss," Sunday laughed and stood up, wiping a run of egg yolk from the corner of her mouth. "Let's go into the village and put a curse on those that had you killed."

"It was a hundred and seventy odd years ago, Sunday. They'll all be dead and buried now."

"Oh yeah, I forgot. But show me the ducking pond."

"I will, I'll never forget it. The place where I sold my soul."

"On your chair, Missy."

Martha stood and patted the back of her old chair. "Not the chair's fault, Sunday. It was all my own fault. I had a choice."

They left the field, shut the gate and holding hands, walked to the village a quarter of a mile away. It was still early and few people were about. Martha remembered the village well and even though some of the older houses had been pulled down and new ones built, a few of the older ones still stood, including the cottage where she had lived with her adoptive parents. A ruin now, with a partially collapsed roof, the windows were boarded up and the door hung loose on rusty hinges. High, dense weeds and shrubs had long since taken over from a meticulously tended flower garden.

As the two peered through the slightly opened door, a soft voice sounded from behind. Martha and Sunday turned to see an old, grey-haired woman looking at them. She smiled, displaying a mouth with teeth missing.

"Not a place you want to be inside, my dears." the old woman said almost mischievously. "It's haunted. A long time ago a young witch lived here with her parents. She killed them both so wickedly. She put curses on them both and they died horribly. She was found out and put to death on a ducking chair at the village pond. She went to hell. Some say that at midnight on the day she was executed, she roams the village to put a curse on anyone foolish enough to be outside on that night. Many have perished on that night over the years. Nobody dares knock the place down, because it's said that she put a curse on the place and anyone who knocks it down will die a horrible death. So don't dilly dally here, my dears. You'd best move on and leave this evil place."

"It's an old wives' tale," Martha said good-humouredly. "I bet she wasn't a witch, just a foolish, high-spirited young woman."

The old woman shook her head vigorously and did a fake shiver. "Oh no, my dear, it's true. My great-great-grandmother was there on the day they put her to death. She saw the young witch put a death kiss on three men at her execution. Her father, a government official and a young lad she was courting, who had spurned her. They all died within the week, and of gruesome deaths."

Martha laughed and turned from the ruined cottage. "All poppycock, old woman. It's just a lot of rubbish, a tale that gets exaggerated as the years go by."

"It's not young lady. Martha Brooks was her name and she was an evil witch. It's true, you take my word," the old woman protested.

"Her name was Martha Budd, not Martha Brooks. She was adopted by the Reverend Jonas Brooks and his wife, Elizabeth. They beat her regularly and starved her. Locked her in a dark cupboard for hours on end. She was raped by the Reverend many times. Her adoptive parents deserved to die."

"Oh no, no, that's not true, my dear. They were wonderful loving patients. God fearing and well liked in Towton Meadows. You've been ill advised. What's your name, anyway?"

Martha started walking away, but stopped after a couple of strides and looked at the bewildered old woman.

"Martha Budd, that's my name. It was never Brooks. Goodbye, old woman. I wish you well, but don't ever sell your soul." Martha grinned and carried on walking.

Sunday followed Martha and turned to look at the old woman. The latter was motionless, like a stone statue, eyes wide and mouth open.

"You've got her thinking, Missy." Sunday laughed as she caught up.

"More ammunition to the story." Martha laughed.

"I've often wondered where you go on a full moon every twelve months."

"You never guessed, then, where I go?" Martha laughed.

Sunday looked at Martha with narrowed eyes. "You don't. I know you don't, Missy. You're kidding."

"I'm a ghost, remember, Sunday. We do things like that. You probably do as well, don't you? It's what we are expected to do, isn't it?" Martha added as Sunday's expression was still a look of confusion. Martha started giggling and Sunday hooked an arm into hers, with the usual boisterous giggle she made. A few yards back, the old woman was still rooted to the spot, her old wrinkled face a mask of mystified disbelief.

A few minutes later and the two stood at the side of the large village pond. Not much had changed since Martha had seen her last human life day at the pond in 1643. A duck island had been made in the middle, to protect the many feathered varieties from prowling foxes.

A metal sign board was erected near the spot where Martha had taken her last breaths on that fateful day, so long ago. The old wooden supports that had held the ducking chair were rotted and covered in green slime, but had denied the passing of time to be removed into history.

Sunday looked up at the sign, but with no great reading ability, she let Martha read the inscriptions that were still clearly legible. After finishing, Martha stepped away and was shaking her head.

"They executed my friend as well. Maisy Duckworth. Murdered here as well. She was even less a witch than me. Her name is after mine. I've never known all these years. I hope she didn't sell her soul like I did."

"How many are named on the sign?" Sunday asked.

Martha did a quick count and sighed dejectedly, shaking her head. "Seven. My name is third on the list. Martha Brooks, put to death 1643 for indecency and witchcraft. So three more poor wretches followed Maisy and me."

"Indecency, Missy? What did you do?"

"The same as you and me do in private, Sunday. Maisy and I loved each other, that's all. We got caught one day by my adoptive parent and three of her nosey friends, having fun in her bed. I was beaten black and blue again. Before I was pushed into the cupboard that night, Reverend Brooks raped me again, as his wife watched."

"I would have killed him as soon as I was let out of the cupboard," Sunday hissed.

"I should have. I cursed her anyway and she died soon after. I gave him the kiss of death just before they put me under the water for the umpteenth time. He wanted me to repent and ask forgiveness. I hope he suffered before he went to Hell."

"According to that old woman it sounds like he did, Missy."

"Poor Maisy. I led her on, to be honest, but she was never a bad person. No more a witch than any other girl her age. She was sixteen. I was eighteen. Maybe I was a witch, but not poor Maisy. I hope she didn't sell her soul."

Sunday took Martha's hand and gently tugged her away from the duck pond. They walked from the village in silence as the sun was taken over by cloud and made Sunday shiver slightly. Martha put an arm around Sunday's waist and knew the chill was now being felt by her friend.

When they reached the gate to the field, both noticed it was open and not shut, as they had left it more than two hours earlier. A quick look to the right of the gate where the bow top was positioned, they noticed smoke whisping up into the overcast sky. Someone had re-lit the fire that had died down after Sunday had boiled her eggs. A further glance and the bulky figure of a man was stretched out in Martha's chair. Other people were sitting around the fire, talking and laughing.

Sunday tugged at Martha's arm and whispered to her, "It's those Irish gypsies again, Missy, but more of them. They're spoiling for a fight. You go on and talk to them, I'll go around and come up at the back while they aren't looking. Have you got a knife with you?"

"No, I'll borrow one of yours," Martha replied. Sunday pulled one of her knives from a boot and passed it over.

"Get near to the big one sitting in your chair. He needs the kiss of death this time," Sunday said as she left Martha to walk towards the group of gypsies.

All eyes turned as Martha was spotted walking towards the group. From the chair, Michael Flannery lifted his sixteen stone bulk and pointed at Martha. He laughed and nodded towards a woman sitting around the fire.

"Get yer arse up, Molly O'Hara, and deal with this English madam. She's one of the toffee-nosed wenches I told you about. The darkie woman will be coming, no doubt. Josie can take care of her. I want to watch as you two stuff the crap out of 'em."

Martha approached warily and noticed a large, big-busted woman climbing to her feet as the other gypsies started laughing. Another woman, younger, but looking equally as aggressive as her friend, jumped down from the bow top where she had been lying. Her blouse top was unbuttoned and she was fastening it up. Behind her, a trouserless Joseph Flannery appeared looking red faced and dishevelled.

Martha stopped a few feet from Michael Flannery and flicked her head at the woman fastening her blouse up. "Get away from my cart and take that buffoon with you and make sure he doesn't leave his pants behind."

"I was going to let him shag me, you English bitch, but now he can shag you instead," the untidy, but attractive black haired woman hissed.

"I'll shag you first, Josie Duffy like I was just going to do, then I'll shag her." Joe Flannery grinned as he started pulling his pants on.

"Save it fer her, Joe Flannery, I'm not in the mood now. I just want to knock her teeth out first, then you can shove your dick up her." Josie Duffy laughed as she stepped threateningly towards Martha, fists clenched.

"She's mine, Josie," the big-busted woman shouted as she marched at Martha. Molly O'Hara was rolling up her shirt sleeves as she walked. The laughter from the watching gypsies shrieked out, as Martha turned to look at the overweight woman striding towards her. Her instinct was to turn and run, but she knew that somewhere close, Sunday would be ready to strike. Her hand reached for the knife Sunday had given her and in an instant, the big woman stopped and looked towards Michael Flannery. He laughed and quickly pulled out a knife and tossed it towards Molly O'Hara.

"Pick it up, Molly, and slit her English throat," Flannery called and flopped back into the chair and started laughing. Molly O'Hara reached down to pick the knife up, but another knife thudded into the grass, an inch from Flannery's knife. The startled woman stiffened and looked around, leaving Flannery's knife on the grass.

"Pick it up, lady, and say your prayers at the same time," the husky accented voice called. Sunday appeared in the background, another knife held, ready to throw. All the sitting gypsies suddenly scrambled to their feet and glanced at the tall figure of Sunday, a few feet behind.

Martha smiled and scooped up the two knives on the grass in front of her. With a deft flick of her wrist she threw one of the knives to Sunday. Bewildered eyes watched as Sunday plucked it from the air, with nonchalant ease. The gasps of astonishment were loud.

Josie Duffy stared wild-eyed at a grinning Martha, then turned to look at a smiling Sunday. Molly O'Hara started whimpering, expecting to feel a knife blade in her body. Her eyes stared helplessly at a stunned Michael Flannery. His brother, Joe, had let his pants drop to his ankles, scared to move a muscle in case a knife came his way. The other gypsies stood rooted, nervous frightened eyes watching the hands of the brown-skinned woman.

"Any of you stupid, illiterate buffoons so much as breathe and it will be the last breath you take," Martha said as she stepped towards a dumbstruck Michael Flannery, still seated in her chair. "I think you are intelligent enough to understand my friend is better than anyone you have ever known at throwing a knife. She will kill you in a blink of an eyelid."

"She can't kill all of us, you English bitch, with just two knives," sneered Michael Flannery as he glared at Martha.

The knife thudded into his hand as it gripped the arm rest and the squeal of pain echoed high into the air. Flannery's hand was fixed to the arm rest, spilling blood. He was squirming as Martha reached him and withdrew her knife.

"I'm almost as good as my friend, but she's always going to be better, Mister Flannery," Martha grinned as she wiped the blood off the knife across the whimpering man's pants. He was about to climb from the chair, but a firm hand from Martha pressed against his chest, pushing him back. Her face lowered and to the man's surprise, a soft, wet kiss was planted on his unshaven, ruddy face. His frightened eyes stared into Martha's and he saw a red glint flash quickly in her eyes.

A few feet away, a bewildered Josie Duffy was felled by a savage blow to her face from Sunday. Flat on her back, the gypsy woman stared up at a towering, smiling Sunday. Blood trickled down her cheeks as her prostrate body was grabbed by the scruff and pulled effortlessly along the grass towards the field gate. Sunday dumped the frightened woman in the gate entrance in a heap and signalled to the other gypsies to follow. Without hesitation the bewildered gypsies ran quickly, then carefully walked around Sunday's menacing figure.

Hopping along, trying to pull up his pants, Joe Flannery was glad to have escaped the fury of the two English women. Molly O'Hara struggled behind, half carrying a crying Michael Flannery, holding his bleeding hand. Sunday stood in the gateway, with hands on hips.

"Come near me and my friend again and you die. Do you hear me?" Sunday said calmly. Molly O'Hara looked at Sunday nervously and nodded. Cursing under his breath, Michael Flannery glared at Sunday.

"We'll come for you both one night, black woman, while you're sleeping and slit your throats," Flannery snarled.

Sunday was smiling at his threat. "I don't think so, mister. You'll be dead within the week and on your way to Lord Lucifer."

Flannery glared at Sunday. "Who the fuck's Lord—whatever you called him?"

"Lord Lucifer. He'll take you in the next few days, because I know you'll take his offer."

"Fuck you, darkie, you English bitch. Go to hell," Flannery replied as he was pulled away by a frightened Molly O'Hara, glad to be walking away unmarked.

"Wrong, mister. I'm not English, I'm French and you're on your way to Hell, believe me." Sunday scoffed as she watched the pair struggling along the lane. Flannery was shouting abuse, but Sunday shut the gate and turned away.

Martha was cleaning her chair of Flannery's blood when Sunday walked back to the bow top. The pair embraced and kissed, then stood back to look at the old oak chair.

"Do you think he'll die tonight, Missy?" Sunday asked.

"Tomorrow, probably. This time tomorrow he'll be dead, that I know. A knife fight, too much ale, a ball shot in his brain, or a heart attack. Even a horse kick to his head. My chair never fails to end the life of anyone who tries to hurt me. It happens."

"You impressed me with the knife throw. You're good." Sunday laughed.

"I had a good teacher, Sunday. Anyway, you impressed me by catching the knife," Martha said as she took hold of Sunday's hand.

"It was so easy, to be honest. Since I went into Blingoburbia and got blessed by Sorceradabra, I feel stronger and quicker. My reflexes are much better. I could hear those gypsies around the fire, whispering to each other, word for word. I hope I can pass it all on to Vardan."

"You will. He will be a mighty warrior in the years to come. We must teach him to become a master of his craft. I'm pleased for you Sunday."

"You mean that, Missy?"

"Truly. I want to be involved. I want to be his second mother."

"You will be as much a mother to him as I will. But promise me one thing."

"What's that?"

"If he is ever naughty, don't make him sit on your chair."

The giggles could have been heard in Blingoburbia as Martha and Sunday relaxed and rolled together on the damp grass. After a few minutes they stood and Martha pointed to where Watson was tethered.

"We have to pack up and move on. Time to go."

"Where to, Missy? I'd like to go back to America one day, but I think it might be best to stay in England until—" Sunday took Martha's hand before finishing. "Until 1826, when we get the Mark of the SWAN. Just in case there are no Blingos in America."

"I think there are, Sunday, but I agree. We'll do our Uptopper duties here in England and Vardan will be born in England. Not a bad place to be born, unless it happens to be Towton Meadows or a place like Gremlins Green."

"Oh, Missy, don't remind me. Year after year of standing in those peat bogs."

"We stay in England, then?"

"England, or France. Either will please me," Sunday remarked.

"Agreed, then. Let's get old Watson harnessed up and set off again."

"Where to Missy?" Sunday asked, taking Martha's hand.

"North. I went up there a long time ago, to a place called York. Lucifer sent Fimber and myself, to Marston Moor, where a big battle was to take place. Nice little villages and open green fields. We passed over a river I remember, just east of York. I was thinking we could rest up there, for you to have the baby."

"Sounds good to me. We have to take him under the water, and sprinkle some spreckle- dust on his head, after he comes up."

"You're agreed then, Sunday?"

"Definitely. York it is, Missy."

They harnessed Watson, then climbed up onto the bow-top. Martha took the reins and flipped them. Watson took the weight and pulled away willingly.

"And we will use the Blingo parchment, that Sorceradabra gave us, to find a time gap," Martha remarked.

"On a full moon, Missy. And a long way from Lord Lucifer."

"He or his brothers, have the ways and means to find us, Sunday, but as long as we are careful, and have the protection of the little people, we should be alright."

"Do we go before my baby is born?" Sunday asked.

"I think you should have him first. Find the river I mentioned, take him under, and then sprinkle the spreckle-dust over him. It will keep his little body safe. As soon as he is a few weeks old, we go through a time gap."

"You know best, Missy. I trust you. Do you know what to do? I've seen you reading the parchment, but I can't understand the markings. I'll have to learn how to read."

"I'll teach you, Sunday. It appears easy enough to understand. We wait till a few seconds before midnight on a full moon. We both call out the year we need to go to, holding hands and touching the things we need to take with us. We have to stand within a circle, no more than eight yards from a trapdoor. That means we have about sixteen yards in diameter. We have till eight seconds after midnight on the full moon. Only those who have been spreckled, can travel through a time gap."

"Don't know what you mean by diameter, Missy, but I know you do. So we can take our little cart and Watson as well?" Sunday asked.

"Yes, it says so. He's been spreckled."

"So what year do we go back to? I'd like to find Jacindra, and have a good talk to her. We could find out how she escaped from the devil."

"I read about a battle in the year 1066 not far from York. She would have been an immortal then and possibly around at the time. Or we could ask to go back even further."

"How far back is 1066?" Sunday asked.

Martha did a quick calculation and spoke.

"Seven hundred and fifty years. A long, long time back."

"Let's go back to that year. If there was a battle, people will have been killed. Jacindra might have been there." Sunday said, and squeezed Martha's hand and settled back.

Martha smiled and nodded. "Sorted then. We find the river, where you can have the baby. Then we find a trapdoor and get everything ready, on the night of a full moon."

"I hope my little boy will be safe, when we go through this time gap."

"After he is spreckled, he will be, Sunday. The Blingos have blessed your body remember. As soon as you give birth, we sprinkle the stuff from the bottle over his body and carefully lower him into the water. When he comes back up, his body will be protected. We wait a few weeks for him to gain strength, then we go through the time gap."

"Are you worried, Missy?"

"A bit," Martha replied.

"Frightened to be honest."

"Me to. Do you think we will arrive at the river, near York, where Vardan will be born?"

"I hope so. I just hope it won't be anywhere near Gremlins Green, or Towton Meadows," Martha said hopefully.

"I trust that old man, from Blingoburbia. He was so pleasant and gentle, when he touched my body. I stood before him naked and I felt comfortable. The feeling I got as this sensation rippled through my body, was off this earth."

They started laughing at Sunday's remark, as the bow-top cart trundled along the track. They were holding hands and hoped they had not been over-heard. They both glanced upward, expecting a great flock of ravens to appear, but there were none.

"You know Missy, when I was pregnant with my first two babies, I didn't have this wonderful feeling inside my body that I have now. I had been raped and brutalised and I dreaded giving birth. I'm carrying a warrior child now, and his father was so handsome, tall and brave. I'll give him the sabre his father gave me. I know he will grow to be as brave as his father, Captain De Lacey."

Chapter Eighteen
York, England

April 1066
Vardan took his first breath as the distant bells of a church near York rang out a few miles away. The bow top was tucked into a hedge on a lane to the east of the thriving market town and Sunday was standing up to her waist in the shallows of a river, just a couple of feet from the grassy bank. The baby boy had been born under the surface of the cold river water, then Martha had taken Vardan from Sunday's body and held him under for a few seconds, then lifted him up and sprinkled spreckle dust over his body from the little bottle Sunday had been given by Sorceradabra.

"He's strong and healthy, Sunday," Martha smiled as she removed the umbilical cord and wrapped a shawl around his pinky brown body. A slap to his bottom and the shrill wailing sound startled nearby birds, who took to flight from the bushes. Sunday took Vardan from Martha and lifted him above her head in outstretched arms.

"He looks so defenceless, Missy, so vulnerable. I can't believe he is finally here and this little wrinkly body will grow to be an immortal warrior," Sunday cried as she pulled him down and held him gently, but firmly. "And he's spreckled like we are, so we'll bury the bottle by the river, so we know where he was born. It will be a special place, where a great warrior was born."

"We'll do that, Sunday and we'll teach him everything he needs to know. I will teach him how to read and write and you can teach him everything he needs to know about the skills of looking after himself. He will be a true immortal warrior when he is fully grown."

Martha pulled Sunday from the river and sat her down on a blanket. It was a warm spring day, an almost cloudless blue sky. Sunday was naked and put the boy to her swollen breasts. He suckled quietly as the young women watched with pride. Martha helped Sunday to pull on her clothes, then found a place below a tree and buried the bottle. A rustle of leaves from a bush made both of them turn in surprise.

A slim, girlish figure emerged from the bushes, garbed in woven sackcloth type clothes, with long golden blonde hair and a necklace of coloured beads hung around her shoulders. A gold clasp, just below one shoulder, held her clothes in place. A braided leather belt around her slim waist held a leather scabbard with a dagger encased. Footwear that was of leather straps turned around her lower legs, to a sole of thicker leather.

Martha and Sunday stared wide-eyed at the young woman, who stared back with deep blue eyes. Nothing was spoken for several seconds between the three, then the young woman calmly moved forward, a hand extended, a smile on her pale face.

"Who are you and why do you come to our lands?" The woman's accent was strange, but of old English.

"We could ask you the same." Martha replied as she shielded Sunday and Vardan.

"I am Erika Haralda of the Nors Egersund tribe. My father is an elder of the Nors Egersund people. You don't look like Angle, Jute or Celt women, our enemies. One of you is a strange colour."

Martha stared more intently at the young woman and shrugged. "Nors Egersund, what—who are they?"

The young woman moved a hand to the dagger, but resisted pulling it out. Sunday stepped to Martha's side and handed Vardan to her. Bending down, she scooped up one of her knives, which she had earlier laid down, before entering the river. The woman took a step back and clasped her dagger. Sunday held her knife ready to throw. Martha, with Vardan in her arms, started shaking her head in alarm.

"No, no, don't pull it out. You will die. Please! We mean you no harm."

Erika Haralda hesitated and relaxed her grip on the dagger's handle. She saw the brown-skinned woman's eyes glint red and knew she was facing a warrior woman. After a thought, she raised her arms wide in supplication.

"I mean you no harm, but you speak a strange tongue and I have never seen a woman of this colour. You, like me are the same colour, your comrade is the colour of the ground that grows with grass. I am of the Nors Egersund. What tribe are you?"

Martha and Sunday exchanged glances, then looked at the pale-skinned woman again, at her long blonde hair and the strange clothes. Martha sighed and handed Vardan back to Sunday, who had lowered her knife.

"We have no tribe. I'm English and my friend is French, or at least that's her language. Where are you from, Erika Haralda?" Martha asked, politely but confused.

"From here." Erika raised her arms and signalled around the area of the river bank. "On the land we stand on here and for many miles in all directions. We defend our land from enemies who would take it from us. Some Saxon tribes and the Angles come from the south to raid our land and steal our crops, take our young women and make slaves of our young men. We were once great in numbers, but we have lost many of our brave fighters to these godless barbarians."

Martha stared at Erika Haralda and started shaking her head again. "Are your tribe's people called Vikings? I read about them when I was a young girl."

Erika Haralda had a faint smile on her face and started nodding slowly. "We were originally from a land east across the great sea. We were called Vikings and came to this land many years ago. We settled here and built our houses, schools and fertilized the land to grow crops. We fought off tribes from the north called the Celts and Jutes, then from the south we were raided by the Saxons, Angles, the Mercians and others. Not far from where we stand now, my people fought with the Britons who lived on these lands against invaders from across the great sea who came to conquer, but we fought them back and sent them away. We had come here to settle and live peaceably and adopted these lands to live alongside the Britons. For many years we lived together, worked together and shared our skills. A fierce tribe from the south, called the Iceni, are like us, the Nors Egersund, and we fought together. They were once led by a great queen called Boadicea, who fought many battles against the Romans. She was killed by the Romans and her tribe savagely reduced in numbers by the Romans. One of her daughters now leads the Iceni, but she is very strange. She never looks any older when she comes to our camp." Martha and Sunday exchanged glances. Sunday spoke first.

"Is her name Jacindra?"

Erika nodded. "That is her name. You know her?"

"No, not yet," Martha replied quickly. "We have only heard of her."

Sunday, with a sleeping Vardan in her arms, looked at the blonde-haired young woman intently. "Have you seen this Jacindra?"

"Yes, I have seen her. I am told that like her mother, she is fierce and without equal in combat," Erika answered. "Like you, who has just had the baby, Jacindra is tall and powerful, but her skin is pale like mine. Her hair is golden and very long."

"Where is your camp? Near here?" Martha asked.

"Towards the east, about three miles. My people move around, because of the tribes raiding our camp. We are now down to less than two hundred, but when I was little there were over five hundred of us."

"So why are you here today on your own?" Martha asked.

Erika smiled and looked to both sides to where she was stood. She waved an arm and from bushes to either side, two young men stepped out, both with bows and arrows at the ready.

"If I thought you were of our enemies, you would now be dead, but we would have taken the child and brought it up as one of our own."

"The 'it' is a boy and his mother is not an enemy," hissed Sunday as she glared red-eyed at the two young men. "And why are you on your own?"

"We go out in threes to hunt and scout our lands. In the old days, it was not necessary to scout, but we have to do it now to survive. We saw your strange cart at the side of the field and your horse tethered and you, naked in the river. I told my brother Odda and my cousin Ulvik to stay hidden."

Sunday held Vardan closely as the two bearded and long, fair-haired men walked from their cover. A few words from Erika to them and they lowered their weapons. Both wore upper clothes of sheepskin and baggy, well-worn dyed leather pants. Swords were hanging from leather belts and each had a dagger to hand. One had a battle axe strapped to his back.

"My name is Martha Budd and my friend is Sunday Brown. Her new-born boy is called Vardan," Martha declared as she noticed the anxiety in the three strangers' faces.

"Your clothes are strange. I have never seen such things before," Erika remarked as she admired Martha's attire. The two young men had wandering eyes, roving across Sunday's and Martha's womanly bodies. Erika dug an elbow into her brother's ribs. He winced and stopped staring. Odda mumbled something to his sister and she grinned.

"Odda says he has never seen two such beautiful women before. There are only a few younger women left in our camp. There is little choice now for them, or indeed for we women. We fear that our tribe, the Nors Egersund, will not be here in a hundred years' time."

With Vardan at Sunday's breast once more, she let a shawl drop and walked naked to the bow top. Martha held her hand as they walked, followed by the three hunters. Erika walked close behind Sunday to prevent her brother and cousin having unrestricted sight of the long-limbed brown body of the tall and strange woman.

As soon as Sunday had put clothes on and taken a seat in Martha's chair, the roving eyes of the two men faltered. Vardan was sleeping again and Sunday was relaxed. Martha had invited the newcomers to inspect the bow top. Erika was amazed at the various utensils that were inside the cart, especially the copper and brass items that were in regular use. A hand-held mirror glass took Erika's attention. She stared at her image for long moments, amazed and somewhat bewildered.

"Take it, you can have it. We have another," Martha offered.

"It's—it's unreal. What is it?" Erika asked. "I can see everything so clearly."

"We call such things mirrors. It is made of glass."

"Glass? What is glass?" Ulvik, the taller of the two men, but shorter than Sunday, asked as he stood looking in amazement at the side of Erika.

"Not sure, to be honest," Martha replied. "It has never crossed my mind. We take such things for granted."

Martha happily showed the three hunters various items in the bow top and was taken by their almost innocent wonderings. After a few minutes, Odda spotted the two muskets that were partially covered by cloths. He touched one and stared wide-eyed at the long, sleek weapon that was almost as long as he was tall. The slim, long-haired hunter, ruggedly handsome with battle scars on his arms and face, looked at Martha with curious blue eyes.

"It's called a musket. We use it for shooting deer, hares and rabbits. Sometimes people," Martha laughed. The three stared at the musket as Martha picked it up in safe hands. She picked up a few ball shot and packets of powder. Outside again, she took Vardan from Sunday and passed over the musket, powder and shot.

"What does it do? You hit deer and rabbits with it?" Odda asked, looking confused.

Sunday had removed the ramrod and slowly, deliberately put ball and powder into the barrel. Three pairs of eyes watched, mystified. Sunday raised the barrel and waved the three back, out of harm's way. Sixty or seventy yards away, scampering quickly across the field, a big buck rabbit was seen. Sunday pointed at the rabbit, took aim and paused, her eagle eyes focusing.

The crack of sound exploded and the rabbit fell dead. Loud gasps sounded as the three hunters stared in utter amazement. Sunday lowered the musket and set off to collect the dead rabbit. With the rabbit held by its back legs, a smiling Sunday passed it to a stunned-looking Odda. He took it, shaking his head. Words were quickly exchanged between the three hunters and nervous eyes then stared at the tall brown woman.

"How? How? What is it called again?" Erika asked nervously.

"A musket. It wins battles. It kills and maims. Have you not seen one before?" Sunday asked as she reloaded. The others shook their heads and said nothing. Another rabbit appeared, running from a hedge, further away this time. Sunday took aim, followed the unknowing little animal with the barrel and fired. The rabbit dropped dead. More gasps of astonishment and head shaking. This time, Ulvik ran to collect the rabbit, his long, straggly fair hair flowing in the breeze, held in place by a broad head band. He returned with a wide smile on his weather-beaten, bearded face. He held the rabbit up proudly.

"Where can we get such weapons?" he asked gruffly.

Martha walked forward, holding a sleeping Vardan. She exchanged a few words with Sunday and the latter then held out the musket to Ulvik. He didn't know what to do and looked across to Erika. They spoke quietly, then Erika turned to Martha.

"Why do you offer us this noisy, but mighty weapon?"

"You said you have enemies who raid your lands. Not just one tribe, but others and your numbers are reducing. We have two such weapons that we use occasionally, but we can get two more if we want. Take them and our shot and powder and we will show you how to use them," Martha replied.

"Why do you want to help us? We can't repay you," Erika said quietly.

"Take us to your camp and tell us what you know about Jacindra of the Iceni. That is all repayment we seek," Martha replied.

"My father, Berkak, knows of Jacindra of the Iceni tribe. They are far to the south east of our lands, but every four years they travel north to trade with us and other friendly tribes.

"There are women at our camp who will help you with your boy. If you kill a deer with the noisy fire stick, we can take it back and feast tonight. Two rabbits will not feed almost two hundred, but we can make broth with them. You will be very welcome."

"Find me a deer and I'll kill it," Sunday grinned.

"There are a few not far from here, but they are usually too quick for our arrows. They hear us coming," Odda said as he held one of the dead rabbits.

Less than an hour later, Watson was pulling the bow top along a narrow track at the side of the river. Odda and Ulvik walked at the side, excitedly chatting between themselves, as

Erika sat beside Martha on the driving seat. Sunday was breast feeding Vardan in the back and thinking of the chance meeting with the three strangers, who knew of Jacindra.

Finished feeding her son, Sunday suddenly tapped Martha's arm. Martha pulled Watson to a halt and looked at Sunday.

"I can hear deer," Sunday said quietly. "Not far away over to the left."

Martha nodded, Erika glanced to her right and tried to see the deer. There was no sight of them. She shook her head.

"I will send Odda and Ulvik to see," she said. "They might be able to take one down if the deer do not hear them."

Sunday tapped Erika's aim and smiled. "They're over to the left, like I said. I'll go and take one down with my musket. Just me, no one else. I'll call as soon as I have it. Your brother and cousin can collect it. I'll have done my bit."

Quickly loading one of the muskets, Sunday quietly slipped from the bow top and disappeared through the bushes. Martha smiled as she saw the puzzled looks on Odda's and Ulviks faces. They had slipped arrows to their bow strings, but a flapping hand from Erika had stopped them following Sunday.

Minutes passed and the only sounds to be heard were of birds and a few bees, searching for plants to pollinate. The silence around the bow top was unnerving for the two young men, who wanted to leave and show off their undoubted hunting prowess. Erika watched patiently as she craned her neck to see where Sunday had gone. Martha was still smiling.

The crack of the musket echoed through trees and bushes. Odda and Ulvik jumped slightly. Erika stood and looked to her left. The call followed and Erika flicked her head at the two men. They dashed off through the bushes to find Sunday. A few minutes passed, then the beaming face of Sunday appeared, her musket carried low in one of her hands. A short way behind, Odda and Ulvik came into view, carrying a dead deer.

"We eat well tonight," Erika smiled as she welcomed Sunday with a hearty slap to her shoulder. Sunday smiled and glanced up at Martha. The knowing thought between them passed unnoticed by the three young Nors Egersund hunters.

The camp was tucked well out of the way, with swampy ground circling a wooded hillside and one edge below a one hundred foot high rock face. It was shielded by the trees and had good resistance to any winds that blew. A motley group of shanty dwellings had been constructed and a well eaten grassy paddock held a few horses. To the far end of the paddock a large area of land held crops, separated by a four-foot high fence from the camp. Chickens ran free, clucking at dogs and children. In the centre of the camp, a larger, thatched-roofed building stood with a thin wisp of smoke filtering from a chimney.

Heads turned in surprise as the bow top cart trundled in, led by the two young men carrying the carcass of the deer. Children ran to the cart and followed it to the large building in the centre. Several adults appeared from the building and watched as Erika jumped down from her seat, with Martha at her side. Gasps of surprise were made at the sight of the taller woman at Erika's side and dressed in strange clothes.

A crowd had gathered within minutes, tribe's people running from jobs they had been doing on hearing of the newcomers' arrival. As soon as Sunday appeared and joined Martha and Erika, further gasps of astonishment rang out. The brown-skinned woman was taller than most of the tribe's menfolk and several of the women stepped back in awe.

Odda and Ulvik laid the deer on a patch of grass and smiled with pride. Erika put the two dead rabbits on top of the deer and stepped back. One of the taller men cautiously stepped forward and looked at the two strangers with concern. He was Berkak, Erika's father and had a similar scarred face to the two young male hunters. His hair and beard was going grey and had beads woven into several long strands. A coloured head band held his hair in place. A hairy cow hide was draped around his shoulders, held by a large, engraved gold brooch.

Knee high sheepskin boots had rough baggy woven pants tucked inside the tops. He looked every part the tribe's chieftain. In one hand he held a tall, stout wooden staff. Notches were cut into the sides. Odda walked to him and they embraced quickly. Berkak stepped back and returned his stare to the two tall women. Odda spoke quickly.

"Father, we brought these two women to the camp, because they have things to show you. The dark one has just given birth to a boy. They have a weapon that makes a loud noise and is a sort of fire stick. It kills much better than an arrow. They are not of our enemies, we are sure of that."

Berkak switched his hard stare from Martha and Sunday. He hushed the watching tribesfolk and looked more closely at Sunday. She was his height, a situation he had never experienced with any woman from his tribe. Only one other woman he had seen in his life, was similar in height to the strange, but beautiful, brown-skinned woman. He stared hard at her and thought he saw a quick glint of red in her eyes. Satisfied the woman was no immediate threat, he turned his hard stare on Martha and felt a hint of joy, that this pale-skinned woman was not of his height, but still taller than any other of the tribes women.

Erika stepped forward and touched her father's arm. "Father, they are not enemies. The tall one killed the deer and the rabbits. She has a boy child. They come to our camp as friends. They have wonderful things in their cart. Like Odda said, they have fire sticks that kill and we can have them if you tell them about Jacindra of the Iceni tribe. That is all they ask in return."

Another older man stepped forward and looked with concern at Martha and Sunday.

Stockier, but shorter than Berkak, he was similarly dressed and also held a tall staff in one of his hands. A short sword was held in his leather belt.

"They might still be spies, Berkak. The Angles and Mercians use such of their women to snoop and take information back. You know this from past history. I say kill them and be done. We can't take chances," he growled and glared at both women, a hand with an iron clasp around the wrist, reached to his sword.

Sunday was lightning quick and pulled out one of her knives and threw it at the rough-looking man's feet. It thudded midway between his feet and raised loud gasps from everyone watching. A second knife came out as quick and was levelled at the astonished man's body. He looked at the first knife embedded in the ground inches from both feet, then at the second one ready to be thrown. His terrified gaze then caught a flash of red in the woman's fierce eyes. He was not sure what to do next, but moved his hand away from the sword.

Berkak put a hand out and tugged the man back a step.

"Hundorp, let's not be hasty. If my daughter says they are friendly, let's give them the benefit of the doubt. The brown one could just as easily have put her knife in your chest. They have brought food and we should be grateful."

"On your head then, Berkak," growled the smaller tribesman. "But I will watch her."

Sunday grinned and walked forward to pull her knife from the grass. Hundorp scowled.

With daylight fading, the Nors Egersund women had prepared food around various fires. The deer had been roasted on a spit and vegetables boiled. Rabbit broth was a side dish. Sunday was ravenous and wasted no time in starting her meal. Martha cradled Vardan and sat away a little from the main body of hungry tribespeople. Erika had noticed Martha sitting on her own with Vardan and took a plate of food to her, with a goblet of wine.

"You must be hungry, Martha. I haven't seen you drink or eat anything since we met," Erika remarked and handed the food to Martha.

Martha was gently rocking Vardan and smiled, but shook her head. "I'm not hungry. I am fine and am just happy at seeing your people enjoying the meal."

"You must eat. There is plenty left. At least take a drink of wine. We make it from berries and certain plants we find. Our men can get drunk on it very quickly. It's good."

Martha shook her head and patted Erika's hand. "Really, I'm not hungry and I sipped some water not long ago," Martha lied.

Erika nodded and smiled. "Can I hold the little boy? He is so lovely. Dark hair and his eyes are so piercing. I had a son three summers ago, but he was taken by the Angles when they raided our last camp. He was blessed with eyes of different colours, one blue, one green. It is said that a boy with different coloured eyes will be a leader when he is grown. The Angles also killed twenty of our men, including my husband. We are struggling now to survive. I lost my brother that day, as well as my son and husband."

Martha carefully passed Vardan to Erika and realised the young woman was used to holding babies. Vardan put a hand to Erika and gripped two of her fingers. She laughed.

"Hey! He is so strong. He will be a powerful man when he is grown. Your friend is so lucky to have given birth to him. I wish you all well." Erika handed Vardan back and kissed his head. She put a hand to the top of his head and looked up to the darkening sky. A lone bright star shone and Erika put her head back and spoke a few words in a strange language Martha did not understand.

"That is the North Pole Star and we respect it so much. It guided our ancestors in years past as they sailed to find a proper homeland. I spoke an old verse that our forefathers made before they set out on a voyage. It was also spoken before a battle. Vardan will be guided by the North Pole Star and protected by its powers. It is said within the Nors Egersund peoples that a boy child blessed to the Pole Star will live to be a great warrior. His mother I have seen is a woman of strength and power. Vardan will be special."

Martha kissed Vardan's head and looked up to the bright star. Erika looked up again and from the east, a streaking light raced across the sky with a trail of meteor and star dust in its wake. Both young women gasped and looked at each other. Erika took Martha's hand.

"It is sealed, Martha. Our great God, Odin, has passed his approval of Vardan."

"I am pleased, Erika, for our boy, but what of yours, where will he be now?"

"The Angles are a warlike tribe. They are from the south and take children from camps that they raid. Boys and girls. They erect large stone pillars in circles and a stone altar, where they sacrifice the kidnapped females to their gods. The body of the female is then eaten before the flesh goes rigid. The chief of the tribe eats the heart to give him extra strength."

Martha shook her head and gently squeezed Erika's hand.

"They're evil. I know someone who is probably their god. Can you not unite with other tribes and fight them, take back your stolen children?"

"My father has had talks with elders of some of the peace-loving tribes, but most are frightened to resist the Angles, the

Mercians and the Celts. There are also warlike tribes from the west. The Hengoed tribe from the dragon country are the worst. Radnor is their leader and he is said to cut off the testicles of his enemies and eat them raw. He has over twenty children and boasts he has supreme virility because of this. My tribe, the Nors Egersund, have fought such warlike tribes, but we have lost so many to the sword or the spear. I would like to find my son Tordal! And bring him home, but there are few young men left in my tribe to help me on such a dangerous mission."

"When do the Angles come to steal food and crops?" Martha asked.

"Before the winter sets in. They are lazy and don't grow the food they need. They prefer to steal what they need. Two of the chief's sons usually come with a small army. They rape our women and if we don't hand our food or crops over, they kill. We can't defend ourselves any more. We will have to move camp again before the winter, go further north."

"Would you let Sunday and me help you fight these raiders?"

"How? You're two women, not trained warriors. You'd be slaughtered."

"We have four good friends who would help us." Martha replied.

"Just four? It would take more than four extra fighters, Martha."

"You saw Sunday with one of the muskets, didn't you? We are both expert shooters, Sunday better than me and we have two hand pistols as well. And Sunday has a sabre that is a bit unusual."

"A sabre! Hand pistols! What are they? "

"Modern weapons, Erika. And a sabre is a type of sword, but very, very lethal in the right hands. After the meal tonight, let Sunday and me talk to your father. Tomorrow we will show you our weapons. You have already seen the musket, tomorrow we will show you the others. Sunday will need to sleep tonight after her meal. I will take breast milk from her and look after Vardan while she sleeps."

"What about you? When do you sleep?" Erika asked, looking confused.

"I get by, don't worry about me."

Erika stood and smiled at Martha and Vardan. She took the plate of food away and walked back to the feast. A few words with her father, who looked across to the bow top where Martha was sitting with Vardan and she went to speak with her brother.

A half-moon was high in the sky when the feast had finished and most of the Nors Egersund had gone to their beds. Martha had explained her suggestion of help for the tribe and Sunday had agreed without hesitation. Vardan was asleep and Sunday had lit a fire a few yards from the bow top. Erika, her father, brother Odda, cousin Ulvik, elder Hundorp and another tribe elder, Tonstad, came to the bow top quietly. They settled by the fire and looked at Sunday and Martha.

A half hour later and Martha's suggestion of help had been heard and agreed by all but the obnoxious Hundorp, who still thought the two strangers were spies. He and Tonstad had departed for their beds, but Berkak smiled and nodded agreeably to Martha and Sunday.

"You have to convince Hundorp and Tonstad that you are serious about helping to rescue my grandson, but I believe you are both genuine. Sleep well tonight and in the morning you can show my people, and especially Hundorp, that your weapons are good enough to take on the Angles when they come to raid our camp," Berkak said and turned, followed by his son and nephew.

Erika stayed a while longer and embraced Martha and then Sunday. She took a peep at the sleeping baby Vardan, then quietly walked back to her lodge.

Sunday took a breath and rubbed her eyes, then yawned. "God's truth, Missy, I'm tired but my belly is full. I wish you could have eaten some of that venison, it was off this earth."

"No matter, Sunday. We'll take some milk for Vardan then you go to sleep. I'll keep a good watch out."

Sunday stretched and embraced Martha. She let Martha take milk into a bottle, then climbed into the bed and was asleep in minutes. Martha sat in her chair and looked at the sleeping figures of Sunday and Vardan. In less than two months, the little boy had become a large part of her strange world.

The Next Day

Berkak, Tonstad and Hundorp watched in bewilderment as Sunday fired one of the muskets at a target, fixed a hundred yards away. Odda and Ulvik were less in awe, having seen Sunday's actions the day before. Others in a crowd of tribespeople were also bewildered at the power of the new weapon the two strangers had brought with them. Martha reloaded Sunday's muskets as the latter did her almost flawless shooting practice. Martha fired a few shots off, missed a couple of times, but still received gasps of disbelief from the onlookers.

After the muskets had been used, Sunday and Martha fired the pistols at set targets and then handed them to both Odda and Ulvik. For the first couple of tries, the lads missed by a mile, but then settled down and eventually got used to the recoil. Ulvik was the better of the two and was loath to give up his pistol or musket when another of the young men stepped forward to shoot.

In all, about twenty of the men took turns to shoot, until Sunday decided it was time to conserve ammunition. Most were disappointed to stop shooting, but Sunday explained that ball shot and powder should be used sparingly. Even though they had plenty to hand, there was no chance of getting new supplies. Berkak accepted the situation and decided his best marksmen would be handed the four weapons. Odda was disappointed not to be one of the four marksmen, but his deft touch at reloading was of the best and he would be on hand to reload for the chosen four. The four marksmen would practice occasionally to fine tune their shooting abilities, with care not to waste ammunition.

Vardan had been taken by a woman from the tribe who had breast milk spare after her recent childbirth and Sunday was left to demonstrate her knife-throwing skills. Within a couple of hours, three or four of the young men stood out from the rest and instructions were given, to smelt knives similar to the one Sunday used.

In return for displaying her shooting and knife-throwing skills, Sunday was given instruction on firing from a bow. The tribeswomen made the arrows and watched with pride as the tall, dark-skinned woman quickly became a competent bowman. Berkak watched admiringly as Sunday improved almost faultlessly, shot after shot. Even Martha's bow efficiency was admired by the men. By the end of the day, hundreds of arrows had been fired, recovered and used again.

Martha had been unable to draw the bow string back to a proper firing position at first, but a few hours later she had almost mastered the craft. Sunday, however, had astonished everybody with her strength at pulling the bowstring back fully, almost from her first attempt. Accuracy came gradually until she had become one of the best bowmen. The men marvelled at her strength and consistency. A few had an eye for the woman, to the annoyance of their own women and eventually Sunday was looked upon as a threat by a few. By dusk, the activity was over and everybody settled down to eat a meal. The women had cooked the food, and filled dishes were handed out around the camp fires. Sunday needed no prompting and set to as soon as she had a wooden dish in her hands. Martha had taken Vardan to the bow top to settle him down and to avoid being seen not to eat or drink.

After a few minutes, Erika climbed onto the bow top with a dish of food for Martha. Vardan was asleep and Martha put a finger to her lips. The two women jumped down and settled on the grass by one of the rear cart wheels. Erika offered the food dish and was surprised the meal was once more refused. Her eyes were searching for answers.

"Tell me what's wrong, Martha. There is something not right, I know," Erika asked.

"I can't eat, Erika. My body cannot take food," Martha replied calmly.

"Or drink. You don't drink water or wine, I've noticed."

"I can neither drink or eat. I am not like you or normal people. I'm different."

Erika put the food dish down and looked at her new friend. "You and Sunday and the baby are not from our time. I've guessed that much. The weapons you have—there are no such weapons anywhere. My father and some of the elders are confused. Nobody has said or guessed anything yet, but I have. Your clothes and the way you speak and like I have just said, the weapons. I think you come from a time in the future. But I can't understand about Sunday. She eats and drinks normally and I've seen her go behind bushes to pee. Not you, though. Sunday has the strength of a man and she fires the bow as though she has done so for years. Some of the younger women are talking about her. Not in a bad way, but they are starting to wonder. Tell me, Martha. I will say nothing."

Martha took Erika's hand and nodded slowly. "You're right, Erika, about the future. We come from a time many years ahead. I was born in 1625. Sunday was born in 1751 or 1752. Vardan was born in 1816. I think we are now back in 1066. We came here through a time gap. We have travelled back seven hundred and fifty years."

The numbed silence was almost deafening as Erika tried to understand what Martha had told her. She looked up at the bow top and thought of the sleeping child. Martha knew what she was thinking. Erika said nothing for a whole numbing minute then turned to face Martha.

"It's not possible, Martha. You're not making sense. You being born in 1625 and Sunday in 1751. If Vardan was born in 1816, it means Sunday was… over sixty when she gave birth…" Erika's voice trailed off.

"Sixty two or three," Martha said.

"How? It's nonsense. No woman can give birth in her sixties. Everybody is dead by that age," Erika replied.

Martha smiled, sighed and shook her head slowly, deliberately. She took Erika's hand.

"I tell the truth, Erika. Sunday and myself are of the undead. Wandering spirits, lost souls, of a time for us, in the distant past, but here now, near York. I was really and truthfully born in 1625 and Sunday over a hundred years later. We met on a ship in the Atlantic and became friends. We have been the closest of friends ever since and will always be. Vardan is half human, half of an undead mother. He will be immortal when he is fully grown. We – Sunday and me – sold our souls to the devil, or a son of the devil. I was killed by people from my village, on a ducking chair in 1643, for being a witch. Sunday was killed by musket shot in 1773. This creature called Lord Lucifer took our souls. He might be listening to me right now."

Erika stood with tears rolling down her face. She scuffed them away and looked at Martha, her face ashen and disbelieving. Slowly she started walking away. After a few steps, she turned, scuffing more tears away.

"Not possible, Martha. I'm a simple Nors Egersund woman, who can't read or write, but I know what you have said cannot be true. I'll see you in the morning." Erika walked away and left Martha staring after her.

A chill wind started and the skies darkened. Flashes of lightning lit up the dark, then the thunder rolled. Martha knew what was coming and prepared herself. A few moments later and a solitary figure appeared in front of her. Not the hideous cackling screeches of Lord Lucifer, or the winged flapping and mockery he emitted. This figure emerged from a shimmering red mist that prevailed all around the immediate area. A mix of animal and human; a head topped with wide curved horns to each side. It stood on hoofed feet.

Martha watched bewildered and with some degree of fright.

"Martha Budd. A long time since I have seen you," the figure said huskily.

Martha stared at the figure with wide eyes. She tried to focus but could not recognise the voice or the identity of the grotesque figure. It looked at her with piercing red eyes. Martha's eyes glinted red.

"I don't know you. I was expecting Lord Lucifer," Martha replied nervously.

"One of my brothers. The most evil of my brothers. You know me as Fimber O'Flynn."

Martha took a breath and stared intently at the figure. "You're—you're at the bottom of the sea."

"I will be in years ahead. I have that to come. Right now I am doing my duty for my father, Satan. Lucifer will take over from me in 1160 for his six hundred and sixty-six years' rule. He passes over to Mephistopheles in 1826. You have ten more years before he passes over to Mephistopheles. 1826 is an important year for you and your friend, Sunday Brown."

"I know, it's the year we can—"

"Take the Mark of the SWAN," Fimber interrupted with a sardonic laugh. "Escape from my brother's clutches. He will try and stop you, take your last favour and send you to the torture chambers. He will do that, Martha Budd, unless you are clever, very clever."

"What can I to do to stop him?" Martha asked.

Fimber laughed and shook his head. "I can't help you or tell you. It is something you have to work out yourself. I taught you as much as I could when we travelled together. Remember the things I told you. I gave you the answer. Go back into your memory and work it out."

"We chose to come here in 1066. We are going to try and find Jacindra. I followed the instructions on parchment, given to us by the Blingos."

"Yes, you were given a parchment by the Blingos, many years in the future. On that parchment are the names of places where time travel is possible. You found one by chance, but you might never find any of the others. They are not all in England. Each one can be found on the parchment. You have a special one with you, an infant called Vardan. He will grow to be the most feared and deadliest of my father's enemies. Satan and my brothers will try to kill him. Vardan's life will always be under threat, there will be no safe place for him, unless he knows where the time travel openings are."

"Why are you here, Fimber? You're a son of Satan, a devil. Why?"

Fimber laughed and shook his head. "My name is Drebmif, the seventh of seven sons of Satan. Because I am the seventh son, I cannot be killed outright, I have immunity to my father's demonic powers, so I decided I did not want to do his bidding anymore. I was tired of the repugnant tasks I had to do. The evil abominations I was expected to carry out, because I was a son of Satan. He couldn't have me destroyed, so he gave Lucifer the job of getting rid of me, without actually killing me. For many, many years Lucifer tried his best to get rid of me, but I was always one step ahead, until that day on the *Tintagel* when he finally caught me off guard. He sent me to the bottom of the sea, where I would remain for a thousand eternities."

"You changed your name to Fimber O'Flynn. Why that name?" Martha asked.

"Very simply, I took the first letter from my name and turned the others around. It sounded Irish, so I simply chose an Irish second name."

"Why are you here then, in 1066 and near York?"

"I am still doing my father's bidding, Martha. I still have ninety-four years left of my six hundred and sixty-six years' duty. We have to gather souls, as you know and send them on to Satan. There is a battle to take place near here in four months' time. A place that will be known as Stamford Bridge. The English King, Harold Godwinson, will destroy a Viking and Scottish army led by his brother Tostig and Hadradi, a Norse chieftain of the Jorvik tribe. Over three hundred boats will bring Tostig's and Hadradi's forces to York, along the Humber river and then up the Ouse and Derwent rivers. Hadradi's younger brother, Magnus, and a Scottish chieftain, Paul Thorfinson, will bring other invaders overland from Northumbria. An army of nine thousand will face the English Army led by Harold. They are expecting to meet no opposition and march on to York and burn the town, kill hundreds of innocent people and take many young women as prisoners. King Harold's fighters will surprise them and slaughter over seventy per cent of the Scottish and Norse invaders. Both Tostig and Hadradi will be killed, but hundreds of King Harold's men will also die. Hadradi's son Olaf and what is left of the invading army will run to the boats to escape, but only forty of the boats will be needed to take them back to sea. After the battle, Harold will take his tired fighters south, to face a Norman invasion. Five weeks' forced march to a place called Hastings, where Harold will then meet his death."

"You want me to point out dying fighters, like Lucifer made you and me do?" Martha said flatly.

Fimber shook his head. "No. No, lassie. Not here in 1066. You haven't actually been born yet, or your friend, Sunday Brown. So it is not your duty yet to do such abhorrent work. That is what I do with others like you, who have sold their souls."

"How can I protect Sunday and her son from your brothers?"

"Only one of my brothers can harm you at any one time, during their six hundred and sixty-six-year spell of duty. That is, except in the last year of the term. Lucifer will pass over duties to Mephistopheles in 1826 on the night of the summer solstice in June, but for the next one hundred and eighty-two and a half days to December the twentieth, the two will be together all the time. During these last six months, Lucifer and Mephistopheles will be at their most dangerous. Each will take the best of the chosen female souls to mate with, to produce offspring for duties on the Uptop lands. You have already been selected. They will both take you in turn. I mentioned that many centuries ago, one lost soul escaped the clutches of my brothers, using trickery and sorcery."

"Jacindra," Martha interrupted.

"Yes. She died in 65 AD, mortally wounded in a battle against the Romans and just before she died, sold her soul. She spent three hundred and thirty-three years working for Satan and then escaped. It was in the year 400 AD."

"So Jacidra has been free for six hundred and sixty-six years?"

"Precisely, and that is why you and Sunday are here in this year of 1066. It was fated to happen. She died a thousand years ago this year. She was twenty-four. The fiercest woman warrior of her day. Your friend Sunday Brown will meet her soon. As we speak, she is travelling north with members of her tribe, the Iceni. She can help you, Martha Budd. That is all I can say other, than to remind you that in 1826 your test of wisdom, courage, strength and determination will decide if you can escape from Lucifer and Mephistopheles. Remember all I have told you, Martha Budd."

The red mist hovered for a few moments and the figure of Fimber O'Flynn dispersed and vanished in the night air. Martha looked around, but her old friend had gone. From the bow top she heard a sound and saw Sunday's head appear over the side. Rubbing her sleepy eyes, Sunday looked down to where Martha was sitting on her chair.

"I heard voices, Missy. Yours and a man's voice, or it sounded like a man's voice. Grating, more like," Sunday said quietly and quickly climbed down.

"Fimber O'Flynn. He came in a red cloud and then disappeared," Martha replied.

"With seaweed wrapped around his head," Sunday joked.

"No. He came, but he came in the form of a devil. He was so ugly, hideous and mal-formed. Horns on his head and large hoofed feet. He told me about Jacindra and that she is on her way north with her tribe. We came here by a time travel gap and the year is 1066. We've come back seven hundred and fifty years in time and Fimber O'Flynn is the seventh son of Satan."

Sunday rubbed her eyes again and sat down in front of Martha. She gave a loud sigh and stared at her friend with bewildered eyes.

Martha took her hand gently, her own dead eyes with a hint of despairing incredulity. For several minutes she explained to Sunday what Fimber had told her. Sunday listened without interruption and stared impassively.

"You mean, somewhere on that parchment Jobsdone gave us, there are places where there is a time travel gap."

"Not exactly, Sunday. This year, 1066, is a thousand years since Jacindra died. Six hundred and sixty-six years since she escaped from the devil's clutches. You and she were destined to meet and that time is almost here. A battle is coming, at a place called Stamford Bridge and hundreds and hundreds will be killed. That's what Fimber said. Nine thousand Jorvik fighters against this English King and his army, but most of this Jorvik tribe will be slaughtered."

"So we have to do more soul picking?"

"Not here, it's not our time."

"Did you tell him about me and Vardan?"

"He already knew. They always know these things."

"What now then, Missy? Pack up and leave?"

"No. We help these people here to fight off the Angle tribe who come to rape, steal and kill."

"I agree, but then what? Where do we go?"

"Back to 1816 through the time gap. Read the parchment like Fimber mentioned. We have only used it to find the entrances to Blingoburbia and where we do Uptopper work. Somewhere in the script are listed time gap places. That's why we were told never to let Lucifer get his hands on it or now, obviously, none of Satan's sons."

"They never will, Missy. But what about Fimber O'Flynn, what happens to him?"

"When his duty spell finishes in 1160, he will probably go back to the bottom of the sea and stay there for ever, unless I can find a way to get him out."

"Make that a 'we', Missy. I'll help to get him out. And by then we'll have Vardan to help us."

"Sorted, then, but now you go back and get some beauty sleep."

Sunday climbed back into the bow top and yawned. "Back to my dream again. I was riding a horse at the side of Captain De Lacey and we were going to a castle where he lived."

Chapter Nineteen

September 1066

Weeks of shooting and archery training had restored confidence within the Nors Egersund tribe and the mood in the camp was at a high level. Both Sunday and Martha had become experts with the longbow. With her improved vision and extra strength, Sunday could send an arrow further than any of the men, to the wonder of almost all, except Hundorp. He had begrudgingly accepted that the tall, brown-skinned woman was not a spy for a rival tribe, but he had reservations about the woman's remarkable weapon skills. He himself was a fierce fighter and had killed many an enemy in fights with the battle axe and sword. Practice with weapons was one thing, using them in combat was another. He often laughed at the thought of Sunday fighting like a man; she was a woman and women cooked and looked after the tribe's children.

Berkak had no worries with Sunday. She was a good mother to her young son, but she was also confident and skilled with weapons and he guessed that in the face of an enemy she would fight without hesitation. With Vardan, she was not lacking in her care for the boy. Several of the Nors Egersund women helped with his daily requirements and enjoyed taking turns to satisfy his needs. Sunday and Martha had gained the tribespeoples' respect. Only the brooding Hundorp held doubts of the two women.

In the late afternoon one day, two young boys came racing into the camp, breathless and agitated. The older of the two lads ran to where Berkak and other men were fitting flint heads to arrows the women had made. Ardal, a tall fair-haired boy of fourteen, dropped to his knees and pointed backwards.

"The Angles are coming, Berkak. We saw lots of canoes by a river four miles away and many horses pulling carts. Lots of fighters with spears and swords. Korgan and me watched them making a camp. Then we ran back here."

Berkak took two coins from his pants and handed them to Ardal. "Give one to Korgan and well done, boy. Now go tell all the men I need to see them immediately."

A half hour later and Berkak had given his instructions to the assembled Nors Egersund men who had been trained in the recent weeks. Just over a hundred were armed and ready to fight, but instead of defending their own camp, the task now was to attack the Angles' camp that the two boys had seen earlier. The two muskets and two pistols had been handed to the best four marksmen. Sunday, Erica and two other young women fighters were to join the men, all with longbows, swords and battle axes. Martha was to remain at the camp to keep Vardan safe. Everything had been planned in case of taking the fight to the would-be invaders. Everyone carrying a longbow had a quiver, stock full of arrows. As well as a longbow, Sunday carried her sabre. The curved cavalry sabre had been looked upon with envy by all the men carrying a typical Dark Ages' sword.

Hundorp had scoffed at the strange sword Sunday carried. He had wielded his broadsword a few times to boast of its undoubted power, impressing a few of the younger men who were to take part in combat for the first time. Sunday had declined to show off and walked with the three other women as the small army set off. Erika was at her side and nudged Sunday as they followed the men.

"Hundmp is never happier than when he is picking fault with others. He is a true fighter and is unafraid in combat, but he has a chip on his shoulder. He wanted to be our tribe leader, but he was voted out. My father is as good in combat, but cleverer than Hundorp. He keeps our people together. He knows we are going to struggle to avoid being totally wiped out in future years, but he is a good man and a good leader. He desperately wants to get my son, Tordal, his grandson, back from the Angles, but fears he will die before he can."

"We'll get him back, I promise," Sunday remarked.

"How can you say that, Sunday? You don't know these barbarians. They're beyond reason," Erika replied.

"I understand this type of men. I was a slave on a ship once and this bigger ship attacked us and beat us, but our captain was a thinker as well as a good fighter. The other ships fighters robbed us of all our food, jewels and guns, but luckily they didn't kill us all. They sailed off and left us with nothing but our smaller ship. The captain was called Suarez and he rallied those of us who hadn't been put to the sword and we managed to get back to port. By a fluke of chance, this other lot who had robbed us, were also at this port. Suarez put together a bunch of his best men, including me and we captured the other captain's brother and a son outside a tavern. He tied the two up and put nooses around their scrawny necks and stood them on a couple of stools, the hanging rope over a tree branch. Suarez then calmly walked back to the tavern and in front of his opposite number and about thirty of his cutthroats, he simply told the other captain that unless he handed over his ship for our smaller one anchored in the bay, he would hang his son and brother. Three hours later, we were sailing on the tide with a fully stocked and armed ship. The other captain got his son and brother back and our old ship. The next day Suarez waited for our old ship to leave port and then blew it to bits.

"That is how you get your own things back."

Erika and the other two women had listened to Sunday and nodded with interest.

Sunday didn't have to say anything else. Erika looked at her with narrowed eyes.

"I think you mean, we should take two of the Angles captive and bargain for my son. Is that what you mean?"

"Exactly that, but not just two captives, we take six. Gives it a better chance. If they refuse to bargain, we kill one captive at a time and send them the head back."

There were gasps of revulsion from two of the women, but Erika nodded and walked forward to reach her father leading the group. A short break was taken as Sunday described what she had told Erika and the two other women. Hundorp had listened and found himself nodding at what Sunday had said.

He suddenly realised he was agreeing with the woman he had never trusted.

"We take twice that many captive and kill two at a time," he growled with menace.

"I agree," Sunday replied and saw a smile of approval on Hundorp's bearded face.

"Very well. You two take care of that little bit of mischief, but no killings unless I say so," Barkak said firmly. "Take four men to help. Any Nors Egersund fighter is worth two of any Angles; twelve captives it is."

The group set off again in good spirits, with regular glances at Sunday from the men, who were in awe of her presence within the war party. Erika was smiling at the thought of getting her son back. Even Hundorp had stopped complaining at everything Sunday did or suggested.

Two scouts who been sent ahead earlier, suddenly appeared ahead, carefully running back.

"A half mile ahead, the Angles are at camp like Ardel and Korgan reported. They are lying around eating and drinking. No sentries posted," one of the scouts remarked.

"How many are they?" Berkak asked as he waved his men to crouch down and rest.

"Not certain but we think about three hundred, maybe four hundred," the same man said.

"Four times more than us, but we have surprise on our side." Hundorp said glibly.

"We've trained for this day for weeks, so we attack straight away," Berkak remarked and signalled his men into the three groups they had decided. Ten minutes later and the three groups were in place, fifty yards apart. Torches were lit and the archers' slotted arrows with oil-soaked cloth fixed over the flint heads.

The four men holding the muskets and pistols were to hold back and shoot at any of the Angles who broke free and were within range. Odda and Ulvik were to reload the firearms for the shooters. They had practiced well and could reload three times in a minute. If a shooter fell, either Odda or Ulvik would take up the weapons. Sunday and her three female friends were to stay together in one of the three groups. Hundorp and twenty-five of the men were to hold back with broadswords and battle axes at the ready. As soon as the archers had sent fire arrows into the Angles, who would panic and run for cover, Hundorp's group would rush forward and slay the enemy at will. Archers would then fire their arrows at selected targets, avoiding hitting their own men.

Berkak waited 'til his three groups were ready with fire arrows lit. He held his wooden staff high and everybody watched and waited. The staff came down and eighty fire arrows sped high into the late afternoon sky. A second volley of eighty arrows followed within seconds, and a third and then a fourth. They caused the panic Berkak had mentioned and hoped for. Two hay carts were fired and set ablaze. Tents were fired and screaming Angles fighters ran in terrified blind panic. Berkak's staff was raised again and then dropped quickly, sending Hundorps twenty-five screaming battle axe and broadsword fighters, into the melee, hacking and thrusting. Forty of the archers now took up swords and raced after Hundorp's men.

Sunday and the remaining archers waited and watched for a chance to fire again. The four men holding the muskets and pistols waited patiently to shoot any of the Angles who broke from their hastily erected camp. They did not have to wait long. A group of Angles who had snatched up weapons were charging at the Nors Egersund archers who had followed Hundorp's men.

The two muskets fired and two Angles fell, with red hot shot in their bodies. The two pistols fired at two of the nearest Angles and one fell dead with a ballshot in his head. A few seconds later and all four firearms were fired again. Three more Angles fell and stunned into disbelief. Thirty or forty of their disbelieving comrades stopped running and looked around for support. The arrows struck them at will and a dozen fell dead. The remaining Angles, panic-stricken, turned to run back, but four shots rang out and two fell dead, two more wounded. The remaining terrified Angles broke and ran for cover. Three or four fell with arrows in their backs. The two musket men picked off two more Angles fighters.

A hundred yards ahead, Hundorp's men had slaughtered all before them. Twenty dead Angles had been torn apart and many more severely wounded. The arrows still rained down and one archer was picking the enemy off, one at a time. Sunday was in her element. Of thirty arrows she had carried, sixteen had found human targets, eleven of them killed.

Angles had run in all directions, some diving into the River Derwent to hopefully escape the slaughter behind them. In the distance, the sounds they heard were loud cracks and screams of their dying comrades. A thick pall of black smoke gathered over the Angles camp and horses that had been brought north had bolted. Dead and injured bodies lay everywhere in bloody heaps. Hundorp's men were killing at random. Heads had been cut off and limbs hacked away in merciless savagery. Twenty-five Angles women who had travelled with their men had simply dropped to the bloody ground, screaming for mercy, at least six of them bleeding from wounds. Two of the women were silent, ashen-faced and bewildered, but apparently ready for death, both trying to appear fearless.

Hildred Grimwalder and her seventeen-year-old daughter, Kristen, huddled together as they watched the bloodbath mercilessly taking place around them. In a moment of sheer panic, one of the other women, seeing a Nors Egersund axeman with his bloodstained Dane's axe held high, ready to kill again, scrambled to her feet and started running to nearby trees. The arrow thudded into the rear of her neck and she fell face down. Sunday grinned and slotted another arrow to her longbow. Erika had seen Sunday fire the arrow and shook her head.

The axeman saw the woman drop dead and cursed loudly. He turned to face the terrified Angle women and selected one to kill. Hildred Grimwalder pulled her daughter close and covered the girl's head. The Nors Egersund axeman raised his large Dane's axe and glared fiercely into the blue eyes of the older woman. The axe was raised high and two strong fists gripped it tight, ready to smash it onto the woman's head. The arrow struck the Nors Egersund man in his shoulder and he dropped the axe, falling to his knees.

Sunday smiled with satisfaction, then pulled one of her last arrows out and slotted it to her longbow. Erika smiled as her eyes fixed on Sunday's. There were nods of agreement between the two young women.

Within an hour the Angles had been routed. Over a hundred of their people lay dead, dozens more wounded. Eight Nors

Egersund had died and a similar number wounded. Other Angle tribes' raiders had perished in the River Derwent, trying to flee.

The remnants of the Angles had escaped and fled. Thirty-two of the Angles had been captured, including twenty of their women. Their leader, Joseph Grimwalder, was one of the captives, taken as he and one of his brothers, Peter, had tried to rescue his wife Hildred and daughter, Kristen. Peter had later escaped himself, but another brother, William, had perished to the broadsword of Hundorp and had been beheaded. Joseph Grimwald had been wounded twice in one of his legs and was unable to walk. His powerful arms were wrapped around his wife and daughter as he and his fellow captives were rounded up.

Jubilant Nors Egersund fighters gathered around the terrified and sullen captives. The two musket men proudly held their rifles aimed at the bewildered prisoners. The two pistol men were as equally proud as they strutted around, with loaded weapons. Between the four shooters they had killed over twenty of the Angle raiders.

Joseph Grimwalder was a beaten man. He had led four hundred and six of his well-trained fighters and over twenty women to raid the Nors Egersund camp in the northern territories. The Angles had raided the Nors Egersund camps before and had seen the normally peace-loving people as an easy touch. Trudging along the river bank with the other captives to the Nors Egersund camp four miles away, he feared for his wife's and daughter's lives.

His injured body was supported by two of the Angles men, each with wounds themselves. There was no sympathy from their captors as they were prodded and forced to march along. One of the Norse Egersund fighters was of interest; a tall, brown-skinned woman warrior who had a longbow around her shoulders and a curved sword with a noticeably blood-stained blade.

Four of the captors held strange weapons. Joseph Grimwalder had seen some of his fighters fall to an injury with no enemy fighters nearby. No arrows sticking from body wounds. He had heard strange noises in the distance and a split second later one of his fighters fell, dead or wounded. Long pieces of wood with metal attachments were carried proudly by the enemy fighters.

Over an hour later and with the light beginning to fade, Grimwald and his captive people were ushered into an animal pen and then bound hand and foot, with no gentleness. The two men carrying the long wooden fire sticks, were left to guard the captives.

After a half hour, with camp fires lit and sentries posted at intervals, Berkak ordered that the Angles' leader was brought to be interrogated. Hundorp wanted to have him butchered in front of the other captives, but Berkak dismissed the idea. Joseph Grimwalder had feared he would be killed and had seen the hatred in the eyes of some of the enemy fighters.

Berkak fixed his tired eyes on Grimwalder's pained, bearded face. He had seen the stocky man before, with a bearskin rug fastened around his upper body and a half round, riveted metal helmet. He had seen the Angles' chieftain mercilessly cut down some of his people in previous raids, including women. Berkak knew Hundorp and other elders wanted to kill the callous leader and take their time doing it.

Both men spoke in slightly different tongues, but could understand what the other said. With grunts of impatience from Hundorp, Berkak looked intently at Grimwalder and at the man's badly injured leg. He sniffed with contempt and looked once more at the man's face.

"You have my grandson and others of my people. You took them in one of your last raids. You will have them returned," Berkak said matter-of-factly.

"Or else what?" hissed Grimwalder.

"Or else you all die one at a time," Hundorp snapped with venom. "And you die last and I'll make sure it takes a week."

"You don't frighten me, you're just vermin," sneered Grimwalder.

Hundorp stood and pulled a burning stick from the blazing fire. He took it to where Grimwalder was lying and held it at arm's length. Berkak tugged Hundorp's sleeve, but the latter pulled away and stabbed it at the trussed mans injured leg. The scream cut into the evening air and startled everybody nearby, including the other captives. Grimwalder writhed in agony, but Hundorp was not deterred. He pushed the burning stick back into the fire and brought it out after a few seconds. Grimwalder watched with terrified eyes.

Hundorp held the burning stick a few inches from Grimwalder's face, then turned to one of his men a few feet away. "Bring the girl," he bellowed.

Berkak looked at him in alarm. "We don't hurt women."

"You don't, Burkak, and if you don't agree you won't get Tordal back alive." Hundorp laughed and put the stick back into the fire. "I'll get your grandson back, my way."

A couple of minutes later, the screaming daughter of Grimwalder was dragged across the ground by two of Hundorp's men. They dumped the girl in front of her father. Hundorp moved to the fear stricken girl and reached down and ripped the clothes from her upper body. Naked above the waist, the girl let out a pitiful scream as Hundorp pulled the burning stick from the fire and held it towards her breasts.

"I'll ask you politely, you filthy murdering bastard. Are you going to have our people returned?" Hundorp growled as he waved the stick at the screaming girl. From the animal pen, a woman's voice shrieked out hysterically. Hundorp grinned and looked at Grimwalder.

"Her mother, I reckon, the one she was holding on to for dear life when we brought her here. I'll ask you one more time. Our people you stole. We want them back."

"Go fuck yourself. My daughter is Angle and we don't scare easily," Grimwalder hissed. The girl screamed again. Her next scream made her father kick and writhe madly as the skin on her right breast seered off in a bloody mess. The smell of burning flesh hit everybody's nostrils. Her mother's voice shrieked out again from fifty yards away.

Grimwalder tried to reach Hundorp with his trussed feet, but they were stamped on by the latter.

"You evil bastard, I'll cut your balls off and make you eat them," snarled Grimwalder.

Hundorp laughed and pulled a knife from his belt. He stuck the long blade into the fire and stepped back. Everyone watched the knife, including Sunday and Martha, who had heard the screams and had come to see what was happening. Erika was with them. She dashed to her father, her face a mask of horror.

"What is happening, Father, what have you done?"

Berkak glanced at his daughter. "We're trying to get Tordal and the others back."

Hundorp stepped to the fire and withdrew the knife. The tip was glowing red and Hundorp grinned. Without a pause he walked to where Grimwalder was lying, the latter's eyes seething with hatred, but also with terror. Hundorp knocked the man's helmet off and grabbed a handful of his hair.

"I'll ask you again, one more time. Do we get our people back?"

Grirnwalder coughed up a mouthful of spit and duly spat it in Hundorp's grizzled face.

"They're Angles now and better for it. If you don't kill me, I'll be back and I'll take the time to personally cut your heart out," Grimwalder hissed and spat in Hundorps face again.

The latter grabbed Grirnwalder and roughly dragged him closer to the fire. Suddenly there was a call from a few yards away and Sunday stepped forward. She was holding both of the pistols. Everybody stared at the tall, brown-skinned woman. She walked to where Hundorp was holding his knife towards Grimwalder's lower body.

"I'll get the answer you want. Get the girl up on her feet," Sunday said to Hundorp.

Kirsten was hauled up and still bare breasted, with a large area of one breast burnt red, she stood whimpering and shaking. Sunday spotted a basket full of apples and pointed at them.

"Pass some over," she called to a man standing next to the basket. He picked out four and walked to Sunday. She lifted the sobbing girl's hands and put an apple in each one. Then she made the girl hold her arms out. The girl dropped the apples, so Sunday struck her sharply across the face. Once more she put an apple in each of the girl's hands and raised her arms. The girl was terrified, but held the apples firmly. Sunday picked an apple up and held it with her thumb lower and fingers at the top. She nodded to the girl and at the apples. Carefully the girl copied Sunday in holding the apples.

Pistols in her hand, Sunday marched thirty yards away, stopped, and turned and raised the first pistol. Everyone was watching in silence. Sunday took aim and before anyone could blink, the pistol cracked and one of the apples was split into shreds. The gasps of astonishment echoed around the immediate area. The girl screamed and dropped the remaining apple.

Sunday marched back, picked the apple up and slapped the girl again. This time she put the apple on the girl's head. It fell off and the girl was slapped harder. The apple was put back on her head and the girl desperately held herself as rigid as she could. Once more to stunned silence, Sunday marched away, this time going ten yards further.

Grimwalder had watched everything, but now he called out as the pistol was raised and held out in an extended arm, towards his terrified daughter.

"Stop the mad woman, stop her. She'll kill my daughter. You'll get your grandson back."

Hundorp shook his head and glared at Sunday. He was not going to be stopped from removing Grimwalder's testicles with the red hot knife. He crouched and was about to cut the man's pants away with the knife, but a loud pistol-shot to his side and the knife was blasted out of his hand. He screamed in pain and fell backwards. Sunday pulled ball shot and powder from a pocket and as she walked to a cursing Hundorp, she reloaded one of the pistols.

Hundorp was scrambling to his feet, but the pistol was levelled at his own testicles.

Sunday stopped five yards away and laughed at the cursing tribe elder.

"He said you get your grandson back. I believe him. If he lies about doing it, then cut his balls off. You keep him here and he sends two of his men back and they bring your people back. If they don't return, what you do with this lot you've taken prisoner is your business," Sunday said and lowered the pistol. She handed the pistols back to the two men who had earlier used them in the attack on the Angles camp.

Hundorp sniffed and scowled contemptuously at Sunday, but he knew she had done what he had failed to do and get a commitment from Grimwalder. He returned to the latter's daughter and pulled her back to where her father lay injured. The girl had pulled her upper clothes in place and flopped at Grimwalder's side, sobbing pitifully.

The red hot knife of Hundorp's was levelled at Grimwalder's lower body. Hundorp knelt down a couple of yards away and glared at the man.

"The darkie is good at what she does, but I'm very good at what I do. You want to keep your balls, make sure your men return with our people."

With the Angle prisoners secured in the animal pen and guards posted, the Nors Egersund tribespeople went to their beds. Sunday and Martha climbed into the bow top; Sunday ready for sleep as soon as she had settled Vardan, Martha sitting in her chair.

"Time to move on, Sunday," Martha said quietly.

"What year and where?" Sunday asked as she yawned.

"Seven hundred and fifty years ahead."

"How, what do we do, Missy?"

"We came to the year 1066 in the river. We go back again the same way, I hope. You, me, Vardan, Watson and our cart. We all came that way, so I'm assuming we go back that way."

"What about Jacindra? We never met her."

"I think the time isn't right just yet. She was travelling north, according to Fimber, so another time another place. Get some sleep, Sunday, and we'll set off at dawn."

Dawn broke with heavy rain falling, but Martha and Sunday had already packed everything and harnessed Watson to the bow top. They trundled away from the Nors Egersund camp before any of the tribe had awoken. Even the men guarding the Angle captives had fallen asleep, but a pair of wary, frightened eyes watched as the cart moved away towards the river. Kirsten Grimwalder lay between her father and mother in the animal pen. Her ankles and wrists trussed, she had not slept during the night, her injured breast keeping sleep at bay. The strange brown-skinned woman had saved her father from being mutilated and probably saved her own life. She watched until the cart disappeared from her sight.

A tear rolled down her dirty face. She wished she could have left with the two women and travelled to wherever they were going. Her life was a misery. Travelling with her deranged father and a mother who protected him and helped to raid the camps of peace-loving people, taking innocent people by force and reducing them to slavery and ill-treatment, even death. She was pleased her father had suffered at the hands of the Nors Egersund. Her love for him had gone after she had seen him raping young girls who had been captured in raids the Angles had made. The previous evening she had hoped the brutish Nors Egursund man had sliced her father's testicles off. The brown-skinned woman had saved him from being mutilated, but he would still suffer that horrendous torture. The boy who her father had taken in an earlier raid had been killed on the way back to their camp. He had escaped and run away, but had been quickly recaptured. Her father had beaten the boy to an inch of his life.

The three-year-old boy had had eyes of different colours and Kirsten had looked after him for a few days before he ran away. A few hours after being recaptured, the boy, with a broken arm and blinded in one eye, had fallen into a river and drowned.

Kirsten looked with hate-filled eyes at her father as he slept a troubled sleep on the wet ground of the animal pen. He was a sleeping dead man. The Nors Egersund brute would have his day in the weeks ahead.

The heavy rain made it hard work for Watson to pull the cart along the wet ground.

Sunday had jumped down and moved to Watson's side to help the willing horse move along, but with the river in sight, a hollow in the ground caused one of the cart wheels to become stuck. Watson pulled on his harness as Martha gently tried to urge him along and Sunday tried to heave the wheel out of the hollow, by pushing with her great strength, but the wheel sank deeper into mud.

"It's no good, Missy, the wheel is sinking deeper," Sunday called as she scrambled upwards from behind the front wheel she had been trying to pull upwards. Martha jumped down and looked at the part submerged wheel. Together they heaved at the wheel as Watson took the strain on his harness. The wheel moved and there was a whoop of joy from the two young women. Then it moved forward a bit more and from the rear, a husky female voice called out.

"Push! Push harder, don't stop."

Sunday and Martha did not look back, but instinctively heaved and pushed harder. The front wheel slowly turned and then it broke free of the muddy hole. With gasps of relief Martha and Sunday looked back. The woman at the rear was mud splattered, but smiling.

"Thank you, err—" Martha called as she stepped away a stride. The other woman wiped her muddy hands on the sides of her bare upper legs and walked forward. Straightened and flicking her long golden hair back, she stepped confidently towards Martha and Sunday. She was the same height as Sunday, the same age, pale-skinned and attractive. Her hair was held in place by a band of engraved silvery metal. Around her shoulders, held in place by a gold brooch, was a reddish cloak of woven material. A thin, silky white vest over firm breasts that could just be seen through the material. A brown cowskin skirt, cut with tassles that was just above her knees. Strapped to her upper calves were bands of soft leather, criss crossed upwards from booted feet.

"My name is Jacindra. I am of the Iceni tribe," the young woman said calmly. "You are not from this time. You travel alone with no men to protect you. You are both of the undead."

"We are. And so are you, Jacindra." Martha said politely.

Jacindra nodded, her blue eyes settled on Sunday. "You are a warrior woman, I can tell. You come from a far land?"

"How did you guess?" joked Sunday.

Jacindra's eyes narrowed and she looked puzzled.

Martha laughed. "My friend jokes, but she does come from a far land."

Jacindra nodded slightly and looked at Martha. "You're from Britain though. Where?"

"A place called Towton Meadows, in the south," Martha replied.

"Wessex. You're a Saxon?"

"Probably, but it's in Berkshire."

Jacindra looked doubtful, but smiled. "I am from the east, in the fenlands. The Romans killed me a long time ago, not long after they killed my mother. She was a queen of the Iceni. Her name was Boadicea. She hated the Romans as I did. They left Britain six hundred years ago with their tails between their legs. Just before I died, I sold my soul to Beelzebub, one of Satan's sons, in return for paradise in eternity. He lied to me but I tricked him three hundred and thirty-three years later and escaped. Since then I travel these lands and slay the devil's offspring. There are many of them, but there are those who fight with me. What are your names and why are you here in Northumbria, in a year before your own times?"

Martha looked from Jacindra to Sunday, who she knew was carefully scrutinising the Iceni woman. "I'm called Martha and my friend is called Sunday. We came to the year 1066 by choice. We came through a time gap and brought a baby boy with us. We dropped into a time gap when Sunday was giving birth a few months ago, in the river ahead."

Jacindra picked up on the mention of childbirth and looked up at the bow top. If there was a baby it had to be inside the bow top.

"The baby is asleep in your strange cart?" Jacindra said.

"Yes, he's sleeping. His name is Vardan," Sunday replied.

"He is an immortal, then? There are only a few such beings on this earth. Can I see him?" Jacindra asked, looking at Sunday.

Martha looked at Sunday, who nodded. Then she climbed into the bow top and carefully lifted the sleeping infant in protective arms. Jacindra looked up and smiled. Martha handed him down to Sunday. The latter held him carefully, allowing Jacindra a full view of his dark features, black tousled hair and pinky brown skin. He was wrapped in a soft blanket.

"He is so beautiful. So boyish." Jacindra remarked.

"His father was a cavalry officer who died in battle," Sunday said proudly.

"Died in battle? Which battle?"

"Waterloo, in a country called Belgium," Sunday replied. Jacindra looked puzzled again.

"Gaul. I think it was called Gaul, before it was called Belgium," Martha interrupted

"Maybe it was in Belgae, a country my mother visited when she had meetings with the Salians and the Franks. But there are many tribes in Gaul who, like my tribe, the Iceni, fought the Romans in many battles. Our friends of the Trinobantes tribe in Mercia fought the Romans alongside the Iceni. Together we defeated the Romans at Mancetter, but we lost hundreds in the battle. The Romans had help from the Jutes and the Angles tribes from Germania who had been promised large areas of our lands. I kill any of the Jutes or Angles that I come across."

"We've just helped a tribe near here fight a raiding army of Angles. We beat them and sent them running," Sunday said proudly.

"Which tribe did you help?" Jacindra asked as she gently ruffled Vardan's dark hair.

"They are called Nors Egersund. Only about two hundred left now," Martha replied.

"They are descended from the Vikings. I've heard of them. They had over two thousand tribes people many years ago, just like the Iceni, before the Romans came to Britain. In battles with the Roman invaders and others sold into slavery, we have lost three quarters of our people. Can I hold your son for a few moments?"

"Of course, as long as you don't steal him," Sunday said good-humouredly.

"I wanted sons, just like my mother, but neither of us had any. I have had sons since I have been undead, but not before I died," Jacindra remarked and carefully held the sleeping child.

He stirred and opened his eyes, looking into the deep blue eyes of Jacindra. For long moments the two held the gaze, then Jacindra kissed him on the forehead and passed him back. Vardan closed his eyes and drifted back into sleep.

"Do you see your sons?" Martha asked.

"Sometimes, but they are all over the world, fighting the forces of evil. I saw the look in the boy's eyes just now and felt the power in his young body. He will be a great warrior, but you must look after him before he leaves you. The offspring of Satan will try and kill him."

"We know, and they will not get a chance to harm a hair on his head," Martha replied.

"He is lucky to have two mothers," Jacindra said and reached forward to touch Vardan, keeping her hand gently on his head. "I pass over the blessing of Boadicea and for Vardan to be safe from harm and for him to be a great leader of men."

Sunday kissed her son and smiled. "Will we meet again?"

"We'll meet again, but in your time. I travel through time like you do and we will meet when you both receive the Mark of the SWAN. I have known of you both and there are things we can share. Go back to your time and we'll meet again."

Jacindra pulled the red cloak around her body and walked away, as Martha and Sunday watched in silence. There was no look back and in moments she was gone from sight.

Martha put Vardan back to his bed and climbed onto the driving seat. A flick of the reins and Watson took the weight of his harness, pulling steadily towards the river. Sunday walked at the side of the bow top, her eyes searching the area ahead, where Jacindra had walked. Martha was looking for Jacindra as well, remembering it was exactly a thousand years since Queen Boadicea's daughter had been killed. She knew it had been fated for her and Sunday to pass back in time to meet Jacindra and for Vardan to be touched by the warrior woman.

The bow top reached the river bank and Martha let Watson pull the cart into the shallows.

Collecting Vardan, she stepped down and took Sunday's hand once more. The two held Vardan, stepped into the water and waited.

"Back to 1816 then, Missy?" Sunday asked.

"1816 Sunday and then we look forward to 1826, when Vardan gets spreckled again," Martha replied.

Chapter Twenty
Aire and Calder Canal
West Riding of Yorkshire

July 1826

The new waterway twisted its way east and west, below a low hillside where three boys had been playing and practicing archery since the mid-morning. Hundreds of small dark figures toiled in the sun below the hillside, some filling any of the dozens of horse-drawn carts with soil and rubble, others still digging and carrying excavated material to ever increasing piles for removal. Six months earlier and there had been three times the labour force on the site. The boys had been sitting for a few minutes, watching the workmen.

"I don't want to be a labourer when I'm a man," Vardan declared as he picked up his longbow. His arrow thudded into the circular target laid over a hay bale and nestled at the side of his fourth shot, a few minutes earlier. The two boys he practised with watched in awe at their friend's excellence with the longbow. Edward Longley and Billy Tordoff had smaller bows and both had fired three arrows, but only the latter's second arrow had hit the mark, but several inches from the middle.

"How can you shoot like that, Vardan?" Edward asked ruefully as the boys walked to retrieve their arrows.

"My mother taught me and my Aunt Martha. I started with a bow like the ones you use. I was six when I started. It's easy as soon as you learn how to pull back the drawstring."

"Let me try again, Vardan. I'm sure I can do it," Billy said and put his own bow down. He was a stocky lad with shoulder-long fair hair, a year older than Vardan. He took the longbow from his friend. He huffed and puffed, steadied himself and raised the longbow. Vardan passed him one of his arrows and stepped away.

Billy slotted the arrow in place and gripped the bow's thicker middle. He pulled on the taught string, but it only twitched back a couple of inches. He pulled again, but failed to increase the pull back. He tried a third time, his chubby face flushing red. The arrow dropped from the string and his friends laughed.

"Fuck, fuck!" he cursed, handing the longbow back. "It's not bloody possible. I'm bigger than you, Vardan and a year older. How do you do it? You're not normal!"

Vardan picked up the arrow and slotted it to the drawstring. His lips touched the waxed string and he narrowed his eyes. The arrow sped from the longbow and struck the canvas target almost in the centre. Billy and Edward gasped.

"Robin Hood couldn't do that every time," Edward laughed, shaking his head.

"No one could beat Robin Hood," Billy scoffed as he turned to walk away.

"You're jealous, Billy Tordoff. You and me will only get jobs as labourers, digging ditches or hauling rocks like our dads have been doing on yon canal this past year. Or grafting our arses off down a black hole of a pit. Vardan will be able to pick and choose what he does. He can read and write and speaks French as well as our Yorkshire lingo. He's cleverer than us," Edward remarked as he slotted another arrow to his bow. It sped away and glanced off the top of the hay bale. "Yes! I hit the hay bale this time."

Vardan took aim again and his arrow followed the first ones into the centre of the improvised target. Billy Tordoff had stopped a few yards away to watch. He sighed dejectedly as he saw Vardan's sixth arrow hit centre. He flopped down onto the grass to wait for his friends.

"My dad's going to get a job at the local pit when he finishes on the canal next month."

"Where's your dad, Vardan?" Edward asked as he walked with Vardan to collect the arrows.

"He was killed at the battle of Waterloo, a few years ago. He was a cavalry officer. I'm going to join the cavalry when I'm older. I want to ride in a cavalry charge like my father did and kill lots of enemy soldiers. I'm going to be a Lancer and call my horse Loire after my Uncle Vidal. He was a friend of my father and his horse was called Loire."

"Why not call your horse after your father?"

"Because his horse was called Vardan. Might be a bit confusing."

"Oh, yeah, it would be. Vardan is not English, though, is it?"

"French. My mother is French."

"She and your aunt Martha are real bonny women. My dad says so. My Ma is a bit jealous of them. She says they never look any older, or get any fatter. Why don't you live in a cottage like most people?"

"Because we move around a lot, different places. Anyway, we're off soon, along the lanes towards York. Meeting some friends my ma and aunt know."

"You're coming back to Knottingley, though, aren't you?" Edward asked as they walked back.

"Not sure, Eddie. My ma wants to go to America. Before I was born, she lived over there. There's this place called Louisiana and they speak French as well as English. They've even got big snakes and alligators. I want to kill an alligator with my knife and make things from its skin."

"Do you think I could go to America? We could meet up."

"I'll ask my ma if you can come with us," Vardan replied as he slotted an arrow to his longbow. Edward pointed to a field gate, sixty or seventy yards away.

"Bet you can't hit the gatepost," Billy Tordoff called.

"How much?"

"I'm skint, but two duck eggs," Billy called across.

"Done. Top foot of the left gatepost, in the middle."

"If you miss, what do I get?" Billy asked.

"A shilling."

"You ain't got a shilling, you fibber."

"My ma and aunt have. Lots, even gold sovereign and jewels. They keep them in a secret place in our bow top."

"You're fibbing, Vardan Brown. Only kings and queens have jewels," Billy scoffed.

"Then my ma and aunt are queens. They're rich. And you better have two duck eggs."

"I can get them easy enough. I often pinch them from a farm I know."

Vardan sniffed and took an arrow out and slotted it to the longbow. Billy and Edward stood to his side and watched as Vardan put his lips to the drawstring and took a breath. He effortlessly withdrew the bowstring as Billy watched with envy. The arrow ran swift and true and struck the left side of the gatepost, near the middle top. Without a moment's pause, Vardan quickly slotted a second arrow to his bow and the arrow sped away, this time striking the right post, middle top.

The other two boys were dumbstruck and stared wide-eyed at the two arrows embedded in the gateposts. Vardan walked and withdrew his arrows. His face was beaming.

"Two duck eggs for each arrow," he quipped with a wry grin.

"Yeah, two for each post, Billy," Edward agreed.

Billy Tordoff sniffed and reluctantly nodded. "In two years' time, I'll be better than you, Browny. I'm gonna practice every day."

"You could practice every day for the rest of your life and never be half as good," Edward scoffed and patted Vardan's back. Billy huffed and walked ahead in silence.

The Following Day

"Ma, why are we going to York?" Vardan asked as he brushed Watson.

"To see a place we visited a long time ago. And in two weeks' time we have an important meeting with some friends," Sunday replied as she cooked a meal over a fire.

"Do I know them?"

"Not really, it's a long time since your aunt and I saw them."

"Can we come back to Knottingley afterwards?"

"Your aunt and I have decided to return to America. You'll like it over there, lots to see and so much space. It's a new country and it needs young men like you will be."

"I like England, though, Ma. I want to join the army when I'm older and get into the cavalry like Pa did. There's probably no cavalry over there."

"Oh, there is, Vardan. I promise. They have soldiers just like there are in England."

"Will you still do jobs like you and Aunt Martha do here? I've seen you clearing the places where people tip rubbish, or where the ground is covered with brambles, weeds and nettles and then put it all back. Why do you do it?"

Martha had been sitting in her chair, reading, and looked across to where Vardan was cleaning Watson. Sunday looked at Martha, shrugged and walked to her, holding a hand out. They took each other's hands, looking at a curious Vardan. He smiled, collected his horse items and let Watson wander away to continue grazing.

"I also wonder why you hold each other's hands from time to time. We're not normal people, are we? Billy Tordoff said I was not normal. And Edward Longley asked me why you and Aunt Martha don't ever look older or get fatter. And why doesn't Aunt Martha ever eat or drink, or go to sleep? I'm old enough to be told things, you know."

Martha smiled and looked at Sunday, who had feared the day would come when Vardan started asking questions. She indicated for Vardan to come closer. He took a stool at her side and sat down. Sunday was kneeling at her other side.

For the next half hour, Martha explained what had happened to her and Sunday. Vardan didn't say a word, he just sat and listened to his aunt. Martha finished speaking and settled back in her chair. Her blue eyes had watched Vardan closely.

"You're a ghost, then, Aunt Martha?" he asked calmly.

"Yes, Vardan, I am," Martha answered.

"Is my ma a ghost as well?" Martha glanced at Sunday and then back to Vardan, his young face almost expressionless.

"Your mother did die, Vardan, but she recovered to be able to eat, drink and sleep, just as you can do. You are both very able-bodied people with very special powers. You can never die."

"You mean I'm immortal."

Martha looked at Sunday for support. Sunday half smiled and nodded agreeably.

"Yes, Vardan, you're immortal, like your ma."

"So in a fight I will never get killed?"

"Unless you lose your head in combat. There are those who will try and kill you, but you have the same powers. There are others, though, who will be like you and not evil like your enemies. You will have to find them and join forces."

"Where will I find them, Aunt Martha?"

"They will find you, Vardan. Your mother and I met one of the good immortals not long after you were born. Her name is Jacindra and she died a long, long time ago, before your ma and I died. She is a warrior woman and hunts down the evil ones. Find her and travel together."

"Am I powerful now, a proper immortal warrior?"

"Not yet, Vardan. Around the year 1840, you will be fully grown and ready to seek out the evil ones. Your body will finish growing then and like your ma and me, you will never look any older. It can be good, but not all the time. There will be things you will miss."

"Do you miss these things, Aunt Martha?"

"Oh yes, Vardan, I do. I would have been long dead now and hopefully in heaven, but because I sold my soul, I have to travel the earth, doing the devil's bidding. I wish I had never done it and had just died and gone to heaven."

"Why do you hold hands with my mother?"

"Because we learned, from some little people, good people, that when we hold hands, the devil or his children cannot hear what is being said."

"Who are the little people you mention?"

"You will meet them before you go your own way. They are the ones who we clear up after. They come from Blingoburbia."

"Can I see them when they come out again?"

"Not sure, but we'll ask. We have to see them on the eighth of August. It's a special day for your ma and me, we receive the

Mark of the SWAN. The SWAN is their symbol and it allows entry to Blingoburbia for bearers of the mark."

"Will I have the mark?"

"When you reach twenty four, yes, but probably not before, unless it is offered."

Sunday had listened and smiled at Vardan, reaching out her other hand. He took his mother's hand, squeezing gently, and smiled at her.

"I understand what Aunt Martha has told me, Ma and I'm pleased that I am like you. Will I be welcome in Blingoburbia when I am grown?"

"I'm sure you will, Vardan. They need protecting from the many other tribes of small people, because as there are different tribes in the Uptop world, some good, some bad. There are good and bad tribes of small people."

"What is Jacindra like? Is she a good warrior?" Vardan asked.

"A truly great warrior. Beautiful, tall, with long golden hair. She is from a tribe called the Iceni and they had many battles with the Romans, hundreds of years ago. Her mother was a queen of the Iceni people. Boadicea and she died fighting for her people."

"I'll fight the bad people, Ma. I'll fight with Jacindra at my side." Vardan stood and walked to the bow top. He collected his longbow and arrows and set off to practice his archery. Martha watched him go and smiled.

"He will be so strong when he is grown, Sunday. You must be very proud of him."

"More than life, Missy. He is your child as well and we must protect him from danger."

Martha stood from her chair and kissed Sunday on the head. "We have to go soon, Sunday. Time to receive our Mark of the SWAN. We could find the river where you gave birth to Vardan and let him see where he was born. Then let's see if we can find the Nors Egersund camp."

"It was a long time ago, Missy. They will all be dead now," Sunday laughed.

"I know. Seven hundred and sixty years ago."

Sunday laughed and shook her head. "Vardan is that old!"

"I suppose you could say that. But I think of him as a ten-year-old boy," Martha replied. "Unless he asks, we'd better just let him carry on thinking he is ten years old, not a little old man with a white beard and a walking stick." The two shook their heads and started giggling as they started to collect things together for the journey to York.

As soon as they had packed things for the journey, Sunday decided to go and buy eggs, bread and milk. Martha sighed and realised it was one of the things she missed, buying food for a meal. Sunday kissed her and set off along a track. It was warm and a blue sky had a few cotton wool clouds drifting slowly overhead. Watson had wandered to the far side of the field he was in and Martha set off to bring him back. She stopped for a few minutes to sit on the grass and reflect on what they had to do.

Twenty minutes later, she was leading the horse by a short rope and noticed a man outside the bow top. Tying Watson to a fence rail, Martha hurried to where the man was standing. He had his back to Martha and was looking up into the cart. He heard Martha approaching and turned to face her, but spoke loudly to someone in the cart.

"What do you want, mister?" Martha called, stopping a few yards away.

The man stared wide-eyed at Martha, then looked up into the bow top. He spoke again, loudly, and a dirty face appeared from within the cart. Martha had never seen the men before and signalled for the second man to get down. He was fat, with untidy, greasy fair hair. He scrambled down immediately. A moment later, another man, thinner, taller and of a similar age to the fat man appeared, holding the tin box that Sunday kept her valuables in. Looking older than their late thirties, scruffy and unshaven, though all had heavily whiskered, ruddy faces, the three looked sheepishly at the young woman. The tall man, in a well-worn woollen jacket and baggy trousers, carefully opened the lid to the box. His dirty face twisted into a smile as he saw the contents.

"Fucking hell, Sam. Your Billy wasn't kidding! There's a fortune here in gold pieces, let alone the jewels. Probably duds, I reckon, but we might get a guinea or two fer 'em at a trader's.

Give the woman a slap and let's piss off, before the kid and the other woman comes back."

Martha stepped forward and made a lunge at the nearest man, but he was quick and avoided her, kicking out and catching her in the stomach. It wasn't pain, but the ferocity of the kick that sent Martha stumbling away and tripping over the bow top cart rails. It was the first man Martha had seen who had kicked her and he dived after her, to wrestle her back down as she tried to gather herself. The fat man joined him and together they pinned her to the ground. A few feet away, the man holding the jewel box was still ruffling through the contents. He pulled out a gold chain with a ruby dangling from it.

"Harry, give us a hand here. We'll shag her before we piss off," Sam Tordoff called as he clamped a hand over Martha's mouth.

Harry Bennet dangled the ruby from a dirty hand as he sat on Martha's chair. "We'll get a few bob for this, Sam. It's bloody massive, pity it's just a piece of junk."

Sam Tordoff was holding the struggling woman down and glared at Bennet. "Fuck the trinkets, Harry, all I want is a share of the gold pieces. Give me and Paul a hand to strip this bitch, then we'll all have a go, but me first."

Harry Bennet closed the box lid and put it on the chair. He rushed to help his two friends, who had managed to pull Martha's skirts to her upper body. She struggled to stop her underclothes being removed, but they were ripped from her and strong hands pulled her threshing legs apart. Sam Tordoff unbuttoned his pants and pulled them down as the other two men looked on, with Martha helpless to resist.

"Give her a good 'un, Sam and be quick, I'm as hard as hell." Harry Bennet laughed as he pushed down aggressively on Martha's writhing body.

"Hold her still, then, Harry, I'm nearly in," Tordoff replied as he shoved his penis hard up Martha. He thrust a few times, then relaxed, moaned and withdrew with a loud gasp of delight. He took over from Bennet to hold Martha down, as his friend removed his own pants.

Bennet found it hard to penetrate the struggling woman, but a fist from Tordoff struck Martha in the face and it gave his excited friend the few moments needed to enter the young woman. Bennet took his chance and thrust into Martha forcefully as his two friends laughed and renewed the pressure on her body. It was hopeless struggling, so Martha relaxed and lay back to let the rapes finish. Bennet reached his climax and pulled out to allow the third man to take his place. Paul Lupton had already unbuttoned his pants and gladly took his place between Martha's legs. He was slower than his friends and they laughingly mocked his laboured efforts.

The knife struck him in the head and the gush of his blood spurted over Martha's face.

It took a few moments for the other two rapists to realise what had happened, but Sam Tordoff let go of Martha as Lupton's body slumped forward over Martha. Tordoff scrambled to his feet and pulled a knife from his jacket, turning to see where the knife thrower was. He saw a figure running towards them from thirty or so yards away. He grabbed Harry Bennet and pulled his terrified friend from Martha.

"It's that darkie bitch, Harry. Get the box and run," Tordoff called as he faced Sunday's figure, approaching fast.

The arrow sent him staggering sideways and he crashed into the side of the bow top. Harry Bennet screamed and grabbed for the jewel box, but an arrow struck him in the chest and he dropped to his knees.

Wounded and bleeding, Tordoff slumped to the ground as Sunday reached Martha, who was struggling up, wiping blood from her face. A few feet away, Harry Bennet pitched forward onto his face, the arrow pushed through his body and the arrow head protruding from his back. Vardan arrived with another arrow slotted to his longbow.

Tordoff looked around at the dead bodies of his two friends and then up at the three figures staring at him. He pulled Vardan's arrow from his side, screamed with pain then threw it away.

"You'll all hang for this, you mad bastards. I'll have you arrested by the end of the day, the kid as well. I'll watch them string you all up and laugh my cock off."

Martha had wiped most of the blood from her face and walked to where Sam Tordoff was sitting by the bow top. She reached down to him and offered her hands. He sniffed and hesitated, but Martha took one of his grubby hands and he allowed himself to be pulled up.

"Take a seat on the chair and let me tend the wound," Martha said, but Tordoff resisted and tried to pull away. Martha persisted and pulled him gently to her chair. He reluctantly sat down, wincing with pain from the arrow wound.

"I'm still going to have you arrested for cold blooded murder," Tordoff hissed.

"The three of you raped me, don't forget. You can be hanged for that," Martha replied as she touched her lips with two fingers. Before he could resist, she touched her fingers to the side of his fat face. He stared at her and shook his head.

"Your word against mine."

Sunday stepped forward and laughed. "My word against yours, mister, and my son saw what you were doing to my friend. We'll take our chances with a magistrate. Now I think it best if you just go and get on with your miserable life. We'll bury your two friends before we go."

Tordoff stood from the chair and scooped up his knife. He sniffed again, wiped snot from his running nose and trudged away. He had walked about fifteen yards then turned and raised the knife in his uninjured arm. Sunday had turned to help Martha with her blood-soaked clothes, but Vardan was watching Tordoff with hawk-like eyes. The knife arm went up a bit more, but the arrow sped away and struck Tordoff in his throat. He fell backwards in a heap into thick bushes. Sunday and Martha heard him fall and turned to look, then ran to where Tordoff had fallen. Blood was gurgling from his throat and his eyes were glazed and rolling.

"He was going to throw the knife, Ma," Vardan said as he arrived.

"We should have taken it from him," Sunday said as she put a comforting arm around Vardan's shoulders. "You did the right thing."

"I just killed two men, though, Ma."

"They were bad men, Vardan. Bad men," Martha said as she hugged the boy.

"Will I go to Hell now?"

Martha and Sunday shook their heads and said, 'No,' in unison.

Chapter Twenty-One
The River Derwent

August the seventh 1826

Martha found the place where the little bottle was buried and scooped it out patiently.

Sunday looked into the pebbled shallows at the side of the river, holding Vardan's and Martha's hands. A few moorhens at the far side dived every few seconds to find grubs. The morning was dry but cool and the surface of the river had a few ripples rolling along.

Vardan looked up at his mother and aunt. "Why are we here?" he asked wonderingly.

"You were born here, Vardan," Sunday replied. "We buried the little bottle that held spreckle dust and it was sprinkled over your tiny body. I was standing up to my waist and you popped out and your aunt Martha held you, then spreckled you."

"I was born in a river, so I was wet through and I was spreckled?"

"Spreckled and very wet, but you will be able to survive in any sea, river or lake, anywhere in the world," Sunday said with pride.

"How soon. Now?"

"When you are fully grown. Tomorrow your aunt and I will take the Mark of the SWAN. Then we can go into Blingoburbia and help the little people. We have already been spreckled with star and moondust and I think you will receive the Mark of the Swan."

"What does spreckling do?" Vardan asked.

Martha smiled at him. "It protects you and it makes you small when you enter Blingoburbia. When you return to the up top, you go back to full size. Spreckling is a reward for good behaviour. The Blingo people can only come up to the Uptop lands if they have been spreckled. They are normal people who breathe and eat and so on, but they live in the earth in a wonderful land of tunnels and large caverns. Like your mother and me, they live for a long time, but they are not owned by any of the devils. There are other little people who are in league with the devil, but such as you, an immortal, can help them by ridding their queendom of the warlike little people. When you are fully grown, you will have a lot of work to do, both up here in the up top and down in Blingoburbia. You were specially chosen to be able to do the tasks that an immortal warrior can do."

"Why can't I do these tasks now, Aunt Martha? I'm stronger than other boys of my age. I can fire an arrow further and more accurately than them."

"Because you're not ready or old enough yet, Vardan. There are a lot of skills you need to learn. Be patient and in a few years you will be ready. Help your mother and me to find a camp we visited many centuries ago and in the morning we will meet the Blingo people."

The following day with the bow top tucked into a clearing a couple of miles further along the track at the side of the river, and Watson tethered, the three set off to try and find the Nors Egersund camp. Martha and Sunday knew it was a hopeless task, but it passed some time for the rest of the day. Vardan carried his longbow and arrows confidently, his eyes watching for any sign of danger, to the amusement of Sunday and Martha.

They sat for a while on a fallen tree that had blown down in a storm, Martha and Sunday watching Vardan shooting his arrows in practice. They marvelled at his skill with the longbow, almost every arrow hitting a target they picked out for him. His mother had suggested a broken branch, hanging limply from where it had broken away from the main branch. It was eighty yards distant and Vardan had boasted he would hit the slim section still holding it to the main branch.

Vardan grinned and touched the drawstring with his lips. His eyes narrowed and his fingers flexed. Then a movement under the tree caught his attention. A man was standing below the tree. He relaxed his grip and turned to his mother.

"There's someone below the tree," he called. Sunday put a hand up to shield her eyes and peered intently across the field. Sure enough, the tall figure of a man was standing motionless where Vardan had spotted him. He appeared to be carrying a musket slung over his shoulder. Sunday told Vardan to stay where he was, but to keep an arrow at the ready and for Martha to stay with him. Her hand gripped one of the knives she always carried.

As she steadily walked across the field, Sunday realised the man did have a musket slung over a shoulder, but he also had two pistols tucked into a belt. His clothes were odd and reminded Sunday of a tribesman from hundreds of years earlier. Twenty yards nearer him, Sunday gasped in surprise and recognised a young man from the Nors Egersund tribe. It was Odda, the brother of Erika and son of Berkak. His blonde hair was the same straggled length to his shoulders. The eyes the deep blue of most of his tribe.

He smiled as she approached and walked to her and thrust his arms around the startled brown-skinned woman. From back along the field, Vardan tweaked the drawstring of his longbow and held the steel tipped arrow at the ready. Martha touched his arm gently.

"They're embracing, Vardan, it's somebody your mother knows."

"I don't kill him then?"

"No, you don't kill him." Martha replied firmly.

Sunday held away and looked into the dead blue eyes of Odda. There was no life in his eyes and his face was a whiteish grey colour. His tunic was bloodstained and there was a finger missing from one of his hands.

"I knew you would come back, Sunday. I've waited for so long," Odda remarked and slumped down to the grass, putting the musket down carefully. Sunday beckoned across to Martha and Vardan. A few minutes later and the three were at Odda's side as he sat with his back to the tree. He explained what had happened to his tribe and brought tears to Sunday's face as she listened. Martha had taken one of his hands and held it gently.

"They were all killed, wiped out?" Sunday asked tearfully.

Odda nodded, "Even the children. King Harold had sent messengers to all the villages around Stamford Bridge, to rally men old enough to fight the Vikings. Myself and thirty of our men went to help Harold and his army fight off the Vikings. Hundreds more men from other villages rallied to help the English Army and succeeded in driving the Vikings away, but only myself and four of the thirty from my tribe survived."

"When did the Angles and the Jutes attack your camp?" Martha asked.

"Six months later, in March the following year. We had fewer than forty strong enough men left to defend our camp. There were over four hundred of them. We had little ammunition left for the muskets and pistols you gave us. We killed about a hundred of the enemy fighters, but after the ammunition was finished they swarmed all over us, hacking and stabbing. They butchered everybody, men, women and children."

"You were killed?" Sunday asked.

Odda nodded solemnly. "One of the last to die, but I had killed four of them with my battle axe. They crucified my father, sister and Hundorp and hacked off their legs above the knees. They bled to death. Erika never screamed. They made me watch it all. Then they started cutting my fingers off, but I was near death when they started. I heard a strange voice in my ear and it offered to give me paradise in eternity if I sold my soul. I was in so much pain and I didn't want to die. I agreed and then I died. Erika had told me that you two had done that just before you died. She asked me not to do it, but I wanted to live. I wish I had never agreed to let the devil have my soul. He was called Drebmif and he gave me five favours, but if I use them all, I leave paradise and become a slave for eternity."

"How many have you left?" Sunday asked.

"Four."

"Then hold on to them. Never let the devil have them all back," Martha said. "Drebmif is one of the sons of Satan, but not the worst one. We have one called Lord Lucifer and he is vile and totally evil. Drebmif was banished to the depths of the sea for refusing to carry on the heinous tasks Satan ordered of his seven sons."

As Martha spoke, the sky darkened and streaks of lightning ran across the sky, followed by a crash of thunder that seemed to shake the ground. Odda looked alarmed, but the others just waited; they knew what was coming. The breeze stiffened and then he appeared, cackling and hovering. Lucifer swirled around a few feet from the ground, his evil red eyes watching Vardan, who did not look the slightest intimidated.

"Your boy is growing stronger with the passing of each full moon. I buy him from you and give you all the favours back," Lucifer called as he looked over Vardan's young body.

Sunday stepped forward and laughed. "Not for a thousand favours, Lucifer, you vile creature."

"I'm Lord Lucifer to you and mind your tongue, Sunday Brown. A thousand favours then and I promise Gertlump will never get her hands on you," Lucifer cackled as he hovered commandingly.

"Send that evil green dwarf to me, Lucifer and let's see who trembles in her boots," Sunday scoffed defiantly. "And Vardan will never do your bidding."

"Very well, Sunday Brown. Then you do my bidding for as long as I want, you and Martha Budd. And who is this wretch?" Lucifer cackled as he cast red eyes over Odda.

"Not one of yours, Lucifer. He belongs to your younger brother, Drebmif. Since you sent Drebmif to the bottom of the sea, he wanders the lands without purpose. We'll take him if he is not wanted."

Lucifer sniggered and swirled around Odda, who was trying not to appear frightened. Their eyes fixed and Lucifer started laughing. Odda felt threatened and began to tremble.

"He looks weak and useless. Fit only for my torture chambers. I see he has four of my younger brother's favours left. You can have his miserable soul for two favours, but he does my bidding for ever, as and when I want."

Sunday looked at Martha and without hesitation they both nodded agreeably. Lucifer pointed a taloned finger at Odda and took two of his favours away. Odda fell to the ground as the power was temporarily removed from his weak body. Martha dropped to his side and lifted his head to her lap. Lucifer shrieked in delight and raised his scaled body higher. He looked at Vardan again, but the boy held his nerve and smiled with contempt.

"He looks at me with fire in his eyes. Name your price, Sunday Brown and I'll take him and let you return to your previous life. No more wandering the lands, waiting to do my bidding. You live normally and then die normally. I give you your life back, but I take the boy."

"Never, Lucifer. You'll never take my boy. He will grow into a man and become an immortal warrior. He will fight your kind until the earth melts. Whatever happens to me, Vardan will carry on his duty. That duty is to destroy evil. He was born to it and he will do it without hesitation, he and others like him. You know who they are and they will never run away. He is protected by the greats and there is nothing you or your despicable brothers can do to change that."

Lucifer cackled and whirled menacingly over Sunday's head. "Before the year is out my brother Mephistopheles will take over from me and he is no different. You are doomed, Sunday Brown, and we will take your boy. I was going to bestow on both you and Martha Budd the ultimate pleasure of bearing my children and taking you both for my wives and removing you from soul hunting duties, but now you will carry on doing my bidding and Mespostopheles will make sure you do such work for his six hundred and sixty-six years of duty to the great Lord himself, Satan. There is a war to take place across the great sea in forty-five years' time and the two of you will be there, slaving for my brother. That is, unless you give me the boy and a certain parchment your friends, the little people, gave you. Then you will be free. Otherwise you go to this war and when it is finished and thousands are killed and souls are collected, Mephistopheles will send you to the torture chambers. When you get there I will personally see that you slave for ever on the slopes, every minute of every day of every year. Gertlump waits impatiently."

"We're not frightened of you Lucifer. We survived the peat bogs and we will survive your orders of soul collecting and that ugly green dwarf does not frighten me, but you will never take Vardan," Sunday replied.

"You will hand him to me or my brother one day, Sunday Brown. I'll have your last favour and then you will do as I ask. Give me the boy now and the parchment, then you and Martha Budd will be free. No more bidding, no more peat bogs, otherwise you go to the next battle and the one after that and so on. I see you have picked up another of our lost souls. Odda of the Nors Egersund. He will make no difference to your plans, he wasn't strong enough to die normally, like you he sold his soul to hang on to something of a life. My father, Satan owns the lot of you and you are ours for eternity. Give me the parchment and the boy. This is your last chance, Sunday Brown."

"Go back to Hell, Lucifer. You can't touch my boy, you have no claim on him and you'll never get your hands on the parchment," Sunday sneered.

"Very well, then you and Martha Budd will carry on soul searching for ever. Odda Haralda will do the same and my weak younger brother Drebmif, or as he calls himself, Fimber O'Flynn, will rot at the bottom of the sea. Give me the parchment and your son and you can all go back and die normally and Drebmif can come up from his watery grave."

Lucifer cackled hideously, lifted himself higher then swooped at Odda, who threw himself to the ground. Martha and Sunday stood their ground a few feet away, shielding a bewildered Vardan. With a final mocking cackle, Lucifer lifted high and disappeared.

Martha gave a hand to a terrified Odda and pulled him up. Odda picked up a Dane's battle axe he had been holding and made sure the musket was over his shoulder. Sunday smiled and stepped to him. Vardan held back, his eyes searching the tall fair-haired man, wearing the strange clothes.

"You have kept the musket all these years, Odda," Sunday said as she reached to the old, but well preserved firearm. Odda took it from his shoulder and handed it to Sunday.

"I've cleaned it and looked after it just as you showed me. The other one was taken by the Angles, but there was no shot or powder left. I hid this one before we were overrun in the battle that killed all my people."

"We can get some shot and powder and see if it still works. That is, if you want to travel with us," Martha said as she handled the musket after Sunday.

Odda looked around and thought for a few moments. He saw Vardan looking at his Dane's axe and smiled. He carefully passed it to the boy and nodded. Vardan had slung his longbow over a shoulder and took the long-handled battle axe. He wasn't sure what to do with it, so Odda smiled and took it back. He waved the other three to step out of the way and pointed to a low tree branch, about ten yards away.

"The middle of that branch," he said and raised the axe. With a mighty heave he hurled the axe at the branch. It twisted two or three times in flight, then thudded into the branch and sent a shock wave along the timber. Vardan watched with disbelieving eyes as the blade stayed deep into the wood.

"That would fell a horse, never mind a man," gasped Sunday.

"It's felled many a man, but never a horse, I like horses too much," Odda grinned as he walked to fetch the axe.

"What do you say, Odda? Do you want to travel with us?" Martha asked.

"If you're all agreeable, I'd like to," Odda replied.

Martha looked at Sunday and then to Vardan. Sunday nodded with a smile. Vardan's face didn't show any sign of approval, but after a few moments he nodded. They all laughed, back slapped and embraced.

Vardan looked at the strange warrior and once more at the Dane's axe. Odda saw his gaze and put a friendly hand on the boy's shoulder.

"If you want, I'll make you one and teach you how to throw it."

"I'd like that and I want to be as good as you," Vardan said happily.

"I'll make sure you're better than me, that will make me happy," Odda replied and put an arm around Vardan's shoulder. He looked at the youngster as they followed Martha and Sunday across the field, to the bow top.

"Your clothes are funny, though. My ma and aunt will make you some new ones," Vardan said thoughtfully.

Odda looked down at his ancient clothes and laughed. "I'd like some new clothes, because I've worn these for a long long time."

The Following Day
A Minute before eight a.m.

Vardan and Odda watched with interest as Martha and Sunday cleared all the weeds, brambles and debris away from a piece of overgrown ground. Vardan had heard his mother and aunt mention the trapdoors during his growing years, but they had never taken him to one before. He watched with curiosity as a trapdoor was uncovered. Odda, too, was curious and instinctively put a hand to his sword as he saw the trapdoor appear. When it suddenly started to move, both he and Vardan jumped back a step. They jumped further back when two pairs of twinkling eyes peered out from the opening. Odda's sword was now half out of his belt, but a hand reached to him.

"Relax, Odda, they're friendly." Martha smiled tremulously.

The trapdoor opened wide and flopped back with a neat crunch. Two little figures emerged quickly, followed by several others, all carrying empty sacks, and disappeared into the undergrowth, leaving the first two standing at the side of the entrance. Vardan and Odda stared wide-eyed at the two little men, who were equally as curious.

"The smaller one is Vardan and we were expecting the boy, but who is this one?" one of the Blingos asked.

"He's a friend who is a lost warrior and we would like to help him," Martha replied.

"Well, I'm Oldgeeza and this Jimsalad, my trapdoor apprentice and we're here to welcome you all to entrance one million and forty three. The three Dabras are waiting to meet you and so is Her Majesty, Her Greatness Missiquin. It's a special day for you, Martha Budd, Sunday Brown and Vardan. However, your friend cannot enter Blingoburbia, because he has not been spreckled. He must wait on the Uptop until you return."

Martha turned to Odda and smiled at the Nors Egersund warrior. He smiled back and nodded humbly.

"I'll stay up here, Martha, don't worry. I'll keep your horse company," Odda said.

"Take care then and Watson will enjoy your company." Martha embraced Odda and stepped to the entrance. Jimsalad was to take Martha, Sunday and Vardan into Blingoburbia and Oldgeeza let them pass through the small entrance.

As soon as they had stepped onto the ground below the ladder, Sunday started laughing.

Vardan and Martha realised they were now the same size as Jimsalad. Martha had expected it, but Vardan was shocked to realise he had shrunk in height and his clothes had also become smaller to fit his new size. Martha was in awe of the surroundings that was Blingoburbia.

Sunday had explained what it was like, but explaining and seeing were two different facts.

The millions of glow worms placed at regular intervals on the stone sides, created a brightness that Martha had never expected. There was no dirt, no fusty air, and no tight spaces.

Contented Blingos were everywhere, busily carrying out work duties, just as Sunday had witnessed when she had first visited Blingoburbia. Ladders were placed against the stone sides, leading to brightly coloured little houses, carefully constructed and disappearing into the distance to all sides. Nice food scents wafted around and Martha felt the first twinges to her nostrils. In almost two hundred years, she had not tasted or smelled food.

The journey to the chambers of the three Dabras took them along tunnels, waterways, hoists and pathways that twisted and turned, uphill and downhill. The little people had learned that three Uptoppers were in Blingoburbia and one of them was the one who had defeated Cerberus Junior, and another had removed Smegtooth the Terrible from Gremlins Green. They waved and cheered as they saw the three Uptoppers passing by their houses.

Martha and Vardan were taken by the friendliness of the Blingos and waved back. Sunday was impatient to get to the three Dabras and strode purposefully along at the side of Jimsalad, giving only an occasional wave.

It seemed like hours that they had travelled deep into the earth and every mile or so they took refreshments. Martha had forgotten what it was like to taste water and laboured her drinking to savour the moments. Vardan and Sunday watched her at times and grinned.

"Aunt Martha takes a long time to drink," Vardan had remarked with amusement.

"So would you if it was almost two hundred years since you last took a drink," Sunday had replied.

"When I drink water, it tastes sweet and I feel a bit stronger for a while," Vardan stated.

"That is probably because you were born under water and when you are fully grown you will be able to go deep into the seas, just like a fish."

"Why is that, Ma?" Vardan asked.

"Because you tasted water before you breathed air. After today you will be even stronger. The three Dabras will give you the Mark of the SWAN, like your Aunt Martha and me. We can't go deep into water, but you can. It will be one of the powers you will have."

Vardan smiled and walked on cheerily.

The chambers came into sight and a fluttering thrill ran through each of their bodies.

Jimsalad had a wide smile on his cherub face. He took a nervous deep breath and it was heard by Martha, who was now at his side.

"Have you been here before?" she asked.

"Er, no, I haven't. We entrance apprentices don't come here. When we do, it means we're ready to move further up the ladder of responsibility," Jimsalad answered.

"Where will you go next, then?"

"To another area in Blingoburbia, a long way from where I live, near York."

"Doing what?"

"To learn about root growing, probably. The rooters make sure all the produce put in the ground by the Uptoppers are kept in good order. Beetroot, onions, carrots, potatoes and suchlike. That is where the others go when they go into the Uptop world with the sacks. We Blingos eat the same things as you Uptoppers, apart from meat. We take what we need and leave the rest for the Uptoppers. When it doesn't rain up top, we water the roots from below. If any Blingos don't water the roots as they should, then they are de-spreckled and have to start all over again as a bottom rung worker. Clearing trash, cleaning ladders, collecting glow worms, repairing roads and tracks, painting houses. It will be at least fifty years before they can earn enough spreckle stars to be able to go up top again. One spreckle star is earned each year, but one is taken away again for any act of misbehaviour."

"They are very strict then, the three Dabras?"

"Oh, no. Not just them. There are five others on the Blingo Council. Missiquin our queen, she sits in the big chair; Poppapil, the doctor; Bossjobs, our engineer; Trapdoor, in charge of all entrances to Blingoburbia and Chief Nurse, Germalina. They sit every eight years to decide all the dos and don'ts of living in Blingoburbia."

"When is the next meeting?"

Jimsalad started laughing and looked at Martha. "Now. Today. There are other up toppers who will be taking the Mark of the SWAN. It is awarded to those who have helped the Blingos or who it is thought will be of a help in the years ahead. Vardan is one of them."

"He's so pleased to be getting the mark, he never stops talking about it."

"We talk a lot about him. The son of Sunday Brown, the warrior who defeated Cerberus Junior. He might be even greater."

They were outside the chambers and Jimsalad stopped and let the three pass through the entrance door. Sunday confidently walked through, followed by an apprehensive Martha holding Vardans hand. The door closed and the three suddenly realised they were inside the heart of Blingoburbia. The incandescent light and warmth was no less inside, than outside in the open expanse of the many tunnels and caverns they had walked and travelled since entering the queendom.

Another door opened and the figures of two Blingos appeared in the opening. Martha and Sunday recognised the smiling faces of Jobsdone and Bossalot, who were the first Blingos they had cast wary eyes on many years earlier.

"Welcome, Martha Budd and Sunday Brown and young Vardan. Your big day has arrived and the eight elders of Blingoburbia await your presence," Jobsdone said as he ushered the three into the room. Bossalot remained at the rear and pulled the doors closed.

A large, polished, octagonal wooden table was in the centre, with one segment raised a few inches higher than the other seven. Gold dividing lines separated each section, running to the centre. There were tall porcelain vases holding almost every variety of flowers around the walls; velvet purple and gold drapes hung in perfect folds down the walls from the ceiling.

Behind the slightly raised section of the table a bespectacled female Blingo sat in her gilded chair, just those few inches higher than her seven companions in their seats. Missiquin, the Queen of Blingoburbia let her twinkling eyes look at each of the three Uptoppers. On a plinth in the centre of the table, on a folded piece of black silk with a gold edging, a beautiful crystal white swan was placed, with its black eyes staring with intensity at the three newcomers. Vardan held the swan's intense stare until it appeared to look to Martha and Sunday. The black eyes stared with depth at the two young women, then relaxed.

"Welcome to Blingoburbia Martha Budd, Sunday Brown and Vardan De Lacey," Missiquin said with a gentle friendliness. She saw a look of surprise on Sunday's face and smiled. "We have followed your progress through the years, Sunday Brown and Vardan's father was a French cavalry officer called Philippe De Lacey. We refer to all Uptoppers with, their full names. Vardan should have been presented to us two years ago for his second spreckling, but we decided to overlook your forgetfulness, because you and Martha Budd were due here today to receive the Mark of the SWAN, so Vardan will be spreckled at the same time."

"Thank you, my son will be your servant," Sunday replied, feeling chastised.

"Very well. Each of the three great Magus will bestow on you and Martha Budd the Mark of the SWAN, which we eight elders around this table grant to those who have proved over many years to be friends of the queendom. On his twenty-fourth birthday, your son Vardan will receive the Mark of the SWAN. Use the parchment to see where the entrance is that will bring him to us. Until then, he can only enter the queendom in the company of either of you, Sunday Brown or Martha Budd. He will, however, be expected to do Uptopper duties as you two have done for many years.

"Train him well, Sunday Brown, because one day he will be a mighty warrior, with the full protection of the three great Magus. There are four of these warriors in the up top world and Vardan De Lacey will be the fifth. You have already met one of the warriors and she gave us a complete account of his suitability. She held him and looked deep into his eyes. He never blinked during these moments and that is a sign that he will never feel fear, never turn away from a fight, never leave an injured friend behind and will strike fear into the evil souls of Satan's children and their offspring. Travel wherever you have to go, but I would like you to be in America in thirty-five years' time. There will be many battles there and thousands killed. Take Odda, the young Nors Egersund warrior with you. We notice he has joined up with you and he is a good man.

"Satan's son, Mephistopheles will order you to do his bidding, as you have done for Lucifer in the years gone by. Make sure none of the dying agree to sell their souls. Touch them on the head with the palm of one of your hands, it will ease their pain and help to prevent them going to the devil. Some will still go that way, but you might be able to save the others. Now go with the three great Magus to receive the Mark of the SWAN, and travel well, wherever you go, doing Uptopper duties and, though it pains me to say this, when you have to work for Satan."

Jobsdone and Bossalot walked forward as Missiquin signalled to them. She rose from her chair and was followed by the elders, Poppapil, Germalina, Bossjobs and Trapdoor, each of the four elders acknowledging the three Uptoppers with smiles and a slight bow of their heads.

Bossalot and Jobsdone carefully lifted the crystal swan from the plinth and brought it to another table, behind the chair where Missiquin had sat. The three Dabras, or Magus, as Missiquin referred to them, were waiting to perform the ceremony of the SWAN. Sorceradabra, Wizadabra and

Magicadabra stood with their backs to the table. The swan was placed on a nest of interwoven golden fibres, which were settled on a crimson silk sheet. Hundreds of glow worms, neatly placed around the walls, cast a glowing silvery sheen around the table and a few scented candles in silver candle holders dispersed a gentle shimmering brightness. Jobsdone and Bossalot took positions at each side of Martha, the first to receive the Mark of the SWAN. She was asked to step out of her clothes and calmly did so. Naked in front of the three Magus, she caught a glimpse of the swan on the table. It had raised its head and the long neck turned slowly side to side. The black eyes glinted in the candle light and very slowly, the head moved forward.

Sorceradabra and Magicadabra lifted the swan carefully and brought it towards a transfixed Martha a few feet away. Wizadabra held a thin silver stick and stepped to Martha. He looked into Martha's nervous eyes and smiled.

"Which arm do you use mainly, Martha Budd?" he asked.

Martha raised her right arm. "My right arm and hand."

"Then you will receive the Mark of the SWAN to your left arm. Afterwards you will be as proficient with your left as your right." Wizadabra put the tip of the stick into a small gold and silver pot holding a clear purple substance. He then touched Martha's skin with the substance and took a bottle of spreckle dust from Jobsdone. The dust was sprinkled over the purple substance and then Sorceradabra and Magicadabra lifted the swan to Martha's arm. The head lifted and the black eyes glinted. The swan slowly lowered its beak to the spot where Martha had been touched and pecked three or four times, breaking the skin. For the first time in two hundred years, a slight jolt of pain rippled through Martha's body.

Wizadabra brought a hand up and placed the palm over the small wound. He gently pressed down and held it for a few moments. Martha felt a warm surge in her arm and a strange tingling taking place on the wound. Taking his hand away, Wizadabra smiled and gently lifted Martha's arm. He nodded as be looked at the wound. He turned Martha around and let Sorceradabra and Magicadabra inspect the mark. They nodded approvingly. Martha had a swan's figure clearly embedded in the skin.

Dressed again, Martha stepped away and let Sunday take her place in front of the table. This time Wizadabra swapped over with Sorceradabra, to let the latter give Sunday her mark.

The same procedure was followed and a few minutes later a white swan was embedded clearly in Sunday's right arm. Vardan was then brought forward and Magicadabra performed the spreckling ceremony over the youngster's body. He looked disappointed not to have received the Mark of the SWAN, but a comforting arm around his shoulders from Magicadabra, assured the boy he would receive the mark on his twenty-fourth birthday.

The swan had been returned to the plinth on the large table, its moments of life ended until the next lost soul received the immortal mark. Sunday and Martha stepped away to be taken back to the up top world, as the three Magus returned to their respective chambers. Vardan turned his head to look at the swan's black eyes one more time, his eyes fixed for a few moments with the Swan. The Swan's head moved up and down slowly for just a brief moment and Vardan nodded with a wry smile.

As the little group made their way back through Blingoburbia, Vardan looked around with doubtful eyes. He was still unhappy at not taking the Mark of the SWAN, but with Jimsalad taking them back to the up top and at his side, he needed to ask a question.

"How does Missiquin know things so far ahead? She mentioned two battles in America in thirty-six years' time. That's a long time," he asked wonderingly.

Jimsalad answered quickly, with Martha and Sunday also confused. "The three Dabras see everything for forty years ahead. They have large crystal balls that they look into. The balls are fixed to a circular brass base with lots of inscriptions marked on it. There are moveable brass pointers that can be turned to any of the inscriptions and as soon as the message is picked up in the crystal ball, a vision can be seen. They have the power to see things we normal Blingos can't see. Not everything, you understand, but big happenings in the up top world. That is why they know what you humans are doing or in your cases, the undead. Missiquin is told everything. It's her right to know everything."

"She called the Dabras, the Magus. Why?" Martha asked.

"Dabras is a nickname we normal Blingos call them, because all their names end in Dabra. Magus is what very extra specially talented mortals are called. Wizards, Sorcerers and suchlike," Jimsalad replied, wondering why these Uptoppers did not know this. He skipped along cheerfully and waved to friends he saw along the way.

"Why doesn't Missiquin have a husband, a king, to help her rule Blingoburbia?" Sunday asked.

"She did, a long long time ago. He was captured by some of Satan's creatures, who invaded our underlands centuries ago. Two undead humans handed one of Satan's sons one of the parchments they had been trusted to keep safe, in return for favours you are all given. On it were the entrances to Blingoburbia and one night of the full moon, Satan sent an army of his creatures to capture the king and slaughter as many of our people as they could. It was terrible. Whole colonies were wiped out. So, the old parchments were destroyed and new ones prepared with a whole lot of new entries marked. Only the very purest of undead humans are trusted with a parchment. We have many enemies who are in league with the devil. You have already met the evil Boggimps. Satan puts his fiercest creatures to guard his territories where the Boggimps, the Hobgoblins, the Trogladytes and other armies of wicked little people live. You defeated one of his deadliest guardians, Cerberus Junior, and that has made you respected warriors, who are welcomed in Blingoburbia. To be awarded the Mark of the SWAN is the highest honour possible, but it takes tens of years to get it." Jimsalad smiled at Vardan, who was hanging on every word he spoke.

"When I win the Mark of the SWAN, I will fight and kill as many enemies as I can," Vardan remarked and received a back slap from Jimsalad and hugs from his mother and Martha. "We will never let Satan get his evil hands on the parchment," he added.

"As you found out not long ago, it has places marked where there are time gaps for you to enter. These time gaps can be used by Satan's creatures if they have one of the parchments. Guard them for ever. You can only ever have one."

"Have you heard of a warrior called Jacindra?" Sunday asked.

"Yes, but I have never seen her. She is one of four immortals who are trying to find our king. There were eight of these time warriors, the most we can have, but four have been killed in battles with Satan's offspring."

"The immortals can kill Satan's creatures, though?"

"Oh, yes, and they do, far more than they have lost, but there are hundreds of these hell creatures. They are all over the Uptop world you call Earth. They do Satan's work and commit indescribable evil. Jacindra and the other three immortal warriors travel all over to combat the hell creatures. In time, Vardan will be offered the chance to join the immortals. You also, Sunday Brown, I guess. That is all I can say. When we get back to my entrance and you pass through to the up top, you go your way again. I might not see you again, but I will always think of you and where you are. Keep the parchment safe, it has all the answers to your questions, all the entrances to Blingoburbia and of the time gap places."

They arrived at Jimsalad's entrance, number one million and forty three, and waited 'til Jimsalad opened the hatch. One by one they climbed out, Vardan desperately hoping he would regain his normal size. He stood in the fresh air and looked quickly at his feet. He breathed a sigh of relief when he saw that his feet were two and a half feet further from his face. Sunday and Martha started laughing at his jubilant expression.

Odda was sitting on a fallen branch a few feet away and smiled as he saw them return through the entrance. He hugged and back slapped them one by one, his eyes searching their bodies for the Mark of the SWAN. He couldn't see them and wondered why.

"Where are your swan marks?" he asked.

Sunday pushed up her sleeve and looked at her swan mark with a contented smile. Martha did the same and saw her mark clearly. Vardan and Odda were confused. They all looked across to Oldgeeza and Jimsalad who were sitting on the fallen tree branch. Both were grinning.

"Only those with swan marks can see them on others' bodies," Oldgeeza said with amusement. "Vardan has been spreckled, but he has not had the mark so he cannot see the swan yet. It helps to protect you here in the Uptop world, so none of Satan's offspring can tell who you are."

Vardan huffed and frowned. "I can't wait till I'm twenty-four. Fourteen more years. It's not fair."

"By the time you receive your mark, you will be fully grown and ready to go out on your own. Time will soon pass," Martha said and put an arm around his shoulder. He smiled and nodded.

Chapter Twenty-Two
Central Wales

December 1826

A seven-foot snowdrift blanketed one side of the bow top as it nestled against a hedge on a leafy lane a couple miles south of Defynnog. Sunday and Vardan had enjoyed a meal of rabbit and potatoes, cooked over a crackling wood fire, while Martha and Odda had watched with muted interest.

Leaving Martha and his mother clearing pots and pans, Vardan had walked to where Odda was practicing throwing his Dane's axe at a broad oak tree. After his umpteenth throw, the axe was embedded in the tree and Odda had walked to pull it out. The arrow thudded into the tree just an inch from the steel blade and narrowly missing Odda's hand, gripping the axe handle. Odda jumped back in shock and yelled in anger.

"Damn you, Vardan Brown! You're a menace with that bow, you could have killed me."

"You'd be dead now, Odda, if I wanted to kill you. My shot was off target, I wanted the arrow to be touching the axe's head," Vardan laughed as he walked to collect his arrow.

"You're just too good, young boy. We should have had you on our side when we fought the Angles, we might have won."

"There were too many of them though, when they came back, weren't there?"

"Like I said, we were outnumbered ten to one at first, but when our ball shot and powder ran out and we had killed over a hundred of them, they had killed ten of our fighters. They still had lots more than us. They slaughtered the remainder of my tribe," Odda said as he walked back to his throwing position.

"You looked after the musket and the pistols all those years, with nothing to fire."

"They captured one of our muskets, but there was no powder or shot left anyway, all it could be used for was a club. I often think what battles back in those days could have been won with a hundred of the muskets."

"My ma was a pirate on a ship on the high seas and they always used muskets and pistols, never bows and arrows," Vardan said as he slotted another arrow to his bow.

"Or battle axes, I guess," Odda laughed as he lifted the axe ready to throw.

The sky darkened and there was a flash of lightning. Vardan looked upwards to the grey brooding sky and sighed heavily. "Lord Lucifer," he exclaimed.

The crash of thunder followed and then the ravens, hundreds of them darting across the sky in a huge squawking flock. Odda and Vardan held their weapons and turned to glance across the snow-covered field to where the bow top was positioned. Martha was sitting in her chair, Sunday standing at her side, waiting for the inevitable appearance of Lucifer.

This time it was not just Lucifer, but another grotesque figure as well. Mephistopheles, a brother of Lucifer had appeared by the bow top. The two devils hovered a few feet from the ground, leering at the two young women, Lucifer as usual making his unmistakable cackling laugh.

"You thought I had forgotten you both," Lucifer sniggered.

"You're like a bad smell, Lucifer, unpleasant and easy to forget," Sunday returned glibly.

"Mind your tongue Sunday Brown, you offend me immensely," Lucifer snarled and lifted his body to hover directly above Sunday. "I have more pleasant things to look forward to now than thinking of you. A long sleep to regain my strength and powers that are almost exhausted, and centuries away from ignorant wandering souls like you. My brother is trained now and takes over our father's tasks soon and then I am rid of you. I've come to take your son with me. I made you an offer not long ago and I want him. You get all your favours back in return. And I want that chair from you, Martha Budd and I'll give you your lost favours back."

Martha shuffled uneasily in her chair, but started shaking her head. "You're not taking either to Hell, Lucifer. The boy or my chair. You can't steal them, you know that. Fimber told me that a long time ago."

Lucifer swirled around in a rage and pointed a taloned finger at Martha.

"That brother of mine was useless. He's where he belongs and he'll remain there, turning into a fish. I've seen what the chair can do and I want it so I can sit in it and regain my strength. All your favours back for it. And the boy. My father will put him to good use, I promise. We'll leave you alone then, to wander the earth 'til you rot. No more biddings. That's a good exchange."

Sunday stepped towards the hovering devils. "That exchange stinks, like you, Lucifer and you'll never take my son, or Martha's chair."

Part of the snowdrift against the bow top slithered off and made Sunday jump. Lucifer cackled and pointed at the fallen pile of snow.

"You will be free to go to warmer lands, Sunday Brown. No more of this silly white stuff, no more freezing nights, like you suffer now. No more finding souls for me or my brother. The boy and the chair and we go away for ever."

Mephistopheles moved a few feet away from Lucifer and hovered nearer to Martha, his red eyes staring at the chair. He turned and looked at his brother.

"Why do you want it, Lucifer? It's just an old wooden chair," Mephistopheles remarked.

Martha smiled, shrugged and stood up from the chair. "Tell him what it does, Lucifer."

"Like my brother said, Martha Budd, it's just an old wooden chair, nothing else."

"True. Just an old wooden chair, so why do you want it?" Martha said calmly.

"Because you have sat in it for two hundred years and I need a chair to sit in while I sleep to regain my strength. I'm too old to take you now, I should have had my way with you before now, so I'll take your chair instead. You get your favours back, I get the chair."

Martha sniffed and looked at Lucifer. She glanced across to Sunday, who was slowly nodding. Martha smiled and then nodded. Sunday turned and climbed onto the bow top, disappearing inside.

"Very well, Lucifer, give me the four favours back and you get the chair," Martha said.

Mephistopheles hovered above Martha and nodded his head impatiently.

"Let me sit in it first, Martha Budd. It's a chair, nothing else. No secret weapon or anything dangerous. You get your favours back, my brother gets the old chair, you go on your way for ever."

"Take a seat then and make sure it's safe to sit on. Then I'll have my favours back," Martha said.

Mephistopheles lowered his figure to the ground and sniffed. Lucifer glared at him.

"Be careful, brother, Martha Budd is clever and I don't trust her," Lucifer remarked as he, too, lowered himself to the snowy ground. Mephistopheles grinned and looked at Martha.

"My brother is tired now after his six hundred and sixty-six years of duty. He's never been a fool and neither am I. The chair is not worth four favours. I'd only give one back for it, but he has to answer to Satan for squandering the favours, not me. If it has any special powers I will find out. I can tell when fools like you are being deceitful. Step away."

Martha moved away a few feet to let Mephistopheles sit in the chair. Lucifer watched his brother taking his seat on the old chair. Martha's face was expressionless.

After shuffling around on the chair for several seconds, gripping hard on the arm rests and lifting up and down on the seat to test its strength he stood and picked it up, inspected it, then put it back down. Mephistopheles was satisfied the chair posed no threat. He smiled and looked up at his brother.

Martha sighed and flicked her head to Lucifer. "Sit on it, then, Lucifer and test it. Then I get four favours back and no silliness."

"I say forget it, brother," Mephistopheles said, shaking his head. "Satan will go mad if he finds you've swapped four favours for this battered old chair. You said we were taking these two women today, not arguing over a chair. I'll take them both myself after you've gone to sleep. Test it yourself, give the woman her four favours back and let's go, its freezing cold here and I hate snow."

Lucifer strutted to the chair and flopped his frame into the old chair. It creaked under his weight, but it held him comfortably and he nodded. After a few seconds of shuffling around and pressing up and down, Lucifer relaxed and leaned back. Martha raised a hand to him, palm up, and stepped to him. He sniffed and smiled dryly.

"My brother's right, Martha Budd. The chair is old and not worth four favours, so you get just one back. I'm sat on the chair now and in possession. Here's the favour back." Lucifer tapped Martha's palm once and started cackling. Martha felt the weight of the favour on her palm and clenched it into her fist. She smiled at him, kissed two fingers on her other hand, then quickly tapped the side of Lucifer's startled scaly face with the fingers.

"I knew you would cheat me, Lucifer, so I've just repaid your detestable cunning and taken a favour back from you. I'll use it to get Fimber O'Flynn from the bottom of the sea. In the meantime, you can go back to hell, if you don't perish before you get there."

Lucifer cackled and started to rise from the chair, but a few yards away, Sunday dropped to the snowy ground, holding the sabre of Captain De Lacey. With a wild guttural scream, she charged at the bewildered devil, sabre held high. A few feet away, Mephistopheles started to face Sunday, but he instantly screamed in pain as an arrow thudded into his body. With a swift flap of his wings, he rose quickly upwards, as another arrow narrowly missed his legs.

Sunday had reached Lucifer and with a mighty sweep with the curved blade at his red scaly body, she cut deep into his flesh. He screamed and fell face forward from Martha's chair as dark red blood oozed onto the snow. Another swipe with the sabre and Lucifer took another deep cut. He screamed pitifully and slashed out at Sunday, who was bringing the sabre back to strike again. Four razor-sharp talons ripped across the brown skin, gouging deep into her body. Sunday fell backwards, but held onto the sabre. Lucifer was seriously injured, but gathered himself to attack the prostrate woman. Mephistopheles was circling several feet above the pair, ready to help his brother, but wary of being hit by another arrow.

Lucifer scrambled up and snarled loudly, dark red blood pouring from his wounds. Then an arrow struck him in the neck. An instant later and a battle axe thudded into his back. He screamed with anger and pain, but had just the strength to raise his body from the ground.

With every ounce of his ebbing strength, he managed to climb upwards, but as he turned to go higher another arrow struck his body. He was about to fall again, but strong hands grabbed out and heaved him higher.

Mephistopheles gathered his injured brother and took him to safety. Vardan had run forward and fired another of his arrows but it ran out of flight as Mephistopheles swept out of range. The youngster cursed and ran to where his mother lay injured on the snow-packed ground. Martha was tending Sunday, but Lucifer's poison-tipped talons had ripped open her body. Sunday lay with her head on Martha's lap, her face a mask of agony.

"Will she die, Aunt Martha?" Vardan asked as he knelt at his mother's side.

There was a grunt from Sunday and she reached a hand to Vardan's face. "No, I won't die, son. I'm already dead, remember, but unfortunately I now feel the pain of any injuries."

"You hurt the devil, though, Ma, I saw you cut him with the sabre."

"I did and I was hoping I could. It proves the sabre has the power to hurt the devil and his kind. We must never lose it. Your arrows and the battle axe hurt him as well. We all did well."

"I think Lucifcer was spent," Martha remarked. "He kept saying he was tired and had to sleep. The other one is a different matter, though. Fresh and dangerous, like Lucifer was when I first met him. Fimber O'Flynn told me that each of the sons of Satan do six hundred and sixty-six years of duty, before another one takes over. This new one might be worse than Lucifer."

"I need a new battle axe now," Odda grinned. "I left the last one stuck in his back." They all laughed, even Sunday, who winced with the effort. Martha sighed and pursed her lips with worry.

"I don't think my chair is powerful enough to kill Lucifer, or probably any of the creatures from Hell. Humans, yes, but not their kind. Sunday cut his body deep twice and he took at least two arrows and the battle axe. Any one of those would have killed a man. But at least we know we can hurt them. To kill them we have to cut off their heads, or pierce their eyes with a knife or a sword."

"Sabre, Missy. Mine's a sabre," Sunday moaned.

"Sorry, Sunday. A sabre or a sword. And your arrows, Vardan, have to pierce their eyes."

"What about a musket or a pistol, Martha? A ball shot in the eyes as well?" Odda asked.

"I think so, Odda, but from a distance, unless you fire point blank. We all have to become expert with those weapons and we have to get hold of muskets, pistols and gun powder."

"I still have one of those you gave me. It might still fire," Odda remarked.

"It travelled seven hundred and fifty years through time. Might not still work," Martha said thoughtfully. "We have to get newer ones."

"Where do we get them?" Odda asked. "Who sells them?"

"We find a gunsmith. There are such people around."

"A gunsmith?" Odda looked puzzled. "And what with? We have no money or anything to trade with. No cows, pigs or sheep, or even chickens."

Martha laughed and patted Odda on an arm. "Times are different these days, Odda. You lived centuries ago, remember."

"Very well, but what do we use to buy them?"

Martha looked at Sunday and they both smiled.

"What we have to do now is find a ship to take us to America. There's a port a few miles away and there should be ships available. As soon as Sunday is fit to travel and the snow has gone we can travel south, to the coast. We have to go to America and find places where there are going to be battles.

We have to try and stop wounded soldiers selling their souls," Martha replied as she put cloths to Sunday's wounds.

"Will I be able to come back here when I'm twenty-four, Aunt Martha? I have to go into Blingoburbia again, remember," Vardan asked, looking concerned.

"We have the parchment. It has the entraces to Blingoburbia all over the world, even America. But we all have to carry on doing Uptopper duties. We have to help the Blingos."

"It takes a long time to get to the chambers of the elders, though. We were ages getting there," Vardan remarked.

Odda looked at the boy with narrowed eyes.

"No, you weren't. I had only been sat on that tree branch for a short while, talking to the little man. No longer than it takes to boil an egg. Not much longer anyway."

Vardan started laughing and shook his head. "You must have fallen asleep, most likely and woke up a few hours later, thinking we had only just gone. No use leaving you on guard duty at any of our camps, we'd all wake up in the morning with our heads cut off."

Martha and Odda laughed and Sunday tried but felt the pain in her body, so she reached a hand out to Vardan. He wasn't sure what he had said that had made them laugh, so he shrugged and climbed to his feet, picking up the bow.

"I'm going to make a snowman and fire arrows at it and pretend it's one of them devils," he muttered and walked away.

"He's good with the bow," Odda remarked. "The best bowman I've ever seen and he's still a boy. I'm just going to make sure I'm always on his side if there's ever another battle."

"There will always be battles, Odda," Martha said as she tended Sunday's wounds. "We have to be at any there are, to try and stop the wounded selling their souls."

After a half hour, Odda rose from the rekindled fire and picked up his own bow to go and find Vardan. Martha reached for Sunday's sabre and handed it to him.

"Take it with you, Odda, just in case those two devils are still around."

"Do I have the sabre's powers?" Odda asked.

"No, but Vardan does. It has his father's blood on the blade. Only Sunday and Vardan have the power of the blade, but otherwise it is a cruel weapon and you've lost your battle axe. This is wild country we are in and there might be bad people around."

"I'll find the boy and bring him back. Keep Sunday warm, we'll be back soon." Odda took the sabre and slung his bow over a shoulder.

He had walked for fifteen minutes through the deep snow with no sign of Vardan. In the distance, he could see steep, snow-capped high hills and rough terrain with rocky crags everywhere. It was a no-man's-land and not for the faint hearted. He put his hands to his mouth and let out a piercing call. His voice raced across the white landscape and eventually hit a rocky cliff face and echoed back. He stared into the blinding whiteness, but there was no sign of Vardan. Once more he called out. Again, after a few moments his echo came back. He trekked for ten more minutes, his eagle eyes searching every crag, frozen stream and in the nearing distance, the high, snow-capped hills. He pulled his bow from the shoulder and slotted an arrow to the string.

The screeching monster hit him savagely from behind and knocked him to the snow-covered ground. He dropped his bow in the fall and lay, momentarily stunned. The greenish creature attacked him again and raked his body with large, razor-sharp claws. It swooped up into the cold light grey sky and turned after a hundred yards to attack again. Odda's sheepskin top was torn to shreds, but he scrambled up and grabbed for his bow, a few feet away. He slotted another arrow to the string and saw the flame-red eyes glaring. He had no chance to focus against the crystal white background and quickly released the arrow. It struck the head of the dragon but missed the creature's eyes. The large figure faltered in flight and suddenly turned upwards again, making a loud hissing sound.

Odda was now composed and waited; the seventy-foot long dragon did a half circle a hundred feet above and prepared itself for another swooping attack on the small figure below. Odda pulled the sabre from his belt and raised it, ready to strike at the flying green monster.

It snorted a blast of orange fire from its nostrils and started the killing dive, the long spiked tail threshing behind the powerful scabrous body. The curved sabre was held ready, but as Odda took a breath and prayed to Odin, his god, an arrow sped towards the diving dragon. The wooden missile hit the dragon on its under belly and within a few moments a second arrow struck the dragon. It screeched loudly, but continued its dive towards Odda. He stood with the sabre held ready, but a wild swing at the creature missed and as the huge body swept by, the long spiked tail swung sideways, knocking Odda several feet across the ground, sending him crashing against fallen jagged rocks.

Young Vardan was at his side in moments and snatched up the sabre. Odda was stunned but managed to roll onto his side and to the cover of the rocks. The dragon had lifted its great body up again and powered away once more to renew the attack. It did another half circle a hundred yards distant, then dropped its head to attack again. Odda was still stunned from his fall, but Vardan stood firm, holding his mother's sabre. Odda watched the youngster brandishing the sabre and noticed that along the blade a trail of blood was visible, but he knew he had not struck the dragon. On the tip of the blade a bright light flashed for a split second, then vanished and the blood stain also disappeared.

Roaring in at speed, the dragon's eyes saw the boy fifty yards ahead, with the shining steel blade held high. A burst of poisonous sheet flame was spat out from the dragon's mouth and it hit Vardan full on, but he held on to the sabre. As the jubilant creature swooped by a transfixed Vardan, the long pointed tail thrashed right and left and hit the boy as he wiped the burning poison from his face. He was catapulted yards to one side and like Odda a few minutes earlier, he crashed against the rocks.

Odda had recovered slightly and dashed to drag Vardan's semi-conscious body behind the rocks where he had fallen. The two injured combatants regained their senses and peered over the rock where they were protected. Odda, less injured, blinked as he realised another creature had appeared. He rubbed his eyes to check he had not imagined it, but there were now two of the large flying creatures and guessed they were considering another attack.

"Fafnir and Draca," he growled.

Vardan looked at him with sore eyes, but only had half vision. "Who? What?" he muttered, still dazed.

"Fafnir and Draca. They are the Hell Dragons. They are lifelong mates, Draca is the male and Fafnir the female. They were sent by Lucifer and his brother to kill us, at least me. They want you alive."

"How do you know their names?" Vardan asked as his sight recovered.

"My ancestors, across the great eastern sea, were plagued with them centuries ago. They are called by different names in different lands. Here in the lands of the Britons they are called Mordant and Cyberacid. They eat cattle and pigs, even horses."

Vardan took another peek over the rocks and saw the two large dragons, but they had settled on the ground and were bellowing into the cold air. The second dragon, slightly larger, appeared to be nudging the other with its head. A few moments later and the first dragon bellowed louder and appeared to be scratching at the ground. Two blasts of fire from each dragon at the ground and then the smaller one started scratching furiously at the scorched earth. A few minutes passed and then the smaller dragon settled itself in the excavated hole and disappeared to the top of its body.

"What is it doing?" Vardan asked dubiously.

"At a guess, I'd say relieving itself, like cats do," Odda replied, shaking his head.

"We could run back now and escape."

"No chance, Vardan, not on snow. They'll see us running and they will come after us and they can fly, we can't."

"Yeah. I don't want squirting with that stuff again, it stings, but suppose they wait to attack again?"

"It gets dark in two or three hours, we can try to get away then," Odda replied.

"Good, because one of them was bad enough. Two and we've no chance."

Fifteen minutes later and there was movement where the two dragons had settled. Now, the larger dragon started clawing the excavated earth back into the hole. Vardan and Odda watched as the two dragons furiously nudged each other for a minute, before standing away and shaking their huge bodies. The one that had attacked Vardan and Odda lifted and immediately roared loudly and then appeared to urinate over the area where the earth had been disturbed. The second one, the larger dragon, did likewise and took longer. After another session of nudging and bellowing, they both sent sheets of fire to the earth, where they had urinated. Both large heads turned to look towards the rocks where Vardan and Odda had been dumped earlier. They immediately dropped to the ground, hoping the dragons had forgotten about them. Their hopes were shattered when both dragons took off at great speed to attack them with a vengeance.

For several minutes the dragons spat huge amounts of poisonous fire at the two partly concealed figures, making up to a dozen dives at their position in the rocks. Both fired arrows at the dragons, both scored hits, but the dragons just shook them off. With only two arrows left between Vardan and Odda, the angered creatures suddenly pulled away and lifted their huge bodies into the cold snowy air and in one swoop, swept high and disappeared.

Two minutes later and two nervous heads popped up and peered over the rocks.

"What d'ya think? They gone, huh?" Vardan asked, still rubbing his sore eyes.

"I reckon so. But you took a shot in the face, didn't you?"

"Yeah, and it hurts like nothing I've felt. Good for you that you can't feel or smell it, because it stings and it stinks," Vardan replied as he rubbed his eyes again.

Odda had stood and noticed pools of the yellow substance collected in gaps in the rocks all around them. He prodded a finger into one and it sank three inches into the smoking residue. He pulled his finger out and carefully looked at the thick, yellowy liquid.

"Fadra's poison. We could rub it on our arrow beads. There is a tale from my tribe's ancestors that it also has healing powers, rubbed onto a wound. On its own it is like an acid and hurts when touching skin, like it did to you just now, but mixed with crushed hemlock, a rival poison, the two compete with each other and make a healing compound. On their own, deadly, but mixed together, harmless. We need to collect as much as we can."

"Good idea, Odda. We'd better go back and get some pans to collect it in."

The two climbed out from the rocks, looked around carefully, then set off at a pace across the snowy ground.

They arrived at their little campsite, with Martha pacing around, Sunday asleep, covered in a blanket under the bow top. As soon as she saw them, Martha ran and threw her arms around both. She stepped back after a minute and shook her head.

"I thought you had had an accident, got wounded or something," she exclaimed.

"We did Aunt Martha. Two dragons attacked us," Vardan replied excitedly.

He explained what had happened and Martha listened intently. She nodded.

"They're the same dragons your mother and I encountered at Gremlins Green, years ago. Mordant and Cyberacid. They've guarded Satan's lair for hundreds of years. What did your people call them, Odda?"

"Fafnir and Draca. The yellow stuff is called Fadra's poison. Letters from the two dragon names."

"And mixed with hemlock it makes a healing solution?"

"Yes. Our ancient warriors of the Nors Egersund and other tribes used it to treat wounds after a battle. On its own, like Vardan found out, it bums the skin and can kill, but not today, because Vardan is protected by his spreckling."

"Go and collect some, then, boys, but be careful. Sunday is very ill and we have nothing to lose by putting some on her wounds. It's dark soon and you should be safe and the snow will give some light. And you said one of the dragons dug a hole, sat in it and then the other one filled the hole?"

Odda and Vardan nodded and spoke together. Martha smiled.

"They were probably doing what cats do, having a pee then covering it over," Martha smiled. "Even dragons have to take a pee, I suppose."

An hour later and Odda and Vardan had found the rocks where they had sheltered from the two dragons. With a large copper tub, mugs and rags to squeeze out the liquid, the two set about filling the vessel. It took two hours to fill the copper tub with the still-warm poison, safely contained and sealed. Vardan looked across the snowy ground to where the dragons had dug and then filled the hole. He looked at Odda, who was holding the copper tub.

"How do dragons have baby dragons?" he asked.

"Not sure, but I think they lay eggs. Why?" Odda looked back with narrowed eyes.

"Suppose that dragon was laying eggs."

"And suppose you and me get away from here before they come back."

"We could go and take a quick look. It's dark now, but we can still see."

Odda sniffed and pulled what was left of his torn sheepskin around his body. "Madness, Vardan, sheer madness. We escaped earlier, they might be back and I haven't got a battle axe."

"No use against one of them, Odda. You only get one chance with an axe. I'll go, you stay here and keep a watch." Vardan picked up his bow and made sure the sabre was tucked into his belt, then set off to reach the spot. Odda cursed and put the copper tub down safely, then ran after Vardan.

A couple of minutes later and they found the place where the dragons had filled the hole.

Odda was looking around with a part fearful face as Vardan started pulling at the broken earth. Within a minute he had joined his younger partner and together they scooped out the broken, but warm, loose soil. Vardan had had to put a cloth over his lower face to reduce the stench of the dragon's urine. Odda grinned as he wasn't affected by the obvious smell.

An hour later and they stopped digging. Three beautiful spotty browny-green eggs were unearthed. Seven or eight inches long each and with a broad circumference, they were undamaged and all warm. Vardan gingerly touched them and held a palm over the eggs.

He looked at Odda with wanton eyes. Odda started shaking his head. "No way, Vardan. We can't. Not dragon eggs."

"We could keep it warm and hatch it. Keep it and bring it up. Train it to carry us."

"It's a dragon, Vardan, not a dog or a cat. They eat other animals, not to mention humans. It could eat you and then you'd wake up one morning inside its belly."

"Just one of the eggs, Odda. Take some of this soil with the dragon pee in it. Keep it covered up until it hatches."

"Martha and your mother will make you take it back."

"Aunt Martha might, but not my ma, she's like me," Vardan laughed.

"No one's like you, Vardan. No one."

"I'll take one of my tops off and make a sack. Put the soil in and cover the egg."

"I'll carry the copper pot back. You bring the soil and the egg. That way, if the dragons come looking, they'll go for you and not me," Odda said, shaking his head. "We'd better cover the other eggs up before we go."

As soon as they had replaced the soil and Vardan had put his egg in the makeshift sack, they set off back to the bow top. Odda was for ever looking around, fearing the dragons would come to find them. As midnight loomed they arrived back to find a worried-looking Martha. She lay at the side of Sunday, who had lapsed into unconsciousness. Before it had got dark, she had wandered the area and found bunches of hemlock. Already crushed, she had boiled the poisonous plant over the fire and kept it heated.

Odda put the copper tub down and spooned out an amount of the poisonous yellow substance. Together, he and Martha prepared the potion, while, unknown to his aunt, Vardan had taken the dragon egg and the special soil into the bow top and carefully hidden it in his own wooden box, where he kept his belongings. Satisfied that egg and soil were carefully covered and warm, he looked at his injured mother. He took one of her hands and kissed it gently.

"Sorry, Ma, I want you to get better. Odda and me brought some dragon stuff back that will make you better. Ma and Odda are outside getting it ready. I found a dragon egg, Ma and I'm going to help it get born, then when it's older, I will ride it into battle."

Martha climbed into the bow top with the prepared potion and looked across to Vardan, still holding his mother's hand. Odda watched from the ground.

"Ride into battle, Vardan? You have to get a horse first," Martha said as she moved to Sunday's side.

Vardan glanced at Odda, who frowned and shook his head.

"I will, Aunt Martha. A powerful horse like my father rode into battle."

"Let's get your mother better first. We have to get these terrible wounds healed before infection sets in. Lucifer slashed her deep and bad with his poisonous claws."

"If she dies, Aunt Martha, I'll kill that devil."

"Your mother won't die again, Vardan, but she's badly wounded. We'll save her."

Three Days Later

More snow had fallen and the bow top was almost covered in a curtain of white. Inside, under warm blankets, Sunday had still not opened her eyes. Martha had been at her side throughout and now held one of her hands.

"I envied you, Sunday, when you came back from Blingoburbia that day after being blessed by Sorceradabra. You could eat again, smell again and even take a pee. Now, though, I wish it was me and not you lying injured. I don't feel pain and I don't eat, but I'd swap places with you without a pause. Odda is certain a poultice he made will work on the wounds."

"It better do, Missy, because my bum hurts, lying down all the time," Sunday whispered. Martha jumped and stared at Sunday's face.

"You're awake, at last."

"I'm dead, remember, and I feel dead." Sunday grinned and stretched.

"Odda made a concoction of stuff his people used to treat wounds. It might have worked."

"Riding on dragons and dragon eggs. What was all that about?" Sunday asked, rubbing her eyes.

"Dragons and eggs? You must have been dreaming, but Odda did put some stuff from a dragon in this thing he made to treat your cuts."

"I knew I had heard someone mention riding a dragon."

"Oh, that was Vardan. He was talking about riding into battle."

"That was it then. Where is he, anyway?"

"Watching Odda make another axe handle. They're going out when the snow has gone to find iron ore. Vardan wants a battle axe. Odda is going to show him how to make things from iron ore."

"Sounds we found a gem in Odda."

"He's good. He knows things we never knew about, or we've forgotten. He will teach Vardan all his skills. When your son is fully grown he will be a man you would not want to face in battle."

Sunday reached a hand out to Martha. "He's your son as well, Missy."

"I know he is, Sunday. I love him as my own."

Chapter Twenty-Three
Fan Fawr, Wales

April the eighth, 1828

"He spends a lot of time sorting things around in his box," Martha said as the three finished clearing the area on top of an entrance to Blingoburbia.

"He's just tidy, Martha," Odda said and hoped he didn't look sheepish.

"I looked in the box a while ago and it smells horrible, all sorts of stuff inside that he's collected. There's even some soil in a rag. Lord knows what he has soil for," Sunday laughed as she cleared the last of the debris.

"Twelve-year-old boys are a law unto themselves. Best to leave them to their treasure and just keep the lid closed. The box is a mess and probably does smell, but thankfully I can't smell it," Martha grinned.

"Do you know what the soil is for, Odda?" Sunday asked.

Odda shrugged and sat down on the warm grass. "You better ask him, it's his business."

"I think you know," Sunday remarked, looking intently at Odda.

"Well, I do, Sunday, but you'd better ask him." Odda was glad he had not lied.

Sunday was about to reply, but the trapdoor tweaked and a pair of twinkly eyes peered through the crack. The hatch cover opened wider and the beaming face of Oldgeeza looked up into the bright April morning. The three stepped back and let the Blingo entrance keeper step out, followed by Jimsalad the apprentice and dozens of other little people, who quickly scampered away, carrying their sacks.

"A good April morning to you all," Oldgeeza said cheerily. "A big day for you all and one everybody in Blingoburbia have been looking forward to."

Martha, Sunday and Odda looked at each other, bewildered faces on each.

"Why is that?" Martha asked, staring at Oldgeeza.

"The big day. April the eighth and the day Draig Goch breathes his first breaths of Welsh air. The first little one we will have seen in a thousand years. You must all be proud, especially young Vardan. He has cared for Draig Goch all these months. He was a bit naughty taking one in the first place, but there are two others which is normal. The third one has always been unwanted by the mother. She only has two teats and the third one, usually the weaker one, gets no milk and dies," Oldgeeza said wistfully.

"Draig Goch? What, who is that?" Martha asked, surprised.

"He will be called Dragon Goch. The first baby dragon to be born in these parts for a thousand years," Jimsalad said, looking slightly surprised Martha did not know.

Martha and Sunday looked stunned, but Odda had a wry grin on his bearded face.

"We found three dragon eggs that time we had that bit of trouble, just after Sunday was badly wounded by Lucifer. Vardan took one of three eggs Fafnir laid in this hole she dug."

"Fafnir!" Martha and Sunday exclaimed together.

"Fafnir is a Norse dragon who was slain by Odin, a Viking chief, hundreds of years ago," Oldgeeza interrupted and saw Odda nodding in agreement. "Satan bought her soul from the gods to be a mate for Draca, or Cyberacid as he is known in the up top world."

Martha and Sunday looked at each other.

"There are two dragons in Ireland that guard the camps of the Boggimps, the Hobgoblins, the Trogladytes and Smegmadytes. Are these the two dragons here in Wales?" Martha asked tremulously.

"More than likely," Oldgeeza replied.

"And my son has one of their eggs?" Sunday asked disbelievingly. She looked towards the bow top, as did Martha.

Without further questions, the pair set off for the bow top. Odda, Jimsalad and Oldgeeza followed.

Vardan was sat in the bow top with the dragon egg safely nestled on a cushion on his knees. He stared in surprise at the five faces looking up at him. The egg was clean, with dozens of overlapping triangular shaped ridges on the surface. Vardan held it tightly.

"It's a dragon egg," Sunday said to a wide-eyed Vardan.

"I know. It's mine. I've been looking after it."

"Future warriors can have their bare backsides slapped, you know," snapped Sunday.

"Yeah, well, it's worth it as long as you don't make me get rid of it."

"Where are you going to keep it, have you thought of that? It's going to be a lot bigger than a dog, or even a horse."

"I can keep it then, Ma?"

"And you clean up after it and it sleeps outside," Sunday replied, shaking her head.

"Odda will make me a cage for it, won't you Odda?" Vardan asked pleadingly. Odda nodded slowly.

Oldgeeza smiled and looked up at Vardan. "It's time for your little friend to come out and face the world, Vardan. Can I hold the egg?"

Vardan stood and carefully handed the egg to the little man. Oldgeeza took it and stepped away a few feet. Vardan jumped down and kept wary eyes on his precious dragon egg.

Oldgeeza held the egg carefully and looked across to Jimsalad, his apprentice. The latter reached into his tunic and withdrew a small bottle. It had a purple liquid inside and Sunday remembered she had seen the substance before in Blingoburbia. Oldgeeza took the bottle, opened it and very carefully poured some over the egg. He then found a soft piece of grass and placed the egg on it and stepped back. Everybody looked on with muted interest.

A minute passed and nothing had happened. The large, crusted egg was the focus of attention with six pairs of eyes watching closely. Then it wobbled slightly. A murmur started from the six watching and eyes widened. More wobbles and the egg rolled away a few inches. It did a half turn and then started rolling slowly down the gentle incline of the grassy ground. Six sets of legs followed until the egg stopped and then went calm and still.

Another minute passed, but no one had spoken. The egg started wobbling again and the murmurs started once more. More wobbles, stronger this time and everyone held their breath. Eyes were willing the egg to break open, but there was another lack of movement. Finally the silence was broken, with a sound of scratching from inside the egg. It moved again and then the tiniest bit of egg was punctured by a small spike. The spike moved around and a crumb of egg shell broke away. Another spike appeared and moved around, more shell dropped off.

A wet pink snout appeared in the tiny hole and pushed. More shell broke away and then a full head appeared. Clear liquid seeped out and the head was followed by a long neck and then a scaly, reddish brown body. The egg burst open and the full wriggling body of the baby dragon fell out onto the grass. A squeak emitted from the open mouth and everybody clapped.

Oldgeeza stepped to the squeaking, wriggling baby dragon and poured some of the purple liquid over its body. He took another bottle from Jimsalad and opened it. Then he sprinkled the silvery and gold powder over the dragon. Draig Goch had been spreckled.

Oldgeeza carefully lifted the little dragon up and walked it to the entrance of Blingoburbia. All followed the little man and watched spellbound as he gently lowered it a few inches into the entrance. A slight warm breeze wafted out and the dragon sniffed the air.

"It's a she and a healthy little specimen. You did her well, Vardan," Oldgeeza said to the astonished youngster. Vardan took the dragon from the little man and held her protectively.

"What do I feed her?" he asked.

Oldgeeza handed the purple liquid bottle to Vardan. "A drop of this in her milk, no more, and for six months. Cow's or goat's milk is fine and twice a day. After six months feed her live mice, shrews, frogs or toads, weasels, even lots of tadpoles. She will grow steadily and can live outdoors after three months. At a year old, take her to a high cliff and simply let her go. She will drop for a hundred feet and then her strength will take over and her wings will flap, then her body will suck in air and away she goes. She will fly around to find food, so you will not see her for days, but as long you handle her carefully and get her used to your scents, she will never be far away wherever you are. But from a year old she will grow quickly and by the time she is three years old, she will be fully grown. There will be days, even weeks, when you will not see her. Female dragons are excellent hunters and are totally independent. Bring her to Blingoburbia in August, on the eighth day, and she will be spreckled again."

"When will she be able to carry me?" Vardan asked.

"When she is about two years old, start climbing onto her back. Get her used to having a weight on her back. Make a leather harness to fit around her neck so you can hold on. Expand it as she grows. Use a definite call to get her attention. They have excellent hearing and can hear you from great distances. She will know who is calling and come to you, but will not come to the ground unless she knows there is no danger. In time, stand on a high ledge and practice jumping on to her back as she passes by."

"Is she a fire breathing dragon?" Sunday asked.

Oldgeeza smiled and nodded. "Oh yes, very much so."

Everyone handled the baby dragon until it tired and closed its eyes. Vardan collected her and took the sleeping dragon back to the box in the bow top. He emptied out the stale soil and put a soft, folded blanket inside. A few minutes later Martha climbed into the bow top with a small bottle, filled with warm milk.

"She needs a feed before she goes off to sleep. I've put a drop of the purple liquid in. Don't know what it is, but Oldgeeza says it's got special growing and healing powers. It worked on your mother's wounds, so it will be fine." Martha handed Vardan the bottle.

"Aunt Martha, when she grows fully I'll ride her all over the lands and sea."

"I know you will, Vardan. Look after her and keep her safe until she is strong enough to fend for herself. Your ma and I will help. Odda says he will make a strong cage for her until she gets too big. We are going to get another cart and a horse so old Watson won't have to pull too much weight. You and Odda will live in it."

"Are there any other Welsh dragons, Aunt Martha?"

"Don't know, Vardan. Probably not nowadays, apart from the two you and Odda saw. I think there were lots of them in the olden days, but they got killed by knights, I think."

"DeeGee will never die Aunt Martha. I'll protect her."

"DeeGee! Is that what you are calling her?"

"I can't say the words the Blingo called her. Draig Goch. He said it in a funny voice, so I am using the two letters, D and G together. Until I can say it how Oldgeeza says it, I will just call her DeeGee."

"So be it, Vardan. DeeGee it is," Martha laughed and left Vardan with his dragon.

Four Months Later

Draig Goch lay on a small hillock overlooking the river, where the two bow tops were sited by the side of the River Neath. Her eagle eyes were watching the two horses, grazing a hundred yards away. Watson and Loire were peaceably eating the meadow grass, oblivious to the young dragon's eyes watching their every movement. A warm sun had risen early in a cloudless blue sky on the early August morning. It was a few minutes to eight and Vardan was walking across the meadow to collect Draig Goch.

She turned from the two horses and saw her young master with a small chain in one hand, a small bag in the other. Her head lifted and she tried to summon the effort to blow a warning from her developing nostrils. After three failed attempts she relaxed and switched her steely red eyes to the more neutral, flickering green eyes that she used when her hunting mood or danger mood was less evident. She knew the boy would be bringing her a couple of mice or a lovely fat toad. He was no threat and she had grown used to his strange scent. There was a toad in the bag, but also a field mouse. Vardan took the mouse out first and dangled it by the long tail. Draig Goch hated these silly antics by her master and snapped it away swiftly. Her eyes watched the bag and saw the movement inside. It was bigger and her mouth drooled. The unfortunate toad tried to escape the boy's clutches and wriggled in fear.

The long neck darted forward, the jaws opened and the terrified toad was history. Vardan had pulled his fingers away a split second before the small razor teeth snatched the toad. He tapped Draig Goch's snout softly and wagged a finger at her. The eyes quickly flashed red, but just as quickly returned to a flickering green.

Vardan deftly fastened the chain to a small leather collar around Draig Goch's neck and tugged it. The eyes flashed steely red again, but went back to the flickering green a few moments later. With another tug, Vardan pulled the feisty little dragon from her warm berth, though her clawed feet had dug harder into the grass.

"Stop being awkward, DeeGee. You're being spreckled again in a few minutes and it's a special occasion, you should be thankful," Vardan said softly.

The nostrils snorted again, but once more there was no response. Draig Goch dug her claws again in the grass, but this time Vardan reached down and scooped her up. Her back legs dangling, his arms under her belly, Vardan skipped down the small hill to where his mother, Martha and Odda waited by the cleared entrance to Blingoburbia. As Vardan passed by the two horses, the flickering green eyes changed to steely red and Draig Goch took in the smell of the two strange four-legged creatures. Saliva ran from her jaws and a long tongue slipped out to wipe it away.

The trapdoor opened and twinkling eyes peered out. Oldgeeza climbed out first, then Jimsalad and about forty other little people, all carrying the hessian sacks and as usual, they disappeared into the undergrowth and bushes. This time, though, another figure appeared from the entrance and a purple and gold robed, long white-haired older Blingo blinked, as the sun stung his eyes. Wizadabra stretched his arms and took in the fresh air of the August morning. The older Blingo looked around and smiled at the four Uptoppers.

"Aahhh, so lovely to feel the up top sun again. I should come up more often, but we are so busy in the chambers down below. Now here I am and there is a young dragon who requires protection for the first hundred years of life. Draig Goch the name."

Vardan stepped forward, holding the angry-looking young dragon. Her eyes were now steely red and definitely not flickering, the nostrils were working overtime, but there was still no fire coming from her mouth. She wriggled in Vardan's arms to escape from the strange-looking figure with the long white hair, who was smiling at her. When the strange little man reached forward to take her, she spat at him and hissed loudly. The little man pointed a finger at the feisty small dragon and suddenly Draig Goch stopped hissing and wriggling and her eyes returned to a flickering green.

Wizadabra took her from Vardan and lifted her above his head, so the sun could touch the now relaxed small green and light blue body. He passed a hand all over her body, then placed a palm on her head and held it there for a few seconds. Wizadabra then took a bottle of the purple liquid from Oldgeeza and poured a small amount on the dragon's forehead. He put two fingers on the spot and gently rubbed it in. He then turned to Vardan and took one of his hands, put a drop on each of two fingers and placed them on the spot where he had touched Draig Goch. Suddenly a light purplish haze appeared around Vardan's hand and on the young dragon's head, then dispersed after a few seconds. A few moments and Wizadabra stepped away and handed Draig Goch back.

"You are bonded with Draig Goch now, young Vardan. You and the dragon will be for ever as one, even though there will be long periods apart. You will be able to speak to her and she will understand what you say. In a hundred years' time, she will need to be spreckled again, as you will be in twelve years' time. Then you will be ready to go and seek out evil and destroy it."

"Will Jacindra be with me?" Vardan asked as Wizadabra turned to go back into Blingoburbia.

"Jacindra will contact you in twelve years' time. She touched you when you were a baby twelve years ago and passed to you the blessing of her mother, Queen Boadicea. Your mother, Sunday Brown, and your aunt, Martha, have a parchment that marks where there are time gaps through which you can all travel. After you are fully grown, you will be able to pass through at these places on your own and do work to combat evil. But beware, Vardan Brown, it is dangerous work and those who you will take on, are creatures that will show no mercy. Like you, they have special powers, but theirs are the powers of evil."

"I will have Draig Goch to help me," Vardan said humbly.

"Yes, but so do the creatures of Hell. Every type of heinous serpent, reptile and fiendish monster. Go carefully, Vardan Brown, and help your mother and aunt to find dying souls and try and persuade the poor wretches not to sell them to the devil's sons."

"Will Odda be an immortal warrior in time?" Vardan asked as Wizadabra took the first step through the trapdoor. The old Magus stopped and looked across to where Odda was standing at the side of Martha and Sunday.

"He has the merits to become an immortal, but Jacindra will choose her partners," the old man replied, waving Odda forward. Odda stepped towards him.

"You are Odda Haralda of the Nors Egersund tribe. We have seen you roaming these lands for hundreds of years and you never sinned or killed without reason. You have the fighting skills that are needed. In thirty- five years' time, if you continue to help as an Uptopper, we will consider you for spreckling and then to become an immortal. Work well, Odda Haralda, and we'll meet again."

Wizadabra was gone. Oldgeeza was sitting on a tree stump and Jimsalad was holding the little sleepy dragon. Vardan had found a field mouse and held the little creature to Draig Goch's nostrils. The jaws snapped and the mouse was gone. Everybody jumped at the lightning speed of the dragon's mouth. A couple of seconds later and she was fast asleep again.

"Unbelievable," Sunday said as she stared at Draig Goch. "I can't blink as quick."

"She will be very, very fast when she's fully grown," Oldgeeza remarked and looked at Vardan. "You will have to be clever to control her, Vardan."

"I will, and where I go she will follow," Vardan replied confidently.

"Not always, Vardan. Dragons only have one master and that is freedom. You will always be second best. Take her now and look after her needs. There will be no thanks from her, she will always take rather than give, but she is your dragon, you are her servant and she will take care of you when you are in need."

Vardan collected the sleeping dragon and walked back to his bow top, the others all watching. Oldgeeza smiled and looked at Sunday.

"It's a long long time since there was a dragon in our lives, and an Uptopper like Vardan. Only every thousand years do they come along. My people are happy again that we have those we can call on to help keep Blingoburbia a place of peace and harmony. There are those sent by Satan to harm us and they have done so. When you and Martha took care of Cerberus Junior and King Smegtooth, we knew we had Uptoppers again to help us. So many of our people have been slain by Satan's progenitors, but in Jacindra, you two and with Vardan and Odda, there is hope for our queendom to flourish once again."

"Who are your main enemies, old man?" Odda asked.

"The Hobgoblins, led by King Ergosnatas and Queen Pooka, the Boggimps, the Trogladytes and the Leprechauns. They are all protected by Satan and his sons. They have been our enemies for hundreds and hundreds of years. The Hobgoblins used to be our cousins, but Missiquin, our Queen and her sister, Mizpooka, fell out after our king was captured. Mizpooka was furious when Missiquin married Massakin, who she wanted to wed. Mizpooka betrayed Massakin by having him captured by Ergosnatas and his Hobgoblins. He is still a prisoner in Hobgob Hollows. One day we will release him from his dungeon."

"Why does Mizpooka call herself Pooka?" Sunday asked.

"Because in Blingoburbia, everyone other than the three Magus has eight letters in their names. Mizpooka is no longer a Blingo so we took three letters from her name. She has vowed one day to get them back, by conquering Blingoburbia."

"Do these other tribes have people like the three Magus that are in Blingoburbia?" Martha asked as she listened with interest.

Oldgeeza smiled and nodded. "Yes. His name's Satan. He has similar powers to our three Magus and he has seven sons who can each perform great feats of sorcery and magic. Though one son, his youngest, Drebmif, disobeyed Satan and was banished. You travelled with him for many years. We believe he calls himself Fimber."

"He's a good man. He's lying at the bottom of the Atlantic and slowly turning into a fish," Martha said sorrowfully.

"We know, Martha Budd, but there is nothing we can do. However, there is one who can help him," Oldgeeza said.

"Vardan," Sunday interrupted.

"Yes. Your son has been given powers to go to the deepest depths of the oceans. Drebmif is a good man and we are sorry to hear what happened to him. When Vardan is fully grown, he and Draig Goch will be able to rescue Drebmif from his watery prison. Now, my friends, I have to leave you and go help find items for the queendom."

Oldgeeza disappeared to find the other Blingos and Jimsalad took his place on the tree stump, to keep a watch on the entrance.

"Where now, Missy?" Sunday asked as they all sat around a fire waiting for a pan of water to boil, so that clothes could be washed.

"We carry on with our Uptopper duties and stay in Wales. Vardan needs to find food for Draig Goch while she is growing. We can all help with that. In twelve years, Vardan will receive the SWAN mark and Odda will be spreckled. Then we go to America."

"What about this new devil, Mephistopheles? He'll be just as evil," Sunday remarked.

"We do our duties as normal and hope there are no battles to attend before the ones that will happen in America in the future. Thousands will be killed over there, unfortunately."

"Will Draig Goch come with us?" Odda asked.

"She'll be fully grown then and can fly anywhere in the world," Martha replied.

"Can't imagine that son of mine not wanting her to come to America," Sunday laughed.

The water had boiled and they had started washing clothes. Odda laughed and started nodding. "Vardan with his dragon will be a one man army in a few years' time."

"With you at his side, Odda, after you get the SWAN mark," Sunday added.

"So we stay here in cold wet miserable Wales for the next few years, then sail across the Atlantic to America and try and persuade dying soldiers not to sell their souls?" Odda said.

"Exactly; and do our best to prevent those evil devils getting the souls of the poor men," Martha answered ruefully.

"Back to my side of the Atlantic and lovely warm weather," Sunday laughed as she scrubbed her clothes. Odda and Martha nodded agreement.

Chapter Twenty-Four
Fan Hir, Wales

August the eighth 1840

The top of the small mountain was covered in a thick swirl of mist that swept downwards to the floor of the Beacons, running for miles in every direction. Fan Gihilrych, another small mountain a few miles to the east, was clear of mist and a bright sun warmed its top. A few horses grazed on the rough moorland grass, also dotted with dozens of sheep.

High above the Beacons, a large creature with a light blue, scaly belly and a dark greeny-brown cover to its top and back, made its umpteenth swoop across the rugged moorland.

Almost eighty feet from head to the tip of her long tail, Draig Goch was hungry after sleeping for three months. Steely red eyes watched the smaller animals fleeing for their lives as she circled, a hundred and fifty feet above. Her red eyes picked out an older, fat ewe, lagging behind other younger and faster sheep. The dragon snorted, dipped its mighty head and began a deadly descent at lightning speed.

The terrified ewe was snatched up by mighty clawed feet and whisked away to the dragon's lair, tucked into a wide gap on the rocky face of one of the mountains. Inside the dark lair were scattered bones of several animals the dragon had devoured in times past; there were even human bones.

Two horse riders, returning to their base after an early morning hunting session, had seen the dragon take off with its prize and the bigger rider, a dead deer strapped across his horse's rear, pointed a finger towards the distant hills.

"She's awake again, Odda. Her first kill in months and better this time than a two-legged one. I'll go up and see her after we've done. I'm looking forward to getting the Mark of the SWAN," Vardan said as the two bow tops came into sight.

"I get spreckled today, but I wish I was getting the SWAN as well. Another twenty years for me." Odda frowned.

"Soon pass. Then we can go together to find and kill Satan's hell creatures."

No sooner had Vardan's words finished than a fierce slash of lightning ripped into the ground in front of both horses. The terrified horses reared then dropped down. Thunder followed and again the horses reared, but both riders held firm.

"Mephistopheles," Odda cursed as he waited for the devil's son to appear. "He chooses his moments. It's nearly time to see the Blingos."

The reddish figure appeared and snarled loudly as he took shape before Vardan and Odda.

At the same time, several other figures appeared to the side of the grinning demon. Different sizes, some small, others as large as Odda and Vardan, different creatures, but all fearsome-looking, grotesque figures. Mephistopheles started laughing as he saw the looks of bewilderment on the two young men's faces.

"Vardan Brown and Odda Haralda. You talk with stupid and boastful hopes of your ambitions to kill my father's fighters, or hell creatures, as you call them. I thought it was time to introduce you to a few of my father's hell creatures. Between them, they have slain many of your kind over the centuries. True, two or three of yours have survived, but that is going to change. I can put a force of over two hundred of our fighters together against your pathetic little rabble of how many? Four, five or six? I will wipe you all out within the next fifty years and then I'll send my armies of little people to wipe out those stupid creatures in Blingoburbia. My brother Lucifer was too soft with your mother and Martha Budd. He should have put them in our torture chambers a long time ago, but Lucifer sleeps now to regain his strength and I am not as easy going. Take a look at a few of the hell creatures you will face in the years ahead." Mephistopheles turned and nodded towards his evil brood.

Both Vardan and Odda looked across at the motley group of hell creatures. Every pair of demonic eyes stared back. Half had never been human; they were mutants derived from the breeding between Hobgoblins, Boggimps, Trogladytes, Leprechauns and others of the small warrior tribes and of humans. Mephistopheles singled out one of his fighters and told him to step forward. The creature had once been human, but now had the haggard, scarred, red-eyed face of a monster. He held a bloodstained scimitar-type sword in one hand.

"Meet Vlad the Impaler. He was the fiercest warrior of his day, four hundred years ago. He killed hundreds of his enemies by himself. Hacked off their heads and put them on stakes outside his fortress. Hence his name, the Impaler. He had the devil's blood in him from the day he was born. He's done that to at least twenty of your so-called immortals. He wants your mother's head on one of his stakes and Jacindra's on the one at its side."

"He's good then?" Vardan grinned, refusing to be intimidated.

"One of my best, Vardan Brown, at least of those that were once human. Meet another of my best, but he is not of human blood." Mephistopheles ordered another hell creature forward. He was small but heavily built. A large head on a muscular body. Yellow eyes and fanged teeth. Large hairy bands, a short sword in one, a steel headed spiked club in the other.

"He's Trogtrol, Chief of the Trogladytes. Sworn enemy to your friends, the Blingos. He and a hundred of his men raided an outpost of Blingoburbia six hundred years ago and slaughtered over a thousand of the stupid imbeciles. Two hundred years later he wiped out another colony of Blingos."

"So he's good as well?" Odda now called from his horse. Trogtrol made to step towards Odda, but a finger from Mephistopheles pointed at the ferocious-looking dwarf.

"He's impatient to get at you, Odda Haralda, but today is not the time and you are not yet an immortal. He can have your soul another day and I want to see him do his worst. Now get away, the pair of you and be thankful I don't let these hell creatures loose. One day I will and I want to watch you both beg for mercy, but I need you both to be immortals. Like I said, they have slain many immortals over the centuries, one day they will kill you two, but first I want your women, Sunday Brown and Jacindra."

Without another word, Vardan and Odda pushed their horses forward and through the group of hell creatures, who begrudgingly parted to let them pass. They rode on for about fifty yards then both turned to look back. There was no sight of Mephistopheles or his warriors.

Later That Day

It seemed hours since Vardan and Sunday had passed through the entrance to the queendom at eight that morning. They had been taken to the Magus's chambers by Jimsalad and Sunday had watched proudly as her tall, muscular son had received his Mark of the SWAN. Vardan had been spellbound by the crystal swan as it did to him what it bad done to his mother several years earlier. The swan's eyes had fixed on Vardan's eyes for long moments, much longer than other recipients in previous times.

All three Magus had been present at the ceremony, to bestow on the powerfully built young warrior, his immortality. He had sworn an oath to defend innocents and the good against evil. The purple liquid had been poured onto his forehead and left to trickle down to his mouth. He swallowed and took it into his body. For several moments his body was frozen and he stood naked before all watching. All three Magus stepped forward to place a palm on his head and silently speak a command to the newest immortal.

The ceremony had finished and Jimsalad had taken the pair back to the entrance. Outside in the up top world again, Sunday, Martha and Vardan had watched as Odda was spreckled by Oldgeeza with the moon and silver dust.

Odda had earlier been envious of Vardan's journey into the queendom, but now as the tingling sensation of his spreckling had flowed over his body and he had taken his first steps to his own immortality, he was happier and embraced his friend warmly.

"I feel good now. It was worth waiting for. You're further ahead than me, Vardan, but one day I will take the journey you made today."

Vardan put a friendly arm around Odda's shoulder and laughed.

"They pour this purple stuff over your head and it trickles down into your mouth. It tastes absolutely horrible and your body freezes. You've got that to look forward to."

Odda laughed and shook his head. "Right, that's it for me. I'll stay as I am so I can't taste anything and feel warm rather than cold."

As the two joked, Martha stepped forward with spades and rakes and pointed them to the area where the Blingos had just returned to the queendom. Both frowned and shrugged, but took the implements to take their turn at covering up.

Sunday watched and started laughing. "Two beefy young men, the world's best battle axe and best bowmen and probably the best riflemen and you have to clear up and get your bands dirty."

Vardan scowled and looked back at his grinning mother and aunt. "You forgot that I'm also the world's best dragon rider."

Draig Goch had feasted well and was lying on her side, ready to fall asleep. The husky voice echoed through her cave lair and she stirred. The great body lifted and the head pointed towards the daylight a few yards ahead. There was a hissing snort and a brief spurt of orange and yellow flame from her mouth. She hated being disturbed.

"Don't do that, DeeGee. It smells foul and it's not funny," Vardan growled.

"I was going to sleep," Draig Goch replied as she turned her head to nibble at an itch.

"I saw you earlier, taking that sheep. That's allowed but you were looking at the horses as well. I've told you, no horses. Sheep, cows and oxen, but not horses. You might take mine and that will get you in my bad books."

"Put a mark on it then and I'll know not to take it."

"No horses, DeeGee. That's an order. Understand?"

Draig Goch finished her itch and sniffed contemptuously. "All right, no horses, but I'm bored staying around here. You promised me travel, so I'm going to sleep again, until you're ready to take me somewhere better. Wake me up when you're ready to go."

"Heard of America, DeeGee?" Vardan asked as he rubbed her wet snout affectionately.

"Is it warmer than this miserable place?"

"Never been, to be honest, but my Ma has and she says it's warmer."

"When are we going?"

"Soon. There's a load of battles to be fought and we have to go to do our duty."

"How far is this America?"

"Across a big ocean, my ma says."

"Do I get a ride on one of them floating things?"

"No, you fly. You're too big to carry."

"Are there any dragons in America? It's not nice, always on your own?"

"Not sure, but probably. It's a hundred times bigger than Wales. Anyway, I'll call you when we're ready, but I need some more practice in the meantime at riding on you. I want to dive deep into the sea, deep down," Vardan said as he turned to leave.

"I hate that. It's wet and cold. I sneeze for days afterwards."

"You get fish, big fish to eat. You like that. Seals and dolphins, tasty, huh?"

Draig Goch sniffed and settled down again. "Yeah, well, that's true, I suppose, but there better be some dragons in this new place. America. And it better be warmer, Vardan Brown, or I'm coming back here."

"No horses, DeeGee, if you get hungry. If you eat mine you're in trouble."

Draig Goch sniffed again and licked her lips. She loved chasing horses. They ran faster than sheep and cows and there was a thrill when she stopped playing and snatched one. There was a land to the south of her cave lair where hundreds of the things roamed freely. When she woke up again, she would take another flight there and bring one back. They were smaller than the ones Vardan Brown and his friend rode; hairy and fat, but delicious.

Chapter Twenty-Five
America
Far North East Mississippi

March 1862

Odda was thrilled as his third shot smashed another of the ten bottles he and Vardan had put on a felled tree trunk. The British Enfield rifle he proudly held was his prize possession. Vardan had missed one of the bottles, but had hit two of his three. On their way to America on a British merchant ship carrying weapons and supplies to the Confederate Army in Alabama, the four travellers had befriended an arms dealer from London in England. Martha had been the target of Jacob Davids, the good-looking Jewish arms dealer, on the *Plymouth Rover* which had carried Martha, Sunday, Vardan and Odda to America.

Martha and Sunday had persuaded Davids to sell them a case of new Lee Enfield rifles and another case of powder and shot. On arrival at Mobile and the waiting rebel commander there, the missing cases of rifles and munitions was offset by several gold coins and a night of passion with Martha and Sunday, for the young grey-coated major.

Driving their two bow tops on the road north from Mobile, it was noticeable that the majority of the rebel soldiers heading to Tennessee and the pending battle at Shiloh, carried ancient flintlocks and fowling guns. The new Lee Enfield rifles Martha and Sunday had acquired through their feminine charms, were more deadly, accurate and could be reloaded twice as quick. In the remaining years ahead during the civil war, such weapons would be decisive.

The four had crossed the state line into northern Mississippi and had settled the bow tops in a quiet recess off a leafy lane, a stone's throw from the Tennessee River. Martha and Sunday had gone to buy supplies, leaving Vardan and Odda to watch the bow tops. A scouting party of Union soldiers had been watching the two young men shooting their rifles. The blue coated northerners carried old Springfield carbines, but better than the muskets most southerners possessed. A sergeant on a fine bay horse pressed his mount forward to go and speak to the two strangers. Dillon Conner was the son of Irish immigrants and no lover of anybody who supported suppression of lesser mortals. He hated the English with a vengeance for invading Ireland in years past. Though he had left Ballyshannon in Ireland as a young boy, he still had great respect for the Irish.

Looking down at Vardan and Odda, his eyes were more on the fine new rifles the pair were holding. His curiosity was also on the long hair both of the young men sported.

"Where are you going, lads? I take it you're with the two carts?" Conner grunted as he flicked a thumb at the two bow tops.

"Tennessee, sergeant. We have business just over the border," Vardan replied politely.

"Over the border? Are you joking? Just whereabouts over the border?"

Vardan looked up at the Union sergeant and shrugged.

"Not sure exactly, sergeant, we're just deciding where to go next."

Conner sniffed and his eyes narrowed. "You're English?"

Vardan nodded. "Yeah."

"And your friend, is he English?" Conner asked switching his keen eyes to Odda.

"I'm from Yorkshire," Odda answered for himself.

"Last time I heard, mister, Yorkshire was in England. So two English fellers over here in the southern states and I hear the rebels down here are buying guns and stuff from England and the two pieces you're firing look fairly new. Lee Enfield, huh?"

Both Vardan and Odda nodded slowly without replying.

Conner waved his four men across and the riders quickly cantered their horses over.

"Davey, Laurie, go see what's in the two gypsy carts. Search 'em good." Conner ordered. The two troopers obeyed the sergeant's instruction and rode the fifty yards to where the bow tops were positioned. Vardan looked up at the suspicious Union sergeant.

"Our carts are private property, sergeant. We have nothing to hide," he said carefully.

"Then you have nothing to fear, mister. What at yer both called?"

"I'm Vardan Brown, my friend's called Odda Haralda."

"What sort of name is that? Not English," Conner mused.

"Like I said, I'm from Yorkshire, but my ancestors were from Norway," Odda replied. "Vikings, to be exact."

Conner turned to the two remaining troopers and laughed.

"Hear that, you two? A fucking Viking over here in America." As Conner spoke one of the other two troopers called to him from one of the bow tops. He pulled his horse around and signalled to his two men.

"Cover them and don't let them out of your sight," Conner hissed and rode away. Both cavalrymen pulled out their old carbines and aimed them at Vardan and Odda.

A few minutes later and the three cavalry scouts rode back, the sergeant with a broad grin on his unshaven face.

"A crate with British rifles in. Lee Enfields and a few Brunswicks. Powder and lead shot. You got some explaining to do, fellers. Gun running is serious trouble," Conner growled.

"We're not gun runners, we bought them legitimately back in Mobile," Vardan replied.

"And you got receipts for them?"

"Somewhere, yeah. My ma will have one someplace."

Conner looked around and then laughed. "Your ma? Invisible, is she, Englishman? I don't see any woman."

"She and my aunt went to buy supplies. They'll be back."

"Your ma and your aunt, eh? They left you two little boys playing with your toys. In this country, feller, Americans at your age are farmers, builders or soldiers, not kids trying to be soldiers. Put your English guns down and stand away. You're going back with us to face army justice and probably a noose. I hate gun runners just as much as I hate the fucking English."

Vardan stepped back a stride, but as he did, with lightning speed he raised his rifle, aiming at the sergeant's belly. The startled Union sergeant was taken by surprise and pulled his nervous horse back a stride. The two troopers with the carbines were now behind their sergeant's body, unable to see Vardan. Odda had not had time to reload his rifle and stepped behind Vardan. He quickly reloaded as the soldiers were unsure what to do.

"You just proved you're gun runners, mister and I'm gonna have my men shoot the both of you," Conner hissed and steadied his horse. He made a gesture to his men to shoot, but Odda's rifle was now aimed at the nearest trooper.

"They fire, sergeant, and you die first," Vardan called with intent.

"Two shots between you. We've got five," Conner almost screamed.

From the bow tops a female voice called across the field. Sunday had her longbow at the ready and an arrow slotted. Her better hearing had heard the Union sergeant. At her side, Martha had also snatched up a longbow and had her arrow sighted to one of the bewildered troopers. The four mounted troopers were unsure what to do, but four carbines were now at the ready.

Conner glanced across the fifty yards and started laughing. "Two bloody fancy-looking women with bows and arrows? Are you fucking mad?"

Vardan still held his rifle to Conner's belly and started grinning. "Take your hat off, sergeant, and hold it above your head."

"You're fucking dead, mister," Conner hissed.

"You will be if you don't raise your hat," Odda now called. One of the troopers had seen the two women with the raised longbows and called across to Conner.

"Sarge, those arrows are pointed at us. The women look as if they know what they're doing," red-haired Davey Barnes called nervously.

"Shut the fuck up, Davey. I'm not taking my hat off fer no fucking English bastard."

The arrow ripped off Conner's hat and carried on past the startled troopers. The sergeant fumbled with his reins and the horse did a quick buck and unseated its rider. Conner fell with a bump and screamed. He tried to scramble up, but a second arrow thudded into the ground between his knees. He let go of the reins and the horse bolted.

The four troopers instantly pushed their hands up in surrender, two of them dropping their carbines. Conner looked up and then across to where both Martha and Sunday stood with longbows at the ready. The embarrassed sergeant stayed on his knees. Odda and Vardan had their Enfields aimed at the troopers.

"We're not gun runners, sergeant and we're not fucking English bastards. We have no interest in your war and just want to move on. Go get his horse, Odda," Vardan called and lowered his rifle. Odda turned and went to fetch the horse. Vardan picked up the two carbines and handed them to the troopers who had dropped them. They were accepted sheepishly.

"Sarge, they're okay. Let's leave them and get off," Davey Barnes called. Conner had taken his horse back, dusted his pants down and glared at Barnes.

"You're American, Davey. I'm Irish and I don't trust the English," Conner scowled.

"They could have killed us. That Negro woman could have killed you," another of the troopers called out. Conner swung his body into the saddle and pointed at Vardan, his eyes warily glancing at the still raised longbows.

"If we see you lot near here again, you won't get lucky the next time."

Conner spurred his horse and set off hastily, followed by four grinning troopers. The red-haired one touched his hat to Vardan and Odda, then waved across to Martha and Sunday, who waved back.

A Month Later
Near Shiloh Church, Tennessee.

They stood looking east from the battle-scarred church building. It was an area referred to as the 'Peach orchard' and the destruction was immense. Hundreds of soldiers in grey uniforms and hundreds more in blue uniforms lay dead or mortally wounded. Along the Hamburg River Road, dead horses lay along a two hundred yard stretch in mutilated heaps. Gun carriages wrecked and supply wagons minus wheels, tipped onto their sides, some still smouldering, several hours after the last shots of the battle at Shiloh had been fired. Local people mixed with the scattered remnants of both armies, searching for fathers, sons, brothers and friends.

A short distance away, leading to the Tennessee River via Dills Branch Stream, another nicknamed area called the 'Hornet's Nest' that had seen the worst of the fighting at Shiloh, held almost a thousand dead and wounded from both sides. So many bodies, it was possible to walk for long stretches by just stepping on corpses without touching the ground. Progress was impeded by the many dead horses littering the many battle sites between Owl Creek to the west and Lick Creek to the east.

The four stood in abject shock at the carnage all around. Screams for help from the dying rent the still, almost bloody air of the battlefield. For Odda, it was his first introduction to mass killings that ran into hundreds, even thousands. A warrior from the eleventh century, he had only witnessed casualties that ran mostly to two figures and just occasionally into three figures. For Vardan it was worse. It was his first visit to a battle site.

Sunday was watching a small group of figures working together over a hundred yards away. Eight in total, four smaller, four larger. Her eagle eyes picked them out easily and she could even hear them talking between themselves. One of the shorter ones seemed to be in charge. Of the larger ones, a giant figure looked up with cruel eyes and growled.

"Hell creatures," she declared, pointing to where the eight figures could be seen. "Soul collecting, I reckon, for their lord and master."

Martha, Vardan and Odda glanced across the battlefield.

"You're right, Sunday. Eight of them," Martha said. "A huge one, three normal size, four short ones and one of the shorter ones ordering the others about."

"Trogtrol," Vardan said as his keen eyes picked out the short stocky figure.

"You know that creature, then?" Sunday asked.

"Me and Odda had the unfortunate experience to see him and a few of the hell creatures back in Wales a few years ago."

"I remember the day," Odda declared. "Mephistopheles stopped him showing us how tough he is. There was another one, taller, who impaled his victims on stakes outside his castle."

"Vlad the Impaler. One real ugly looking specimen, carrying a strange-looking sword," Vardan added and looked back to his bow top. "I think I'll go get my sabre, something tells me it might be needed."

"I think I might need my battle axe," Odda grinned.

"Alright, boys. I think I might need a longbow. I'll stay back a bit and keep you two in sight, just in case," Sunday said and followed Vardan and Odda. Martha shrugged and called out to the three.

"Fetch my chair, I might need it," she laughed. "On second thoughts, I'll get a longbow as well and stay with Sunday. Leave you two fellers to have a word with those despicable creatures."

Trogtrol's yellow eyes saw the two walking across the battlefield. He nudged the hell creature at his side. Vlad the Impaler looked up from his demonic work and spotted Vardan and Odda approaching. He picked up his scimitar and smiled. He had thought of a confrontation with the two young upstarts every day since he had first set his evil red eyes on them in Wales, years earlier.

Another hell creature was watching. Ergosnatas, the vile Irish Hobgoblin chief, had heard of the two who were friends of his loathed enemies, the Blingos. He had heard the mother of one of the pair had defeated Cerberus Junior and another had killed King Smegtooth the Terrible. Ergosnatas needed to impress Mephistopheles, who he knew favoured Trogtrol as leader of his group of hell creatures. He and Trogtrol had never been friends and had to avoid confrontation, for fear of being sent to the torture chambers for disobedience.

"Kill the fair haired one, but take the dark haired one captive. Mephistopheles wants him alive to hand as a present to Satan," Trogtrol ordered. All but Ergosnatas grunted agreement to the powerful hairy dwarf's instruction.

"They usually have two undead women with them. Keep a watch for them, but don't kill either if they appear.

Mephistopheles wants both for wives," Trogtrol barked. "This is a day I've wanted for years."

Eight pairs of evil eyes watched the two young warriors striding confidently across the bloody battlefield of Shiloh. Each hell creature wanted to be the one who killed the long faired-haired fighter, the one holding a battle axe. Trogtrol moved a half pace in front of his group; he needed to be the one who killed the invader. He held his spiked club firmly in a strong hairy hand. His other held the Roman sword with which he had slain hundreds of his enemies.

Both Vardan and Odda knew they were not going to be welcomed with hearty back slaps or hugs. Odda glanced at his big friend and spoke quickly.

"Straight in, Vardan, and no mercy. While you're striking the first one, have the next one in mind. I'll take the short one in front, you go for the taller one with the hat and the broad blade. After those two, we take the others as they come, including the giant. Are you nervous?"

Vardan kept his eyes forward and nodded. "A bit. My first battle."

"I know, it was the same for me, peeing myself," Odda laughed.

"I'm glad my pants are brown," Vardan replied dryly. Odda laughed louder.

The eight hell creatures watched, with Trogtrol now a stride to the front. Behind him, Vlad the Impaler set his dead eyes on the tall muscular figure of Vardan, his scimitar held ready. At the rear came Attila the Hun and the giant Mongolis.

Several yards away, a scaly red figure grinned as it looked up from stealing another soul from a dying soldier. Mephistopheles would keep out of the way of his elite squad of ferocious guardians. These were the best of the hundreds of slayers that his father, Satan, held in service.

They had served Satan well in the short time Mephistopheles had been on duty for his father. His brother Lucifer had never been let down by the same hell creatures during his spell as Hell protector and provider. Although from an original number of ten, the elite squad had lost two to the immortals in the earlier centuries. He wanted Vardan captured, to be taken away and trained to be one of his feared warriors. To fight and slay the immortals, the hell creatures had to be the best.

Trogtrol was ready for battle. He intended to remain the best of Satan's hell creatures. He had slain hundreds in the past, mostly lesser individuals such as the Blingos, the Gnomes and the Pixelves. To capture the son of the destroyer of Cerberus Junior would be a real prize. He hated collecting souls for Satan, it was work for the feeble undead. He was a hell warrior and should have been an immortal warrior. If he could not be one of the latter, he would kill them instead.

The head of Vlad the Impaler hit the bloody ground after one lightning swift stroke from Vardan's sabre. Vardan kicked the severed head aside and wielded his sabre again. Plodgum the evil Enforcer of the Smegmadytes was next. He let out a blood curdling scream and ran at Vardan with his trident and razor wire netting. Unfortunately, he tripped over Vlad's severed head and fell in front of Vardan. The curved sabre flashed again and a second head dropped to the ground. Attila and Mongolis waited at the rear if they were needed.

A few feet away, Trogtrol was in a fierce fight with Odda. The two smashing at each other with their weapons, the battle axe narrowly missing the hairy dwarf's large head, but taking one of his pointed ears off. In return, his spiked club had battered Odda about the body.

The first arrow struck Plebtooth the Terrible, King of the Boggimps in the middle of his head, making him squeal with anger and pain. He grabbed the arrow shaft and pulled it out with a large blob of hairy green jelly-like flesh attached. The second arrow hit him in the eye and sent him sprawling backwards, dead and flat on his back.

Ergosnatas the Hobgoblin, jumped over the headless corpse of Plodgum and dived at Vardan with his broadsword slicing through the air. Sabre and broadsword clanged together and both warriors pulled away quickly to strike again.

Odda had grounded a hissing and cursing Trogtrol and raised the mighty battle axe to chop the dwarf in half. He would have succeeded, but as he brought the axe down, a growling figure jumped onto his back, clawing at his body with razor-sharp talons. Mephistopheles had seen his hell creatures being killed and flew across the battlefield to stop the slaughter. He was too late to stop a fourth hell creature dying. Banshee executioner, Drumbad the third, took arrows in two of his three eyes and like Plodgum a few seconds earlier, ended up on his back, another slain hell creature.

Odda was hurled several yards from where Trogtrol had faced being chopped in half, and landed on top of a Union howitzer, that hours earlier had blasted red hot canister at the flagging Confederate rebels. His back was raked to the bone and he slid from the big gun and over the dead body of a blue-coated gunner, who had lost a leg as well as half his face.

Mephistopheles glowered at the four remaining hell creatures and cursed loudly, his rantings echoed across the battlefield. Trogtrol scrambled to his feet and stood, head bowed to his screaming master. Likewise Ergosnatas and hulking giant Mongolis. The latter, Genghis Khan's bestial torturer, whose favourite delicacy was to tear out an opponent's heart and eat it, washed down with a goblet of blood from the victim's body. Attila stood stiffly but erect, each hand grasping a sword. His red but fearsome eyes watching the young warrior who had slain two of the elite hell creatures.

Vardan moved to where Odda lay over the dead Union soldier and carefully lifted him to his feet. A dazed and wounded Odda picked up his battle axe and turned to face the remaining four creatures. Vardan cupped his hands and blew breath into them, making a loud, shrill noise. He repeated the call twice more, this time louder and directed to the north east. He stopped and scanned the evening air. A few yards away the remaining four hell creatures and a leering Mephistopheles, were ready to strike again at Vardan and the wounded Odda.

Suddenly, a loud shrieking noise echoed across the sky and eyes turned to look upwards.

The swooping figure of Draig Goch came into view, mighty wings spread wide and her armoured body thrusting power into every muscle. She saw the seven figures three hundred feet below and picked out her dragon master, supporting his injured friend. The other five, she guessed, confronting her young master a few feet away, were not friendly. She roared loudly and dived at the five awe-struck hell creatures. At tremendous speed the massive green and blue body swooped earthwards. A long spout of poison flame was unleashed and four of the hell creatures dived for cover. Mephistopheles held his nerve and warded off the flames with a raised hand, but the whoosh of air as the large fire dragon swept by, unsettled his hovering body and he stumbled. He ordered his remaining four fighters to stand away.

Having lost half of his hell creatures, he had no wish to lose the rest. He had underestimated the fighting skills of Vardan and Odda, and also knew that the two killed by arrows to the eyes, were shot at long range by others, almost certainly Sunday Brown and Martha Budd. With a fire dragon to contend with as well, and knowing the power of such beasts, he had no choice but to skulk away. His time would come again.

"I will send fifty against you next time, Vardan Brown and I will have dragons. You were lucky this time, but I will have your head cut off and put it on show at my father's torture chambers." Mephistopheles ordered his four hell creatures away and dejectedly they trudged from the battlefield. Then the ranting son of Satan vanished in a red haze.

Vardan waited 'til Draig Goch had settled on the ground and walked to her. He rubbed her snout and smiled.

"Thanks, DeeGee, you came quick."

"You called three times. I'm not deaf, you know. I heard you the first time," Draig Goch replied with a hint of sarcasm. Vardan laughed and patted her snout.

"Just testing you, lady. I need to know how quick you respond."

"Was I good?"

"Very."

"Then you're happy, I'm happy and now can I go?"

"Yeah, off you go then and don't leave town. I might need you again."

"I'm sure you will, Vardan Brown, holder of the Mark of the SWAN," Draig Goch replied, then shook her mighty body, took in a lungful of air and lifted away, disappearing into the oncoming night.

An hour later and Odda had received attention to his cuts from Martha and Sunday. The yellow fire poison matter that had healed Sunday's wounds would do the same for Odda. As soon as Odda was settled on his bed, Martha, Sunday and Vardan left him, to continue finding dying soldiers. They had found a few and persuaded them not to sell their souls. With nightfall, but still the cries of wounded men at different places, the three continued their work until turned midnight. Vardan and Sunday needed sleep and tiredly left Martha to resume finding soldiers to let go of life peaceably. She toiled on the battlefields 'til dawn.

There were as many bloodied blue uniforms on the Shiloh battlefields as there were grey when the final numbers had been totted up. Confederate General Albert Johnson had been killed and would be the highest ranking officer to lose his life in the civil war. Union commander Ulysses Grant, would in later years become President of the United States. Just over three thousand five hundred between both armies were killed, almost the same on each side. The second highest death toll in the battles of the civil war, behind Gettysburg in Pennsylvania.

Six Months Later
Boyle County, Kentucky

His wounds healed, Odda had decided he could teach Vardan no more battle axe fighting skills. They were equally matched with the big Dane's axe weapon. So too with the rifle and pistols. It was with the longbow that Vardan had the edge. His bigger frame and extra strength meant he had the power to send an arrow further than his not small friend. However, neither had the skill of Sunday with a throwing knife. As much as they tried, neither could match Vardan's mother in accuracy with a knife.

A few miles from Perryville, the two bow tops were tucked into a small copse of trees off a farm track. It was the first week into October and surprisingly warm for an autumn day.

Both horses were peaceably grazing in a nearby field and Martha and Sunday were roasting a chicken over a fire. Several potatoes also roasted in the fire. Sunday was content to let Martha do the work, while she sat on Martha's chair, sipping wine.

Odda and Vardan were practicing their various weapon skills. They had spent an hour with their longbows and had swapped over to the Enfield rifles they had brought up from Alabama. While Vardan had the edge with his first seven or eight shots at targets they kept moving further away, nimble fingered Odda could reload his rifle four times a minute, to Vardan's three.

From a hundred yards away on the farm track, two Union soldiers had heard the firing and had ridden to investigate. They pulled their horses to a halt and looked across to Vardan and Odda. One of the soldiers stared intently and shook his head.

"Fucking hell, Laurie. It's them sods we saw a few months back near Shiloh. Up here now in Kentucky. What the fuck are they doing?" Davey Barnes muttered.

Lawrence Brubaker looked with similar intensity and also nodded. "Spying Davey for the rebels, that's what I think. Fucking rebel spies. Too much of a coincidence."

"Nah. They're not spies, Laurie. Probably gun runners like the sarge said, but not spies. Let's go see and tell 'em to fuck off before Conner gets his Irish arse over here."

"They're fucking good with those British guns though, Davey. Did ya see how quick they reload?"

"Too good, Laurie. We could do with shooters like those two on our side. Let's go talk to 'em?"

Brubaker hesitated and looked around. "Suppose Conner and the others come though? He'll probably accuse us of being collaborators."

"Collab—collab what?"

"Collaborators, you dumb fuck. Siding with the enemy." Brubaker laughed, shaking his head.

The pair kicked their horses forward and cantered across the field. As soon as they had ridden twenty yards, both Odda and Vardan heard the horses. They turned and waited. Odda quickly reloaded his rifle, but did not raise it. Vardan also held his rifle low.

"We meet again, fellers," Davey Barnes said carefully, his eyes watching both closely, his free hand touching the butt of his revolver in its holster.

"Passing through, soldier, like last time. Heading north all the time," Vardan replied, looking up at the wary soldier.

"Gotta tell you to move on though, mister. Braxton Bragg's rebels are a few miles away and itching for a fight. Not safe around here. Best you move on," Barnes said firmly.

"Take us a couple of hours to pack up," Vardan replied.

"We'll help you get moving and away from here. Go west, it'll be safer," Barnes said.

"Fair enough. You can have something to eat if you want, my ma and aunt are cooking a meal in the trees over there." Vardan pointed. "Chicken, roast potatoes and stuff."

The troopers looked at each other and smiled. Davey Barnes nodded. "Sounds good, Laurie. Can't hurt, I suppose."

Brubaker sighed and shook his head.

"If Conner comes we'll get shot, but I'm hungry and we had no breakfast."

Ten minutes later and Brubaker and Barnes were tucking into the food, along with Sunday and Vardan. Eagle-eyed Davey Barnes had hardly taken a breath as he ate, but eventually looked at Vardan and then to Sunday. He downed a tankard of wine and wiped his mouth.

"Ma'am, you don't look old enough to be his ma." Barnes nodded towards Vardan.

Sunday wiped her mouth and smiled. "We black women don't age as quickly as white women, soldier."

"You eat well, though ma'am. I see your friend isn't eating though, nor yon feller." Barnes flicked a thumb to where Odda was bringing the two horses to the bow tops.

"They have a tummy bug from yesterday. They're off food for a bit."

"Hope the chicken isn't bad," grinned Brubaker as he listened to Sunday.

"Fresh this morning, don't worry, fellers. We aren't spies and we don't poison people," Martha said as she took the plates to wash. "There's coffee ready if you want."

"No offence meant, ma'am, it was the best grub I've had in a month," Brubaker replied as he stood up. "I'm Laurie Brubaker and my pal is Davey Barnes. We're from Boston, the pair of us. Known each other since we were kids."

"Oh, we were up in Boston a few years back," Sunday stopped and realised what she had said. "On business, that's all."

Brubaker and Barnes looked at each other than at Sunday.

"A few years back, on business? You could have only been teenagers," Davey Barnes, said looking curious. "And I thought you had just come over here from England when we saw you earlier this year."

"We're older than we look, Davey. Like Sunday said, she doesn't age much," Martha said, hoping her reply would be accepted.

"Let's get you hitched up, folks, and get you on your way," Brubaker said as he decided not to waste more time. His doubts could wait for later.

Watson and Loire had been hitched to their respected harness and most items packed into the bow tops, but a call from Davey Barnes made everybody look around.

"Sergeant Conner and other riders coming, Laurie," he said stiffly. "That Irish sod can sniff trouble ten miles away."

Brubaker cursed and looked quickly at Sunday and Martha. "We didn't eat anything, we just saw you and ordered you to pack up and leave."

"We'll say nothing, don't worry," Sunday replied as she flopped back into Martha's chair. They all nodded and waited for Sergeant Conner and four other riders to arrive.

The black-haired Irishman jumped down and handed the reins to one of the riders. He stomped across to where his two sheepish-looking troopers were waiting.

"You two better have a bloody good reason for being off your horses. And an even better reason for tittle tattling with the enemy," Conner growled as he pointed an accusing finger at the four with his two subordinates.

"We just helped them pack their things, sarge, to get them moving, that's all," Davey Barnes said appealingly.

"These are the same lot we caught back in Tennessee, just before Shiloh. I can remember, even if you two miserable misfits can't. Have you checked their carts for more guns and ammunition?" Conner blasted, glaring at Barnes and Brubeker. They both shook their heads.

"We just saw them, sarge. We don't think they're gun runners," Barnes replied. Conner waved a hand at his mounted soldiers.

"Johnson, get down and check the bloody carts. O'Riley, Butler, get your Spencers out and cover these four spies. If one even sneezes, shoot the bastard." Conner pulled his revolver out and waved the barrel at Odda, who had finished with the horses. "Over here, mister, and stand where I can see you."

Nothing was spoken for two or three minutes, until the soldier searching the bow tops jumped down from the second one, shaking his head.

"Nothing, sarge, other than the ones we saw last time," Charlie Johnson called and walked back to his horse.

Conner cursed and shook his head. "They've hidden the cases somewhere. Johnson, get your arse off and inform Colonel Webster that we've arrested rebel gun runners and spies near Doctor's Creek. We need a platoon sending, to search the area."

Charlie Johnson stopped and looked at the sergeant. "Sarge, Colonel Webster is hard pushed to put a unit out just now. He's using what spare men he has to get drinking water to our lads, ready for the fight and I don't think this lot are spies or gun runners. They're just a bunch in the wrong place at the wrong time."

Conner stared wide-eyed at trooper Johnson and spat his next words out.

"They were at Shiloh, Johnson, might I remind you and I'm giving you an order, soldier. Get gone."

Johnson swung up into the saddle and kicked his horse away without further protest. As soon as he had disappeared, Conner turned on Martha and the other three 'spies.' He spotted the coffee pot and marched to the fire and snatched up a tin mug, pouring himself a good measure. Sunday jumped up and out of the chair, offering her seat to the belligerent sergeant.

"Sit down, sergeant, and calm down. We're not going anywhere now, by all accounts," Sunday said politely. Conner grunted and took a drink of the coffee.

"Too bloody right, lady. You and your bunch are staying right here, 'til Johnson gets back with twenty men to search this area. I know you're ferrying guns to the rebels and I'll damn well prove it."

Davey Barnes picked a mug up and poured himself a coffee. "Sarge, there's a water shortage in these parts and I heard General Bragg had mentioned grabbing as much of it near here to deny the bluecoats getting it. These lot aren't spies."

Martha stepped forward and took the coffee pot from Davey Barnes. Conner had taken Sunday's place in the chair and flicked his fingers at Martha, for a top up. He was grinning.

"I'll have the four of you shot before the day's out. English madam. Bloody English, always conniving and double dealing. Well, Dillon Conner is no fool, I'll tell you that, lady. I'll drink your coffee and to hell with accepting gifts from the enemy. You won't be needing it now. Just tell me where you've hidden the guns and I'll put a good word in for you. Your men will be shot and you and the black woman will be sent to jail for twenty years' hard labour." Conner swatted a fly from his head, but the insect resisted and flew back.

Martha put the coffee pot down and touched two of her fingers to her lips and moved to the side of Conner.

"I'll get the fly off you, sergeant," Martha said and reached her hand to his head. He stared hard at Martha but she touched her fingers to his face and gently touched his dusty skin. The fly took off again. Conner pushed Martha away and threw the remaining coffee he hadn't drunk towards Sunday's feet. It splashed onto her boots. Sunday just smiled.

Two hours later and Major Frederick Schumacher bowed gracefully to Martha and Sunday. The Union officer apologised to the two beautiful young women and gently kissed them each on a hand as he turned to leave. He had arrived with a small troop of horse soldiers after a breathless Charlie Johnson had ridden to the command post of General Alexander McCook and explained the reason why he had been sent. Colonel Webster had been present and with no junior officer available, he instructed Schumacher to investigate.

As Martha, Sunday, Vardan and Odda looked on gleefully, the Union soldiers made a futile search of the area for the cache of weapons Sergeant Conner insisted were hidden. Major Schumacher had never seen the Irish sergeant before that afternoon and he was determined that the obnoxious Dillon Conner would be in the first wave of northern soldiers, foot or horse, that would face the rebels.

Davey Barnes and Laurence Brubecker were given the job of escorting the two bow tops away from the immediate area, where battle was imminent. They had orders to take the four non-combatants towards the Ohio River, a few miles to the west. After an hour, though, the two young soldiers pulled their horses up and decided it was time for them to ride back and rejoin their unit.

"You should be safe here, Martha," red-haired Davey Barnes declared. The rebels are away to the east and south, so get to Springfield and then go north to Lexington."

"Be careful, Davey Barnes and you too, Laurie Brubecker. Don't go getting killed," Martha said and blew the two lads a kiss each. Sunday did the same and waved as the young soldiers rode off.

"Glad you gave that stuffy sod the kiss of death, Missy," Sunday grinned as she flipped the reins to get Watson moving.

"He deserved it for being so arrogant and bullish. I just wonder when he gets his comeuppance and how."

"Is there a time limit on it?"

"Not sure, to be honest, but he's a living dead man right now," Martha laughed.

Three Days Later
Perryville, Kentucky

For a full day from early morning on the eighth of October, to almost midnight, the two armies attacked each other almost non-stop. Chaplin Hills to the west of Perryville took the main barrage of the fighting. Hundreds of cannon blasted grape shot, cannister and ball at blue and grey-coated soldiers. A large number of the Union army was made up of raw recruits who had never fired a gun in anger. Over fifty thousand of the northerners had foot slogged to the small Kentucky town. Less than twenty thousand southerners faced them. Of the latter army, most were battle hardened and this worked greatly in their favour as the day went from dark to light and back to dark.

Hundreds of the young northerners, excited the day before to be part of the oncoming battle, ran from the battlefield hours before it ended. Most of these had run out of ammunition or drinking water, with no new supplies readily available.

Attacking a row of cannon, with empty musket rifles and just a bayonet fixed, was suicide. The young blue-coated lads turned and ran. No one could blame them.

It was the same for the older grey-coated soldiers. Most of these were by no means old men, but they had fighting experience and they had water. If their leader, General Braxton Bragg, did one thing right, he had gathered valuable drinking water for his troops, in an area of Kentucky that had had no rainfall in weeks. Unfortunately for the Confederates, he was not as skilled a strategist as his opposite number.

Don Carlos Buell was one of the Union's better generals. He delegated better than Bragg and afforded his commanders latitude. Braxton Bragg was hesitant and not an opportunist.

Neither a sin in normal life, but these were blood and thunder battle conditions. Chances had to be taken. General Buell wisely took chances and in the end, it counted. Neither general could boast he had won the day, but the Union commander would have taken the field again the following morning. Confederate Commander Bragg decided to withdraw his troops.

Three days after the battle, General Braxton Bragg had taken the remnants of his confederate army through the Cumberland Gap, many miles to the south east and into northern Tennessee. He and his men would fight another day.

Had he not floundered with bouts of indecision earlier in the day, General Bragg would have won a great victory with his outnumbered troops. He had gained better positions around the small town of Perryville, had sufficient drinking water and ammunition for his men and most were not raw recruits. But Braxton Bragg was not of the military calibre of his opponent, General Buell. The latter was a brilliant leader, he was highly motivated and a deep thinker. Bragg would never have been a brilliant poker player. He always needed to be certain he had a winning hand. Taking a chance was something he never allowed into his thinking.

Sadly, General Bragg had lost the trust of a lot of his men. He was no coward, he knew how to fight, but he was not the greatest man manager. His second in command, Major General Leonidas Polk, a religious man, was the better military strategist. Robert E Lee would have been better swapping the two around, Polk in charge and Bragg number two. General Buell on the other hand had a team of men he trusted and they him.

As the fighting at Perryville drew to a close around midnight, both armies withdrew. The death toll between north and south was near fifteen hundred, with as many wounded. Blue lying next to grey. Before midday on the ninth, General Bragg had withdrawn most of his troops to begin the march south east to Tennessee. He left a contingent to clear up his non-fatally wounded; the dying would sadly be left and buried later.

Makeshift graves had been dug for both armies' dead, but most no deeper than eighteen inches and by the next nightfall, hogs, wild dogs, foxes and other scavengers were scraping the shallow earth away to tear at the bodies.

Mephistopheles and his hell creatures were doing their damndest to steal souls from the dying, and the son of Satan had brought in elite replacements for the ones he had lost at Shiloh. Other, lesser creatures took orders and laboured to please Mephistopheles. These unfortunate hell creatures would glance across the bloodied battlefield to look at four of the undead, who were also talking to the dying, but not appearing to please their lord and master. He would scream obscenities at them and threaten to unleash his elite warriors to attack and kill the four, but he resisted sending these ferocious elite fighters to follow up his threats. None dared ask why. They had heard of the torture chambers.

Martha and her three companions had toiled laboriously through the day and night, persuading critically wounded soldiers to pass away peaceably and not sell their souls to the devil, explaining what the consequences were. Most agreed, but every now and then, one poor wretch would refuse to listen. Like Martha, Sunday and Odda before, the soldiers wanted to hang on to any thread of hope for a life in paradise.

Eventually Martha found the dying figure of a soldier she only just recognised. He wore a blood-covered blue jacket, but one arm was missing and also a leg. His hair was matted with dried blood mixed with mud and his face was a mask of pain and utter misery. He could barely see and didn't recognise Martha as she knelt at his side and held the hand on his remaining arm. The sergeant's stripes were visible, but stained with blood. Dillon Conner was delirious and asking for his mother. He thought Martha was his mother. Tears welled up in his almost dead eyes and he tried to smile.

Holding the dying soldier, Martha tried to explain to him why she was there. Conner blinked and nodded. He had heard the word 'paradise' and pushed everything else from his tortured mind. Martha shook her head and tried again to make herself understood. Then a fierce grip took hold of her arm and she was hurled backwards several feet.

Mephistopheles cackled with glee and leaned to the dying soldier's ear. A few moments passed and using every ounce of his remaining energy, Dillon Conner smiled and nodded. Martha struggled up and screamed at Mephistopheles, but the foul deed was done. The son of Satan had stolen his thirty-third soul on the Perryville Battlefield. It went into the leather pouch with thirty-two others.

Mephistopheles raised his scaly body and glared at Martha. His evil red eyes glinted.

"I beat you, Martha Budd. The stupid one I just took, will be trained to become one of my elite warriors. He will have a reason to help me destroy your pathetic little band of immortals. I said you gave him the kiss of death three days ago as he sat on your silly ducking chair. He came to me with a smile on his foolish face. He wants revenge and I'll have him trained to be able to achieve it."

The swirling red mist evaporated and Mephistopheles was gone. Sunday and Odda had seen the spectacle and had rushed over. A few moments later and Vardan was there. They all looked at the dead body of Dillon Conner, lying a few feet away. There was a crooked smile on his bloodstained face.

"He sold his soul?" Sunday asked dejectedly.

"I tried to stop him," Martha replied sadly, nodding.

"Foolish man. But the chair's death curse still works after all these years," Sunday grinned.

"That was one time when I wished it hadn't."

"He was a brute, Missy. He deserved it."

"But he hadn't killed anyone in anger, Sunday. He was just a soldier taking orders," Martha reasoned as she took a last look at Sergeant Conner's pained face.

"Yeah, his orders. Anyway, he's done what we did and sold his soul and like we have, he'll regret it."

"Mephistopheles told me he's going to have him trained to be one of his elite warriors and give him the chance to get his revenge for me giving him the kiss of death."

"Well, for his sake, he'd better be good, because that last lot weren't up to much," Vardan laughed as he listened to his ma and aunt.

Odda grinned but shook his head. "I'm just glad that huge creature they had didn't get involved, and the other one holding two swords."

"And the dwarf you were fighting, the boss one. He looked good," Vardan grinned.

"I had him ready to chop his fat body in half, but I'm glad Sunday and Martha had their longbows and glad you called DeeGee. Where did she come from?"

"She said she has found a cave in some mountains to the east. High up near the top. I'm going to find her and practice riding on her again, before she gets lazy."

Odda laughed and patted Vardan on a shoulder. "Best of luck then, my young friend, because that is one feisty little dragon."

Sunday heard Odda's comment and laughed. "Well, if DeeGee is little, I'd hate to be faced with a big one. I'm just glad she's on our side."

Packed up again after spending two days and nights at the Perryville battle site, the bow tops pulled away and headed east towards Virginia. Vardan travelled with them for part of the journey, but would leave to seek out his feisty dragon, Draig Goch.

Chapter Twenty-Six
West Virginia

May 1863

Three weeks after a fierce battle at Chancellorsville, the two bow tops were heading north to Maryland. Vardan pulled his horse to one side and waved at the three who would travel to the next battle site. Sunday called to him.

"A place called Harpers Ferry on some river, Vardan. Don't spend too much time with that Welsh dragon. We might need you."

"I'll be there, Ma, don't worry. Harpers Ferry, I'll find it."

"And don't forget to wash your clothes," Martha called. Vardan laughed and turned his horse south west to ride towards the Shenandoah Mountains, where Draig Goch had nested.

He rode confidently on the big black horse he had named De Lacey, passing several groups of Confederate soldiers heading north. Some would stop and chat to pass a few moments and one group in particular took his attention. They were mostly Negro men but wore no distinguishing uniforms. Soiled clothing mainly and some with no boots or shoes. Vardan had not seen many black people in one group before leaving Alabama and Tennessee and was puzzled as to why these Negro men were heading north. He pulled De Lacey up and called to a couple of young lads, looking no older than their mid-teens. Neither had anything on their feet.

"Where are you going, lads?" he called.

"You a spy, mister?" the smaller of the two called back.

Vardan laughed and shook his head. "No, I'm not a spy. I'm just curious as to why you're walking without shoes on."

"Because we can't afford any, that's why," the other lad replied dryly. "You speak funny, mister. Where you from, the north?"

Vardan laughed again, shaking his head. "I'm from the north, I suppose, but the north of England."

Both youths looked confused and stared up at Vardan. The smaller one shook his head. "England? That's near London, aren't it, where the Queen lives?"

"Yeah. London's in the south though. I'm from Yorkshire."

"Are you a white man? You look different," the same lad spoke.

"My ma is black, my pa was a Frenchman."

"From Louisiana? There are lots of Frenchies down there." The taller one now.

"No, he was a proper Frenchman, white and a cavalryman in Napoleon's army." Vardan grinned, looking at the bewilderment on the youths dusty faces. He reached into a pocket and pulled out some coins. Both looked suspiciously at the offered money on the palm of Vardan's hand and held back.

"A few dollars, lads, should be enough to buy yourselves some boots. Take it, a present from a Yorkshireman."

At that moment the biggest man Vardan had ever seen walked up and scooped the money from his hand. De Lacey spooked at the appearance of the large Negro, but was pulled back by a startled Vardan. The huge Negro stood his ground and waved the two dumbstruck youths to take the few dollars from his massive hand. They gingerly took the money and nodded a 'thanks' at Vardan. Smiling and showing beautiful white teeth, the big Negro patted De Laceys rump, then Vardan's thigh and walked on. He too had no shoes or boots on.

Vardan reached into his jacket and pulled out some more money. He handed one of the youth's two five dollar bills.

"Take this, lads, and give it to the big man. Tell him to buy himself some boots. Go on."

The taller lad took the money and nodded. He started to walk but looked back at Vardan. "He's called Mugwump Mandlu. Six feet eight he is and two hundred and eighty pounds.

"No one knows where he actually comes from, but he tells everyone he's from Zululand in Africa."

"So where are you all going? You didn't say," Vardan asked again.

"We're going to join up with the northerners and fight against the rebels. This white feller called Abraham Lincoln, once said we blacks can be free from slavery if the rebels are defeated."

"So what are your names and where are you from?"

The tall youth had run off to catch up with the big Negro, but the shorter one pointed after the other two.

"He's my cousin Joey and I'm Clarence. We're from Tuscaloosa in Alabama. We ran away ten months ago and if we get caught, we'll get flogged every day for a week. Thanks for the money, mister, we wore our boots out getting as far as here. Anyway, what you doing here in America?"

"Searching for a dragon in yon mountains," Vardan replied, pointing to distant highlands.

The bemused youth shook his head and grinned. "No dragons in these parts, mister. Alligators in Alabama and snakes up here, but no dragons. They're just in fairy stories." Clarence took off to catch his cousin as Vardan watched with a smile. After a minute, he pulled De Lacey around and carried on towards the distant mountains.

The Following Day

The summit towered above Vardan as he stood at the side of De Lacey. Over four thousand feet, but only a small mountain on the eastern flank of America, to the giants in the west of the country, but somewhere on the grassy and craggy slopes, he knew Draig Goch was waiting. She had found a safe hideaway to rest after her infrequent sorties out and about in the time she had been in America. Long sleeps would follow her impromptu flights to scavenge for food in the nearby areas to her mountain lair, taking a buffalo, an ox or a horse to gorge her appetite. She raided well-stocked farmsteads or open prairie at night to avoid detection, sometimes swallowing up hundreds of miles as she ventured further afield, not just to take food, but to strengthen her young muscles.

Tales had spread like bushfire at the mention of a great flying creature that swooped at high speed to snatch up a one-ton bull and whisk it away into the night. Late night drinkers, stumbling home after a boozy session in a bar or saloon, were the main story tellers. The tales became more exaggerated as they were told to smirking disbelievers.

Vardan walked De Lacey to a tucked away grassy pasture, unsaddled him and hid the horsey equipment. Thirty minutes later, standing on a ledge a few hundred feet from the ground he made the call upwards towards the summit. The great body appeared and swooped downwards, piercing eyes latching onto the small figure standing on the rocky ledge.

A circling bald eagle, its own razor eyes watching a pair of young rabbits on the valley floor, saw the massive figure four hundred yards away, turned in panic and flew away at speed. Draig Goch saw the eagle escaping and for a brief moment thought at taking it for a tasty snack, but remembered her dragon master would be annoyed at being kept waiting. Her eyes returned to the waiting figure on the ledge, a mile away.

As usual, Draig Goch made a scary first sweep at her dragon master, waiting to make his daredevil jump onto her back. It annoyed him as she pulled away at the last second, leaving him yelling curses. Her second flight was inch perfect and Vardan made the leap onto her back. The large wings powered effortlessly as man and beast soared away on the wind.

She climbed high and within a couple of minutes, the ground was three thousand feet below. Vardan had learned how to sit without holding on the harness he and Odda had fitted around Draig Goch's broad neck. Several pieces of leather had been stitched together to make a twenty foot long girth harness that fitted neatly around the fire dragon's neck. Hand straps at various points on the harness made it easy for the dragon rider to maintain a strong sitting position.

Wrapping her wings together at the top of her body enabled Vardan to slip back a few feet, so that he was safely secured from falling as Draig Goch took advantage of the air currents and rolled her body around as a javelin would in flight. He had even made special inner leg supports to stop his skin being torn by the sharp scales on the dragon's body. These would just be rolled down over his boots, when not riding Draig Goch.

She was flying north over Pennsylvania and turned her head. "Do you want to see something special, young master?"

Vardan heard her and took a deep breath as the wind sped by. "Like what?"

"Hold on and I'll show you. It's a good way ahead."

Vardan settled back and put his head down against the wind. Draig Goch grinned and raced on as the miles and hours sped by. Pennsylvania gave way to New York State and still she headed north. Eventually Vardan tired of waiting and thumped the top of her neck.

"Where are you taking me? It's getting colder," he yelled.

"Nearly there, young master. Nearly there."

A few minutes later and Draig Goch started to slow and go lower. Vardan peered ahead and realised the air was getting damp. He could feel a drizzle in the wind and gave a shudder.

"I'm freezing, DeeGee, and it's started to rain." He cursed loudly.

"Hold tight, young master. We're there and I'm going down."

Vardan stared wide-eyed at the sight ahead as it loomed through a wet mist. A thunderous roar sounded and freezing water hit Vardan in the face. He screamed and held tight on the hand straps. Draig Goch was in her element and soared thirty feet along the top and width of Niagara Falls, on the border with Canada. In less than ten seconds, Vardan was saturated and holding on for grim death. He had clamped his eyes shut and waited for the end to come. He saw his young life disappearing in a watery grave. He couldn't even speak as the biting cold tortured his body.

Then she climbed. The powerful wings opened fully and water was shed from the great body. A whimpering dragon rider was speechless, shivering and beyond reason. She climbed higher and took him to warmth, catching a gentle air stream. Two thousand feet above the great falls, Draig Goch circled in a great arc and closed her wings to the top of her body. Vardan, with his reserves of strength, slipped underneath and started breathing properly once more.

She was in control and Vardan knew it. Eighty feet long and five ton of animal that could fly at fifty miles an hour and spit poisonous flames fifty yards. But he was also in charge, because this kind of killing machine was a one master fire dragon, with extraordinary powers. She could fly higher than other creatures, could dive to the depths of an ocean and stay under for well over an hour. Her body was so tough, it was as if she had armour plating.

There were other types of dragons, killing machines like Draig Goch, but only a few were built like the Welsh or Nordic fire dragons. Four thousand years earlier there had been hundreds in the world. Now, that number had decreased to about a dozen. Satan and his sons were the dragon masters of at least four of these deadly predators. Two or three lived in China, two more in the northern countries, three or four others, including Draig Goch, in different parts of the world.

"Did you like it, young master?" Draig Goch asked as she powered off back to the south.

"No, I didn't. I'm soaked to the skin. I need to get back, or my horse will wander off," Vardan grumbled.

"I needed to fly this far. It was also a test for you. You only do short distances on my back, you needed to go further, because one day we might need to go even further. You have to be strong to be a dragon rider. You'll be dry by the time we get back to my den."

"If I don't get pneumonia before you get me back."

"Stop complaining and enjoy the ride. One day you will have to fight from my back and use your weapons without holding on to this thing around my neck."

"How do you know things like that? You're just a fire dragon." Draig Goch snorted and did a full upside down turn as she raced south. Vardan held on for his life.

"Just a fire dragon, huh? I know a lot more than you think, young master. I know that Mesphistopheles is training his hell creatures to wipe you and the other immortals from the face of the earth. You need to practice riding my back more than you do. It isn't just a game for little boys."

"How do you know such things?"

"There were three dragon eggs the day you found them, yeah?"

"Yeah. I took one and got you and brought you up, I looked after you."

"So you did, young master. However, the other two hatched and I speak to one of them."

"Only one?"

"Just the nice one. He's a good sort, my brother."

"And the other one?"

"My sister. She's a real bad dragon. Mephistopheles is her master and he has trained her to seek out you and the immortals. He had many of us fire dragons under his command a long long time ago, but one of his brothers, Drebmif, banished them during his six hundred and sixty-six year reign and most died from inactivity and boredom. Mephistopheles is determined to breed more of the bad ones and let them loose to plague the earth, so he and his brothers can dominate the humans. Wipe most of them out, but keep some back as slaves to breed and create a race of hell demons."

"So where is your brother now?"

"The little people you call Blingos have spreckled him, given him the SWAN mark, like they did to me and you, and he lives in a cave near the top of a high mountain in a land to the east, far across the great sea that you sailed on to come here. The mountain is much much higher than the one I live in. I went there once to see my brother."

"So when you're not with me, you fly to far lands? That's cheating."

"Not at all, young master. I am a free dragon, when you don't need me. Sometimes I sleep for weeks, other times I fly away. Besides my brother, I have met other dragons. I am always ready to come to your call, have I ever not done so?"

"No, but—" Vardan started.

"No buts, young master. I am a free dragon, but you are my one and only dragon master. Now settle back and let me get you back to your horse."

Harpers Ferry

A couple of hundred yards from the banks of the Shenandoah river, a mile south of Harpers Ferry, the two bow tops nestled at the edge of a copse of trees. A bright spring sun shone down, drying washing spread over bushes nearby. The horses grazed peaceably but lazily eating the new grass. Over a crackling fire, a pan boiled water and on a spit, a chicken was roasting. Vardan and Sunday were looking forward to a meal of chicken and vegetables.

"Fancy a juicy leg?" Sunday said, offering a perfectly roasted leg to Odda, watching with interest.

"Go boil your head, Sunday, that's not fair. I haven't eaten chicken for eight hundred years and you know it," Odda replied with a sniff of contempt.

"Yeah, just teasing, old friend. I know how you're feeling. I missed eating good food for all those years I was dead. It's a rotten deal." Sunday shrugged and started eating the chicken leg. At her side, Vardan, who had returned from his dragon ride, pulled off the other chicken leg and tucked in to the soft white meat. He grinned and patted Odda on a shoulder.

"I'll eat yours then, Odda, if you don't want it."

Odda scrambled to his feet and skulked off, snatching up his rifle and ammunition bag.

"Don't be so hurtful, Vardan. And you, Sunday. Stop teasing him," Martha said and spooned cooked vegetables onto two tin plates, for mother and son.

"He's a bit prickly about it though, you know. Being of the undead," Vardan said as he gobbled greedily at his food. "He wishes he had gone to heaven instead of selling his soul."

"So do I, Vardan. But like your ma and Odda, I did. We roam the lands and seas and see things we would never have seen when we lived," Martha replied as she stood from her chair to follow Odda. She collected her own rifle and left the camp.

Sunday waited 'til Martha was out of earshot and looked at Vardan.

"We'd best not tease him, son. Remember, we have the best of both worlds. We can live for ever and eat and drink. Odda and Martha can't enjoy good food, as we can."

"He's brilliant with his rifle, Ma. I'm better with the bow, but Odda can beat me with the battle axe and powder and shot. I don't know how he can throw that axe as he does. He never misses. I'm just glad he's on our side."

"He lost his family and all his friends all those hundreds of years ago to the sword and battle axe. His tribe was wiped out. I thought I had had it bad, back in the Caribbean, but people in his day lived horrible lives and died early. Finish your food and we'll catch them up. I'll take my bow, I need to practice."

Fifteen minutes later, Sunday and Vardan had rejoined Odda and Martha. The four spent an hour with the weapons, fine tuning their skills. After her last shot had found its target, Martha decided to walk back to the bow tops to clear up and wash pots and pans. The other three continued their weapons practice. Odda had once more beaten Vardan with the rifle, but in reply, with his mother's bow and arrows, the latter had evened up the score as both had shot arrows at a target. They back slapped each other and walked back, once more as best friends.

Martha had cleaned up, washed pots and brought in the dried clothes. She flopped onto her chair and put her head back, to look upwards at the clear blue sky, with fluffy white clouds slowly drifting by. Her mind went back to the conversation she and the others had had when the chicken was ready to eat. She could not remember ever not being hungry when she had lived with the belligerent adoptive parents, Jonas Brooks and his severe wife. Scraps of leftover food was all she was given and she was made to say grace before they allowed her to eat the stale food. Only when she ran away at fourteen and started stealing food, did she start to enjoy having a full belly. Then the bad times of life in self-indulgent debauchery added to her thefts of food and plaguing the young lads in her village. The day they drowned her on the chair she now sat on. Selling her soul to Lord Lucifer and the despicable job of finding the souls of the wretched wounded soldiers, after the many battles she had attended.

The gruff voice made her jump in the chair and she turned to see a group of untidily dressed men, seated on horses a few yards behind where she was sitting. A tall man, with heavy facial hair and a sweat stained hat topping his head, jumped down and approached.

"Howdy miss, sorry to disturb you, but we have some business to sort with you," the man almost whispered.

"What sort of business? Our two carts causing a nuisance?" Martha replied, standing to face the man and his companions.

"Oh, heck, no, miss. This is a free country and you aren't causing a nuisance. No, your horses in yon pasture, four lovely specimens they are."

"Yes, they are, but what about them?" Martha asked, glancing across to where the four horses were grazing.

"Well, miss, as you might know, there is a bit of a war going on in these parts and horses are needed to pull wagons and others for the Union cavalry. The two big horses fit the requirement for the cavalry and I assume the cobby types pull these here carts."

"Yes, that's right, but who are you and what about the horses?" Martha said calmly.

"I'm Jethro Cartwright and I work for the government as a horse trader, I buy good quality horses for the Union army. I've called to buy your horses for a fair price."

Martha was stunned and stared wide-eyed at the scruffy man.

"The horses are not for sale, Mister Cartwright, so I'll ask you to leave."

He pointed to the four horses, then spat out some tobacco he had been chewing. "'Fraid not, miss. I have this here note that authorizes me and my team to buy horses and take them immediately." He unfolded a crumpled paper and handed it to Martha. "That there note, as you can see, is signed by Major General Sheridan and bears his seal. We have the right to take your four horses today. In return, I'll give you ten dollars apiece for the two big 'uns and six each for the cart horses. That's a fair price for untrained horses. To be a bit extra fair, we'll call it thirty-five dollars. That's a lot of money miss for four average animals."

"Shove your thirty-five dollars, Mister Cartwright and just go. You're not taking our horses, not now or ever," Martha blasted and handed the note back. Behind Cartwright another man dismounted, stepped forward and pulled the former back a step.

"Look, you English bitch, I take it you're English with that voice. Take the money and get out of our way. We're taking your old nags and that's it. If you got a complaint write to

General Sheridan and sort it with him." The man called four other men forward and pushed past Martha. The men dismounted and handed the reins to a fifth man.

Martha grabbed the arm of the second man, but he turned and pushed Martha and she tripped and fell to the ground. Cartwright stepped forward and helped Martha back to her feet. The five others walked to the pasture, holding halters and ropes.

"Sorry for that, miss, Ed meant you no harm. He's not the most patient of men. Two of the others are his younger brothers and the Thompson boys are all the same, bullish and hot headed. Take the money, miss, and we'll be on our way." Cartwright declared. Martha shook her head and stepped back. As she did, Vardan, Odda and Sunday returned to the camp. Immediately two rifles were raised and an arrow slotted to Sunday's bow.

Jethro Cartwright wheeled around and called after the four striding to the four horses. They stopped and looked back. Ed Thompson began walking back immediately. The other four men stopped in their tracks. One reached for a hand gun in its holster, but the arrow thudded into the ground, six inches from his nearest boot. The second arrow struck his holster and the man gasped in shock and threw his arms wide.

"The third arrow kills your man, mister," snarled Sunday as the arrow was already in place. Cartwright stared in disbelief and raised his arms.

"You're in big trouble, black woman. We have a legal document to take the horses."

"Try taking the horses when you're all dead," Sunday replied as Odda and Vardan took aim with their rifles. Ed Thompson arrived back and pointed an accusing finger at Sunday.

"That was attempted murder and you'll swing," he blasted at Sunday.

"And your actions are attempted theft and assault, I saw you knock my friend down," Sunday replied as her finger twitched on the drawstring, the arrow ready.

"I'll knock you down, nigger woman, if you don't back off," Thompson hissed and started walking to where Sunday was standing with her bow. Before he could reach Sunday, Vardan stepped forward and put a palm upwards at Thompson.

"That's my mother you're insulting, mister, and if you want to walk away unharmed from our camp, you'll apologise to her."

"Drop dead, sonny. Ed Thompson apologises to no one," Thompson laughed and made to push Vardan out of the way. The swiftness of his action stunned Thompson as he fell flat on his back from a punch to his jaw. He glared up at Vardan and started to scramble to his feet. As soon as he was up, he rushed at Vardan, but a side step by the latter, sent him sprawling to the ground, this time onto his belly. Vardan stepped to the grounded man and grabbed him by the scruff, pulling his heavy body up. Thompson took a swing at Vardan, missed and a second punch from Vardan felled him once more.

"Now you say sorry to my mother, mister, or you get some more of that," Vardan snarled.

Thompson looked up through dazed eyes and tried to focus, but all he could see was the large figure of Vardan standing over him. Jethro Cartwright had watched the fracas and moved to where Ed Thompson lay on his back. He reached down and grabbed the man, hauling him to his feet.

"He meant no insult, young feller, but I'll apologise for him. Besides, you hit him hard and he obviously can't speak 'til he gets his senses back. He can take a seat for a few minutes, then he'll apologise," Cartwright stated, but Thompson waved a dismissive hand at Vardan.

"I ain't saying sorry, Jethro. This lot are in real trouble now. We go back and report them for attempted murder. We got the law on our side," Thompson growled.

Martha now stepped forward and pointed to her chair.

"Sit down, mister and take a rest. I'll get you some water."

Jethro Cartwright nodded and helped Thompson to the chair, a few feet away. He was still dazed and allowed himself to be sat down, but he was cursing and stabbed a finger at Vardan.

"You caught me off guard, kid and I'm going to make you regret it. We're taking the horses, either today or as soon as we get back here with more men." Thompson rubbed his sore jaw and sniffed contemptuously. Martha returned with a tin cup of water that was hastily taken and downed almost in one gulp.

"Get me another one, English woman, and think yourselves lucky we didn't kill you all and take the horses without handing over any money."

Martha returned with another cup of water, almost snatched from her hands. She touched two fingers to her lips and smiled at the obnoxious man slurping at the water. Politely she touched the side of his head and smiled when he pushed her hand away.

"I was just touching a bruise, mister, I meant no offence," Martha said politely.

"Touching a bruise I have gets you no sympathy. I meant what I said. We're gonna come back with more men and take the horses. Now get out of my way." Thompson ranted and pushed his heavy body from the chair.

Calling his brothers and the other men, Thompson and the group remounted and stiffly rode away. Vardan and Odda watched carefully, until the group had disappeared.

"We best pack and leave here, before that lot come back with more men," Martha called as the four stood in delayed shock at what had happened.

A half hour later and the two bow tops were trundling away from the riverside camp, Odda and Vardan riding their horses, Martha and Sunday driving the two cart horses.

An hour later and they passed through Harpers Ferry to the bridge over the Potomac, where they could cross into Maryland and then continuing north to Gettysburg in Pennsylvania. Four sets of eyes carefully watching the land to all sides, for any sight of Thompson's riders.

Disaster struck a couple of miles from the small town of Burkettsville. Martha and Sunday in the front bow top were sharing a joke as to when the death kiss that had been planted on Ed Thompson's face would become true. Concentration lapsed in a fit of giggles and the bow top struck several scattered rocks. Watson panicked and heaved the cart to the side, but in a shuddering crash the cart tumbled off the track and into a gully with a dislodged wheel.

The young women jumped down, Martha rushing to a frightened Watson to calm him.

Sunday cursed as she saw the wheel lying on its side. Vardan, who had been riding De Lacey and leading Odda's horse, jumped down and tied the horses to a hitch rail. He and Odda ran forward and stared in disbelief at the broken axle. The lads immediately dropped into the gully to try and lift the dead weight of the bow top. Even with Sunday adding her weight, the bow top was still too heavy for the three of them to lift high enough for Martha to slot the wheel back in place. An hour of heaving, lifting and cursing, the bow top remained lop sided.

Almost exhausted, and tempers frayed, the four dropped down in the gully to take stock. "It weighs over half a ton, we'll never lift it high enough," Vardan gasped.

"I thought you were immortal and had the strength of a bull," Odda grinned as he playfully patted Vardan's shoulder.

"I was putting more weight in than you, my Viking friend," Vardan snapped.

"You're bigger than me, Mister Immortal," Odda laughed.

"Stop bickering, you two. It doesn't get the bloody thing upright," Sunday hissed and threw a stone at the broken bow top. "Go fetch your dragon, Vardan and get her to lift it out of this rotten ditch."

The three others looked at Sunday and then she Martha and Odda looked at Vardan, their heads nodding. Vardan was about to respond, but turned as three figures appeared a couple of feet above them.

"You folk need a hand?" a young Negro lad asked as he looked at the four travellers. Four sets of eyes stared upwards and nodded simultaneously. There were amused grins on two of the Negros' faces. The third man towered above them and grunted an acknowledgement.

Vardan realised he had seen the huge Negro before. He nodded a greeting.

"You gave us money fer boots, mister, some time back. We remember you. Look." The lad raised a booted foot and smiled at Vardan. He nudged his friend, who did likewise. "We all bought ourselves new boots. We owe you a favour. Mugwump doesn't say much but he's grateful as well." The young lad looked up at the huge Negro, who nodded.

"It's too heavy to lift up. We were thinking of going for help," Sunday said as she put a hand up to the big Negro, who hauled her out of the gully. He smiled and put a hand out to Martha, who accepted the offer. Mugwump Mandlu dropped into the gully and took a deep breath, then nodded at a bemused Vardan and Odda. They stood to his side and took holds on the underside of the bow top. Mugwump looked at the two young Negro's.

"Git down here, Clarence Watkins and you too, Joey Watkins, and git that wheel on when we lift," he growled with a voice like thunder.

Vardan and Odda braced themselves and gripped harder to each side of Mugwump. The big man breathed out and gripped with his huge hands.

"On three, lift, fellers and I mean lift," he said tersely. "One, two, three."

Vardan and Odda lifted for all they were worth, but their efforts were secondary as between them, Mugwump snarled loudly and heaved upwards. The bow top held stubbornly for a few moments, but another snarling heave from Mugwump and it lifted. The two lads were nimble and quickly pushed the wheel into place.

Vardan and Odda fell backwards after their efforts, but the big man thumped his chest and bellowed loudly. His mighty voice made Martha and Sunday step back quickly. A few seconds later and Mugwump stepped to the back of the bow top and turned facing backwards. He gripped the underside as Martha dashed to the front to hold Watson steady. Vardan and Odda tiredly took a similar position at Mugwump's side and took deep breaths. On the second count of three, Odda, Vardan and Mugwump heaved backwards. Martha pulled Watson's bridle and slowly the bow top started moving. A few minutes later and the ordeal was over. Back on firm ground the bow top was out of the gully.

"Thanks, mister," Sunday said and gently kissed the big Negro on the cheek. Mugwump smiled and displayed a mouthful of even white teeth. After a hug from Martha, Mugwump smiled and pointed to his new boots.

"I bought the largest pair I could find. They are a bit tight, but better than none at all. That wheel needs attention though. You should find a wheel smith to repair it."

"Where are you three going anyway?" Sunday asked.

Mugwump sniffed and looked across to Vardan. "Like Clarence told him a while back, we're heading north to join the Union Army. We want to be free men and get decent jobs and raise families under our own roofs, not slaving for a living under white men's rules."

"So why come so far north?" Vardan asked. "You could have joined up back in Georgia or Tennessee."

Clarence shook his head and smiled. "We could have, but as blacks fighting for the north, if we get captured by the Confederates, we would be shot as traitors. We've heard that the Union Army is taking black volunteers and forming new regiments. We want to fight for our freedom."

"So you've walked hundreds of miles. You told me the last time I saw you that you're from Alabama?" Vardan replied and saw the look of surprise on the faces of his three companions.

"That's right, mister, and worn out our clothes and boots. You helped us a lot, giving us some money. We bought new boots and had a bit left for some food," Clarence said.

"Any money left?" Sunday asked. Clarence, his cousin Joey and Mugwump shook their heads humbly. Sunday turned and climbed into the back of her bow top. A minute later, she jumped down and pressed five dollars into each of their hands. The three looked at the money and then one by one they hugged Sunday for the gift. A tear broke free and trickled down Sunday's face. Mugwump smiled and deftly wiped it away with his large fingers.

The riders appeared on the track and made all seven look backwards. Twenty Union horse soldiers and a few civilian riders galloped towards the two bow tops and the seven startled onlookers. Ed Thompson rode straight to them and pulled his horse up just a few feet from Vardan. A sergeant did the same and almost nudged Mugwump, before jumping from his horse. Close behind, a young lieutenant casually rode to the group and ordered his troop to stay back. The troopers spread out in a line, pulling carbines from scabbards.

Ed Thompson pointed at Vardan and looked to the lieutenant. "This is the thug that attacked me, Lieutenant. He needs to hang."

The lieutenant looked down at Vardan and nodded towards Thompson. "Is that right, mister? You assaulted that man? He is employed by the Army of the United States and therefore protected in that capacity. I'm Lieutenant James Hickey and sent with these men, under instructions from General Kilpatrick to take suitable horses from civilians to be used in service. You were offered good money, I believe, but refused to cooperate."

"He insulted my mother and refused to apologise. He attacked me, I defended myself," Vardan stated. "And none of our four horses are for sale. My mother told him that."

"You have no choice, mister. I see two excellent horses tied to a hitch rail. We'll take them and leave the two cart horses. That's final. Ten dollars each for the two riding horses and no action against you for assault. Sergeant Brady, get two of your men to take the horses. Mister Cartwright, hand over twenty dollars to these people."

Jethro Cartwright nudged his horse forward and reached into a saddle bag for the money. Sergeant Brady, a stocky red-haired man, a revolver drawn, signalled to two of his men to collect Vardan and Odda's horses. They dutifully jumped down, carbines in hand passing reins to colleagues and started walking to collect the horses.

In the time it took to blink an eye, Vardan reached up and grabbed Ed Thompson, pulling him from his horse. Odda hurled himself at the startled lieutenant and Mugwump grabbed the bewildered sergeant, throwing the latter's revolver towards one of the young Negroes. Joey Watkins snatched it cleanly and held it with a glint in his eye. Sunday turned and dived into the back of the bow top and gathered her bow and arrows.

The line of young cavalrymen raised their carbines, but with nervous horses turning around unsettling their riders, none dared fire a shot. Ed Thompson screamed at the troopers to open fire, but they resisted and looked at both the lieutenant and the sergeant for instructions. Vardan turned Thompson around and with one mighty punch, sent the man staggering backwards several feet, finishing up on his back in the dust.

Odda held Lieutenant Hickey firmly and took a revolver from his subdued captive. He pointed it towards the mounted troopers, who were still confused. A few feet away, Joey Watkins held Sergeant Brady's revolver at the row of troopers. A few feet further away, standing on the back of the bow top, Sunday had a target in line for her first arrow.

Having lost the advantage, Lieutenant Hickey looked around and realised some of his men would die if shooting started. To his side, Sergeant Brady, a former street fighter from New Jersey, and not small, at close on two hundred pounds, glared at the giant Negro who had grabbed him. He looked across to the lieutenant for instructions.

James Hickey was a West Pointer and had never seen action. Twenty-two years old, he had an older brother who had fought at the first Bull Run and then at the battle of Perryville. Young Hickey was desperate to prove himself in a fight, but for the first time since leaving West Point, he found himself faced with a life threatening incident and it was definitely no fun. He glanced quickly to his sergeant, a fearsome man with a reputation for bravery, he also having fought at Perryville and before that at Pea Ridge in Arkansas. Yet Sergeant Brady was also disarmed and the man had fifteen years' experience in the army. The people he had faced here were a bunch of women, illiterate Negroes and civilians. He wished he was safely back home in New Hampshire on his father's farm.

Martha now stepped forward and walked to Vardan, who was hovering once more over the obnoxious Ed Thompson. She pulled Vardan away and walked with him to where Odda was holding the young lieutenant, but still with the revolver aimed at the mounted troopers. Sergeant Brady had decided that he was no match for the big Negro, despite his brutal fighting experience of bare knuckle fighting and carefully pulled away. He looked to Joey Watkins for the return of his revolver, but the youngster just grinned and waved the barrel at him. Brady cursed and dusted himself down.

On the back of the cart, Sunday still had an arrow fixed on one of the mounted troopers, her quiver of other arrows at the ready. Hoping his chance of not being killed before he actually rode into battle was diminishing by the second, Lieutenant Hickey signalled to his riders to stand down and lower their carbines. The troopers breathed a sigh of relief.

Embarrassed, dusty and trembling slightly, Lieutenant Hickey looked disbelievingly around. He caught Vardan's eye and tried to appear confident, assertive.

"Look, sir, I can up the price for your horses. I can give you a signed note and promise you that they will be returned to you free of charge at a later date should they not be needed. Thirty dollars for the two. What do you say?"

Vardan smiled and shook his head. "Sorry, Lieutenant, but they're still not for sale. We need them just as much as your army does. It's your war, not ours, we're just passing through. We're British and we don't take sides."

Sergeant Brady pointed at the three Negroes. "So why are you travelling with blacks, mister? They hardly make you neutral. They're slaves and should be back where they belong. On a plantation. We're fighting a war against the rebels to free these nig—" Brady's voiced trailed off before he said the word 'nigger'. Mugwump glared at him and scoffed.

"You no better than the whites from the south, mister. Men like you fight for money, not for the livelihoods and welfare of us blacks, or niggers, as you were gonna say. Me and my two friends are hoping to join up and become volunteers in a coloured regiment, ready and willing to fight the Confederates. Now having met you and these other blue coats and these other whites with you, I think we made a mistake coming north. You're trying to steal these English people's horses and that's not what freedom is about. They gave us money to buy new boots and food. They not bad people. I heard Mister Lincoln is a good white man, but some of you are no different to the whites from the south." Mugwump turned and patted both Vardan and Odda on their backs. Then called to Clarence and Joey. The latter tossed the revolver back to Sergeant Brady and followed his two friends.

Suddenly, from behind, Ed Thompson screamed and ran at Vardan, who had his back to him. He had drawn his own hand gun and levelled it to shoot. On the track, Mugwump wheeled around and instantly hurled himself at Thompson, who was just a few yards away. Thompson fired off two shots at Vardan, one missing, but the other hitting him in the side. Seeing the large figure of Mugwump approaching, Thompson turned and fired. Too big to miss, four bullets struck home, but the giant Negro carried on and struck the enraged Thompson squarely and bowled the screaming man over. Reaching down, Mugwump, bleeding from the bullet wounds, grabbed Thompson and heaved him upwards and above his head, then hurled him against rocks a few feet away.

Mugwump staggered back a few steps, then dropped to his knees, his head bowed in agony, but Thompson had drawn a large knife and dazed, staggered towards the Negro. His arm went up ready to strike, but a first and then a second arrow struck his body, then a volley of bullets sent him sprawling back into the rocks. Sergeant Brady had emptied his revolver at Thompson and then ran to where Mugwump was kneeling. His respect for the big man was unquestionable and he put an arm around the broad shoulders. Vardan arrived clutching his side where he had been hit by the bullet and also dropped to Mugwump's side.

Slowly, Mugwump slipped down and allowed himself to be supported by Vardan. He had taken two bullets in his chest, one in the neck and one near his heart. Within moments others arrived, including Clarence and Joey Watkins. The youths were crying and stood head bowed above their dying friend. Martha reached Mugwump and knelt at his side.

Vardan looked at his aunt and they locked eyes. Mugwump was seconds from death and his eyes also locked with Martha. She lowered her head and whispered into his ear. He blinked through dimming eyes and very slowly shook his head, his fading eyes staring at Martha in doubt.

An almost blinding flash of lightning followed and then the thunderous roar that scared the cavalry horses, who took off in panic. The skies had darkened and everybody turned to stare upwards. Martha whispered again in Mugwump's ear and this time, he managed a smile and nodded slowly.

Mephistopheles hovered above Martha and glowered at her in glee. He held the soul pouch and dangled it loosely in his taloned fingers. It already contained the soul of Ed Thompson and he wanted a second. Martha looked up at him and smiled.

"Take him, Mephistopheles. He's yours for the time being, but I want him back," Martha said calmly.

"And why would I give you back such a beautiful specimen, Martha Budd? He will be one of my hell warriors in time. You tell me why?"

"Because your father wants my last soul and that will be the price. My soul for his and you can't refuse, can you, or Satan will banish you, like he did to Fimber O'Flynn."

"When? When do you give it back?"

"Not just yet. I'll let you know."

Mephistopheles cackled and swirled around a few feet above Martha. He pointed a long scaly finger at her and his evil eyes glinted a brighter red. "Soon, Martha Budd, soon, I want you back in my possession. In the meantime, I will start this wretched man's training. He's slipping now and I'm taking his soul before it disappears." Mephistopheles swooped to the side of Mugwump and grabbed his soul, dropped it in his pouch and then was gone. Martha kissed the big Negro's face and stood up, watched by the others around the body.

"You spoke to him, miss," Sergeant Brady said as he also stood up. "He saved this young feller's life." Brady nodded towards Vardan.

"He was brave, sergeant, he gave his life without a thought," Martha replied and wished tears would come.

"We need men like him on our side. A pity that bastard shot him. I hope he goes to hell." Brady pointed to the bloodstained body of Ed Thompson.

"He's on his way, sergeant," Vardan chipped in, holding his side.

Sergeant Brady looked across to where Lieutenant Hickey was waiting and smiled back at Martha and Vardan.

"Git yourselves away quickly and leave young Hickey to me. He's fresh out of military school and clueless. I'll sort it. Stay off these type of roads though. There's gonna be more trouble in the coming weeks and no place for the likes of you lot. Go back to England is my advice." Brady started walking away but stopped and looked at the two young Negroes, standing by Mugwump's body. "Hey, you two. If you really want to volunteer to fight on our side, there's a captain a bit further north putting together a few Negro regiments. The Fifty-fourth and Fifth Massachusetts. Find him and sign up. Tell him Frank Brady sent you."

Clarence and Joey watched tearfully as the cavalry troop rode away. They were lost and almost without hope, but Martha walked to their side and put a comforting arm around both in turn. They scuffed tears away from bowed heads.

"You can travel with us if you like, lads. Save boot leather and we'll feed you in return for a few jobs. Wha'dya say?"

Martha remarked. There was no hesitation from the youths and they nodded with smiles.

"First job then is to help bury your big friend," Vardan said as he listened to his aunt. "I'll get spades."

An hour later and Mugwump was buried and lots of rocks stacked on his grave. A simple wooden cross was wedged in place and the six stood together, looking down at it. After a few minutes they solemnly walked away, but Clarence, the more talkative of the two youths, spoke quietly to Martha at his side.

"You spoke to him, miss, before he died. I saw his eyes looking at you. He was the biggest man I ever saw and the strongest, but he was religious. He said his prayers every day and never missed. He would give you his last crust of bread. What did you say to him?"

"I told him we would meet again. He would be safe with us, or with the other three if I wasn't around. He'll be fine, don't worry," Martha replied quietly.

"Everything went still and quiet while you spoke to big Mugwump. It went dark, the thunder and lightning. Real scary, did you feel it?"

"Yes, I did. It happens sometimes." Martha walked on.

"Do you believe in God, miss? In, you know, Jesus?" Clarence asked unashamedly.

"I didn't when I was younger, but I do now."

"What about the devil? Is there such a creature do you think?"

"Oh, yes, definitely. Absolutely."

"Mugwump will be okay though. He's not bad, he'd help anyone. Break bones if he was picked on by some no-good thug, but he's never been bad. He'll be in heaven now."

Martha sighed and knew Vardan had heard Clarence. They exchanged glances and reached the bow tops and the horses. Clarence climbed up with Martha as Joey took a seat at the side of Sunday. Vardan and Odda rode steadily at the sides as they continued their journey north. As they passed where they had buried Mugwump, Martha looked back sadly.

A Month Later

Clarence and Joey jumped down from the bow tops and were hugged warmly by their four friends. They had tears in their eyes as they said goodbyes. Vardan had grown close to the talkative Clarence and embraced him for long moments. Joey, the much quieter of the Negro youths, had sat at Martha's side mostly on the journey through Maryland. He stared in surprise as the latter handed him a silver cross and chain she had worn around her neck for years. He took it and bowed his head humbly, clutching the necklace in a hand.

"Thanks, Missy. I'll treasure it 'til my dying day, I promise."

"I know you will, Joey. Look after yourselves, and good luck in finding your coloured regiment. We'll think of you both and your friend Mugwump." Martha kissed him and climbed back up to her seat and flipped the reins to walk Watson forward. Behind Martha, Sunday set Loire off and waved to the two youths, a final gesture.

They were near the Monocasey River, a couple of miles from Taneytown on a warm June day, as they left Clarence and Joey behind. The lads were still eager to join the Union Army and had been told earlier that day by a small group of union horsemen, that the captain they were seeking was over near Emmitsburg to the west, where around a hundred Negroes had gathered.

"They're just boys, Sunday. Innocents," Martha said as they stopped for a break a couple of hours later, near the banks of the river.

"They must have walked a thousand miles to sign up, Alabama is a long way behind," Sunday said as she sipped coffee from a mug.

"That's more than the length of England and Scotland together. And it would be hard doing that distance sat on our seats, letting the horses do the work," Vardan remarked as he heard his mother and Martha talking.

"I can't imagine what it would be like being a slave," Odda said as he listened.

"I can." Sunday said shaking her head. "I was a slave girl from the age of twelve 'til I went to sea, but even then I was still a slave 'til I learned how to fight. Starved, raped and beaten before then. Not anymore."

The other three fell silent at Sunday's remark, until the horses stirred, having heard sounds some yards away. Sunday and Vardan heard the sounds at the same time and stood up, grabbing their weapons; Sunday her bow and Vardan his rifle. Martha and Odda then snatched up their rifles. All four peered anxiously around trying to see the danger, then stared in muted shock as the tall figure of a long-haired woman appeared, walking towards them. She wore a flowing red cloak over a cotton tunic to her knees, leather straps around her lower legs, holding sandals to her feet. Around her shoulders a longbow and a quiver full of arrows. From her waist a short Roman type sword hung. A broad smile and friendly eyes.

"Sunday Brown, your grown son Vardan, Martha Budd and Odda Haralda. You're all a long way from Britain," Jacindra called, her arms open.

"You, too, Jacindra," Martha and Sunday replied in unison with a laugh. They embraced Jacindra, then stepped back to look at the ancient warrior woman.

"Missiquin and the three Magus sent me to find you. There is trouble developing with the rival tribes to the Blingos and other peace-loving small people. Queen Pooka of the Hobgoblins is planning to invade Blingoburbia again, as she and Ergosnatas did hundreds of years ago. Missiquin's evil sister is determined to take the queendom from her. We immortals are few in number and now need your help to stop the Hobgoblins invasion. It's also time for Odda to receive the Mark of the SWAN. After you attend the dying at the next battle, near Gettysburg in two weeks' time, you are all needed to join up with my other immortals and return to the queendom," Jacindra said with concern.

There were nods of agreement from the other four and Jacindra embraced them again.

Vardan smiled and pointed to the mountains, behind them.

"We have my dragon to help us. She will strike fear into the hell creatures." He grinned.

"I have heard of her, Vardan and she is mighty and you have trained her well, but her sister and three other hell dragons are loose. She needs to be blessed again by the Magus to help protect her. Odda needs the same protection."

"How many other immortals have you?" Sunday asked.

"Three others. With myself, you, Vardan and Odda, we will be seven," Jacindra replied. Sunday, Vardan and Odda glanced towards Martha and Jacindra saw their eyes. She smiled at Martha sympathetically and put a comforting arm around her shoulders.

"Sadly, Martha is not of fighting blood, and we need her to remain as an Uptopper to continue the work that you have done up here for so long. Our need is for a born fighter to help combat the hell creatures. Strong, fearless, courageous and willing to go to the ends of the earth to do our work. Some time ago we had Jehanette Romee with us, but she was killed in battle against Lucifer's fighters in France. You might know her as Joan of Arc. We found out later she had never fought in a battle before the French burned her at the stake. So, Martha, it would be no good for you to face these demons."

Martha smiled and nodded. "I understand, Jacindra, though there is one who might be suitable to become an immortal. He died recently, not far from here. He's called Mugwump Mandlu and he is all the things you mentioned. He chose to sell his soul to Mephistopheles and that demon is going to train him to become one of his fighters. I said I would give my last favour back to release him from Hell. Mephistopheles agreed."

"If you do that, he'll send you to the torture chambers, you know that. There is no escape," Jacindra said, shaking her head.

"I know. But Mugwump will be good with your fighters," Martha replied thoughtfully.

"Think carefully, Martha. You can roam the lands for a thousand years as an undeader, but once in the torture chambers, there is no one to help you, for ever."

"Who are the others with you?" Sunday asked. "You said there are three others."

"There is Yoshitsune, who was the greatest Samurai swordsman in Japan, hundreds of years ago. Robert Rogers from here in America, a hundred years ago, a natural hunter and born fighter. And a Chinaman called Yue Fei, who was the fiercest warrior of his day, seven hundred years ago. I have fought with him on many occasions and he can kill without using a weapon. His hands and feet are deadly, but like Yoshitsune, Yue Fei is an expert swordsman. These are the immortals who are left to fight the hell creatures." Jacindra moved to Martha, embracing her warmly. "If you give your last favour back, we will find a way to get you out of the torture chambers, we will try everything," Jacindra said, and saw Martha smiling and nodding. Vardan, Sunday and Odda were nodding agreement.

Gettysburg Battlefield, July 1863

Three days of almost non-stop fighting ended in the semi darkness of the late evening of the third day. Casualties on both sides were high. Over three thousand men and boys lay dead, over fourteen thousand wounded and more than five thousand captured or deserted on the Union side. The Confederates had suffered slightly worse; four thousand dead and eighteen thousand wounded. They also had had five thousand captured or deserted.

The Confederates, though starting with a hundred less cannon than their opponents, with just under three hundred pieces, had lost fewer batteries at the close, but not enough gunnery personnel to fire them. Union Major General Alfred Pleasonton's cavalry chargers had done their duties well, cutting through the Confederates' defences with precision. The better trained Union cavalry had lost many men during the battle, but with half their number dead or dying at the end of three days' brutal and relentless fighting, the will to carry on had wained.

The Confederate Cavalry Commander, Jeb Stuart, a brilliant horseman, but less disciplined in his actions than Alfred Pleasanton, was exhausted after three days of fighting and though ready to ride against the enemy again with equally exhausted troops, overall Commander Robert E Lee decided otherwise. He had lost seventy per cent of his gunners and his cavalry would have had insufficient cover fire to charge the Union guns.

At all of the battle points near the little town of Gettysburg, the two hills, Little and Big Round Top, the Peach Orchard, Cemetery Hill, Culp's Hill and on the Wheatfield, dead horses and men lay everywhere. Generals from both sides surveyed the various sites and almost telepathically decided to withdraw their respective forces. Neither blue nor grey won at Gettysburg. The American Civil War would rage on for two more years and thousands more infantry, cavalry and artillery men would perish on different battlefields.

Mephistopheles was jubilant. The pickings on the Gettysburg battlefield were plentiful and just turned midnight he had almost filled his pouches. He had spotted Martha and also the tall figure of Jacindra working with the others, trying to persuade dying soldiers not to sell their souls. He had several of his hell creatures nearby and his main enforcer, Trogtrol, the fearsome dwarf leader of the Trogladytes, was hoping he would be released from soul collecting to attack the immortals. Mephistopheles resisted Trogtrol's pleas to attack them.

One hell creature kept glancing across to where Martha and her group were working. The huge figure of Mugwump Mandlu plodded along the bloody battlefield in a daze, obediently following orders to point out dying soldiers. Mugwump's sorrowful eyes watched his fellow hell creatures feverishly and gleefully pointing out the poor wretches, lying in bloodied heaps so near to death. By dawn, their able-bodied colleagues would return to collect the dead and wounded. In the few hours to first light, some of the screams of the dying soldiers would have ended in misery.

Mugwump looked down at the crumpled figure of a young Negro youth, lying with a leg missing and terrible body wounds from shrapnel. Joey Watkins lay on his side, the remaining leg doubled up to his chest. He saw the giant lumbering figure staring down at him and raised a hand with his last dregs of energy. He coughed blood from his mouth and spoke quietly in laboured words.

"Take this, Mugwump. It's a silver cross and chain, the English lady gave it to me. I can just see you, but I know you're dead. She was dead like you. Clarence told me, he guessed she and the others were ghosts, like you are now."

Mugwump looked across to where Martha was kneeling at the side of a dying infantryman and stared intently at her. Within moments she looked up and their eyes fixed. In less than the time of a heartbeat, a sudden chill wind blew across the battlefield and a streak of lightning struck the ground, followed moments later with a loud crack of thunder.

Mephistopheles flew across to where Mugwump was standing and hovered menacingly a few feet above the giant Negro.

"His soul is mine and you are wasting time, Mugwump Mandlu. Step away and let me take his soul before he's gone. And don't touch that thing in his hands, it's a cross and it has been touched by Martha Budd and she has been spreckled by the Magus."

Mephistopheles slammed his scaly figure down and pushed Mugwump away from the dying youth. He swiftly lowered his head and put red hot lips to Joey's ear, but hissed and slashed his long taloned fingers at Mugwump's leg. Searing pain exploded through Mugwump's body and he fell to his knees.

"He died, you useless imbecile. You lost me his soul and you'll pay dearly," Mephistopheles ranted.

"He was my friend and you were not getting your hands on him," Mugwump replied and reached to Joey's hand, taking the cross and chain. His great body instantly shook and was pitched backward several feet, but he still clutched the cross and chain.

Mephistopheles raised his body several feet from the ground and bellowed loudly across the battlefield. There was more lightning and thunder, then a small army of hell creatures raced to where their master was calling them. Trogtrol was at the front, swords in both hands.

A hundred yards away, Jacindra had seen and heard Mephistopheles and signalled to Vardan, who was several yards further back.

"Get your dragon, Vardan, and be quick," Jacindra called as Sunday and Odda raced forward, carrying their weapons. Vardan responded immediately and put both cupped hands to his mouth. His voiced swept upwards and away to the south west. The hell creatures hesitated and their evil eyes followed the sound across the darkened sky. Mephistopheles hovered menacingly over Mugwump, who now had Martha running to his side.

"Throw that cross away, Mugwump Mandlu, and you will not be punished," he hissed.

Martha shouted at the big Negro. "Don't, Mugwump! It's a cross and the sign of decency and goodness. I'm spreckled and I've touched it. They fear symbols of goodness, but I didn't realise a simple silver cross held that much fear for them. Don't let it go, hold it."

Mugwump was in pain on the ground, his legs and body trembling, but he held the cross tightly even though it was burning into his hand. Martha had reached him and instinctively lowered her head and kissed the side of his face. Suddenly, Mugwump's body stopped trembling and the cross stopped burning into his hand. Martha leaned back and touched the hand clutching the cross. Gently she pulled it from Mugwump's grip and dangled it from her own right hand. As it swung lightly, the hell creatures stared in muted shock.

Jacindra stepped forward and the hell creatures took a step backwards.

"It's how I escaped from my hell sentence, over a thousand years ago. I had a silver cross my mother, Boadicea, gave me. Beelzebub, the devil at the time, wanted it and I tricked him to let me return from hell, if I gave it to him. I made a wooden copy of it and painted it to look like silver. Only silver hurts these fiends, unless gold is touched by a soul who has been spreckled. I escaped with just seconds to spare before Beelzebub realised he had been tricked. They throw such things into the fires of hell, to stop immortals having them." Jacindra pulled a silver cross from her chest and smiled and pointed to the row of hell creatures. "This is the cross my mother gave me. It protects me in battle. Look at their faces, they know the strength of the cross is as good as any power they have."

Above them, Mephistopheles raged and circled in anger. He screamed at his hell fighters to attack, but they held back in fear of the crosses held by Martha and Jacindra. A stab of a finger at one of his creatures and the unfortunate warrior was burned to ashes in front of his group. The others grunted and moved a step forward, weapons raised. A few yards away, Jacindra waved to her four friends to stand ready. Sunday had slotted an arrow to her bow and targeted Trogtrol's eyes. Odda had his battle axe similarly aimed at a hell creature's head, a sword in his other hand. Vardan held the sabre of his father at the ready and knew he would kill at least three of the hell creatures, before he found himself in trouble. He eyed Attila as his first victim. The long-dead barbarian slayer had his evil eyes on the tall immortal warrior, who had foolishly made a loud call to the heavens a few moments earlier. The gods would not help him this day. Attila had been the greatest warrior of all time. Vardan's head was his.

The sky darkened and every pair of eyes stared upwards. Draig Goch swooped at the group on the ground below her and picked out her young dragon master. Vardan held his arms up and waited. The great beast took him in an instant and swept upwards at speed. The clawed foot holding him moved forward and Vardan grabbed one of the leather straps around his dragon's neck. He scrambled upwards and around her neck.

"Be careful with that sword of yours, young master, don't stab me with it," Draig Goch hissed as she circled a thousand feet above the Gettysburg battlefield. "I take it you want me to frighten that group of odd-looking little beasties facing your mother and aunt?"

"No, DeeGee, I want you take them all for a ride and make their day."

"Careful, young master. Sarcasm annoys me."

"I don't want you to frighten them. Blast them with some of your poison fire." Vardan scowled as he gripped the harness tightly with his free hand. "Get me close enough to swipe a couple of their heads off. And don't burn my mother or any of my lot."

"You told them to keep out of the way, yeah?" Draig Goch called as she prepared to dive. Vardan didn't answer. "I'll take that as a no then. Brilliant."

Mephistopheles saw the great figure diving like a javelin and cursed loudly. Trogtrol, Attila, Mongolis and three others held their ground, but the rest of the hell creatures turned and ran. The screaming curses of Mephistopheles followed them across the darkened battlefield. Vardan pointed to the running hell creatures.

"Get them, DeeGee! Get me close and to the front, I'll drop off and then blast them, then go up."

"You want me to warm them up, huh?"

"There's at least twenty of them, DeeGee," Vardan scoffed.

"Get ready to jump then, and keep your head down," Draig Goch said as she levelled off a few feet above the ground, eighty yards in front of the fleeing hell warriors.

Vardan timed his jump almost to perfection, but stumbled as he landed and dropped his sabre. Draig Goch immediately blasted out a sheet of almost white hot poison flames that hit the half dozen front runners. They screamed and fell backward in a burning heap, the following group stumbling over the charred bodies. Vardan snatched up the sabre and ran at the fear-crazed hell warriors as they approached.

The first swipe took off the head of a Hobgoblin, the second took the head from a barbarian chieftain, who had ridden with Attila the Hun on many of their murderous raids against innocent villagers in Germania, centuries earlier. A bearskin-wearing Mongol warrior, who had served with Genghis Khan in the thirteenth century, was less intimidated by the young immortal and drew his sword. Vardan sliced off a third head from a hell creature and then faced the brutal-looking Mongol. The latter charged head on and with his metal shield, pushed Vardan back, swinging the sword at him, but missing. Vardan took a breath and made ready to a take another swing from the enraged warrior. The sword hissed through the cold night air, missing Vardan's head by a hair's breadth.

They faced each other now, crouched, heads bowed, circling. The Mongol lunged and stabbed his razor-sharp sword. Vardan parried it and stepped away, the Mongol lunged again and caught Vardan's leather wrist strap, slicing through it almost to the skin. They stared wild-eyed and circled again, this time Vardan anticipating another lunge from the muscular Mongol. The sword didn't stab forward, but came around in a half circular sweep that took Vardan by surprise. He lost his footing and had to raise his sabre arm to parry the sword's swing with his blade. He took the full force and swiftly leaned backwards to escape another swipe by the Mongol's sword. The momentum of this wild move from the Mongol put him off balance and with lightning speed, Vardan wheeled around and sliced the warrior's head off.

Vardan snatched up the metal shield the decapitated Mongol had dropped and began jumping up and down, waving his sabre. He had slain four hell creatures in less than as many minutes and the thrill swept through his body. The sound above him made him look upwards to where Draig Goch was shaking her head at him, as she hovered thirty feet above.

"I suppose you're a bit happy, then, young master and enjoy jumping up and down like a brainless fool, or do you need me anymore?"

"Stay around a while longer, DeeGee and be ready to do that poison flame thing again if needs be, there are still a few of them over there." Vardan nodded towards the hell creatures who had not fled. Draig Goch sniffed.

"It uses up a lot of energy to spit all that poison out. Go and chop their heads off and save me the effort."

Vardan glanced across to where Trogtrol and his friends were waiting and shrugged. "Nah, they look a bit annoyed right now. Just one more fire breath before you fly away."

"Very well, but that's it for tonight. I need to go back to sleep," Draig Goch sniffed and flapped her mighty wings, rising into the air once more.

"Stay around then, and wait and see if I need you again," Vardan called after her.

Vardan lifted the metal shield and gripped his sabre tightly. He carefully walked back towards Trogtrol and Attila, both warily watching the young immortal as he approached.

Sunday, Jacindra and Odda all faced the remaining hell creatures, weapons at the ready.

Mephistopheles was cursing and hovering, but his evil eyes were watchful of the fire dragon circling five hundred feet above. Trogtrol was waiting for the command to attack the immortals, but his master angrily kept him and the other, braver hell creatures back.

Vardan proudly displayed the shield he had won and saluted his friends with the sabre. Sunday was beside herself with pride and sighed contentedly as he stood once more at her side. Jacindra tapped him on the shoulder with her own sword and smiled.

"You did well, Vardan. You killed a few more hell creatures. You and the dragon are paired well. I salute you," Jacindra pointed her sword upwards.

"What now?" Vardan asked as he stood between his mother and Jacindra.

"We bargain for Martha's freedom," Sunday said and stared at Mephistopheles. The son of Satan swirled around and pointed at Vardan menacingly.

"Give me him and the dragon and Martha Budd will go free. You can also take the big Negro over there." Mephistopheles pointed from Vardan to Mugwump. The latter had recovered from his injury and stood behind the other hell creatures, not sure what was expected of him.

Vardan stopped his mother from answering and pulled Martha to his side.

"Release her, Mephistopheles. She is not a fighter. No threat to your fighters. You've had years of service from her in collecting souls, time to let her go back."

"I want her for the torture chambers unless you agree to join my hell fighters. I also want the dragon and the crosses the Iceni woman and Martha Budd hold. Then she is free. And the chair Martha Budd possesses. I want it for myself, I want its powers."

Martha stepped forward and looked at Mephistopheles. "You can take my last favour and be done. I'll go to your torture chambers and stay there for eternity. In return, my friends, take Mugwump Mandlu and I'll give you my cross and the chair."

Trogtrol pushed forward and shook his head. "Master, give me the order to kill these obscenities and then you can have everything. You don't have to bargain, you are the almighty and powerful. I, Attila, Mongolis, Ergosnatas and the other two here are your best warriors, we have never lost a battle with the immortals, we can train others to be as good, we can wipe these pathetic creatures out once and for all. You have dragons that can be as good as that one up there." Trogtrol pointed into the night sky, where Draig Goch waited.

Mephistopheles swirled around again and dismissed Trogtrol with a flick of his hand.

"I have dragons, Trogtrol, but I need a dragon master like the son of Sunday Brown to train them, or do you think you can ride a dragon like Vardan Brown does?"

"No one can beat me in battle, Master, but I am not a dragon master, but we have others in far lands who are as good as Vardan Brown. I say we kill them right here and you can have it all. Then we invade the queendom and wipe out the Blingos, who gave these creatures their powers. After the Blingos we slaughter the Pixelves and then the Gnomes. You will rule the whole world above and below ground, you and your brothers."

"True, very true, Trogtrol, but do you think you, Attila and the other four standing with you can kill these four immortals, who, remember, have a little teeny weeny dragon flying around up there, waiting to wipe you all out with one breath? They can't kill me, but what do I tell my father, the great Satan? That I have failed to do his bidding? He will send me to join my brother Drebmif at the bottom of the sea. I don't really want to turn into a fish, do you?"

Trogtrol bowed his head and stepped back in shame. Mephistopheles hovered and then looked to Martha, who was watching him closely.

"So be it, Martha Budd. I will take you and your chair and the cross you have and the one the Iceni woman wears around her neck. My older brother, who was tricked by her will be even redder in the face when he learns I have the silver cross of Boadicea. Satan will reward me for my brilliance. I will have the pick of any female souls who come to hell. That fool Mugwump Mandlu can go with these others. He will never be a proper fighter. In the short time I have had him, he has done nothing else but moan and groan and wish he hadn't sold his soul. He is too big and clumsy. Take him, Iceni woman, he's yours, and pass over your silver cross. Put it on the ground with your spreckled cross, Martha Budd. Trogtrol, go get her chair. Say your goodbyes, Martha Budd. You have one minute."

Tears flowed down Sunday's face as she and Martha embraced. Jacindra, Odda and Vardan waited to embrace Martha and in turn they kissed and embraced her. Mugwump had walked across and his big arms wrapped around Martha's body for several moments, until she gently pushed away.

Vardan stepped to her and whispered a few words. Martha looked up into his eyes and smiled, nodding slightly. They touched hands and held for brief moments. Then a hideous laugh sounded from a few yards away and the reformed grotesque figure of Gertlump the Boggimp appeared in a red haze at the side of Mephistopheles. Martha stared in disbelief and hesitated, as the stubby green fingers of the Boggimp woman gestured for her to walk forward.

Sunday ran to Martha and threw her arms around her shoulders. Martha paused and kissed Sunday on the lips, then gently pushed her away. Gertlump grabbed Martha roughly, turned the frightened woman and shoved her towards the red mist, laughing loudly.

Gertlump finally had one of the two undead human women for her torture chamber, who she had never stopped thinking about since they melted her many years earlier. Half of her wish had now come true and the other half would follow as time moved on. Martha Budd was hers to do with as she pleased. The red mist disappeared and Martha was gone.

Epilogue

The five undead warriors left Gettysburg in the early hours of the fourth day. Sunday and Jacindra sat in the front bow top pulled by Watson, Odda drove the second bow top and Vardan was riding De Lacey and holding the reins of Loire. Mugwump's large frame was too big for him to sit with Odda, so he walked at the side, silent and bewildered.

For two hours at the front, neither Sunday or Jacindra had spoken, then a large rabbit bolted across their path. Sunday pointed and called out.

"Breakfast. We need to eat. I'm hungry."

"You can eat then?" Jacindra said.

"Yeah, like you, Vardan and I can eat. Odda has to have the Swan mark soon then he can join us. Poor Mugwump will have to wait like we all had to do."

"I couldn't eat for more than four hundred years, until I was befriended by the Blingos and they guided me to be the immortal I am. Like you I was an Uptopper looking after entrances to the kingdom."

"The kingdom? You mean the queendom," Sunday interrupted.

"No, it was a kingdom hundreds of years ago, but King Massakin was captured by the hell creatures after almost all the Blingos were slaughtered by those demons."

"Yes, I remember now and the Queen's sister turned traitor and wants to rule Blingoburbia. That's why that ugly dwarf Trogtrol wants to wipe the little people out and join her on the throne."

"Exactly, Sunday. Myself and a few immortals rescued Missiquin, the two Magus and some of their people and took them to safety. That was hundreds of years ago and year by year they have rebuilt their underground world."

"You said two Magus, or Dabras as they are nicknamed. There are three of them."

"There were two Magus hundreds of years ago, but as the number of Blingos grew a third one was needed. A third Magus was chosen by the Swan and took his place at the chambers in the year 1333. In the year 1999, the first one, Sorceradabra, will retire from the chambers and become the Magus Superius. A replacement will then be chosen by the Swan."

"1333 to 1999. How many years is that?" Sunday asked, her eyes narrowed.

Jacindra laughed and nodded. "Six hundred and sixty-six years. The same number Satan uses, or should I say he copied from the Blingos. It's known as the devil's number, but it is also sacred to the Magus. It was started a year after Jesus died on the cross, in 1 AD."

"I don't understand all those numbers, Jacindra. I never learnt how to read, write or add up. I only know how to survive and fight," Sunday remarked almost disapprovingly.

"That is why you were chosen to become an immortal. Not many of them could ever read or write, but they were all superb fighters and leaders. The other three I mentioned, Yue Fei, Robert Rogers and Yoshitsune are all able to read and write, in other languages. The American, Rogers, could only speak English when he died, but he can now speak Arabic, Mandarin, Spanish and Japanese. It helps when we go in pursuit of hell creatures in different places of the world. We dress according to the clothes that are worn in different countries. We have to mix in and obviously, not in the type of clothes we wore before we died. I choose to wear my original clothes when I seek out new immortals. I hate wearing the fine silk, lace or cotton dresses that women wear today. Those awful bonnets that modern women have on their heads."

Sunday started laughing at what Jacindra had said. "At least with the modern frocks that women wear now, we can hide our swords and pistols underneath."

Jacindra started laughing and playfully patted Sunday's leg. "It's damn hard though pulling a three foot long sword from under your skirts, not to mention a heavy battle axe."

They giggled now and the bow top started rocking. A few moments later Vardan rode to the side and looked at his mother and Jacindra.

"What's funny, Ma? We just lost Aunt Martha and that's too hard to think about." Jacindra and Sunday stopped giggling and nodded sheepishly, sniffing back tears.

"Sorry, Vardan. We're as upset as you, but your Aunt Martha would understand, she was always making me laugh. We'll get her back, I promise. Somehow, we'll do it. There will be a way to rescue her from that evil green Boggimp. You spoke to her just before she was taken, what did you say to her?"

"I told her more or less what you just said. I'll get her away from the torture chambers and back to our family, because we are a family. A family of immortals that will wipe out every hell creature we find. I killed four last night and I'm so so pleased. They deserved to die a second time. We need to have Odda marked by the Swan and big Mugwump spreckled as soon as possible. Where do we find the Blingos?"

Sunday looked at Jacindra as the bow top trundled along the track. The latter looked across to Vardan and smiled.

"Don't worry, Vardan. They will find you when it is time. They see everything we do. We carry on doing our work at the entrances to Blingoburbia and on the eighth day of the month, at eight in the morning, two of those cheery little faces will appear on the other side of a trapdoor, looking up at us. They've done it for centuries at rubbish tips all over the world and they will carry on doing it. They look after us and we do the same for them.

"You will meet the other three immortals very soon and then we return to the queendom and plan our moves against the hell creatures. Odda will take the swan mark and Mugwump will be spreckled as soon as he is approved."

"And we take my Aunt Martha back from the torture chambers. And then I go deep into the sea with Draig Goch and rescue Fimber O'Flynn," Vardan said matter-of-factly.

"One way or another, Vardan, we will get them both back. We will slay the hell creatures and make both the queendom and the up top world safe from Satan and his son's threats,"

Jacindra replied as Vardan rode alongside the bow top on De Lacey.

"We find more immortals along the way," Vardan remarked enthusiastically.

"We find as many as we can, Vardan. The best and bravest warriors. Satan and his sons will build and train an army of hell creatures. We can go back in time to seek out the warriors we need. The Magus gave us the parchment to find the time holes. Your mother and Martha found one that took them back to the time when Odda lived before he was killed. I held you in my arms as a babe, on the banks of a river near York in 1066."

"We can find these time holes to go back?"

"We can, Vardan, and we must. They are in every country and in these countries there were warriors, brave warriors who will serve the queendom and kill the hell creatures. Your mother and Martha gave you a good sound start and you will be a mighty servant of the queendom. I give you my word that a way will be found to take Martha back from the devil. I promise you that," Jacindra added solemnly.

Vardan looked upwards to where Draig Goch was still circling. He raised his sabre and saluted her.

"With Dee Gee, I will find Aunt Martha and take her from Satan's clutches. I am proud to be an immortal warrior, and I will always help to protect the Blingos who bestowed on me that honour. With you, Jacindra, my mother and Odda and other immortals, we will wipe out the Hell Creatures."

Jacindra smiled and raised her sword. Sunday and Odda did the same. The four stood together and watched as Draig Goch bellowed and spit out a sheet of flames, then swooped downwards at speed, lifted her great body and flew away.

"How can we lose with that dragon on our side?" Vardan said, as he watched Draig Goch disappear from sight.

The End